SIZZLE

Barbara Brett

SIZZLE by Barbara Brett

Copyright © 1988, 2000, 2016 by Barbara Brett

Third edition.

Published by Brett Books in the United States of America

Originally published by Zebra Books

Cover design by C. Linda Dingler

Cover art by Daniel O'Leary

For information email Brett Books at brettbooks@brettbooks.com.

Author services by Pedernales Publishing, LLC.
www.pedernalespublishing.com

Library of Congress Control Number: 2016932024

ISBN: 978-0-9899173-3-9 Paperback edition
ISBN: 978-0-9899173-4-6 Digital edition

Printed in the United States of America

For Hy—
And for Jennifer and David, Hilary and Sam,
And for Steven and Eileen, and Haley—
my real-life treasures,
whose love is wealth beyond compare.

Prologue

Spring 1988

WHEN MARIETTA WYLFORD was making love with a man she didn't care for, which was more often than not these days, she found it helpful to close her eyes and focus her mind on the first and last ride she had taken on the Coney Island Cyclone at the age of fifteen. A rather pimply boy named Tommy Something had talked her into it, and when their lead car reached the crest of the first incline, he grabbed her in his scrawny arms and clamped his wet lips on hers. The forces of gravity and wind velocity kept them glued together for the rest of the ride. Unable to disentangle herself, Marietta (she was just plain Marianne back then) clung to him, moaning and shrieking into his mouth as their car hurtled from peaks into valleys and catapulted from valleys onto peaks. Afterward, Tommy swaggered along by her side, convinced that he had given her the sex thrill of her life. She saw no reason to disillusion him by revealing that he disgusted her and that her reaction had been sheer animal panic evoked by speeding through space at such a terrifying rate, especially not after he bought her a huge stuffed panda. In the twenty-three years that had slipped through her fingers since that hot, sticky July night, she had made excellent and lucrative use of that memory.

Now, just when her mind had taken her halfway up the sharpest incline of her imaginary roller coaster, a dense weight plummeted down on her chest, making the air whoosh out of her lungs and into her companion's mouth. She managed to free her lips from his and to whisper as passionately as she could with the little breath she had left, "Don't stop now, darling."

His head dropped onto her pillow.

She lay there for a moment, staring up at the rainbow prisms the crystal chandelier cast on her ceiling in the soft pink glow of the nightlight. Never had she felt such an oppressive weight. It crushed her breasts until they threatened to become concave. But the pain and the pressure were as nothing compared to the icy fear that had begun to pulsate from the dark recesses of her mind and radiate all through her body.

Her tongue darted out and moistened her dry lips. "Darling . . ." she whispered. "Darling...are you all right?"

There was no answer from the slack lips pressed against her cheek.

She closed her eyes and slowly turned her head. It took every ounce of courage she had to open them. When she did, she found herself staring into a pair of glasslike blue eyes that she knew could not see her, would never see again.

"Oh, my God!" she cried. With a strength born of necessity, she thrust off the body and groped for a pulse in his wrist and throat. When chest massage and mouth-to-mouth resuscitation both failed, she succumbed to the horror of the situation, and ran into the bathroom, vomited, and sank down on the floor.

She lay there, curled in womb position on the powder-pink carpet, her head pressed against the hard, cold porcelain of the bowl, telling herself that it wasn't true, that it couldn't be true. But finally she had to admit that it was. That was when the trembling began.

"Do something," she told herself through chattering teeth. "You can't just lie here—you have to do something."

She pulled herself to her feet and walked over to the white-and-gold French provincial telephone on the Lucite table beside the pink marble bathtub. She dialed a number and, while it rang, took a cigarette from a pink Wedgwood box and lit it with a matching lighter.

Be home, she repeated silently with each ring. *Please, please be home.*

On the fifth ring a rather breathless female voice came over the wire.

"Melanie," Marietta said, "Philip Bailey just died while we were in bed. What do I do?"

"Oh, my God! Are you sure he's dead?"

"Of course I'm sure."

"Have you called for an ambulance?"

"Are you out of your mind? I can't have him found naked in my bed."

"Well, you can't just have your maid put him out with the garbage in the morning. You have to call for an ambulance immediately. Any delay would sound fishy to the police."

"But he's in my bed, and he's naked."

"Since when have you been such a puritan?"

"I'm not a puritan. I'm a businesswoman, and I refuse to jeopardize the deal we were working on. God knows, I'm sorry for Philip, but that doesn't change the fact that the stock he was about to sell me will go to his wife now, and she'll never let me have it if she knows how he died."

"Get him dressed. Tell the police and the medics that he was taking a nap."

Her hands began to tremble. "Melanie, I can't touch him."

"You have to. What are you wearing?"

She glanced into a mirror. "One false eyelash and some hair spray."

"First call nine-one-one. Then get yourself dressed as though you were going out to dinner. I'll be over in five minutes. Pray that the cops are slow getting there."

An officer answered the 911 phone on the fifth ring, and sounded so efficient as he took down her information that Marietta was tempted to tell him not to rush the ambulance over, that she had things to do before it arrived.

She hung up the phone and ran into her bedroom to dress. Though she knew it was there, it somehow came as a shock to find Philip Bailey's body still sprawled across her bed. It lay as it had fallen when she had struggled out from beneath it, legs on the side at an angle that would have been awkward even for a contortionist, upper torso flat on its back, arms flung wide in a grotesque welcoming gesture. The eyes were the worst—those staring, unseeing eyes. She knew she should close them, but she couldn't bring herself to do it. Instead, she reached for the silk sheet that had tumbled to the floor and pulled it over his face.

The blue of the sheet reminded her of cloudless spring skies and of heaven. She wondered fleetingly if there was a heaven. Philip Bailey would know by now. But only from hearsay. She doubted very much that he would be an inhabitant.

Not since her days of whirlwind changes during fashion shows had she dressed so quickly. In less than three minutes, her navy Yves Saint Laurent suit looked as though it had never been taken off. Unable to locate her missing false eyelash, she pulled off the remaining one, reglossed her lips, and combed her shoulder-length red hair.

She was picking up Philip's clothing when the doorman rang her on the intercom.

"Yes, William?" she said, praying he wouldn't announce the arrival of the ambulance.

"Miss Danielle is here to see you, Mrs. Wylford."

"Thank you, William. I'm also expecting an ambulance. A friend visiting me has taken deathly ill. It should be here at any moment."

"I'll send the medics right up, ma'am." William's tone held the proper mixture of servility and humanitarian concern.

Marietta had the door open before Melanie could ring the bell. Closing it, she said, "The ambulance hasn't arrived. So far, so good."

"I'll bet you haven't dressed him yet," Melanie said, her brown eyes scanning Marietta's face. She was ten years younger and four inches shorter than Marietta, but her lack of makeup, angular body, and severe attire occasionally made people take her for the older of the two.

Marietta shook her head. "Melanie, I—"

But Melanie didn't wait for her to finish the thought. "Come on," she said, brushing past her and heading for the bedroom. "The *Post* printed another one of its bitchy editorials about the delay in response to emergency calls. The cops will be trying to break the sound barrier for the next few days."

By the time Marietta caught up with her in the bedroom, Melanie had pulled down the sheet.

"Couldn't you at least have closed his eyes?" she asked. Gently, she reached over and performed this final service. "Rest in peace," she whispered, her face suddenly filled with tenderness. Then she turned back to Marietta, all business again. "You'll have to help me. I can't do this by myself."

Marietta nodded. "I'll be all right now. I just couldn't touch him while I was alone."

Melanie picked up Philip's black silk socks from the floor and handed one to Marietta. "I've never known you to be squeamish. In your office, you make life-and-death decisions about corporations and careers every day."

"This is different. I don't like being out of control. It scares me."

The socks were the easiest to put on. The rest of the clothes posed a real problem: Philip Bailey was well over six feet tall and weighed two hundred and forty pounds, more than both women put together. For a moment the two stared at his hulking frame, feeling at a loss. Then Melanie picked up his undershorts from the floor. "Come on. If the Druids could build Stonehenge without modern technology, we can dress a corpse."

"They had more than just seconds to do it in," Marietta reminded her, but she reached for Philip's trousers.

Working together, they slipped the shorts and trousers up past Philip's knees. Then Melanie knelt on the bed, slipped her shoulders under his thighs, and hoisted him up like a wheelbarrow while Marietta pulled the two garments over his buttocks and belly.

"Thank God he considered himself too macho for an undershirt," Marietta said as Melanie eased herself out from under his legs.

By rolling him first on one side and then on the other, they managed to slip his shirt on without ripping it. They decided to dispense with his tie and jacket, on the theory that he would have shed them if he had gone into the bedroom to lie down because he wasn't feeling well. Just as they finished buttoning his shirt and shoving it into his pants, the intercom buzzed.

"The ambulance guys are on their way up, ma'am," William announced.

"Did he have anything to eat here?" Melanie asked.

"A few martinis, some Stilton cheese, some caviar."

"Good. Tell them that. Say he came here to take you to dinner. You had some cocktails first, and then he said he wasn't feeling well. You suggested that he lie down for a while. A little later, when you went in to see how he was feeling, you found him dead and called for an ambulance."

Marietta nodded and ran a hand through her hair. "Do I look all right?"

"You always look all right." Suddenly, Melanie's face paled. "Damn! We forgot to zip his fly." She ran to the bedroom and returned just as Marietta was opening the door.

The policemen were solicitous, the ambulance attendants swift and efficient. Within ten minutes the necessary information had been taken down and they left with the mortal remains of Philip J. Bailey, American publishing genius. The policemen followed the covered stretcher, one of them with Philip's jacket and shoes tucked under his arm.

Marietta closed the door after them and leaned against it. "How was I?" she asked.

"As always, you were magnificent. You had the perfect blend of reserve and concern one would expect from a person who had a strictly business relationship with the deceased."

"Well, it was strictly business. All I was doing in that bed was negotiating a special stock option and offering him a sweetener he'd never get from Harrison Kendricks."

Melanie gave her a level look. "He wasn't interested in any kind of deal with Kendricks. We both know you're the one he wanted to sell *Sizzle* to."

"All right. So I'd had a couple of drinks and I was high on them and on the news he'd just told me. He said he'd gotten some information on Kendricks that was guaranteed to force him to back off. It all combined to make me feel horny." She sighed. "He may have been a genius in the magazine world, but the guy was nothing special in bed."

"Considering what happened, maybe he wasn't feeling up to par."

Marietta dismissed the subject with a wave of her hand and walked into the living room. There, surrounded by the antique furniture she had collected over the years—the ivory-brocade-covered

Louis XVI gilt-wood sofa, the Louis XV beechwood bergères, the tulipwood writing tables and ormolu-mounted worktables, the eighteenth-century paintings and decorations, and the Waterford crystal chandelier—she began to relax. "God, I could use a drink," she said, collapsing on the sofa. "Is there anything left in the pitcher?"

Melanie walked across the room to the bar that had been handcrafted to resemble an elongated Louis XV commode. She inspected the monogrammed Steuben martini pitcher. "It's empty."

"Make us a few, will you?"

"What did you do with the gin and vermouth," Melanie asked, looking around, "polish them off?"

"They should be there." Marietta straightened up and peered over at the bar. "No, wait—Philip made the drinks in the kitchen. He must have left them there."

As Melanie passed the cocktail table, Marietta gestured toward the martini glasses that stood next to a sterling silver tray set out with dishes of crackers and caviar and cheese. "Get rid of this on your way, please. It depresses me."

Melanie cleared the table and disappeared into the kitchen. A few seconds later she was back with the Gilbey's and vermouth.

Marietta had slipped off her shoes and stretched her long legs out on the sofa. She didn't speak until after she had taken two big swallows of her drink. "What's going to happen now?"

Melanie placed the well-filled martini pitcher on the cocktail table within easy reach and curled up on the other end of the sofa. "His family will be notified. There'll be an autopsy to determine cause of death. The fact that he was dressed won't fool the medical examiner, Mari. He'll know that Philip wasn't merely counting sheep when he died."

"Damn. Maybe we should have washed him."

"There wasn't time, and it wouldn't have helped. Don't worry. I'll make a few well-placed phone calls. The news shouldn't leak out. Do you know his wife?"

"We've never met."

"You'll have to pay your respects to her before the funeral and attend the service. Otherwise, she'll jump to conclusions, and so will the public."

"They'll jump to them anyway."

"Not if you make it hard for them. No one can carry it off better than you. When you do visit his wife, though, no matter how itchy you are to get your hands on her shares, you're not to talk business."

"I'll leave that to an emissary," Marietta said, giving her a meaningful look. "We're not going to be able to drag our feet on this, you know. Kendricks's bankers announced his intention to make a hostile raid Monday. This is Wednesday. That leaves us only seventeen business days before the SEC will allow him to start buying up shares."

"I thought you said Bailey had something on Kendricks that was bound to make him back off."

"Yes, but he hadn't told Kendricks—or me, either, damn it. When I asked him what he'd found out, he said that the fewer people who were in on the secret, the stronger his position would be. The only hint he would give me was saying something like, 'Dallas would prove to be Kendricks's Achilles heel.' And then he died before I could get any more out of him."

"So that's why you let him get you in bed."

Instead of responding, Marietta finished her drink and poured herself another. "Philip probably found out some dirt about the newspaper Kendricks bought down there, or about some of his real estate."

"I can't imagine anyone finding anything Kendricks would want suppressed. He's never made a secret of the fact that he's a bastard. He revels in his reputation. The whole world knows he was a mercenary in Africa twenty-five years ago and has used the same killer tactics he learned there to build his publishing empire. He started it off by inheriting his family's newspaper from his brother under pretty suspicious circumstances, but he never tried to hide that fact either."

Marietta brightened. "Maybe that's it. Maybe Philip discovered proof that Kendricks killed his brother."

"As far as I know, his brother never set foot in this country. He died in England. I think Philip was snowing you because he knew it was the only way you'd let him into your bed."

Marietta shook her head. "He knew something, I'm sure of

it. He was too confident, too exultant to have been putting on an act."

"Then if it was something he could find out, I'm sure you can learn what it was too. He must have proof of it somewhere. He wouldn't be relying on hearsay."

"Yes, but where's the proof?"

Melanie shrugged. "In a safe or a safe-deposit box, maybe. Maybe in his desk at the office."

"I doubt that he'd let it out of his sight." Marietta jumped up, almost knocking over the pitcher. "His attaché case! I forgot to give it to the policemen. It's still in the hall closet." She ran from the room and returned a moment later with a brown leather case bearing the gold monogram *P.J.B.*

"As your lawyer, Mari, I have to tell you that you can't open that. It should be delivered to his heirs intact. I'll take it with me when I leave."

"For God's sake, Melanie—"

"Of course," Melanie cut her off, standing up and stretching, "I have no idea what you might or might not do while I'm in the john."

The moment Melanie was out of the room, Marietta opened the case. Its contents were disappointing: an advance issue of *Sizzle* with Diane von Furstenberg on the cover, the late-city edition of that morning's *Times*, a Xerox copy of an edited manuscript, an advertising contract with Tiffany's, a bottle of Maalox No. 2 tablets, a pair of soiled socks. She returned the items, snapped the case shut, and shook her head as Melanie reentered the room.

"Would you like to spend the night at my place?" Melanie asked.

"No, thanks."

"Would you like me to stay here, then?"

"No. I'll be all right. I'll sleep in one of the guest rooms."

Melanie picked up the attaché case and headed for the door. She paused there for a moment, studying Marietta, her eyes full of concern. "Are you sure you're all right?"

"Of course I am." A note of impatience crept into Marietta's voice. "I was shaken for a moment when it happened. That was to be expected. But it was only for a moment." She opened the door, and Melanie walked out into the hall. "Make those phone calls you mentioned and see to it that everything is done exactly as it should be. I don't want any loose ends. I'll see you at the office tomorrow. Nine sharp."

She closed the door briskly. She was in control again.

BOOK ONE

1971—1988

Chapter One

BACK IN THE living room, Marietta picked up the martini pitcher and a glass, opened the sliding doors, and stepped through them. Suddenly, twenty-one stories above Manhattan, she was in an English country garden. There was no need to switch on the floodlights; she knew by heart where every flower bloomed. A soft spring breeze brought the delicate fragrance of the wisteria on the arbor that had been erected a few yards ahead, its lavender blossoms gently swaying like airy bunches of fairy grapes. To her left and right, azaleas burst forth in bright shouts of shocking pink, snow white, and ruby red. Farther on, tulips stood tall and erect like miniature renaissance guards adorned in vermilion and gold uniforms. Though it was tended year-round by a landscaping firm that catered to the whims of New Yorkers who could afford the amenities of rural life in the midst of urban convenience, she had planned the garden herself with the help of William Lancelot Brown-Fenwick. A descendant of "Capability" Brown, the eighteenth-century landscape artist, Brown-Fenwick designed the gardens of some of the grandest estates in England, and Marietta had commissioned him to fly to New York and assist with hers. She had known exactly what she wanted. Her second-grade teacher, Mrs. Greenfeld, had hung at the front of the classroom a calendar with photographs of English gardens. At the end of each month, the child who had earned the most good-conduct stars was presented with that month's photograph. Marietta had received the coveted prize three times, and all through her childhood those pictures had decorated the cracked and peeling walls of her shabby room. She had vowed that one day she would have a garden just like those depicted in the photographs, and now she did, right down to a flagstone path. Except for a few permanent plants—the wisteria, the miniature peach and cherry trees, and the rambling roses that delicately wove their way up the little brick wall that had been erected solely for their climbing pleasure—as each season waned, the huge concealed planters of beautiful flora were replaced by others bursting with blooms of the next.

Marietta stretched out on the green and white chaise longue and took a slow sip of her martini. Up above, she could see the tiny pinpricks of starlight that were piercing the polluted sky. Down below, she could hear the roar and screech of city traffic. She sighed and closed her eyes. This was where, as a child, she had always longed to be when she grew up—close to the stars, with the city at her feet. It hadn't been easy, but then Marietta had always known that nothing worthwhile ever was.

She began life as Marianne Vuckendorn, which should have been a sufficient handicap for anyone, but fate chose to deal her out even more. She had a brutal, alcoholic father who rarely worked, and when he did, he spent all his money on liquor and whiskey-drinking friends. Her mother, too weak willed to leave him, slaved behind the steam table in a lower Manhattan cafeteria, where, on the rare occasions when her boss was in a good mood, she was allowed to take home some leftover vegetables that had been cooked beyond recognition and some dried-out ends of meat. When Marianne was eight and still fantasizing that her father had crept into the palatial home of her real parents—visiting royalty from Europe—and kidnapped her from her diamond-studded cradle, her older brother, then fifteen, was killed by a fellow junkie in an argument over their stash of heroin. When she was twelve and past all fantasies, her younger sister, then eight, died in a fall from a swing in the local playground, which, unlike its counterparts in well-to-do neighborhoods, had no rubberized protective cushioning in potentially dangerous areas. No one bothered to investigate the accident, obviously just another case of a dumb poor kid who didn't watch what she was doing. That death was a turning point for Marianne. She had always known that someday she would escape the vicious cycle that had closed her parents off from hope and kept them tied to apartments in crumbling tenements in the Crown Heights section of Brooklyn, outcasts forever quarantined because they suffered from that insidious social disease, poverty. Now she began to make concrete plans for that escape. Her mother delighted in telling her that the angels had smiled on her face, and even a critical look in the mirror confirmed that her mother was right. She had large, wide-apart eyes the color of fine emeralds, and luxuriant, silk hair that gleamed like burnished copper. Her nose was straight and her chin firm but gently rounded, her cheekbones high and aristocratic, her skin a clear ivory tone unmarred by blemishes or freckles. But if the angels had smiled upon her face, it soon became apparent that they had beamed on her body. For she grew to a height of five feet, eight inches, and to a breadth that was nothing less than the American dream—thirty-eight, twenty-three, thirty-six. Obviously, she was made for better things than Crown Heights had to offer, and she was determined to have them.

Only one other person knew about her plans—Cynthia Danielle. Marianne and Cynthia had known each other all their lives. They grew up in the same apartment house, were in the same class all through school. They shared giggles, homework, secrets, and dreams. Cynthia wanted to escape too, but by a different route. She planned to get a job after high school graduation and attend college at night; perhaps she would even go on to law school. She tried to talk Marianne into following the same course, for Marianne had an extremely quick mind and earned far better grades than she without even trying. But Cynthia's dream was too prosaic for Marianne. Why strive for years to earn a place in the middle class when she could marry far above it without the struggle or the wait? She was convinced that such a marriage was possible. After all, from the onset of puberty she had been pursued by males who were delighted and eager to spend their last cent on gifts and entertainments that might bring her pleasure—in return for the anticipated pleasures she might bring them.

Shortly before Marianne's seventeenth birthday, her mother, whose health had never been good, suffered a massive coronary at work, collapsing into and thoroughly ruining a fresh batch of French-fried onion rings. Though her boss was understandably distressed, his compassion won out in the end and he refrained from deducting the cost of the onion rings from her posthumous paycheck. Naturally, the Vuckendorns had no savings, but with her mother's Social Security death benefits and the help of neighbors, Marianne was able to arrange a small funeral. Returning from the cemetery, her father cried great drunken tears, took her in his arms, promised he would never again touch a drop of whiskey, and vowed to get a job and take care of her for the rest of her life. The next morning he was gone, and so were the eight dollars and seventy-three cents in her wallet, the only money she had in the world. She never saw him again.

Though she earned barely enough as a salesclerk in Woolworth's to support her own household, Cynthia's widowed mother, Shirley, offered Marianne a home, and it was during the year she spent with Shirley Danielle, Cynthia, and Cynthia's younger sister, Melanie, that Marianne discovered the first real feeling of family warmth and ties that she had ever known.

After her high school graduation, Marianne took the face and figure the angels had smiled upon to New York's finest modeling agencies, presenting them under the name she had decided to be known by—Marietta Dawn. She learned to her dismay that though her height was right, she was far too voluptuous for haute couture fashion modeling. A few agency interviewers suggested that she try movies or the theater, but she knew she had no talent for acting. Disappointed but not defeated, she registered with an agency that specialized in providing characters for TV commercials, advertisements, and confession magazine illustrations. She earned thirty dollars an hour, but the work was sporadic and brought with it no social spinoffs that would gain her admittance to the world of wealth she had every intention of conquering.

To supplement her modeling income, she took a job as a cocktail waitress in an elegant midtown piano lounge. There she met many affluent men of varying marital status. Though none was in what she considered the proper financial bracket to be taken seriously, they did come in handy for offering her exotic and expensive glimpses of the life she someday intended to lead, and their gifts of money and clothes she accepted as her due. If one happened to turn out to be expert in bed, she considered it an added bonus, but that was by no means a criterion for continuing a relationship; all too frequently, her worst lovers were her most generous benefactors. Cynthia, who shared an apartment with her in the West Village, was a little embarrassed by her friend's sex life, which began to take on marathon proportions, so Marietta made an effort never to have men in the apartment when Cynthia was there. It was easy enough to arrange, for Cynthia worked full-time as a clerk in an insurance company and attended classes at Hunter College four evenings a week. Though she ignored Cynthia's frequent suggestions that she take some college courses too, Marietta did not neglect her education. She became an avid reader of books and magazine articles about the social set she intended to enter—the people in that set, their lives, their pleasures, their businesses. She kept tabs on all the eligible men worth at least a million dollars a year after taxes. Someday one of them would be her husband; all she needed was the right opportunity. That opportunity arrived on her twenty-first birthday.

She spent an hour that morning posing for a tender love scene that would be used to illustrate a story in *True Confessions.* Her partners for such shots were always aspiring actors who picked up money modeling while they awaited their big break. More often than not, they were so wrapped up in how handsome or dramatic they would look in the photo that they considered her merely a prop. That day, however, she worked with a fellow who was new to her. His name was Craig Campbell, and he had recently arrived in New York, hoping to break into the theater. When Larry Melman, the photographer, introduced them, Craig's eyes wandered over her in a way that made it clear he considered her to be a great deal more than a prop. He began getting hot in the clinches, which were shot in a corner of Larry's studio that had been set up to look like a living room, and more than once Larry had to remind Craig that the scene was supposed to be tender, not passionate.

As they were packing their kits and preparing to leave, Craig told Marietta that a friend who was an insider had given him two invitations to a fashion showing that afternoon. Because the showing was for the press and buyers, not the public, a great deal of free food and booze would be available, a particular attraction for a struggling actor. Marietta agreed to accompany him; one never knew what opportunities might present themselves. They arranged to meet at three o'clock in the lobby of the Plaza Hotel.

Marietta arrived a little early. She enjoyed watching the women, exhausted from a day's shopping at Bergdorf's and Saks, amble in to revive themselves with tea or something stronger in the Palm Court. Someday she would take her place among them. In her camel's hair coat and sand-colored suede fashion boots that had been gifts from lovers, she looked as though she belonged there already.

She almost didn't recognize Craig when he stepped through the revolving doors. In a borrowed gray topcoat and navy-blue suit, he projected the image of a bright young executive on his way to the top, a far cry from the small-town garage mechanic he had portrayed in Larry's studio that morning.

"I use the Stanislavsky method," he confided. "It works even better off-stage."

It was not until they were in the elevator on their way up to the grand ballroom that Marietta learned they were attending a showing of the new line of Lady Sabrina Swimwear. Her heart beat a little faster. Harlan Wylford, the president of the company, was one of the men she had recently added to her "eligible" list. He had built a small business inherited from his father into one of the most popular and profitable bathing suit companies in the country. Lady Sabrina swimsuits were worn all over the world. He was sixty-two years old, and his wife of forty years had died six months before.

Upstairs they checked their coats and Craig handed his invitations to a receptionist, who smiled warmly, checked them against her list, and proffered name tags identifying them as staff members of a magazine called *Trend*. Next, a beaming representative of Lady Sabrina shook their hands and invited them to get drinks at the bar and help themselves to the lavish buffet.

For starters, Craig piled his plate with roast beef, shrimp, and stuffed avocados. "I haven't seen so much food since I crashed a society wedding," he said.

In addition to the drinks at the bar and the food on overladen tables, waiters and waitresses passed through the crowd with exotic hors d'oeuvres and champagne.

Over the rim of her champagne glass, Marietta scanned the crowd. It was predominantly female, women from thirty through fifty, no doubt buyers for swank stores around the country. Dressed in the height of fashion, they all looked like walking advertisements for their stores' designer departments. The men, too, were obviously fashion-minded, and dressed with much more flamboyance than Craig.

Several of the men spotted Marietta and, taken with her beauty, drifted over to flirt with her. She was on automatic pilot for most of the repartee, her attention still focused on searching for Harlan Wylford.

Just before the show began, she spotted him. By that time she and Craig were seated at one of the little tables that had been set up in the ballroom. He was dressed more conservatively than most of the men, wearing a dark gray suit and a blue tie. He stood erect, and though his hair was gray, he looked younger than his years. Marietta was trying to think of a way to wangle an introduction when he walked up on the stage and delivered a short welcoming address. Then it was too late. The fashion show began.

To the accompaniment of music and the sultry, intimate voice of an MC who described each garment as though it were an exquisite jewel, slim, elongated models strolled across the stage and along a runway, displaying a line that ranged from one-piece cover-ups to scant bikinis. The models seemed anachronistic in that vast gilt and ivory room with its huge crystal chandeliers and draped balconies. Harlan Wylford, on the other hand, seemed as though he belonged there or anyplace else that exemplified elegance and prestige. He sat at a table near the stage and watched the models with pride, occasionally making a comment to one of the three men and two women in his entourage. But it was a different expression of his that soon grasped Marietta's interest; every so often, as he watched a nearly naked young woman saunter or strut before him, his eyes would fill with hunger. After forty years of marriage to the same woman and six months without her, he was ripe for the picking, and Marietta intended to be the woman to shake his tree. Only one question remained: how? In a moment Craig answered it for her.

"Would you mind if we left soon?" he whispered, leaning close to her ear. "It's a godawful bore. I never thought I'd see the day when I'd say that about a chance to stare at half-naked women, but they might just as well have put those swimsuits on a bunch of boys. Those models are like sticks."

"Fashion models are always skinny," Marietta reminded him.

"I can't for the life of me see why. Who wants to look at girls without chests in bikinis? The church ladies back in my hometown could have gotten up a more exciting fashion show than this."

That, Marietta realized, was it. She now knew how to shake Harlan Wylford's tree.

"Craig," she said, kissing him lightly, "you're brilliant. You've just given me a marvelous idea."

He gave her an intimate look. "I hope it's that you're ready to get out of here and come back to my place."

"Why not?" she asked. She felt like celebrating.

They took the Fifth Avenue bus to West Eighth Street and walked the rest of the way to Craig's seedy little room on Avenue A. Since, thanks to Lady Sabrina, they would have no need for dinner, he splurged on a bottle of cheap wine and a bag of pretzels.

"Watch out for the cockroaches," he said as he closed the door behind them. He switched on the light, and several of the large brown insects scurried across the worn linoleum. Marietta shuddered and involuntarily stepped backward, into his arms. He hugged her and kissed her neck. "I train them to do that," he confided.

He put the wine and pretzels on a scratched table and went to a curtained closet to hang up their coats. Approaching the aluminum-painted radiator by his cracked window to warm her hands, Marietta soon discovered that more noise than heat emanated from it. When he walked over to her, she saw that he had removed his jacket and tie and rolled up his sleeves. His arms were strong, his neck long and wide, and there were intriguing little curls of dark hair peeking through his open collar.

He ran his hands up and down her arms. "Shall we have our wine before or after?"

Her tongue darted out over her lips, leaving them sparkling and moist. "Why not in between?" she whispered, slipping her arms around his neck. And then they were lost in a long, deep kiss.

Slowly they undressed each other, kissing each part of the other's body as it was exposed, and then they sank down on his lumpy studio couch and made love.

It had been a long time since Marietta had made love with a man who was close to her own age. What Craig lacked in experience, he made up for in vigor. She had forgotten how marvelous it was to feel strong young arms crushing her, ardent young lips burrowing their way into secret places, filling her with shocks of ecstasy.

Suddenly, at the crucial moment, he raised himself above her and looked into her eyes. "I forgot to ask," he said. "Is it all right? Are you prepared?"

She burst out laughing. "Jesus! You *are* new to New York and the century! This is 1971. Yes, I'm prepared—and now, my sweet country boy, I hope you're prepared for me."

She rolled herself over on top of him and pressed her mouth down on his. When she knew his head was spinning from her kisses, she slipped her breast between his lips and eased herself down on him. Then they were lost in an explosion of passion that left them both weak and shaking.

Afterward, wrapped in a glow and the scratchy Indian blanket that served as a cover for the studio couch, they ate pretzels from the bag and drank wine from jelly-jar glasses, telling each other a little about themselves.

Craig spoke with warmth about the large loving farm family he had left behind in Indiana. All his life he had wanted to act, he told her, and though it was a calling his down-to-earth parents didn't understand, they had never discouraged him and had even been proud when he had won a drama scholarship to UCLA. After college he had spent a year studying at the Pasadena Playhouse, and then another acting bit parts in a touring company. Now he had come to New York with the dream of getting a solid off-Broadway part that would win him recognition.

"Do you have any connections?" Marietta asked.

He had a marvelous laugh, deep and rich, and his teeth were white and even. "Are you kidding? A farm kid from Indiana?"

"But it will take years without connections."

"I've got time on my side. When I get to the top, I want to know I got there on my own."

"That's a risky business."

He shook his head. "Not for me, it isn't. Deep inside, I've always known that someday I'm going to make it." Tenderly, he pushed her hair back from her cheek. "Now tell me about yourself."

Usually, Marietta lied about her past to lovers. Sometimes she claimed descent from an impoverished Russian princess who had escaped the Red terror with only her life and a jewel-encrusted miniature of the Czarina, which she'd had to sell in Paris for the price of third-class passage to New York; sometimes she was the granddaughter of a financier who'd jumped from the window of his Wall Street office when the stock market crashed in 1929, leaving the family with debts it was never able to work off. But when she looked into Craig's clear blue eyes, she didn't want to lie. She had the strangest longing to be little Marianne Vuckendorn—or, at least, little Marianne Dawn—again, if only for a few brief moments.

She took another sip from her glass, leaned her head on his shoulder, and told him the real story of her childhood. When she was finished, he slipped his hand under her chin and tilted her face up so that he could look into her eyes. His own eyes were filled with sympathetic pain.

"I've read about lives like yours," he said. "They always seemed so far away before. I wish I could help you to forget."

She smiled, suddenly Marietta once more. "Well, it's far away from me now too. And I'm going to do something to make myself forget. Someday I'm going to be very rich."

"You don't need a lot of money to be happy."

"That's a fairy tale that was started by the rich to keep the poor from asking for their share of the goodies, and you're repeating it with the innocence of someone who never had to go to bed hungry."

His hand slipped down to her breast and began gently caressing her nipple, sending little shivers of pleasure through her. "I wish there was something I could do to make you happy," he said.

She reached down and began caressing him too. "You can," she whispered. "How about an encore performance?"

She didn't have to ask him twice....

It was 2 a.m. when they left his apartment, and the temperature had dropped to thirteen degrees. She had more than enough money for a taxi, but he insisted upon seeing her home, and she knew better than to ask a farm boy from Indiana to let her pay for a cab. So they walked hand in hand, their heads bent against the onslaught of a biting early-November wind that cut off all possibility for conversation.

At her door they turned to each other, their cheeks winter pink, their eyes sparkling from the cold. He took her face between his hands and kissed her lightly on the lips.

"I think I'm falling in love with you," he said.

She laughed. "I think you had too much champagne and cheap wine."

"Wine fogs the brain but not the heart. Can I see you tomorrow?"

"I'll be tied up all day with a special project, and I have to work tomorrow night from seven to midnight."

"I'll pick you up when you get off."

She looked up at him. A relationship with him could lead only to a dead end. It would be years, maybe decades, before he reached the kind of income bracket she wanted. Maybe he would never reach it. Still, she had no plans for the next night. And he was so tall, so handsome. She felt so good in his arms.

"All right," she said, "but you have to promise me that there'll be no more crazy talk about love."

He pulled her into his arms and gave her a kiss that left her head spinning. "Who needs talk?" he asked. Then he kissed her once more and returned into the cold.

She found the bedroom light on and Cynthia asleep, a history textbook open on her lap, a notebook and ballpoint pen on the floor. Quietly, she picked up the books, closed them, and placed them on Cynthia's night table. Then she undressed and climbed into her own bed.

She lay awake a long time, staring into the darkness and making plans for the meeting she intended to have with Harlan Wylford the next day. When she finally drifted off to sleep, her mind was filled with speculations about Harlan Wylford's assets. Her dreams were filled with Craig Campbell's face.

Chapter Two

ARLY IN HER research, Marietta had learned that nothing is ever out of season for the rich. Winter, fall, summer, spring—they can choose their favorite time of year and proceed to follow it around the world. Eager to keep them properly outfitted for that pursuit, the great Fifth Avenue department stores have bathing suits readily available in the middle of winter and ski togs in July.

Marietta was at Lord & Taylor's when it opened its doors the next morning. She hurried to the Bermuda Shop and quickly selected the scantiest Lady Sabrina bikini she could find in her size; it appeared to have been fashioned by a thrifty designer from a few strips of turquoise ribbon. From the department store she taxied to Abet Rent-a-Fur on Twenty-eighth Street, where she rented a luxurious, full-fashioned Scandinavian mink coat. Then she sped back to her apartment, where she rushed to apply makeup, fix her hair, and dress properly for the occasion.

At a quarter to twelve, wrapped snugly in the mink coat, her coppery hair done up in an elegant twist, she stood before the desk of Harlan Wylford's private secretary. The woman had obviously been hand-picked by Wylford's wife. She was a no-nonsense type of about fifty in a gray suit that matched the dull color of her hair, and she looked up at Marietta with a glint of admiration and perhaps a touch of envy in her eyes.

"May I help you?" she asked.

"I'm Marietta Dawn. I'm here to see Mr. Wylford. I'm afraid I'm a little late." Her heart was pounding. What if he wasn't in?

The secretary looked perplexed. "I'm sorry, but I don't have you down in my book, Miss Dawn."

Marietta made a devastating smile. "I'm sure Mr. Wylford has me down in his. Will you show me in, please?"

"Yes, of course." A little flustered, the woman rose and led the way to the inner office. "Miss Dawn," she announced, opening the door.

Harlan Wylford looked up from his desk, obviously puzzled. Before he had a chance to say a word, Marietta swept in, holding out her hand to him.

"I saw you just yesterday at your showing. Surely, you haven't forgotten me?"

He stood up and took her hand, his eyes clearly saying he couldn't believe he had forgotten such a beauty. "Yes, yes, of course. It's so good to see you again." He turned to his secretary, who was still hovering in the doorway. "Thank you, Miss Kravatz. That will be all. No calls, please."

Miss Kravatz slipped out and closed the door behind her. Wylford turned back to Marietta. He was still holding her hand, and now he slipped his left over it too. "I can't believe that I could have forgotten meeting you. You'll have to refresh my memory. May I take your coat?"

"No, thank you. I'm fine this way. And I must admit that I stretched the truth a bit. You see, I saw you at your showing yesterday, but you didn't notice me."

He shook his head, incredulous. "I'd better have my eyes checked."

Slowly she withdrew her hand from his. "May I sit down?"

"Of course, of course."

She settled herself in a comfortable chair on the opposite side of his desk, crossing her legs to show them off for best effect. "I have a business proposition for you."

His eyebrows arched in mild surprise. Up close, Marietta noticed, he was even more handsome than from afar. His hair was a vibrant silver gray, his jaw was firm and square, and only a few lines fanned out from his lively blue eyes. "Really?"

"Actually, it's more a business idea—one that is bound to increase your sales."

"Perhaps you're not aware that Lady Sabrina is the best-selling line in the country."

"Of course I'm aware of that. But I'm also aware that no matter how good sales are, they can always be better."

He nodded. "And how do you propose to go about that here at Lady Sabrina?"

"By improving your presentation, by showing off your wares to the best possible advantage at showings and in advertisements."

"We already do that. We hire the best fashion models available."

"That's the problem. Bikinis and even one-piece bathing suits are made to show off figures, but the best fashion models available are built more like boys than like women. If you single out one or two numbers in each season's new line and have them modeled by someone who has the kind of body every man longs to see in a bikini and every woman wishes hers would look like when she wore one, you'd see your sales of those numbers rocket. Of course, it would have to be just one model, so that those numbers would stand out above all the rest. That person would then become identified with the line, like a trademark."

"That's an interesting suggestion. And I suppose you think that you should be that person."

"I know I should be." She stood up, opened the mink coat and let it fall languidly to the floor, revealing that all she wore beneath it was her new turquoise bikini. She walked closer to the desk, and then turned slowly so that he could have a better view of her full breasts and tiny waist, her firm buttocks and shapely legs. She paused, her legs spread slightly apart. It was there in his eyes again, the hunger she had seen the day before—only now it was raw and naked. His hands were trembling slightly. She licked her lips and asked softly, "If you were a buyer for Saks, wouldn't you order more of this number if you saw it displayed to such an advantage?"

"Yes," he said, his eyes upon the provocative gap between her thighs, "I believe I would."

"Good." Her voice was bright and all business as, her breasts quivering, she picked up the coat, slipped it on, and pulled it as tightly around her as a virgin's cloak. She sat down again. "When do you want me to start?"

"Immediately, of course."

"Wonderful." She stood up, as though ready to leave. "I'll report for work Monday morning."

"Wait." He was staring at the coat as though he were willing it to spring open. "I want to get more of your ideas about this. Let's discuss it over lunch."

"I'm not exactly dressed for lunch."

"I don't mind. We can have it sent in."

"But I do mind. Give me an hour to go home and change, and I'll meet you wherever you choose."

He suggested Le Petit Trianon, one of those elegant little East Side restaurants that are hidden away in brownstones and known only to such of New York's cognoscenti who are either extraordinarily wealthy or who have unlimited expense accounts. Twice, Marietta walked past the establishment, thinking it was a millionaire's residence and that Harlan had given her the wrong address. Finally she spotted the small white-on-black sign in the window to the right of the door: LE PETIT TRIANON, *Reservations, s'il vous plaît.* When she discovered that the huge paneled oak door was locked, she rang the bell. Almost immediately it was swung open by a man who looked as though he and his tuxedo had been designed by a computer that had been fed data on the components of the perfect maître d'.

"May I help you, mademoiselle?" he asked in an accent worthy of Louis Jourdan.

"I'm here to meet Mr. Harlan Wylford."

"Ah, yes. Mademoiselle Dawn. I am Charles. This way, please." She followed him through a thickly carpeted foyer lighted by a cut-glass chandelier with pendant drops, and hung with eighteenth-century landscapes and portraits of the nobility. They entered a small dining room with about a dozen tables, all covered with snowy-white linen and decorated with small bouquets of pink roses and baby's breath in crystal vases. The room was lighted by electric candles in elegantly carved *bras de lumière* affixed to the richly polished cherry-wood paneled walls. Harlan was awaiting her at a table near French doors that looked out on a now winter-bare walled garden. He rose from his chair as she approached, and did not sit down again until Charles had seated her comfortably and had helped her slip off the mink coat, revealing a snug green wool dress with a plunging neckline. He nodded to Charles and told him that the champagne could be served now.

"They have private dining rooms too," he informed Marietta as Charles slipped away, "but I thought you might be more comfortable here the first time we dined together."

She raised an eyebrow and smiled. "You must think we have a great deal of business to discuss."

His eyes held hers. "Must it always be business?"

Her only answer was a noncommittal smile.

Within moments, a waiter arrived with a bottle of Moët in a silver bucket. He extended the bottle for Harlan's inspection and, upon his nod, opened it and poured a little into his glass. Harlan sipped and savored, nodded once more, and the waiter filled their glasses and quietly retreated.

"To you," Harlan said, raising his glass.

"To our association," Marietta countered, raising her own.

Harlan, she found out as they partook of consommé, *poulet farci Parisienne,* julienne of zucchini, potatoes rosemary, *tonille aux fraises,* and demitasse from Limoges dishes, knew how to order an excellent lunch. He was also easy to talk to. Though she was aware that he was primarily fascinated by her face and figure, it became obvious to her that he was also interested in her business ideas and intended to put them into operation, not only because he wished to ingratiate himself with her, but also because he believed that they would prove profitable. When he brought the conversation to a more personal plane, she opted for her impoverished-Russian-princess story rather than for her Depression tale; being a businessman, Harlan might have asked awkward questions about her grandfather's suicidal investments. Harlan listened sympathetically, either believing her or being too polite to reveal by even a blink of an eye that he did not. She kept the details vague and the story short, and quickly changed the subject to one every man warms to—himself.

At three forty-five, when the waiter came along with the special cognac of the house, Marietta brought the conversation back to business. She declined Harlan's suggestion that she start working for him the next day, saying that, instead, she would rather begin on Monday, which would give her lawyer a chance to glance over their contract.

"Contract?" Harlan echoed. "I thought we had agreed on terms," he added, referring to the very generous salary he had offered her.

"Oh, we have agreed." Smiling, she turned her eyes fully on his. "But I think everything should be in writing. Gentlemen's agreements are fine between gentlemen, but you know what they say about women always changing their minds. I don't want any of your business associates to accuse you of leaving yourself unprotected." What she meant, of course, was that she did not want any of his business associates to talk him out of the deal. She leaned forward a little, giving him a better view of her décolletage. "It will be better for us both that way, don't you agree?"

His eyes slid down to her neckline, and he nodded.

She looked at her watch. "It will be just a simple contract, one the two of us can draw up ourselves. I'm sure your secretary can type it up for us in no time when we get back to your office."

He took the hint and signaled for the bill.

Back in his office, Miss Kravatz quickly typed the document they drew up, naming Marietta his head model, whose responsibilities would be to supervise all other models and to model numbers that would become associated with her exclusively. Her starting salary would be a generous thirty thousand dollars a year, and at the end of one year the contract would be renegotiated for more money.

"You know," Marietta said when she was holding the document in her hand, "I really see no need for my lawyer to examine this. I trust you, Harlan. I can't believe you'd try to take advantage of my ignorance of the business world. If you're satisfied with this, then so am I. Let's sign it now and get it over with."

They did so, calling in Miss Kravatz and the head salesman as witnesses.

When the other two had left the office, Marietta tucked her copy into her purse, saying, "I really must be going. I think I've taken up too much of your time already."

"Not by far," Harlan told her. "In fact, I think we should go out and celebrate our agreement."

"I wish I could, but I have to go home and change. I have an engagement this evening." She was pleased to see the disappointment in his eyes.

"Tomorrow night then."

She shook her head sadly. "I'm all tied up for the rest of the week, and I'm going away for the weekend. How about Monday evening after my first day of work? Then we'll really have something to celebrate."

"All right. Monday. It seems a long way off, though." He helped her on with her coat, his hands lingering on her shoulders. She turned her head so that her hair brushed his cheek. He touched it for a moment. "You have such beautiful hair. I've never seen any quite that color. It's probably indiscreet to ask, but is it natural?"

"It is, but most people refuse to believe it. And I'm much too modest to prove it," she added with ravishing smile.

"*I* believe it," he said. His eyes told her that he longed to see the proof himself someday.

She left his office confident that her battle was half won.

She was in high spirits when Craig picked her up that evening at the end of her shift. She had quit her job and was ready to take life in both hands. But first, she wanted to take Craig in her arms. She had never before experienced the feeling that overcame her as she saw him waiting for her at the exit—a sort of quivery melting that started in her throat and ended somewhere near the pit of her stomach. It was frightening but delicious, and making love back in his apartment heightened it to the point of ecstasy. Later, while she lay with her head nestled in the crisp mat of dark hair on his chest, she told him—without providing any details—that, following her woman's intuition, she had visited Lady Sabrina and had been hired as a model. He was pleased for her and sure that her career was on its way. She didn't tell him that a career was far from what she had in mind. She had no intention of seeing him again after that night, but somehow, wrapped in his arms, she couldn't bring herself to tell him that. When he suggested pizza and an off-off-Broadway play the next night, she found herself agreeing. After all, she thought, tracing the fine Grecian line of his lips with her fingertip, what harm could it do?

In the weeks that followed, she was to ask herself that question many times. Eventually, she stopped. She was afraid her conscience might come up with an answer.

Before starting her new job she spent the days learning everything she could about the bathing-suit industry. By the time Monday arrived she was far from an expert, but thanks to the business branch of the New York Public Library, she certainly knew more about it than any other model before or since.

As she expected, there was trouble with the house models, who resented an outsider being thrust into a superior position over them. With the exception of Ed Stern, the chief accountant, who seemed genuinely impressed by her innovative ideas, she faced strong resentment on the executive level too. She knew Ed liked her and had tried to win the others over to her side, but, perhaps because he was gay, he held no clout with them. Actually, she never would have guessed about Ed's homosexuality if she and Harlan had not run into him and his companion at the theater one night. There was something about a look she caught the two men exchanging that keyed her in. She couldn't resist making a crack about it later. It was the first time Harlan was a little sharp with her. Ed was a nice guy, Harlan said. He was good at his job, a hard worker and a loyal one. What he did with his private life was nobody's business. Besides, Harlan went on, when it came to the good qualities that set human beings apart from the beasts, Ed was more of a man than most of the he-men he had ever come across. She wound up feeling a little ashamed of herself, and in the days that followed, aware that Ed was standing up for her against the others, she came to understand and share Harlan's affection for the man.

Fred Gibbs, the general manager, was her most aggressive enemy. He always made it clear—when Harlan wasn't present, of course—that he thought his boss had taken leave of his senses. Though most of the others obviously agreed with Fred, they were more circumspect about their opinions in Marietta's presence. However, her businesslike manner and the sensible yet imaginative and profitable suggestions she always made at conferences soon won the executives' grudging approval. The models' approval she would never win, but they were easily replaced, especially after she pointed out the economy of hiring only freelance models—no need to be bothered with the bookkeeping hassles of withholding taxes, the expense of health and unemployment insurance, the headache of employee relations.

Much to her relief, her prediction came true. Her name, face, and figure immediately became associated with the product, and sales soared higher than ever. Marietta Dawn *was* Lady Sabrina.

But what Marietta Dawn really wanted to be was Mrs. Harlan Wylford. In the office she tried to keep relations with Harlan on a cool, strictly business plane, but he became adept at finding reasons to confer with her just before or after a modeling session, while she was still in one of his temptingly skimpy bikinis. Pretending not to notice the bulge rising on the left side of his fly, she would slowly and demurely slip on the shimmering, clinging jade-green kimono she kept in her dressing room and give him a straightforward answer to the question he had no doubt already forgotten.

Harlan belonged to a rare, almost extinct branch of Homo sapiens Americanus: he had married young and had been devoted and absolutely faithful to his wife of forty years. He knew about love, but when it came to raw sex he was a babe in the woods. Marietta sensed this, and was determined to play on it to her best advantage. She saw him no more than three evenings a week after work—usually only two—and limited those meetings to public though intimate restaurants and lounges. Weekends she spent with Craig. She told herself it was not because she preferred his company but because it was good policy to keep Harlan dangling, panting and wondering.

She found herself living at a peak of excitement she had never dreamed could be maintained. Days spent helping to run an important and growing business were a stimulation for her quick mind and sharp intelligence. Her evenings with Harlan, during which she glimpsed the world of luxury he held the key to, were titillatingly exhilarating. Nights and weekends spent with Craig and in his arms seethed with passion and quivered with fulfillment.

When Harlan asked her to join him for Thanksgiving dinner, she declined, telling him that she would be spending the holiday out of town with old friends. Actually, she and Craig spent the day in the Crown Heights apartment of the Danielle family. It was a delightful holiday, with everyone helping with the cooking and cleanup. Shirley and Melanie roasted a huge turkey, and Cynthia and Marietta brought along their first and almost-successful efforts at baking pumpkin and mince pies. And in Shirley's battered old soup pot, Craig mulled cider according to his mother's recipe. There was a great deal of laughter, teasing, and love around the crowded table in Shirley's cramped, overheated kitchen.

As they were leaving, Craig hugged Shirley and thanked her for inviting him. "This was the closest I've been to home since I came to New York," he said.

Eleven-year-old Melanie laughed and looked around the cramped apartment with its cracked walls, which was situated in one of the seamiest neighborhoods in Brooklyn. "I thought you said you lived in a big old farmhouse with fields of wheat stretching out as far as you could see."

Shirley pulled her younger daughter closer. The wrinkles time and worry had etched around her eyes deepened as she smiled and said, "Home's not a place, but a feeling inside you."

"A feeling you get when special people are around," Craig added, reaching for Marietta's hand.

Because Cynthia had decided to spend the long holiday weekend with her mother and sister, Marietta had their apartment to herself. She could not resist the temptation of inviting Craig to join her. It was the first time they had been together for such an extended period, and she had hoped that it would help her to work Craig out of her system. It didn't. They spent a great deal of the time wrapped in each other's arms in Marietta's twin bed, making love with an almost frenzied passion. Craig had been relatively inexperienced when they met, but he had proved a quick learner with Marietta as his teacher, and now he was able to excite her as no man had ever done before.

In between lovemaking, they bundled up against the cold and wandered the city hand in hand, looking at the Christmas decorations, munching hot chestnuts purchased from sidewalk vendors, ducking into coffee shops now and then for food and warmth. Inevitably, cozy conversations across steaming cups of coffee led them back to the apartment and bed.

Sunday morning Marietta awoke to the delicious aroma of perking coffee and the sizzling of frying eggs, bacon, and hash-brown potatoes. She found Craig in the kitchen standing over the stove, with the table already set for two.

"I thought I'd give you a modified sample of a farm break-fast," he said, kissing her, then piling her plate high. "Mom will give you the full treatment when you come home with me for Christmas week."

Her heart sank. He had hinted at the possibility of her spending the holidays at his home in Indiana before, but she had always managed to change the subject. She was sure that Harlan would ask her to spend Christmas Day with him, and she felt that it would be good strategy to do so. He was ripe for the picking, and Christmas Day would probably be the perfect time to set their relationship on a straight course to the altar.

"What about it?" Craig asked, and sat down across from her. "Will you come home with me for Christmas?"

"You know I haven't been at Lady Sabrina long enough to ask for any time off. Besides, it's probably for the best. Do you really think we could spend a week in the same house with your family without going crazy? I doubt very much that your mother would let me bunk with you, and it will be way too cold for us to go sneaking off to the barn."

"I'd manage something," Craig said with a roguish gleam in his eyes. "My folks are pretty heavy sleepers." He reached for her hand, his look softening. "Promise me you'll try to get the time off. You're all I write home about. Mom and Dad are dying to meet you, and I can't wait for you to meet them."

"I'll try," she said, knowing she wouldn't, and wondering why that thought depressed her so.

Monday evening she and Harlan dined at Le Petit Trianon again. This time, however, he had reserved a private dining room. They did not take the winding staircase to reach it but, instead, followed Charles into a tiny, manually operated, gilt elevator that was illuminated by a Tiffany chandelier. As he slid the door closed and pulled the lever, Marietta was reminded of an off-off-off

Broadway production of a Gay Nineties musical Craig had taken her to. Embarrassingly amateurish, it closed almost as soon as it had opened, but its highlight had been a pretty blonde who sang a heart-wrenching rendition of "She Was Only a Bird in a Gilded Cage."

Charles led them along a burgundy-carpeted, oak-paneled hallway to a highly polished door. With a bow he showed them in, then discreetly disappeared.

Her breath catching, Marietta looked around. In the days of the original owner of the mansion, a minor robber baron who had made most of his millions in sweatshops, the room had probably been a study or a dressing room. Now the panels of the ivory-colored walls were hung with royal blue brocade and decorated with works by early American Impressionists. Marietta spotted among them two mother-and-child pastels by Mary Cassatt and a New York winter scene by Childe Hassam. The furniture was late Empire. Two walnut chairs were drawn up to a table *à deux* covered with a red and blue damask cloth. Across the room, a blue velvet settee stood at a right angle before the fire crackling in a white and violet marble fireplace. In front of the settee was a piecrust table laden with caviar and hors d'oeuvres, and in a tripod next to it, a bottle of Moët lay in its bucket of ice.

"Do you like it?" Harlan asked. He took her coat and hung it in the closet.

"I love it. But what's the occasion for such opulence?"

"The occasion is our being together again."

Marietta laughed and sat down on the settee, draping her arm gracefully across its back. "We were apart only four days, according to my calendar."

"According to mine, it was a lot longer than that."

Instead of answering, she smiled and reached for a wafer and caviar. Harlan opened the champagne and poured it. "I've already ordered for us," he said, handing her a glass. "I wanted us to be disturbed as little as possible by the staff. It's so rare that we have a chance to talk in private."

As they touched glasses, she noticed that his hand was shaking slightly. She regarded it as a good sign. Obviously he wanted to get their relationship on a new level and wasn't sure how to go about it. She hoped he wouldn't be crass and come right out and ask her to be his mistress. She was heartened by the fact that there was no piece of furniture in the room upon which they could comfortably make love. When the time for that came, she wanted to be in complete control so that she could play it for all it was worth.

"You sound so serious," she said huskily. "I hope you haven't gone to all this trouble to cushion the news that you want to fire me."

His laugh was tense. "You know better than that, Marietta. You've done great things for the company. Business has nothing to do with the problem."

"Then there is a problem?"

He drained his glass and walked over to the fireplace. "Yes, but not in a negative sense. It's just that I want to get to know you better, and I haven't had the chance. In the office, it's strictly business—which, of course, is as it should be. But outside the office, I see you only a few times a week, and then it's in a restaurant or a theater where we're surrounded by other people. I feel as though we've never really been together. I—I wanted to do something about it."

"Well, you have—and you've done it beautifully." She spooned some caviar onto a toast round and bit into it daintily. "This is warm and cozy, and I like it very much."

"But it's not nearly enough," he said earnestly. "I want to do so much more." He closed his eyes for a moment, as if praying for courage to go on. "I thought about it all through that long Thanksgiving weekend, and I've come up with an idea. I've rented a villa on the Côte d'Azur for Christmas week. I—I want you to spend the holidays there with me." The last words rushed from his mouth like runners taking off at the shot from a starter's gun.

Marietta had expected perhaps an awkward declaration of love followed by a suggestion that she accompany him to his apartment after dinner; she hadn't been prepared for an invitation to spend Christmas with him on the French Riviera. Her heart began to pound, and she was aware that the blood rushing to her cheeks must be turning them an attractive shade of pink. She had been raising her glass to her lips as he spoke and, regarding him over the rim, said quietly, "Are you suggesting what I think you are, Harlan?" She tried to look and sound disappointed in him.

His own face reddened to the hairline. "Oh, no, nothing like that," he said, rushing to sit down beside her. "It's a villa. You'll have your own room—your own wing if you prefer. All I want is for us to have some time together, time to get to know each other."

"That's all?"

"Absolutely."

She continued studying his face, as if trying to read his innermost thoughts, and it reddened even more.

"You'll love the Riviera," he pressed on. "The beach is beautiful, the shopping is marvelous, and the night life is the most exciting in the world. There's an excellent staff at the villa. You'll have the best food, the best care. Please come. If you don't like it, we can take the first plane home."

For a moment, she remained pensive, pretending to think it over. Then she gently placed her hand upon his. "All right. If the arrangement really will be as you said."

"You have my word."

She finished her champagne. "Why don't you have them bring in dinner now? I'm starving."

Exhilarated, hardly able to contain his joy, Harlan leaped up and pressed a bell beside the fireplace. In a few moments a waiter wheeled in their consommé Rejane.

Throughout the meal Harlan spoke about the attractions of the Côte d'Azur, sounding like an enthusiastic travel agent. Marietta listened, her mind spinning with plans of her own. Christmas was less than a month away. There was a great deal to be done.

Later, when they were leaving, Marietta drew back at the entrance to the elevator, remembering how confined she had felt in that tiny vehicle. With a smile she informed the operator that she preferred the stairs. Besides, she reminded herself as she turned away, it would be best not to be in close quarters with Harlan from now until they arrived on the Côte d'Azur. She would cut down on their evenings together too, and insist that they be spent only in more public places. She wanted him quivering with frustrated desire by the time she got him alone. All the way down Le Petit

Trianon's elegant winding staircase she could feel his eyes on her derriere.

CRAIG HAD SOME choice words about stingy employers when Marietta told him she wouldn't be able to get time off around the holidays. With kisses and sweet diplomacy she convinced him not to cancel his own plans and remain in the city so that they would be together on Christmas and New Year's Eve. Conjuring up visions of how pleased his family would be to see him, she even persuaded him to leave a week earlier than he had originally planned.

They spent the entire night before Craig's departure in a marathon of love on his lumpy studio couch.

"I want to make love to you at least once for every night we'll be apart," he said. His tongue trailed exciting little circles on her breasts.

"I think," she whispered, clamping her legs around him, "that we're well on our way to making it twice for every night."

In the morning there were dark circles under his eyes as he packed his suitcase and prepared to leave for the airport. Marietta traced them gently with her finger. "Your mother's going to ask where these came from."

"I'll tell her I was up all night administering to the needs of a dear friend." He snapped the locks and pulled her into his arms. "I miss you already. Why don't you quit that damn job and come with me anyway?"

"You know that's crazy." She kissed him lightly and slipped from his arms, reaching for her coat and mittens. "You'll be gone only a couple of weeks. Besides, at the first sniff of that fresh Indiana air and the first taste of your mom's cooking, you'll probably forget all about me."

"The hell I will."

They left the apartment, and she waited with him on First Avenue for the bus to the airline terminal. The wind was sharp and biting, and he thought the tears it brought to her eyes were for him. He reached out to brush them away.

"You'll come home with me for Easter," he said. "There's nothing like springtime in Indiana. Everything on the farm comes to life. You'll love it."

She smiled and nodded. It was not the right moment to tell him that if things turned out right, by Easter he would no longer be part of her life.

A bus screeched to a stop, and he kissed her and boarded it. She watched it disappear into the distance. Then, her eyes still smarting from what she told herself was lack of sleep and the wind, she turned away.

Chapter Three

CHRISTMAS FELL ON a Wednesday that year. Marietta and Harlan left New York Sunday afternoon and arrived at Nice's International Airport in the very early hours of Monday morning. Awaiting them was a liveried chauffeur, a husky, middle-aged man whose thick dark eyebrows met over his nose, giving him a rather fierce appearance. His voice was surprisingly mellow, not the growl suggested by his rough features and unsmiling lips. "I am Antoine Levesque," he announced with a thick, rich accent. "Welcome to Nice. I am happy to be at your service."

It was too dark to see the landscape as he headed the black Rolls-Royce along the narrow coastal road, but Marietta thrilled to the shimmer of the Mediterranean beneath the lights of the magnificent yachts, at anchor like huge, graceful seabirds reposing for the night.

At Villefranche, near the tip of the Cap Ferrat peninsula, the headlights illuminated a long white stucco wall that terminated in a high Doric column. Upon its capital a marble lion gazed meditatively toward his twin atop an identical column at the other end of the encircling wall several yards away. Joining the columns was an iron gate, the elaborate design of which could not disguise the fact that it had been placed there for privacy and protection, not decoration. Antoine unlocked and opened it with great flair, and then returned to the car and continued along a gravel road lined with stately palms. At the end of the drive, its white facade almost luminous, stood the Villa Claudine, a two-story house of classical inspiration.

Weary from their travels, Marietta and Harlan mounted the

steps to the colonnaded portico and the door. They were admitted to the main hall by an elderly butler with a fringe of gray hair. He was dressed in full livery and spoke with only a trace of a French accent. His name, he told them as he repeated Antoine's welcome, was Henri. Because of the hour, he had taken the liberty of allowing the rest of the staff to go to bed, but he would awaken them immediately if their services were desired.

Harlan shook his head and assured him that morning would be time enough to meet the staff. "Now, if you'll show Mademoiselle Dawn and me to the rooms I asked you to have prepared for our arrival..."

With a nod that was almost a bow, Henri lifted their traveling cases and motioned them to precede him up the wide, winding marble staircase.

Upstairs, he started along a corridor and said, "As you requested, monsieur, the blue suite for Mademoiselle Dawn, and the green suite at the other end for you. Mademoiselle..." He opened the door of a room that easily could have contained Marietta's entire West Village apartment. "I hope this is satisfactory."

"Most satisfactory," Marietta assured him.

He placed her case upon a luggage rack. "The cook left a cold supper, if you are hungry."

She shook her head. "I'm much too exhausted to eat a thing." She turned to Harlan, who was standing just beyond the threshold. "You'll forgive me if I go straight to bed, won't you?"

He couldn't quite hide his disappointment. "Of course. Have a good night's sleep. I'll see you in the morning."

"Not too early, I hope."

"Sleep as late as you like, my dear." He smiled and followed Henri down the hall to his own room.

A few minutes later Henri knocked and entered with the rest of her luggage. He showed her the bell cord beside her bed and told her that when she pulled it in the morning a maid would come with her coffee and to draw her bath. Her eyes rested on his stooped back as he left the room, and she thought that he had probably been up more hours and was no doubt even more exhausted than she was, jet lag or no jet lag.

Leaving the unpacking for the morning, she undressed

quickly and slipped between the cool silk sheets of the bed. She was asleep almost instantly.

When she opened her eyes eight hours later, it was with that feeling of strangeness that washes over one upon awaking in unfamiliar surroundings. For a moment she lay still, gazing up at the paneled ceiling, which had been decorated in the style of Fragonard—a local Riviera boy who had made good—with rosy-cheeked and dimple-buttocked cherubim looking on benevolently as lovers in ruffled shirts and knee britches poured out their hearts to mistresses in powdered wigs and low-cut farthingales. Slowly she remembered the champagne-gilded first-class flight from New York, the smooth drive in the velvet-upholstered Rolls, the arrival at the villa built in 1922 by the English financier Sir Nigel Northbert for his beautiful French mistress, Claudine du Verre. A mystic who fancied herself to be the reincarnation of Marie Antoinette, Claudine had delighted in decorating the villa in a way that would have made Marie feel at home. The toasts of the Riviera society of their day, Claudine and Sir Nigel numbered among their frequent guests Picasso, Ernest Hemingway, and the Scott Fitzgeralds. When he returned from a business trip and found Claudine in bed with Phillipe Courdeau, a pupil of Picasso who emulated his master in everything but talent, Sir Nigel jumped to the conclusion that Claudine had extended the hospitality of the villa just a little too far, and he shot them both—Claudine through the heart, which proved fatal, and Cordeau in the posterior, which proved embarrassing. Riviera society spoke of nothing else for three and a half days. A jury ruled justifiable homicide and acquitted Sir Nigel. He boarded up the villa and did not return to it until after World War II, when he spent his final days as a recluse, living among Claudine's acquisitions. He left the villa to a grandniece who, combining a romantic soul with a cunning mind, restored it to its original grandeur, hired a permanent staff, and rented it out at great profit.

Marietta stretched luxuriously, then slipped out of bed for a better look around the room she had been too exhausted to explore upon arrival. Cerulean blue, the walls matched the sky tones in the scenes depicted upon the ceiling, and the woodwork and paneling were a creamy ivory enamel. Her high-backed Louis

XVI giltwood bed was flanked by a pair of Louis XV tulipwood and fruitwood tables en chiffonière. Their marquetry, in a symmetrical pattern of butterflies and roses, was exquisitely framed by an ormolu border, and atop each of them rested a lamp made of Louis XV brass chamber candlesticks. Across the room, between a pair of French windows draped in royal-blue brocade, stood a tulipwood writing table of the same period, its cabriole legs decorated with ormolu *chutes* and *sabots*, with foliate marquetry on its side drawers and top. The room also contained three large matching marble-topped Louis XVI commodes, a settee, and three matching fauteuils, upholstered in the same shade of blue as the armless chair at the writing table and decorated with carved floral branches. And here and there were a parquetry worktable, a commode, or a bonheur du jour, with its intriguing cupboard doors and drawers and hidden writing surfaces.

In bare feet she padded to the windows over the savonnerie carpet, its strands of gold, blue, and green woven into an intricate design of rosettes and shells, surmounted by garlands and crowns and fleurs de lys. Parting the drapes, she discovered that her room overlooked a rose garden with a marble fountain complete with a mermaid and spouting dolphins. She stepped out on her terrace for a better look. A balmy breeze wafted the scents of earth and sea to her nostrils. She closed her eyes and inhaled deeply. She had come a long way from Crown Heights.

Leaving the windows open, she returned to bed and pulled the bell cord.

Not a minute later there was a brisk knock on the door and a maid entered bearing a tray. "*Bonjour, mademoiselle,*" she said. "Welcome to the Villa Claudine. I am Colette, your maid."

She was far from Marietta's mental image of a French maid named Colette—young and sexy, with breasts popping out of a snug black uniform, legs encased in black nylons, a saucy cap perched on dark curls that framed a face with smoldering eyes and pouting, sensuous lips. This Colette was a woman of indeterminate years, though, to be kind, Marietta would have put her age at about thirty-five. On her stocky, matronly figure she wore a crisp gray uniform with long sleeves, a high neck, and a hem that descended below her knees. Her shapeless legs were clad in gray nylons and ended in large feet and ugly black oxfords. Her starched white apron was a no-nonsense affair that covered most of her dress front, and there was no perky cap upon her lackluster brownish hair, which she wore in a short, straight bob, caught back on the sides with crisscrossed bobby pins. Her round, large-boned face was scrubbed and free of makeup, and her eyes hovered somewhere between blue and gray.

"I have brought you some *café*," Colette said, approaching Marietta, who was sitting on the edge of the bed. "My father says Americans enjoy *café* upon awaking."

Marietta swung her legs under the covers so that Colette could place the tray above them. "Your father is well informed. Does he know many Americans?"

"He has worked for many." Colette arranged the tray and poured coffee from a silver pot into a Limoges cup decorated with sprigs of violets. "He is Henri. You met him last night. My mother is the cook here. Shall I prepare your bath?"

"Yes, please." It was amazing how easy it was to let others do even the simplest things for one.

Colette crossed the room and pulled open the remaining drapes. "Do you like the salts, the oil, or the bubbles in your bath?"

"Bubbles, I think."

Marietta watched Colette disappear into the bathroom. Sipping her coffee, she listened to the maid busying herself at the tub. Presently the sound of rushing water stopped, and Colette returned. "All is ready, Mlle. Dawn."

"Thank you, Colette. Do you know if Mr. Wylford is awake yet?"

"He has been downstairs for some time. He is waiting in the garden. He has told my father that you will both have breakfast there. Do you wish me to unpack your clothing while you bathe?"

"That would be very helpful."

Marietta picked up her robe and strolled into the bathroom. Not even in magazines devoted to the rich, her favorite reading material, had she ever seen such a magnificent bathroom. Large enough to accommodate a party, its gleaming tiles were the same blue as the walls of her bedroom, but dispersed among them were gold medallions with mermaids, dolphins, and seashells. The thick blue carpet led to the edge of a huge bathtub in the shape and color of a nautilus shell, which was cut into the floor. Two pink marble steps led into the tub, filled by a gleaming gold faucet in the shape of an open-mouthed dolphin, its handles oversized golden starfish. A huge gold clamshell heaped with rosettes of fragrant soaps in every color of the rainbow was set out at the edge of the tub, along with a pile of plush velvety towels. To add to the enjoyment of bathing *à deux*—or perhaps to make bathing alone less lonely in that huge room—the wall at the foot of the bathtub was mirrored, as was the entire ceiling. On one side of the room stood a white-and-gold marble-topped vanity with a three-way mirror and a velvet-seated bench, and next to that, a blue-velvet easy chair beside shelves piled high with luxurious towels of every size in beautiful pastel colors. On the other side of the room, next to a white-and-gold table displaying copies of *Vogue* and *Paris Match,* were a bidet and a gleaming blue toilet bowl, reminders that the rich were only human, after all.

Marietta slipped out of her nightgown and descended the steps into the bathtub, stretching out in the delicately scented bubbles with a contented sigh.

By the time she returned to her bedroom, wrapped from shoulder to ankles in a velvety towel and looking like a Roman empress, Colette was putting away the last of her clothes.

"Will there be anything else, mademoiselle?" she asked.

"Not at the moment. Please tell Mr. Wylford that I'll be down soon."

Marietta chose her outfit carefully—white slacks, a low-cut emerald-green blouse, gold sandals. Though the lighting in the bathroom was better, she couldn't resist applying her makeup at the poudreuse in the bedroom. It fascinated her to think of the long line of beauties who had attended to their strategies there, dabbing perfume between almost-naked breasts, applying a beauty patch to their cheeks, a touch of rouge to their lips and nipples. Finished with her own makeup, she eyed herself critically for a moment, and then opened one more button on her blouse. Some things hadn't changed much over the last few centuries.

Harlan sat in a lounge chair on the patio behind the house. He was paying no attention to the book that lay open on his lap, but gazing expressionlessly at an oval pool in which goldfish darted among the water lilies. A small round table was covered with a mauve linen cloth and set for two.

"Good morning."

He had not heard her approach, and he turned and rose, his eyes brightening with pleasure. "Good morning. Did you sleep well?"

Smiling, she looked up at the sun mounting the sky. "Obviously. You must be famished. You shouldn't have waited."

"The pleasure of waiting for you is surpassed only by the pleasure of being with you."

"I'll bet that's something you just read in that book."

"You'd lose then. It's one of my many discoveries about you since you've come into my life."

"Really? Sometime you must tell me about the others—but only the flattering ones. Not now, though. I'm much too hungry to be impressed by anything but food."

Taking his hand, she led him to the table. He held her chair, then sat down himself. Immediately Henri appeared, pushing a tea table full of covered dishes.

"He must have X-ray vision and a magic wand," Marietta observed, watching his approach.

"It's a servant's job to anticipate an employer's needs and wishes." Harlan, lowering his voice, leaned conspiratorially closer: "Besides, I've already told him what we wanted for breakfast."

"Oh? And what do we want?"

He opened his napkin and spread it across his knees. "Melon, butterfish meunière, shirred eggs princess, Wiltshire ham. And champagne, of course."

"Of course."

As Henri served, she turned and gazed out past the goldfish pond. The view was breathtaking. Terraced gardens led down to the sea below. She longed to forget breakfast and run off and explore, but she forced herself to turn back to the table, the champagne and food, and to Harlan.

Later, they toured the grounds, which were divided into formal and informal gardens and included both an avocado and an orange orchard. Graceful magnolia trees shaded some walks, and stately cypresses, standing as erect as vigilant sentinels, guarded others. A pebbled path between rosemary hedges led to a kidney-shaped swimming pool and beyond that a tennis court. The sea was approached by wide, shallow steps paved with variegated pebbles that gleamed in the sunlight and shaded by mimosa trees which were at the moment in full bloom, their yellow blossoms suffusing the air with a delicious honeylike fragrance.

They descended the steps and silently gazed at the sea. This was not Marietta's first encounter with a large body of water; as a child, she had frequently bathed in the Atlantic Ocean at Coney Island. But it had been difficult to be awed by it in the midst of shouting swimmers, ice cream sticks, soda bottles, and scraps of paper. She experienced no such difficulty here. The clear, brilliant blue was broken only when gentle ripples caught the golden rays of the sun. Far out, gleaming white yachts and boats with colorful sails bobbed along like jewels cast on its surface by some benevolent, gigantic hand. Up above, the sky echoed the color of the sea below, with a puff or two of white cloud scattered here and there to proclaim its separateness and individuality. To the south, jutting out in a golden haze that befitted a peninsula where lived some of the world's wealthiest people, was the Cap d'Antibes.

Before lunch Marietta changed into a bikini and took a dip in the heated pool. Harlan demurred, saying the air was too cool for him, and stretched out on a chaise longue at its edge. She was not only a strong swimmer but also an extremely graceful one, and she delighted in the awareness of Harlan's eyes upon her as her arms cut smoothly and quietly through the water. She concluded with a backstroke in which her breasts kept threatening to pop out of her bikini bra.

"What would you like to do this afternoon?" he asked as she stood before him and slowly toweled herself.

"Tour the area, of course. I want to see every last inch." She intended to keep him occupied with everything but what he hoped for most of all until the one perfect moment.

"Then hurry and change," Harlan said. "We're lunching at the Chèvre d'Or in Eze, a little way up the coast. The village hasn't changed since medieval times and even has some pre-Roman streets."

Back in her room she slipped into a full-skirted white dress with a cowl neck, and brushed her hair until it tumbled over her shoulders in gleaming waves. Downstairs, she found the Rolls pulled up in front of the villa, Harlan and Antoine waiting beside it.

After a few miles on the Middle Corniche, the car was climbing up a mountain to a little village settled upon it like an eagle's nest upon a lonely promontory. Centuries of exposure to the elements left it looking as though the wind had carved it out of the rock. Soon Antoine stopped the car and turned to them.

"I can go no farther," he said. "The auto cannot travel these streets. The rest of the trip you must walk. I shall guide you, if you like."

"That's all right," Harlan told him, helping Marietta from the car. "I know the way. Why don't you go back to the villa and return for us in a few hours?"

Inside the walled village they made their way along the narrow and ancient cobbled streets to the cliff where the Chèvre d'Or overlooked the coast. Harlan said, "From this very spot in days of old, villagers may have stood watching for the dreaded approach of pirates and slave raiders."

Marietta was delighted by the restaurant's rustic charm. Once it had been a private home, and its stone walls and exposed wooden beams maintained the local idea of a warm, homey atmosphere. The bright yellow tablecloths looked like bits of sunshine that had been trapped as it spilled in through the huge windows that descended nearly to the floor. Seated near a window with a magnificent view of the coast, Marietta thought she wouldn't be able to concentrate on her food, but the *oignons à la grecque* and the *tournedos du chef* offered ample competition to the scenery.

After lunch they visited the highlight of Harlan's itinerary, the ruins of the local chateau, arising like a monument to the past from the garden of exotic plants and flowers that encircled it. The hours passed quickly, and soon it was time for a final stroll along the narrow streets.

Tired from their outing, they dined at the villa before leaving for a performance of *La Traviata* at the Opera de Nice. To Marietta, the audience was as fascinating as the production on the stage.

The costumes of the singers could not compete with the Paris and Milan originals on the women who sat listening to them. With all the jewels on display, it was surprising that the room darkened when the house lights were dimmed.

After the performance, the audience poured forth through the doors and out onto the street like a swarm of butterflies suddenly being released from a magnificent cocoon. Each couple headed for one of the Rolls-Royces, Mercedeses, or Alfa Romeos lined up on the Rue Saint-François-de-Paule as though the cars were flowers their antennae were programmed to select.

Harlan suggested a visit to a nightclub, but Marietta was too exhausted to be tempted. Antoine returned them to the villa, where Marietta kissed Harlan's cheek and mounted the stairs, feeling his sad eyes upon her all the way to her room.

The next morning, after a vigorous game of tennis, they set off to see Cap Ferrat. They walked the promenade on its western coast, which they agreed deserved its reputation as one of the most beautiful waterside walks in the world. They explored the picturesque old fishing port of Saint-Jean at the tip of the peninsula, and while there, lunched in the lovely garden of the Residence Della Robbia, recently reopened after its annual two-month siesta. Afterward, they visited the nearby cemetery for a look at the strange, huge statue referred to reverently by the locals as the Black Virgin.

They dined that evening at the Negresco, the grandest of Nice's grand hotels, where key members of the staff were garbed in colorful eighteenth-century uniforms. First they had drinks in the bar, sampling the hot hors d'oeuvres that waiters brought around by the trayful. Then, around nine, they moved into the elegant gold-and-ivory restaurant, Le Chantecler, for dinner.

As she watched him discussing the wine list with the sommelier, Marietta thought that Harlan looked very handsome in his white tie and tuxedo. Were it not for his silver hair and the deep grooves time had etched in his cheeks where dimples must have winked when he was a boy, she could easily forget that he was at least ten years older than her father—if that irresponsible drunkard was still alive somewhere.

The sommelier left, and Harlan turned to her with a smile.

"The Morue Provençale is magnificent," he said. "I'm sure it will be an experience for you."

"You really seem to know your way around the Riviera. Have you been here often?"

He shrugged. "Jane and I came a few times."

She smiled brightly, but her heart was sinking as she asked, "Did you stay at the villa?"

"No. We always took the same suite at the Carlton in Cannes."

Marietta relaxed. She didn't want any fond memories of the virtuous Jane intruding when she put her plan into action. When she first went to work for Harlan, there had been a photograph of Jane on his desk. No doubt taken a few years before cancer struck, it showed a chubbyish woman in her late fifties who looked as plain as her name. Her gray hair had been carefully coiffed, and makeup had been applied to make the most of Nature's gifts, but it couldn't disguise the fact that, aside from large dark eyes that looked rather sad, Nature had been in one of her parsimonious moods when that face was molded. Within two weeks of Marietta's employment, the photograph disappeared from Harlan's desk. Harlan rarely spoke about his wife, but Marietta knew that he had loved her deeply.

"Was Cannes Jane's favorite resort or yours?" she asked, her heart catching again.

He spread his hands. "It's hard to say. I planned trips that I hoped would make her happy, and I think she came along because she thought that they would make me happy." He sighed. "We were sweethearts all through college and married right after graduation. We had everything going for us. It should have been a charmed life, but even though she tried hard not to let it show, there was one great unhappiness that overshadowed everything for Jane—she couldn't have children and she never stopped longing for them."

"How did you feel about that?"

"I wanted children too—I was even willing to adopt, but Jane wouldn't consider it. All I really wanted, though, was for her to be happy."

"I'm sure you succeeded."

"I like to think that I made her as happy as she could be. She certainly made me very happy. I spent almost three-quarters of my life married to her, you know."

"Yes, I know," Marietta said, reaching across the table and placing her hand on his, "and I think it's beautiful." What she didn't add was that she considered it providential from her own viewpoint, for it meant that he had led a relatively sheltered life. Surely, he realized that also and, now, at sixty-two, longed for a taste of the exotic before it was too late.

He turned his hand and closed his fingers over hers. "And I think *you're* beautiful," he said, his voice husky. "We should be talking about you and today, not the past. You look particularly lovely tonight."

She was wearing a strapless gown of forest-green velvet that draped softly over her hips, then cascaded gently to the floor, and she had done her hair up on top of her head, allowing a few romantic ringlets to hint at the gypsy in her soul. Except for gold shell earrings, she wore no jewelry that could detract from the abundance of creamy bosom that swelled above her décolletage.

"You should compliment yourself then," she said. "You suggested that I wear something green."

"I had my own special reason."

"And what was that?"

But his only answer was a mysterious smile that he was to flash now and again all through the evening.

It was near midnight when they left the Negresco. The palm-guarded Promenade des Anglais was quiet, almost solemn as Christmas Eve moved on toward Christmas Day. A chilly breeze blew in from the sea, and Marietta pulled her short velvet evening cape more tightly around her shoulders. Noticing, Harlan started to slip his arm around her, but then dropped his hand to his side.

"I don't think there'll be much night life here tonight," he said. "Would you like to go back to the villa? I asked Henri to have a fire in the library."

"That sounds good," she said, shivering a little.

Antoine, who had been pacing the Rolls slowly behind them, stopped the car and jumped out to open its door.

AFTER HER BEDROOM, the library was Marietta's favorite room in the villa. Its walls were lined with books in several languages, many of them collector's items, gold stamped and bound in leather. Besides these treasures, containing perhaps the wisdom of the ages, there were also books strictly for reading pleasure. The deep leather armchairs were conducive to browsing and dozing. There was a large floor globe and, next to it, on its own rosewood stand, an unabridged French dictionary. Rococo settees flanked the huge marble fireplace above which hung a landscape in the style of Watteau. Here and there on tulipwood and kingwood parquetry tables stood exquisite Meissen figures in their vibrant colors: birds so lifelike that they might have flown in through the window only moments before; dancers frozen in a joyous moment of movement; potpourri bowls whose painted sprays and sprigs would never know the fate of their contents fashioned by nature.

On a teacart beside the fireplace, Henri had set out a supper for two—cold salmon fillets poached in sour cream, watercress sauce, spinach and avocado salad with a dill dressing, Oriental chicken, fruits in brandy, and petits fours. A bottle of champagne chilled in a silver bucket.

While Harlan attended to the champagne, Marietta curled up on the sofa.

"Merry Christmas," he said as they touched glasses.

"Merry Christmas." She looked around the room. "Somehow, it doesn't seem like Christmas, does it? The weather's so balmy, there are no cards on the mantel, and there's not even a tree."

He reached into his pocket and took out a small, flat gift-wrapped box. "Perhaps this will make it seem more like Christmas."

She smiled but didn't reach out for it. "Wouldn't you rather wait till morning?"

"It is morning," he reminded her.

"In that case, let me get your present too." She dashed upstairs to her room and returned a minute later with a package about the size of a shoebox.

As they exchanged presents, Harlan said, "Open yours first."

"Why don't we open them together?"

"Because part of your present to me must be the pleasure of watching you unwrap yours."

Her fingers trembling with anticipation, she undid the silver ribbon and gold paper and slipped out a slim white leather jewel box. Slowly she opened it, then gasped with delight and surprise. Glittering upon the white velvet, where it lay suspended from a braided gold chain, was a brilliant-cut emerald pendant surrounded by a navette diamond cluster.

"Oh, Harlan!" she cried. "It's beautiful, but I really can't—"

"Do you like it?" he asked eagerly.

"I love it, but—"

"Then you must accept it. When I saw it, I knew that it had been made just for you. It's the exact color of your eyes, even down to that delicate blue flame when it's held up to the light. Come over to a mirror and let me put it on for you."

They walked out into the hallway, presently coming to a gilt-wood mirror above a sidetable. She felt his hands trembling as he fastened the catch behind her neck.

"There," he said, gazing at her reflection in the mirror. "Didn't I tell you? It was made for you and no other woman in the world."

It hung above her cleavage like a pointer indicating a treasure. If it was not exactly true that the pendant had been fashioned with her in mind, it certainly seemed true that she had been fashioned to be decorated with jewels.

"You must keep it," Harlan said, his trembling fingertips upon her shoulders, "if only to make an old man happy."

She brought her gaze up to meet his in the mirror and saw the hunger in his eyes. "What old man?" she asked lightly. "I thought this was a gift from you."

"Oh, Marietta! I—"

Quickly, before he could say more, she turned and gave him the impulsive kiss and hug that is usually bestowed upon beloved uncles. "Of course, I'll keep it—and I'll treasure it always." She slipped from his arms before he had a chance to tighten them around her, and then grabbed his hand and led him back into the library. "Now you must open my present, though I must say it looks like nothing compared to yours."

He tore off the paper and seemed genuinely pleased to see the personalized desk set upon its marble stand. "I've always wanted something just like this," he told her.

Marietta shook her head and fingered her own gift. "I liked it when I bought it, but somehow it seems inadequate now. I'll try to think of something more personal and appropriate before we leave. Maybe the next time we're in Nice..."

"I won't hear of it," Harlan insisted.

But Marietta smiled and reached for her champagne. "We'll see," she said.

She enjoyed some supper and another glass of champagne, then stretched languorously and said she thought it was time she got some sleep.

"I'll have another glass of champagne before I go up," Harlan told her.

She said good night and dropped a kiss on his forehead as she passed by. In the doorway she turned to remind him of their plans to go boating the next day. "Don't stay up too late," she advised.

He nodded, his eyes holding a sad, disappointed-little-boy look. She smiled to herself all the way upstairs.

Colette had turned down her bed and laid out her pink silk pajama-and-kimono set. Ignoring those, she opened a drawer in one of the commodes and withdrew a diaphanous black negligee. Hurriedly, she removed her clothes, flinging them across the settee. Walking over to the poudreuse, she admired herself in the mirror above it. The glass reflected the sparkle of the emerald and diamond pendant, but she was pleased to see that the jewels were overpowered by her breasts.

She removed the pendant and then picked up her bottle of Chanel and began applying it lavishly to her breasts, between her legs and behind her knees, on her wrists and inner arms, her temples and the pulses in her neck. She touched up her makeup and, removing the pins from her hair, combed and brushed it till it tumbled past her shoulders in fiery curls. The negligee had wide, flowing sleeves ending in a black lace trim that was echoed in a soft ruffle around its bateau neckline. Two long black satin streamers just below the hollow of her throat were its only indulgence to a possible need for fasteners. Tying them in a girlish bow, she stepped into high-heeled slippers of red satin and hurried down the hall to Harlan's room.

As she had hoped, he had not come upstairs yet. No doubt he was still sipping his glass of champagne, wondering if he would ever have the courage to make an advance to her before their vacation ended. She switched on a lamp on a commode near the door, suffusing the room with a soft, dim glow. Then she pulled open the drapes at the French window opposite the door and stationed herself in front of it. Upon Harlan's entrance, the first thing he would see would be the moonlight streaming through her negligee.

When the door opened at last, a cross current was created and the negligee rippled softly in the breeze. Harlan advanced a few steps and then stopped suddenly, blinking, perhaps wondering whether the champagne had affected his mind.

"I just thought," Marietta said huskily, "of something more appropriate for you." As she started forward, the gown billowed out behind her, displaying her body in all its magnificence.

At first, while she spoke, his eyes were riveted on her face, but then his gaze traveled slowly downward, past the delicate arch of her neck to the luscious swell of her pink-crowned breasts, down to the sensuous curve of her slender waist, further to the intriguing red-gold triangle between her thighs, all the way down her legs, and then back up to her eyes. He gave a strangled gasp. Quickly, he closed the door and leaned against it for support.

For a second, the fear flashed through Marietta's mind that he was about to drop dead of a heart attack, but by the time she reached him, though he still looked dumbfounded, the color was returning to his cheeks. Tilting her head back, her lips moist and parted, she slipped her arms around his neck. Suddenly he was dumbfounded no longer. His arms crushed her against him with a strength she hadn't anticipated, and his lips came down on hers with a bruising force.

At last she was able to pull away. "Gently, gently, darling," she whispered, running her fingers along the lapels of his tuxedo. "And how about getting out of these clothes? Diamond studs and starched shirts are elegant, but not very comfortable to be pressed against."

Within seconds he had torn off his jacket and cummerbund and tossed them in the general direction of a chair, not even noticing that he had missed. But his fingers trembled so violently that he had trouble unfastening his suspenders.

"Patience, patience, my darling," Marietta advised, her voice husky. She took his hands in hers, brought them up to her lips, then placed them gently at his sides. "Let me do it."

He looked as though he might faint with ecstasy as she slowly unfastened the buttons and tossed the suspenders over his shoulders. Then, one by one, taking her time, she removed each diamond stud, setting it carefully on a nearby bonheur du jour. Placing her hands on his chest, she moved them leisurely upward, then opened them outward, slipping the shirt from his shoulders as she did so. The garment fell to the floor, revealing the athletic undershirt beneath it. "Hands over your head," she instructed in the tone of a doting mother speaking to a little boy, and he obeyed as readily as a well-behaved child would. She tugged the undershirt out from his trousers and pulled it over his head. As he brought his arms down, he tried to pull her into them again, but she gently but firmly placed them back at his sides, telling him in the same motherly tone, "Not till we're all finished." It came as a surprise to her that his broad, muscular chest was covered with a mass of hair that was as gray as the hair on his head. Gleaming through it, a monument to long-ago surgery, was a long pink scar that began at his midriff and disappeared into his trousers. Perhaps Craig's chest would look like Harlan's in forty years. But it was a vision of Craig's chest as it looked now, wide and strong, with its crisp dark curls, that her mind had to push away.

She ran her fingers through the hair on Harlan's chest, and then lowered them to unfasten the hook at the waistband of his trousers and to unzip his fly. Moaning softly, he stepped from his trousers as they fell to the floor. Within his white briefs, his penis bulged like a prisoner struggling to be free. She placed her arms around him, slipped her hands inside the back of his briefs and squeezed his buttocks. Then, with one quick motion, she jerked the underwear down over his thighs. His penis popped out like a jack-in-the-box, and his thighs trembled violently. After helping him step out of the briefs, she led him to the bed and made him sit down. She knelt on the floor before him and bent over to remove his shoes and socks, making sure, without allowing the action to appear deliberate, that her hair caressed him. He groaned with rapture.

The job completed, she rose and said, "Now, that's much more comfortable, isn't it?" As he stared almost in a trance, she grasped the satin streamers of her negligee and leisurely pulled them in opposite directions, making the loops of her bow diminish and disappear. Casually she shrugged the gown from her shoulders and let it slide to the floor.

"My God! You're so beautiful!" His voice rose with emotion, and his eyes gleamed with awe and wonder as well as desire.

Never had she felt so sure of herself, so powerful, so in control of her destiny. She straddled his legs and, offering a breast to his lips, grasped him and began to lower her body.

After a lifetime of repression, it was too much for him. She had uncapped a fountain of desire. Moaning, and with a sudden, rapturous cry, he ejaculated prematurely.

For a moment they seemed suspended in time and could only stare at each other. Then he snapped his head away, but not before she saw the glint of tears in his eyes.

"Forgive me," he said. "I'm so sorry, so ashamed."

There was not a doubt in her mind that the future of their entire relationship depended on how she handled the situation. She sat down upon his lap like a little girl, and gently she reached up and pulled his head down, burying it between the warm and comforting softness of her breasts. "Never let me hear you say such silly things again," she murmured. "Don't you know that you just paid me the highest compliment a man can give a woman?"

Slowly he raised his head and looked into her eyes. Her gaze did not waver as she whispered, "I've never been more flattered in my life." She moistened her lips with her tongue, then curved them into a mischievous, confidential little smile as she ran her fingers through his hair. "And on top of that, now we can have the delightful pleasure of lying down and starting all over again. Wouldn't you like that?"

He would indeed.

They reclined on the bed, and this time she let him take the lead. Perhaps because of his long celibacy, beginning well before his wife's death, or because of the many years he had been married to a woman who either had no interest in experimentation or had been too inhibited to admit to one, he was a rather clumsy lover, but Marietta moaned and writhed beneath his kisses and caresses in a make-believe rapture that she knew was convincing, and for the consummation, which came too quickly and was over too soon, she wrapped her legs tightly around him and emitted groans of ecstasy sufficient to restore his pride and even to inflate it.

Her last thought before she fell asleep was that Harlan had a great deal to learn about making love, but she knew that after what she had shown him that night, he would be a more than eager pupil. Contentedly, she stretched her body to its full length and ran her hand over it. And he would want her as his exclusive and indispensable teacher.

The days that followed were divided between sightseeing and sex. Harlan rented a sailboat and they skimmed across the sparkling blue waters, its red-and-white-striped sail puffing out in the breeze like Harlan's chest after one of their morning romps in bed. Intoxicated by the heady fragrance, they wandered through the open flower market on the Rue Saint François-de-Paule in Nice, and Harlan filled her arms with blossoms, telling her she looked like his personal goddess who had brought him the bounty of the earth. They played roulette and baccarat at the Casino in Monte Carlo, and shouted themselves silly at the horse races at Cagnes-sur-Mer. In Cannes they strolled with the world's wealthiest and most beautiful people on the Promenade de la Croisette, and on the Rue d'Antibes, Harlan insisted that she pick out trinkets and Paris gowns in the elegant shops. They took the boat from Cannes to the Ile Sainte-Marguerite, visiting the fortress where, in 1687, Louis XIV had imprisoned the Man in the Iron Mask, who may have been his twin brother, and whose small chapel and double-doored cell with its barred window and its table and gilded chair had been preserved unaltered through the centuries. In Grasse, they visited the Fragonard museum and the house where the artist had taken refuge during the Revolution, and then, nostrils tingling from the sweet scents of orange blossoms, jasmine, and attar of roses, they toured a factory where the essential oils for perfumes were produced. Naturally they were not foolish enough to buy the factory's "genuine imitations" of famous perfumes; Harlan bought her the real things on the Rue d'Antibes. On the way back from Grasse they stopped off in the walled village of Saint-Paul-de-Vence, where the houses on the tunnel-like streets bore coats of arms, and lunched just outside the walls at Colombe d'Or, a rustic restaurant decorated with original paintings by Picasso, Miró, and Leger. They visited Vallauris, the pottery village Picasso made famous, and saw more Picassos at the reconstructed medieval fortress in Antibes that had once been a stronghold of the Grimaldi family. After the Grimaldi Museum, Les Collettes, Renoir's little villa at Cagnes-sur-Mer, seemed humble and bare, but the sight of the artist's palette and wheelchair and the sun-dappled garden where he painted to the last, holding his brush between fingers crippled with arthritis and as gnarled as the old olive trees surrounding him, moved Marietta more than all the Picassos she had seen or would ever see.

When they weren't touring or dining in quaint or elegant restaurants, they were back at the Villa Claudine, making love. Like a wide-eyed child being given the keys to a candy shop, Harlan was hesitant at first about the variations she introduced, but he was always agreeable and ultimately eager. Obviously, he had never before known the joy of bathing *à deux*, and when she invited him into her bathtub, he was so enthusiastic that she sometimes wondered if she would ever bathe alone again. He delighted in soaping her soft, smooth flesh, and then enhanced his pleasure by watching in the mirror above while she did the same to him. Finally, he would pull her down on top of him, his hands sliding over her as she kissed and stroked him, until at last, trembling with desire, he would reverse their position, and she would be lying beneath him, her head resting on a mound of towels, her long hair spreading out in the water, her breasts swaying tantalizingly. Next he would lower himself upon her, the warm, scented water lapping over them gently at first and then more and more vigorously until finally it splashed over the floor furiously as his passion hit its peak. Later, he would dry her delicately with a luxurious towel and tenderly pat talcum all over her, with careful attention to her buttocks, the enchanting crease beneath each breast, and the intriguing area between her thighs—all of which usually led to yet another love session on the thickly carpeted floor.

By December 31, Harlan had come a long way from the clumsy, overeager lover of the week before.

Having tarried in bed and bath even longer than usual, they did not breakfast until almost noon, and as they finished, Harlan told Marietta that he had some errands in Cannes. He invited her to come along, suggesting they could go their separate ways and then meet later, or perhaps she would like Antoine to take her someplace else. Tired from days of sightseeing and nights of love, Marietta opted for remaining behind; they would be leaving on Friday, and she welcomed a quiet day amid the amenities of the villa.

Harlan gone, she poured herself another cup of coffee from the silver pot and relaxed with it on the chaise while Henri came out to the patio to clear away the breakfast dishes. As she watched him, it occurred to her that although he had devoted himself successfully to making her stay at the Villa Claudine a perfect one, she had rarely spoken to him and knew absolutely nothing about him. He turned to place some dishes on his teacart, the wind catching at wisps of gray hair and the sun glinting off his stooped shoulders. A memory of her mother bending over steam trays in that seedy cafeteria flashed in Marietta's mind.

"You work very hard, Henri," she said with a warm smile. "I want you to know that Mr. Wylford and I appreciate all you have done to make us comfortable."

He turned to her, obviously pleased by the unexpected compliment. "But it is my job, mademoiselle," he said, inclining his head in a little bow.

"And one you do quite well. I suppose you're looking forward to retiring soon."

That idea seemed to surprise him. "But no, mademoiselle. I look forward to many more years of service. I have only sixty years of age."

Marietta was stunned to learn that the bent, work-worn old man was two years younger than Harlan. "That's the age when many people start thinking about retirement in America," she said, trying to smooth over a possible insult.

"Then they will be old before their time," Henri said with authority. "Work keeps us young."

She wondered what he saw when he looked in a mirror. "Colette is a hard worker too," she said to change the subject. "She has been very helpful to me. It must be great comfort to you and your wife to have such a fine daughter. Have the three of you always worked together?"

"No, mademoiselle. Colette began working as a maid in l'Hotel Carlton in Cannes ten years ago when she was fifteen. But last year she married her Jean. He is a good man, but a very jealous one. He does not want her working where she will be seen and admired by rich and immoral young men, and so she has come to work with my wife and with me."

It was difficult not to smile at the idea of Colette turning the heads of poor old men, not to mention rich young ones, but Marietta managed to keep a straight face as she asked, "What kind of work does your son-in-law do?"

"He is a croupier at the Palm Beach Casino in Cannes."

She thought of the croupiers she had seen at the casinos. They were all tall and tanned and movie-star handsome, looking as though they had been placed at the gaming tables to encourage women to lose their hearts as well as their money. She had seen many a jeweled beauty giving them the eye, signaling that she was as disposed to drop her pants as her francs. "Surely, Colette has more reason to be jealous of his work than he has to be jealous of hers?"

"But no, mademoiselle. He is a good husband. They have what you call a true love match."

"How very nice for them." Marietta brought her cup over to his teacart, then went upstairs to get a sweater.

In her room she found Colette dusting. She studied her a moment, remembering Henri's words that Colette had begun working ten years before at the age of fifteen. That meant she was twenty-five now, only four years older than she herself was. How incredible! Was it genes or work that had aged her so? And yet she had captured the heart of a croupier. Try as she might, Marietta couldn't imagine Colette lying in the arms of her handsome, jealous Adonis.

"Yes, mademoiselle? Do you wish me to do something for you?"

Color crept up Marietta's cheeks as she realized she had been staring. "No, thank you, Colette," she said. She picked up her sweater and left the room.

Downstairs in the library, she picked out a beautifully illustrated biography of Renoir, tucked it under her arm, and passed through the French windows into the rose garden.

She read for a while there, sitting beside the marble fountain inspired by Bernini, but despite her interest in the subject, she couldn't keep her mind on the book and finally put it aside and began to stroll about the grounds. There was a natural wood that she had not yet explored, and she wandered for a while among gnarled old stone pines, their misshapen branches entwined as though to give them strength to resist the mistral, which had been called by the Romans "the masterly wind." Though an almost fairy-tale wood, it was not as enchanting as the call of the Mediterranean, and she soon found herself walking beneath the flowering mimosas along the low pebbled steps that led to the sea.

It seemed a long time ago that she had stood there beside Harlan, gazing out at the sea for the first time. So much had happened since then. She had explored a world beautiful beyond her expectation, and had tasted a life exotic beyond her imagination. She wanted them both, and she knew that if she handled everything carefully, Harlan would give them to her. In three days they would be returning to New York. She should use this time alone to plan her strategy for the change in their relationship once they were back in the States. It would be a disaster if Harlan should think of her only as a mistress. Gradually, carefully, without allowing him to guess that it was her idea, she would have to bring him around to thinking of marriage. But somehow she couldn't focus on that now. There was something about the crystal-clear air of the Riviera that gave one the feeling of being inside a bubble where time stood still and all problems were suspended for the duration of one's stay. She gave herself up to that feeling, and to the delicious sensations of the breeze gently lifting her hair from her shoulders and the sun warming her face. She gazed off to where the sun drenched the Cap d'Antibes in a golden haze. Craig had once told her that nowhere in the world could the sun be more golden than over a field of Indiana wheat. She would have to tell him he was wrong. And then she remembered that this was something she could never share with Craig.

EARLY IN THEIR stay, when Harlan had consulted her about New Year's Eve, Marietta had told him she would prefer to spend the evening at the villa, alone with him. She had thought that was the answer he was hoping for, and she could tell by his eyes that it was. They agreed to dress for the occasion and to meet in the library at nine for before-dinner drinks.

Harlan was mixing their martinis when she entered wearing her green velvet gown and the emerald pendant he had given her.

"Every time I see you, you look even more beautiful than before," he said, handing her a glass. "Sometimes I'm half afraid that you're a wood nymph or some other magical creature who will suddenly just disappear."

She gave him an intimate smile. "You know better than anyone that I'm only a flesh-and-blood woman."

He shook his head. "*Only* is a word that should never be used in describing anything about you."

They ate by candlelight in the dining room, sitting at opposite ends of the long cherrywood table, covered now with a snowy damask cloth and set with sterling silver and sparkling Limoges china. As Henri served the consommé, Harlan said, "I thought that after all the foreign dishes we've been eating, you might be longing for some home cooking, so I asked for roast beef, mashed potatoes, garden vegetables, and apple pie."

The meal was delicious, but Marietta found that the names of the dishes were the only thing American about them; Marguerite had somehow managed to make everything taste like a French delicacy.

Later, they moved into the library, where a fire took the chill off the evening air. While in Cannes that afternoon, Harlan had bought some romantic American dance records, and he put them on the stereo. It was well after eleven, with less than an hour left of the old year. Not at all sorry to see it slipping away, Marietta went into Harlan's arms for a sweet, slow dance.

They danced in silence for a long time. Then the bracket clock on the mantel caught Marietta's eye.

"It's five to twelve," she said, looking up at Harlan, her eyes sparkling. "Isn't this a wonderful place and a wonderful way to start a new year?"

He stopped dancing and gazed down at her, his hands on her shoulders. He looked almost young in the firelight. "I was hoping," he said, "that we might be starting more than a new year together."

While her heart began to hammer, she furrowed her brow and tried to look faintly puzzled.

Gently, he brushed her hair back from her face. "I mean, my darling Marietta," he said, his voice husky, "that I love you. In these last few days, you've made me happier than I ever thought I could be—than I sometimes fear I have a right to be. You've given me back my youth, my life. I only wish there were something of equal value I could give you in return."

She moistened her lips. "You just said you've given me your love. I'd say that's a fair trade."

"I'm sixty-two. How old that must seem to you! I know it sounded ancient to me when I was your age. But inside, I'm no different than I was then. I still feel the same—Oh, hell! I'm putting this so badly. If only I could find the right words!" He turned away from her and stared into the fire.

She slid her arms around him and rested her cheek against his broad back. "Whatever it is, why don't you just say it? After what we've come to mean to each other this week, how can there be any 'wrong words' between us?"

Slowly he turned around, reached into his pocket, and took out a small black box, which he handed to her. "This is what I went into Cannes for today."

She snapped open the lid and gasped. Twinkling upon the black velvet was a ring with a marquise-cut diamond that must have weighed at least five carats. Speechless, she raised her eyes to his.

"Will you marry me, Marietta?" he asked. "Can you forget about the awful gap between us?"

Never in her wildest dreams had she thought it would happen so quickly, so easily. Her eyes filled with tears.

"What gap?" she whispered.

She held out the box to him, and he removed the ring and slipped it on her finger, his own eyes filling with tears too. "Oh, my darling!" he said. "I promise you I'll make you happy." And then his lips crushed hers in a kiss that left her head spinning.

When their lips finally parted, she glanced aside at the clock. "Happy new year, darling," she said. "We've just kissed through an entire year."

"I can't think of a better way to have spent it," he said, kissing her again.

He opened a bottle of champagne and they drank a toast to their future. Over on the stereo, the record changed and Nat King Cole began singing "Tenderly."

"Dance with me, Harlan?" Marietta asked.

He placed their glasses on the mantel and took her in his strong arms. She liked the way he held her, close yet not too tight. It made her feel warm and comfortable, but not confined or constrained. She closed her eyes and rested her head on his chest. He was a good dancer, and they glided smoothly and easily across the floor. He was a good man too, a kind man. They would be happy together. She would see to it.

When Harlan whispered that he wanted to get married on the Riviera and remain there for an extended honeymoon, she found the idea tempting. Returning to the States as husband and wife might circumvent a great many problems; she knew that Harlan had friends and business associates who would try to talk him out of marrying her. But she was confident of the place she held in his heart now, and confident of Harlan too—he was a decent man, a rare believer in the old virtues; he would not withdraw his proposal of marriage because others might disapprove. Besides, she longed for a real wedding and the time to plan it in—time that would prove to detractors that she had not somehow seduced Harlan and rushed him off to a minister in a weak moment. So she whispered back that from the time she was a little girl she had always dreamed of a real wedding.

"Then you shall have one, my darling," he said, his arms

tightening around her as they swayed to the music. "From now on, you shall have whatever you want."

She closed her eyes and nestled her head against his chest. On the stereo, Nat King Cole's voice sang on, but it was the echo of Harlan's words that rang in her mind: *From now on, you shall have whatever you want....*

Chapter Four

O_N F_{RIDAY} _{THE} _{SUN} seemed brighter than ever, gilding the Mediterranean and surrounding the Villa Claudine with a sparkling halo of light. But Marietta's mind was so filled with happy projects that she looked back only once as Antoine drove them to the airport.

On the flight home Marietta and Harlan made their wedding plans, differing only about the date—Harlan wanted an earlier one and Marietta a later one. By the time their plane landed in New York, they had compromised on the fifteenth of May.

Harlan saw her to her apartment house in a taxi, but she wouldn't let him come upstairs. Exhausted from the flight, they agreed that they would spend the rest of the day sleeping and getting over jet lag. They would see each other sometime Saturday.

Anticipating a lavish tip from Harlan, the cab driver cheerfully lugged Marietta's suitcases up the three flights of stairs. When he left, she closed the door and looked around the apartment. She had always loved the home that she and Cynthia had made for themselves, but now the rooms looked tiny and the simple furniture shoddy. In the center of the white Formica-topped dinette table stood the blue Woolworth vase Shirley Danielle had given them as a housewarming present, and in it was a bunch of daisies. Propped against the vase was a note:

Welcome home, Mari!

  I'll see you after work this evening. We have to talk! Craig has called and called and called!

Cynthia

Craig! He wasn't supposed to be back in town until the Sunday after New Year's Day. Maybe Cynthia meant he had been calling from Indiana. Sighing, Marietta headed for the bedroom. She would have to think about what to tell Craig, but she was too tired to deal with it now. She undressed and fell into her bed.

The room was dark when she awoke hours later, but there were sounds of someone moving around in the kitchen and the delicious smell of frying hamburgers. She slipped into her robe and hurried outside.

Cynthia saw her when she was halfway through the living room, and they rushed into each other's arms.

"It's so good to have you back!" Cynthia cried. "You look absolutely marvelous. What was it like over there? Tell me everything that happened."

Marietta laughed. "Not till I've had one of those hamburgers. How did you know I'd be dying for some good old-fashioned American cuisine?"

"You can thank my woman's intuition and my budget—payday isn't until next Friday."

"Is dinner almost ready, or do I have time to give you your presents first?"

"Oh, presents by all means. There's always time for presents."

"Good. But first I have to chill the bottle of champagne I brought back for us. No one in France would dream of eating hamburgers without it." She rushed off to the bedroom and returned with a bottle cradled lovingly in her arms.

Cynthia opened the freezer compartment of their refrigerator with a flourish. "The wine cooler, *madame*."

"*Merci beaucoup.*"

With great ceremony they made room for the bottle between some frozen TV dinners and French-fried onion rings, then bowed to each other as they closed the door.

"Come on," Marietta said, grabbing Cynthia's hand. "You can open your presents while I get dressed."

In their room Marietta rummaged through her valise and pulled out three gift-wrapped boxes which she handed to her friend.

The smallest box contained perfume.

"Shalimar!" Cynthia cried. "How did you know I've always wanted a bottle of Shalimar?"

"Could it be because you're always spritzing yourself with it every time we walk past a perfume counter?" Marietta asked as she stepped into a pair of jeans and pulled a yellow sweater over her head.

The box next in size contained French chocolates.

"You really are determined to spoil me, aren't you?" Cynthia laughed. "And wreck my figure and complexion too. But every ounce and every pimple will be worth it!" She reached for the third box. "I can't believe there's more."

She sat speechless after removing the lid, and then she reached in and touched the cloud of blue that lay nestled in the box. "A silk blouse! A *French* silk blouse. Oh, Mari, thank you! I've never seen anything so beautiful, never believed I'd ever own anything as gorgeous as this." Lovingly she removed the blouse and held it to her cheek.

"Try it on," Marietta prodded.

Cynthia pulled off her turtleneck sweater and slipped into the blouse, carefully fastening each covered button. "It feels so cool, so smooth, so luxurious!" she said. She wriggled her shoulders in delight.

"And it looks as though it were made just for you," Marietta said, pleased with her choice. The blouse was a perfect match for Cynthia's clear blue eyes, and its simple lines set off her ivory complexion and short-cropped brown curls.

Suddenly, Cynthia wrinkled her nose as an acrid odor invaded the room. "The hamburgers!" she cried. "Shut the stove off, will you? I'm not going within ten feet of anything that spatters while I have this on." She began unbuttoning the blouse as Marietta made a dash for the kitchen.

Later, over tepid French champagne and overcooked American hamburgers, Marietta told Cynthia all about the Villa Claudine and the Côte d'Azur.

"It must have been marvelous," Cynthia said, her voice filled with awe. "It sounds almost like a fairy tale."

"I came back with something a lot more substantial than a glass slipper," Marietta said. She went into the bedroom, took her engagement ring out of her purse, and slipped it on her finger. Returning, she held her hand out to her friend.

"Oh, Mari! It's beautiful!" Cynthia cried. "I didn't know diamonds came that big except in the Museum of Natural History."

Marietta laughed. "We're getting married May fifteenth, and I want you to be my maid of honor."

Cynthia jumped from the table and hugged her. "It's what you always dreamed of, ever since we were kids. Dreams do come true!" Then, with a sudden frown, she stepped back and studied Marietta's face. "But now that you have it, is it really what you want?"

"Don't look so gloomy!" Marietta hugged her again, and poured the last of the champagne. "Of course, it's what I want. I've worked for it harder than any politician ever fought for the presidency. And like a guy who's won the election, I'm not just going to sit back on my laurels now that I've got what I want. I'm going to put all my energy into making it even better. My mind is bursting with plans to help Harlan expand his business and his wealth. I'm going to see to it that this marriage is as beneficial to him as it will be to me. Now let's drink to my success."

"I'd rather drink to your happiness," Cynthia said as they touched glasses.

"It's the same thing, silly."

"I hope so." They left the dishes for later and curled up on the sofa with their glasses. "Do you love him, Mari?"

"Come on, Cynthia! There's no such thing as love—at least not the kind you're talking about. Poets and novelists invented it so that they could make a living writing about it instead of having to slave away at dreary jobs like the rest of us."

Cynthia shook her head. "Love exists, Mari. Ask anyone."

"*Belief* in love exists. It's the great pipe dream foisted on us by the overprivileged. It used to be that the rich could keep the poor in their place by telling them that they were born into poverty because it was all part of God's plan. 'Accept it, be humble, don't covet our huge estates and piles of gold,' they said. 'They only condemn us to an eternity of hell, for it's as difficult for one of us to get into heaven as it is for a camel to pass through the eye of a needle. Be grateful that God has chosen you to live out your life in poverty while you slave away to increase our wealth. Why, you lucky, starving masses, you should pity us, because, for you, the best is yet to come—when you die of malnutrition or of overwork or of diseases you can't afford to get treatment for, you'll be welcomed right into heaven.'"

She laughed and took a sip of champagne, then went on: "It was centuries before the poor caught on to how they were being shafted, and when they couldn't depend upon religion to keep the poor in their place any longer, the rich invented a new creed for them—romance. 'Oh, pity us,' they said, 'sitting here in our mansions, so cold and lonely and miserable among all our useless possessions. Not all the gold in the world can buy us what you have—love. Be grateful, you lucky, starving folks, for when you die of malnutrition or of overwork or of expensive diseases, you will die happy, in the arms of one who loves you.' Bullshit. My mother swallowed it whole hog and died a sick, overworked, overburdened woman who was old long before her time. It will never happen to me. I'm going to beat the rich at their own rotten game."

"I know what I'm about to say is a cliché, Mari, but statements become clichés because they put the truth so clearly: Money really can't buy happiness."

"If it can't, then it can buy a hell of a lot of good substitutes for it. You may find this difficult to believe, but I discovered during the last ten days that it's even easier to be happy in a sun-filled villa on the Riviera than it is to be happy in a cockroach-ridden slum in Crown Heights." She reached over and pressed Cynthia's hand. "Don't look at me that way. I'm not just some evil, gold-digging bitch. Harlan's a good man, and I really like him. I'm going to make him happy both in bed and out of it. Marrying me is going to be the best thing that ever happened to him. I'm not going to take his money and run. I'm going to stick with him, stand by him, and help him increase his fortune, which we'll put to good use. One of the first things I intend to do when we get settled is arrange to send you through college and law school full-time—you won't have to beat your brains out anymore, working and going to school at night. And I'm going to get your mom and Melanie out of that decrepit apartment and set them up in a nice place, wherever your mom wants to live. I'm—Why do you keep shaking your head that way?"

"Because I'm not going to let you do it."

"Why? Do you think the money will be tainted somehow?"

"Of course not." Cynthia smiled and squeezed Marietta's hand. "It's just that—well, we all have our dreams. You've achieved yours, and I'm happy for you. Mine is to make something of myself completely on my own. I'm really touched that you want to help me, but I can't accept that help. It's too important to me that I do things my way. Do you understand what I'm saying?"

"I think you're crazy, but I understand. At least I'll still be able to help your mom."

Cynthia shook her head again. "Don't count on it. I'm sure she won't accept your help, either."

"Do you intend to talk her out of it?"

"I wish she would accept it. But I know her better than that. After all, she's the one who brought me up to be the way I am."

Marietta sighed. "Well, that's not going to stop me from trying. Part of my dream has always been to use my money to help you and your mother."

"Then I hope our refusals will turn out to be the only problems you ever have to cope with."

Laughing, Marietta raised her glass. "I'll drink to that."

There was an awkward pause for a moment, and then Cynthia said, "Actually, there is a bigger problem that you have to cope with—Craig. What are you going to tell him, Mari?"

Marietta felt as though a cold hand had just gripped the back of her neck. She stiffened, but managed to keep her voice casual. "I have time to think about that. He won't be back from Indiana till Sunday."

"He's in the city now. He came back two days after Christmas, said he was lonely and couldn't bear the thought of seeing the new year in without you. He's been calling and dropping around ever since."

Her hand trembling a little, Marietta put her glass down. "What did you tell him?"

"What *could* I tell him? If only we'd thought about the possibility of this happening before you left! Then you could have given me some plausible story to have in reserve. I'm no good at making things up."

"What did you tell him?" Marietta repeated.

"I—at first when he called, I thought he was phoning from Indiana, and I just said you were out. Then he told me he was in the city and asked me to have you call him when you got in." She ran a hand through her hair. "When he called the next night, I said you'd gotten in too late to return his call and then had to leave early in the morning on a business trip. He wanted to know where, and I told him I couldn't remember, that I thought it was someplace down South, maybe Florida or Georgia. I said I didn't know when you'd be back. He thought it was strange that you'd be sent on a trip over the holiday, but I said, 'Who knows how bosses figure things?' Then he took to dropping in to see if I'd heard from you. It was harder to lie to his face, Mari."

"You didn't owe him any explanations."

"Maybe not, but I was here and you weren't, and it was me he kept giving that hurt, puzzled look. Finally, he said he'd called your office and had found out you were on vacation. I was sick of being caught in the middle, and I blew up then, telling him to leave me out of it, that whatever was going on was your business, not mine, and that if you felt like it, you'd tell him all about it when you got back tonight. I'm afraid I was pretty rough on him. I didn't mean to be. It's just that it was written all over his face how much he loves you, and knowing he was going to be hurt left me feeling so damn guilty. Oh, hell. I probably just complicated things for you, and I didn't mean to."

"Don't feel bad. You did the best you could. I'm sorry you got stuck that way." And then Marietta recalled something Cynthia had just said. "You told him that I'd be home tonight?"

Cynthia nodded. "He's bound to show up soon. And when he does, I'd rather not be around. Do you mind if I stick you with the cleanup and get out of here? I'll go to a movie or something."

Marietta's heart sank. She didn't like the idea of facing Craig alone, but it wouldn't be fair to ask Cynthia to undertake the embarrassment of witnessing what might turn into an unpleasant scene. "Of course, I don't mind," she said. "You go ahead. I'll take care of everything."

By the time she had finished washing the dishes, Marietta was thinking that Craig wouldn't come after all. No doubt he had drawn his own—and correct—conclusions about the situation and realized that everything was over between them. Instead of being relieved that she was escaping a confrontation, she felt a vague sense of disappointment. She wished Cynthia had not gone out. She didn't really want to be alone.

At ten o'clock, just when she was thinking of going out herself, perhaps to the coffeehouse two blocks away, the doorbell rang. *Maybe it's Harlan,* she thought, *or Nancy from down the hall.* But even before her trembling fingers had unfastened the door's three locks, she knew who would be standing on the other side.

She had forgotten how his tall, massive frame could fill a doorway. He stood there in his jeans and gray duffle coat, the long red and blue wool scarf she had given him for Christmas wrapped around his neck, his cheeks flushed and his eyes sparkling from the cold, his thick dark hair windblown. In his hand he held a bunch of white chrysanthemums. He thrust them toward her, saying, "Welcome home."

Their eyes held, and she knew he wanted to kiss her and was waiting for her to make the first move into his arms. Instead, she smiled and stepped back so that he could enter. "Thanks. I'll get some water for these. You must be freezing. Would you like a cup of coffee?"

"Sounds good."

She put the kettle on the stove, then busied herself arranging the flowers in a vase and spooning instant coffee into two mugs. He stood framed in the archway that led to the tiny kitchenette, watching her.

"So you were able to get some time off after all."

"Yes. Isn't it ironic how things work out?" She kept her voice light and casual, but it sounded as if it were coming from someone else's mouth. "Why don't you take off your jacket and sit down? I'll be with you in a minute."

As he tossed his coat and scarf over a chair, she suddenly remembered the little box he had given her before he left, with instructions that it wasn't to be opened until Christmas. She had placed it in a bureau drawer and forgotten all about it. The kettle began to boil, and she turned her back to prepare their coffee. She could feel his eyes on her every second, and the water splashed out of the mugs and onto the counter. She wiped it up with a sponge, wishing he would say something and yet hoping he wouldn't. She felt she could deal with anything except the awful awkwardness that was suddenly there between them.

She brought the mugs into the dinette and sat down across the table from him. Not once did he take his eyes from her face. Forcing a bright smile, she raised her mug as though proposing a toast. "Happy New Year."

He ignored his mug and her toast. "I almost didn't come tonight," he said.

"Hard day?" she asked, pretending not to get his meaning.

"I've been coming over here every night for news of you. I guess I made a pest of myself with Cynthia. She's a good kid, and I'm sorry I hassled her, but I was going crazy, trying to figure out what was happening." His eyes searched hers. "Why did you tell me you couldn't get time off?"

"Because I didn't think I could. It all happened quite suddenly after you left."

"But when it did happen, why didn't you come out to Indiana?"

So here it was—truth time. She would try to go slowly, gently. "Because I had a chance to go somewhere really exciting."

"Oh? Where?"

"The Riviera."

There was a pause while all the implications of a trip to such an exotic place hung in the air. She hoped that once they penetrated his brain, he would get up quietly and leave. It would be so much easier on them both. But he seemed to have no intention of making things easier.

Finally he drew a deep breath and said slowly, "I kind of figured it was something like that. At first when the truth dawned on me, I was furious, but then I realized how something like that could happen. I mean, hell—you'd have to be a saint to resist a temptation like that." He forced a smile. "What I'm trying to say, Mari, is that you don't have to tell me about it. It's over. I'm not saying I'm happy about it, but—"

"It isn't as simple as that, Craig," she cut in.

"What do you mean?"

"I mean—" She broke off, unable to stand the way he was looking at her. She had to escape from his scrutiny. It would be easier to say from the kitchen. With a glance at his untouched mug, she pressed her hands to the table and started to rise. "I forgot to put the milk out."

He reached over and put his right hand on top of her left. "Sit down. I take my coffee black—remember? It's not that long since we've seen each other. I haven't forgotten that you take yours black too, or that…" His voice trailed off, and he looked down at his hand, obviously aware that he was feeling more than just her fingers under his palm. He slid his fingers under hers, then lifted her hand and stared at the diamond on her ring finger. Lightly, he ran his thumb over it. "This doesn't look as if it came from a gum-ball machine."

"I guess that's because it didn't. I'm engaged, Craig." It was a relief to have the words out at last.

Slowly, he withdrew his hand. "To the guy who took you to the Riviera?"

She nodded.

Anger flashed in his eyes. "Who is he?"

"No one you know."

"I didn't expect it to be anyone I know. Guys I know take their girls to Central Park to get away from it all, and they can hardly afford a Boy Scout ring, let alone a rock like that. Who is he?"

"Harlan Wylford."

"Who the hell—" A light of recognition began to dawn in his eyes. "Is that your boss—the old guy who owns Lady Sabrina?"

"He's not so old," she snapped, taking her hand from the table and putting it in her lap, out of sight.

"Not so old? Shit. That guy is three times your age. He's got one foot in the grave and the other poised on the edge. Is that why you're marrying him—because you're hoping he'll drop dead from sheer joy on your wedding night and leave you a rich widow?"

Trembling, she jumped up from the table. "I know you're hurt, Craig, but that's still a rotten thing to say. You have no right to talk to me that way."

"No right?" His chair crashed to the floor as he leaped to his feet. "I have all the right in the world. I'm in love with you, and you gave every sign that you felt the same way about me."

"I never told you I loved you."

"You didn't have to. It was in your eyes, in your voice, in your kisses, in the way you made love with me. For God's sake, Mari, grow up! There are more ways to say 'I love you' than with words."

Her anger began to match his. She hated being put on the defensive. "No, *you* grow up! We're living in the jet age. Love doesn't have to have a thing to do with screwing. I warned you. I told you at the very beginning that I didn't want any talk about love."

"People say a lot of crazy things at the beginning of a relationship."

"I don't."

"Why did you keep seeing me?"

"Because I liked you, because we had fun together. Because we were good together in bed."

"And Wylford—were you seeing him too?"

"I could see no reason not to."

The anger drained from his face, and for a second she saw raw pain in his eyes. "Do you love him, Mari?"

First Cynthia, now Craig! "Love!" she cried, running her hand through her hair. "Why does everybody have to talk about love? There are other things in life that are a lot more important if you're going to survive and survive well. I told you from the beginning that I had plans to get them."

"I thought we were going to get them together."

"Then that was your problem. I never gave you any reason to think that." She turned her back on him, unable to bear the agony in his eyes. Why didn't he accept the fact that it was over between them and go home and leave her in peace?

Suddenly, she felt his fingers bite into her shoulders, and he spun her around so fast that she stumbled against him. His cheeks were flushed, his eyes blazing with anger and hurt. "Every time you crawled beneath the sheets with me, you gave me reason to believe it."

She struggled to free herself from his grip, but he wouldn't let her go. His hands tightened. "Look at me!" he commanded.

"Look at me and tell me that it all meant nothing, that you didn't love me then and don't still love me now."

Her heart began pounding. She didn't understand why it was such agony to be so close to him that she could smell the familiar fragrance of his after-shave, see the hairs that glistened at the open neck of his flannel shirt. What she did understand was that she had to say something to regain control, to break the terrifying spell that was overpowering her. Defiantly, she raised her eyes to his and said, "For a farm boy, you sure haven't learned much about life and sex, have you?"

"Is that all I was to you—nothing more than just another goddamn stud in your stable?"

"Let go of me, Craig. You're hurting me!" The anger in his eyes was beginning to frighten her.

"Goddamn it! I want to hurt you. I want to turn you into a human being. I want you to feel some of the pain that's ripping me apart. I—" He dropped his hands, his eyes suddenly filling with tears. "Mari, don't do this to us. Don't do it to yourself."

She rubbed her shoulder. "It's over, Craig. Please go home."

He made no move to leave, but stood there staring at her. "You're really going to do it?" he asked finally, his voice edged with hurt and disbelief. "You're going to marry that doddering old creep?"

Her eyes met his, but she didn't answer. She saw no reason to continue the scene.

They stood that way awhile, their gazes locked. Then he whirled round, snatched up his jacket, and rushed to the door.

"You forgot your scarf," she reminded him.

He glanced over at it, then back at her. "No, I didn't forget it. Give it to your fiancé with my compliments. Maybe you'll get lucky and he'll hang himself with it, making you a rich widow all the sooner."

"That isn't funny."

"I didn't intend it to be." There was no hurt in his eyes now—only anger and a cold, piercing contempt.

In spite of herself, Marietta shuddered. She hadn't wanted things to end on such an ugly, bitter note. "I was hoping we could part as friends," she said softly.

"Were you? Oh, I see. Wylford can't get it up, and you were hoping I'd be available for stud service after the honeymoon. Sorry, honey, I'm all booked up. But if you let me have your number when you're settled in your little honeymoon mansion, I'll pass it around to the guys. I'll be happy to let them know what a great piece of ass you are."

"You goddamn bastard!" she cried, slapping him hard across the face.

"You gold-digging bitch!" His hand shot out and returned the slap. Then he looked down at his hand, as though it had acted automatically and he was surprised at what it had done. When his eyes returned to hers, however, they held no sign of remorse. "My mother always told me never to hit a lady," he said, his voice soft, yet shaking with rage. "But then, you're no lady, are you?"

As she stood there, still rigid from the shock of his slap, he took a last look at her and let himself out. He closed the door so quietly that it was a moment before she realized that he was gone from her apartment and from her life. And then she whirled, grabbed his scarf from the chair, and stuffed it into the garbage bag in the kitchen. "The hell with him!" she said aloud. She felt elated, as though she was also disposing of the last vestiges of Marianne Vuckendorn.

She rushed into the bedroom, opened her bureau drawer, and pulled out the little green-and-red-wrapped package Craig had given her. She intended to toss it into the garbage too, but she couldn't resist a quick look at its contents. With trembling fingers she ripped off the paper and lifted the lid of the white pasteboard box. On a bed of cotton lay a small gold-filled heart suspended from a thin chain. Etched across the heart was one word: *Forever.* The word blurring before her eyes, she closed the box and shoved it deep inside her drawer. Her tears, she told herself, were only for Craig. In spite of all his terrible and unfair remarks, she was sorry she had hurt him.

Chapter Five

Shirley Danielle was fond of telling her daughters that their father, considering them to be the crowning glories of his life, had chosen the most beautiful names he could imagine for them. Their names and memories, she said, were their matchless inheritance. From the time Marietta became a member of the Danielle household, she had been aware that Shirley's devotion to her daughters was something rare and wonderful, and she considered herself fortunate to be included in the warm circle of her love. It was a kindness she would never forget, and now she was determined to repay it. Laden with packages, she accompanied Cynthia on a visit to Shirley and Melanie the Sunday after her return from France.

Shirley's face brightened as she opened the door and saw the two young women standing there. She hugged them and drew them inside, where, after they had hung up their coats, she gave them her customary motherly inspection, complaining that Cynthia looked as though she was working too hard and had lost more weight.

Usually, Marietta found herself the recipient of similar comments, but today Shirley seemed rather baffled by her appearance.

"You look wonderful," she said finally, "as brown as a berry. Cynthia told me you were away for the holidays. Where did you go—Miami?"

"Even better than that, Shirley. I was in France, on the Riviera. Wait till you see what I brought back for you, and hear my news."

They hurried into the living room, where she gave Melanie and Shirley the presents she had bought for them. Shirley sat patiently with her boxes on her lap so that she could have the pleasure of watching Melanie open hers first. The child's eyes grew wide as she unwrapped the little Meissen figure of a shepherdess, the gossamer red silk scarf, and the small bottle of Chanel No. 5. She ran over and threw her arms around Marietta, crying, "Oh, Mari! I love them all! Thank you."

"The perfume's for when you get older," Marietta told her. "Keep it in a dark, cool place."

"The scarf's for when you get older too," Shirley said.

"Oh, Mama!"

"Well, maybe you can wear it to church once in a while," Shirley relented. "But you have to take good care of it."

"I will!" Melanie promised, wrapping it around her neck. Gently, she caressed it with her fingers. "Open your presents now, Mama," she urged. "Let's see what Marietta bought for you."

Smiling, Shirley reached for a box. "I feel like it's Christmas all over again."

Exclaiming over each one, she opened the box of chocolates and the bottle of L'Heure Bleue first. Then she unwrapped and lifted the lid of the large cylindrical box.

For a moment she was speechless. Finally, with trembling fingers, as if she were afraid it might break, she reached in and lifted out the black velvet hat with the narrow brim and short veil. "Oh, Marianne!" she whispered. "I've never seen anything so beautiful."

"I bought it in Cannes," Marietta said, "but the shopkeeper assured me it was sent there directly from Paris."

"A Paris hat! Oh, my." The eyes she turned on Marietta were sparkling with pleasure, but troubled too. "It must have cost you a fortune. You really shouldn't have."

Marietta laughed. "This is one gift you can't make me return. Now let's see it on you. If anyone deserves a Paris hat, Shirley, it's you."

Shirley rushed off to her bedroom and returned a moment later, the hat on her head. Her eyes gleaming and her cheeks flushed, she looked ten years younger.

Marietta surveyed her critically, adjusted the hat so that it dipped down at a jaunty angle over her left eye, and then stepped back to admire the result. "You look just like one of the elegant women on the Promenade de la Croisette."

"What's that?" Melanie asked.

"The Fifth Avenue of Cannes."

"Mom, if Maurice Chevalier comes to Brooklyn and sees you in that, he won't be a bachelor very long," Cynthia teased.

Shirley struck a glamour-girl pose. "That old man? I've got my sights set on Louis Jourdan. One look at me in this hat, and he'll be my love slave for life." She slipped it off her head and looked at it lovingly. "I adore it, dear, but you were really much too extravagant. I wish you could return it and get your money back. When will I ever wear it?"

Marietta took the hat from her hands and firmly placed it back on her head. "You can wear it when you visit your friends—it will give them plenty to talk about because they'll be sure some handsome lover gave it to you. You can wear it when you go to church on Sundays, and you can wear it to my wedding."

"Oh, no. It's bad luck to wear black to weddings, dear." And then Marietta's words sank in and Shirley's face lit up. "Your wedding! When did this happen? Why didn't you tell me the minute you walked in that you were engaged? When are you getting married?"

"May fifteenth."

"Can I come too?" Melanie asked. "I've never been to a wedding."

"Of course you can come." Marietta hugged her. "I couldn't get married without you and your mother and your sister there. You're my family."

Bubbling with plans, Shirley sat on the sofa and pulled Marietta down beside her. "Reverend Philby can marry you at the church, and then you can come back here for the reception. I'll do all the cooking. You girls can help me, of course. We'll—"

Marietta laughed and shook her head. "Not on your life. It's going to be a real wedding with a real reception. You're not going to lift a finger. You'll sit back and relax and enjoy it all."

"But it would be foolish for a young couple just starting out to waste money hiring a hall and caterers. I don't think you and Craig have any idea how much something like that would cost."

"I'm not marrying Craig," Marietta said softly.

Shirley looked puzzled. "Do I have his name wrong? I meant that nice boy you brought here Thanksgiving."

"You have his name right, and I'm not marrying him. I'm marrying my boss, Harlan Wylford."

"Oh." It was as though a candle had gone out behind Shirley's face. "I liked him so much, and he seemed so very fond of you."

The muscles in the back of Marietta's neck tensed, and she felt a headache coming on. "Harlan's very fond of me too."

"I'm sure he is." Trying to cheer up, Shirley reached for Marietta's hand. "Tell me all about him."

Marietta began to relax. "Well, he's tall and handsome and very rich."

"Wow!" Melanie's eyes lit up. "Did he sweep you off your feet?"

"Absolutely."

"I saw a movie like that on TV the other day," Melanie said. "This girl goes to work behind the glove counter in a department store, and she starts dating this guy who works in umbrellas. She thinks he's a clerk, just like her, but he's really the owner's son, learning everything about the store so he can take over one day, and she gets mad when she finds out he's rich, because she thinks he was making fun of her, but he's really in love with her, and in the end they get married. Is that how it happened with you?"

Cynthia and Marietta exchanged a look and laughed.

"Not quite," Marietta said, "but the ending's just as happy."

"How old is he?" Shirley asked.

"Older than I am."

"How much older?"

Marietta shrugged evasively. "What difference does it make? We know we'll be happy together."

"In other words, he's quite a bit older. In his forties?"

Cynthia's sigh told Shirley that she had underestimated. "Older than that?" she asked, frowning.

Marietta leaned over and kissed her cheek. "I love you, Shirley, but it's really none of your business."

"I love you too—that's why I think it is." She turned to Cynthia. "Why don't you and Melanie see how dinner's coming along?" After they left the room, Shirley replaced her hat in the box and turned back to Marietta with the no-nonsense air of a mother. "Now, how old is he really?"

"Sixty-two, and don't even try to talk me out of it."

"Sixty-two? Marianne, what are you thinking of? I'm forty-two, and I'd consider a man that age too old for me!"

"That's because when you think of men in their sixties, you think of the kind of men you know—guys who have had to break their backs to make ends meet and wind up being fossils at forty—hunched over from too much work, gray and drawn from too much hardship, and pot-bellied and bleary-eyed from drinking too much beer to try to forget it all. Harlan's not like that. He had a pampered childhood and adolescence, attended the best schools, inherited his father's booming business and went on to build it into the biggest and best bathing-suit house in the world. Because he's never had to scrounge or worry, he's as hale and hearty now as he was at my age. As far as I can see, the only concession he's made to time is a gorgeous head of silver hair, and it can hardly be called a concession when it makes him so attractive."

Shirley shook her head sadly. "That's where you're wrong. Life is unfair in many ways, especially in deciding who'll be born rich and who poor, who'll reap sorrow and who joy. But rich or poor, happy or sad, no one escapes time's grim toll. The moment we're born it begins its relentless erosion, and though for some, like your Harlan, its ravages may not be visible on the outside, you can be sure it's working on the inside."

Marietta shivered. "I don't want to talk about it. You're being downright morbid, Shirley, trying to turn what should be a happy time for me into something scary. It isn't like you to be so—insensitive."

"I didn't say what I did out of meanness." Shirley smiled but her eyes were filled with tears as she reached for Marietta's hand. "You're like one of my daughters, Marianne. I want the same things for you that I want for Cynthia and Melanie. That's why I'm trying to open your eyes to what you're doing—because I want you to be truly happy."

"But happiness is different things to different people. This marriage will make me happy. It's what I've longed for all my life."

"My mother used to tell me, 'Be careful what you wish for—you may get it.'"

"And mine used to tell me, 'The sky's the limit.'"

Shirley laughed. Then her eyes searched Marietta's. "You're sure this is what you want?"

"I'm sure."

"Then I won't say another word, except to wish you joy with all my heart."

The two women hugged each other, laughing and crying at the same time.

"Everything's going to be wonderful," Marietta promised when they drew apart. "From now on, I'm going to take care of us all. As soon as Harlan and I are settled, I'm going to find a nice apartment for you and Melanie and—"

"But we already have a nice apartment," Shirley interrupted.

"Come on, Shirley! You know what I mean—a beautiful apartment in a safe neighborhood, one where you can walk down the street without fear and with pride."

"Are you sure you don't mean a neighborhood where you can visit us without fear and with pride?"

The words stung. "That's not it at all!" Marietta protested. "I want to do it for you because I love you, and because if I have the best, I want you to have it too."

Her face softening, Shirley reached out and touched Marietta's cheek. "Forgive me. That was a very unfair thing for me to say. I guess it was my own pride talking."

"Then you'll let me do it?"

Shirley shook her head. "I appreciate the offer and I love you for making it. But as you said before, happiness is different things to different people. For me, it's managing on my own." She held up a hand to quiet the protests upon Marietta's lips. "And to quote you again, 'Don't try to talk me out of it.'"

Sighing, Marietta decided to give up for the time being. "You're just like your stubborn daughter."

"What about my stubborn daughter?"

"She won't let me put her through school."

Shirley laughed. "I guess you're just going to have to spend all that lovely money on yourself, but we'll get a big kick out of watching you do it. In fact, I'll be glad to help when it comes to planning your wedding. After all, you're my first daughter to get married."

Before long, Melanie came in to announce that dinner was ready, and the rest of the visit was spent with the four of them seated around the table eating Shirley's meat loaf, drinking Marietta's champagne, and arguing good-naturedly about the lengths of wedding gowns and the heights of wedding cakes.

Chapter Six

I N THE WEEKS and months that followed, preoccupied as she was with work and wedding plans, it wasn't too difficult for Marietta to put Craig out of her mind. She convinced herself that what they had shared had been no more than a pleasant interlude while they worked away at the real goals of their lives. By chance, she had achieved hers first; if it had been the other way around, she told herself, he would have been the one to end the relationship. Once he could see beyond his wounded pride, she was sure that he would recognize that too. In her heart she forgave him for the unpleasantness of their last meeting and she wished him well. Her scanning of the reviews of obscure productions in search of his name was simply a manifestation of that magnanimous spirit. His name never appeared.

Harlan had wanted her to quit her job or take a leave of absence from it so that she could devote herself to planning their wedding and their lives afterward, but she refused. Though she was aware that it could not possibly dispel rumors that she had seduced Harlan and was marrying him for his money, she knew that her physical presence at the office would make it a little harder for those stories to spread. For the first few weeks after the announcement of their engagement, Marietta was aware of silences and wary looks every time she entered a room unexpectedly, a reaction that was followed invariably by profuse warmth. She always pretended not to notice the first response and to be gratified by the second. Actually, both moved her equally to amusement and disdain. When, at the end of January, Fred Gibbs, the general manager, left the company abruptly "to pursue other interests,"

Marietta was sure Harlan had fired him because he was less than enthusiastic about the marriage; Fred had rarely bothered to mask his dislike for her when Harlan wasn't present. Harlan, however, would say only that he had fired Fred for incompetence, something he had been intending to do for years.

Fred Gibbs did not sound the only note of disapproval. There were some awkward moments when Harlan took her to dine with old friends. More polite than Gibbs, these well-bred couples in their fifties and sixties were cordial and gracious, but in unguarded moments their eyes revealed their suspicions of her and their fears for Harlan. It would have been a simple matter to charm the men, but she was worldly enough to know that that would turn their wives into formidable enemies. She chose instead the more difficult but, in the end, more rewarding course of first captivating the women with her wholesome warmth and eagerness to please. Once the women were won over to her side, she didn't have to work hard on their husbands.

If Harlan noticed that his friends were at first reluctant to accept her into their circle, he showed no sign of it. He was as enamored of her as ever, and seemed to live for the weekends, the only time when she would stay overnight at his Fifth Avenue apartment. Though she never allowed it to diminish her ardency, Marietta felt uncomfortable in the bed Harlan had shared with his wife and in the rooms they had inhabited for so many years. She made it clear that she wanted to start off their marriage afresh, in a place of their own, and decorated to her own taste. Harlan agreed readily, and in March, he bought the penthouse apartment she chose in a condominium on Sutton Place. Only then did she agree to take some time off from work, and she devoted those days to the joyful task of decorating the apartment. Her tastes were expensive but excellent, and it was in this activity that Marietta won over the women in Harlan's circle. She would appeal for advice on one of the finer points of interior decoration, and then, without the woman's ever being aware of it, would maneuver her into suggesting her own preferences. Thus, Marietta emerged with the apartment exactly as she wanted it, and with the goodwill and admiration of the women, who were convinced that it was all a result of their own exquisite taste.

Though the apartment was ready two weeks before their wedding date, with the bedroom furnishings assembled, Marietta refused to allow Harlan to make love to her there; perhaps she was being old-fashioned, she said, but she wanted them to start off in it as husband and wife. Her adamancy on the subject endeared her to Harlan all the more.

A few days before the wedding, Marietta set aside her honeymoon outfits and sent the rest of her clothes and personal belongings to the Sutton Place apartment. As she was unpacking there, she came across the little white box Craig had given her for Christmas. She hadn't intended to take it with her, and she realized that she must have packed it unconsciously. Wondering what to do with it, she held it in her hand a moment. Finally, she slipped it into the drawer in which she was arranging her scarves. It was foolish to keep it, she knew, but she couldn't quite bring herself to throw it away; though it wasn't worth very much, it was rather pretty. Maybe, if her forthcoming maid turned out well, she would give her the necklace one day.

ON THE AFTERNOON of May fifteenth, Shirley and Melanie came to the apartment that Marietta and Cynthia were sharing for the last day. There, they all dressed for the wedding. The Danielles had allowed Marietta to purchase their dresses when she insisted it was the privilege of the bride, but she knew that they would accept no other gifts bought with Harlan's money. They had already met Harlan, and he had charmed them all. Marietta had told him that upon the death of her widowed mother, the granddaughter of the impoverished Russian princess, Shirley had taken her in, and he had been eager to make her acquaintance. He and Marietta had taken the three Danielles out to dinner several times, and though a warm relationship had developed, Shirley and Cynthia had made it clear to him that finances were never to be discussed.

Shirley, Cynthia, and Melanie dressed first, so that they could then help the bride. Though Marietta had wanted to buy a gown for her, Shirley had insisted that a street-length dress would be more practical, and they'd agreed on a mauve chiffon with a full, layered skirt, a jewel neckline, and long fitted sleeves. Melanie wore a pink voile dress with a white collar and cummerbund and her first pair of nylons. Cynthia looked magnificent in her rose-colored chiffon gown with its cowl neck that drifted into full-length streamers in back; in contrast, she would be carrying a bouquet of pale-pink sweetheart roses.

The bride was breathtaking. Fashioned of antique-white lace, Marietta's gown began with a demure, high ruffled collar, but after that concession to modesty it clung dramatically to her breasts, tiny waist and sensuous hips, flaring out to the floor at about mid-thigh; it could easily have been a magnificent heirloom handed down through generations of women from an ancestor who was an intimate of Czarina Alexandra. Certainly, Marietta looked every inch a princess in it.

And later, she felt every inch a princess too when the limousine Harlan had sent came to a halt, the chauffeur hurried to open the door, and the Danielles assisted her out and then across the sidewalk and up the carpeted steps of the magnificent Plaza Hotel. There, in the State Suite, before twenty guests, Harlan's minister performed the ceremony. Harlan's hand shook a little as he slipped the diamond-encrusted platinum band on her finger, and she wondered if he were having second thoughts. She stopped wondering when he gently lifted her veil and gave her their first married kiss, about which there was nothing hesitant or indecisive.

Their wedding dinner was downstairs in the Edwardian Room. Everything had been done with quiet elegance and in excellent taste. It had been easy to keep the guest list small. Aside from the Danielles, there was no one Marietta had cared to invite, and Harlan, an only child, had no living relatives; he limited his invitations to his closest circle of friends.

The wedding party was seated at two adjacent tables, and when the first glass of champagne was poured, George Kirk, a senior vice president of First National City Bank and longtime friend who had served as Harlan's best man, stood up to propose a toast. He was tactful enough not to sadden the festivities with any mention that he was a stand-in for Ernest Hathaway, Harlan's old college buddy. Ernest had had a stroke two weeks before and was now lying in a bed at Doctors Hospital, speechless and paralyzed. Nevertheless, George's very appearance as best man brought Ernest to everyone's mind.

After the toast, a trio comprised of piano, violin, and bass struck up "The Anniversary Waltz," and the dance floor was cleared for the bridal couple. Harlan had taught Marietta how to waltz, and she slipped into his arms and closed her eyes, surrendering to the lush dips and swirls of the music. She wondered sometimes how her own generation, which prided itself on knowing everything about sexual stimulation, had managed to overlook the erotic possibilities of the waltz, the rumba, and the fox trot.

As they returned to their guests, Marietta became acutely aware of all the gray heads and furrowed faces at the two tables. If it were not for the three Danielles, the wedding party could easily have been mistaken for a miniconvention of grandparents. Harlan's friends certainly looked at home among the oak-paneled walls, rich golden draperies, and the candlelight that evoked the atmosphere of a bygone age. When they were settled, she would have to try to woo Harlan away from these old and depressing people.

Harlan had taken a room at the hotel so that they wouldn't have to travel that night, and as the door closed behind them, he pulled her close and covered her with kisses.

"I've wanted to get you alone all day," he whispered. "I thought our guests would never leave."

"You'll have a lifetime to be alone with me now," she reminded him.

"A lifetime isn't nearly long enough," he said, his hand moving up to her breast. "You make me wish for immortality."

They kissed again, and his other hand grasped along the back of her gown, obviously in search of the customary zipper. Encountering instead a long row of tiny covered buttons, he groaned.

Laughing at his impatience, Marietta turned around so that he could unfasten the back buttons while she worked on the ones at her wrists.

"The designers of wedding gowns must still be living in the nineteenth century," she said.

"Maybe not. Maybe they're simply aware that anticipation whets the appetite. The wedding gown is the virgin's last line of defense, and for centuries husbands have delighted in breaking it down, button by button. No doubt a man in my business shouldn't admit it, but the wedding gown is probably a much sexier garment than the scantiest bikini."

His casual tone told her it was only chitchat. Still, his mention of virgin brides sent a chill through her. Was he remembering the night forty years before when he had performed the same unfastening service for Jane? No doubt she had been a virgin. Wasn't every bride in those days? Didn't every husband of that generation expect her to be one?

They were facing the vanity, and Marietta's eyes caught Harlan's in the mirror. She saw nothing but love in them.

With a teasing smile, she said, "In that case, perhaps you'd like me to wear this every night."

He shook his head and smiled. "Not you. You don't need any special garment to enhance your sexiness."

"That's because you love me."

"That's because you're you."

She stepped out of the gown and hung it up in the wardrobe. Then she withdrew the pale blue negligee she had sent ahead for her sojourn at the Plaza and, kissing Harlan as she passed by, headed for the bathroom. "Don't go 'way," she whispered.

As she undressed in the bathroom, she couldn't keep her thoughts from wandering back to Harlan's remarks about virgins. She wondered how a virgin would be feeling at a moment like this. Nervous, of course, and frightened but excited too if she was really in love. And as excited as her new husband would be at the prospect of getting her in bed at last, he would be nervous and frightened too, scared he might hurt her or not be able to satisfy her. The whole idea of the wedding night, of starting a life together with first-time intimacy, was outrageously ridiculous. Or maybe, she thought, catching her own eyes in the mirror, it was outrageously romantic.

Don't be an idiot! she told herself, picking up her brush and pulling it through her hair with more energy than necessary. *What's so special about screwing for the first time?*

Certainly, it hadn't been special for her. She had been treated to that experience at the age of sixteen by Bill Norton, the neighborhood rich kid; his father owned the local pharmacy. Bill was nineteen at the time and a sophomore at Brooklyn College. When he gave her the blue cashmere sweater she had hinted at for Christmas, she had known she would have to come through for him. He brought her to his apartment after a date one Saturday night when he was sure his folks would be out. Bill pretended he was a worldly-wise sophisticate, but he was so inexperienced he hadn't even had the sense to have condoms on hand. When she protested, he tried to convince her that nothing could happen to a girl the first time, and he went into a great sulk when she insisted that he find the key to his father's store and swipe a package of rubbers.

While he was gone, she had gotten cold feet and been tempted to run home. The very idea of letting a boy put his penis inside her was positively nauseating. Could there really be women who actually enjoyed such a revolting act? Or was that just a story men spread around to make themselves feel better? She reached for her coat, then remembered the beautiful blue sweater Bill had given her. He had promised there would be many more beautiful gifts to follow *if…* She put the coat down, took all her clothes off, and got between the sheets. Bill was ecstatic when he found her waiting in bed. As he tore off his shirt, she couldn't take her eyes from the bulge in his pants, and when his trousers and undershorts finally dropped to the floor she gasped. She had never realized that an erected penis would be so big. And *that* was somehow going to fit into *her?* Like an animal frozen in the presence of a snake about to strike, she kept her eyes riveted to that huge organ, thinking of it as almost apart and separate from Bill as he climbed into bed. Bill took it as a compliment, his chest swelling with pride; he never guessed that her reaction was motivated by fear, not fascination.

Suddenly, he was all over her, squeezing, biting, kissing, sucking. "Stop!" she cried. But Bill was only nineteen and had lusted after her for the past two years. He couldn't stop; he didn't know how. With a groan of ecstasy, he mounted her and began to thrust. *Oh, God, the pain!* She never dreamed it would hurt so much. Why hadn't anyone ever told her? Why didn't they write about that in those stupid hygiene books? She began to scream. "Cut it out!"

Bill grunted. "Do you want Mrs. Kelly upstairs to hear and tell my father?" He ground his mouth down on hers in a kiss that muffled her cries and made her teeth cut through her lips. And then at last it was over, and he flopped on his back, exhausted and sated, telling her how great it had been. When he finally noticed her tears, he made an awkward attempt at comforting her, promising that she would get to like it after a while. As they were dressing, he noticed the blood on his sheet and went into a panic over how he would explain it to his mother. They decided he should tell her he'd had a nosebleed.

Bill had been right about it getting better after a while. In the five years that had passed since that night, Marietta had learned to enjoy sex, had discovered how to please a man and how to show him how to please her. There had been many partners to practice with.

She put down her brush with a sigh. That first time, however, had very definitely not been special. Of course, the act itself wasn't special—it was the most common activity on earth, indulged in by every living creature—it was the person one performed it with that gave it any significance. Perhaps that was what all the wedding-night hullabaloo was about. She would never know, she told herself, as she reached for her vial of Chanel, and she didn't really care.

But as she applied drops of the perfume to her breasts and thighs, Craig's face flashed before her, his hair tousled from her caresses, his eyes warm with his desire. She looked around the luxurious bathroom, complete with telephone and chandelier, and shook the vision away. Then she slipped on the diaphanous negligee and checked her appearance in the mirror. Suddenly, she didn't like the garment anymore. Oh, she knew she looked smashing. It was the color. Why hadn't she remembered Bill Norton and that damned blue cashmere sweater when she was buying her trousseau?

Harlan was sitting in the wing chair in the bedroom, dressed in a brown silk robe over beige and brown pajamas, and looking every bit as attractive and debonair as Cary Grant playing an English lord. In a stand beside him rested a bottle of Piper Heidsieck. His eyes caressed her as he said, "How do you manage to grow lovelier by the minute?"

She gave him the only answer possible—a smile.

With a contented sigh, he rose from his chair and proceeded at once to the champagne. Extending her glass, he observed, "A wedding tradition that should never be ignored. It launches a marriage on an ocean of joy." He touched his glass to hers. "To us. May we always be as happy as we are tonight."

"Always," she echoed, and raised the glass to her lips.

"I didn't have any food sent up, but if you're hungry…"

"Only for you." She put her glass down and moved into the circle of his arms.

Smoothly, and with a half smile, he opened her negligee and let it slide to the floor. Then slowly, standing at arm's length so that he could admire her nakedness in all its ivory and gold splendor, she returned the courtesy and removed his robe and pajamas. Closer and closer she inched until her nipples brushed against his skin. Swaying gently, she rubbed them back and forth across his chest. Groaning with desire, he crushed her to him, his lips engulfing hers in a kiss that made her head spin. He kissed her eyes, her cheeks, her neck, the hollow of her throat, and then, with his tongue, trailed little circles on her breasts until she moaned in delight. In their haste, they ignored the bed and continued on the wing chair instead, Marietta straddling Harlan's lap as they gave themselves up to the ecstasy of oneness. Faster and faster, she rocked on his thighs, clutching his face between her luscious breasts. *There!* she thought in triumph. *What virgin bride could bring her husband such joy on their wedding night?*

And then softly she began to cry. When Harlan looked into her eyes for an explanation, she told him the first lie of their married life: "They're tears of joy, my darling."

Chapter Seven

BERMUDA, MARIETTA discovered, was made for honeymoons. She and Harlan spent the next two weeks being pampered by the staff of the Inverurie Hotel, swimming in the crystal-clear blue water, sunning on the pink sand, dancing under the stars, and making love whenever and however and wherever they felt like it.

It was on their last night on the island, as they lay in each other's arms in the tender afterglow of love, that Harlan told Marietta he wanted to have a family. Her heart sank, and she was glad that they had made love in the dark, for she knew that her face would have revealed her revulsion to his idea.

"But surely we have plenty of time before we think about that," she said as casually as she could.

His laugh was soft and indulgent. "Spoken in the true spirit of the very young. You have plenty of time, my darling, but I don't. I'd like to get started on our baby as soon as possible."

She had worked long and hard to get Harlan. To share his wealth with anyone else, even a child who would be half her own, was unthinkable. Raising herself on an elbow, she stroked his body, coming teasingly closer and closer to his groin. She leaned over, her breasts dangling on his chest, her hand still making its nimble excursions and approaching its target. "I love you so much," she whispered. "Let me have you all to myself. At least for a year."

With a moan, he grabbed her wandering hand and led it to its destination.

"Please? Just one little year. Say 'yes.'" Her hand gripped, released, stroked, gripped again.

"Oh, my darling! Yes, yes, yes!" he cried. And then he rolled over on top of her, and she pulled him to her with her arms and legs.

Afterward, she fell asleep in his arms, sure that by their first anniversary he would have forgotten his foolish dream of a family.

WHEN THEY RETURNED to the States, Harlan settled two million dollars on Marietta so that she could feel as independently wealthy as her ancestors under the czars. He then suggested that she retire from the business and concentrate on being his wife. She was far too ambitious to be satisfied with such a circumscribed existence, however, and she made that clear to him. In a spirit of compromise, she agreed to stop modeling, aware that in his rather old-fashioned way he did not want others to see her body. She appeared at the office only a few days a week, but was not idle on the other days; she took courses in business administration and studied on her own too. Deploring Harlan's satisfaction with the status quo, she urged him to increase his share of the market. To her delight, by the end of their first year together, he had taken over two of his biggest competitors. But to her dismay, he began talking again about a family.

At breakfast on the morning of their first anniversary, Marietta found beside the croissant on her Royal Worcester bread-and-butter plate a sapphire and diamond necklace with matching earrings that Harlan had ordered from Harry Winston's. She wore them that evening when they dined at the Edwardian Room; Harlan wore the Girard Perregaux watch she had bought for him at Tiffany's. Before they went to bed that night, Marietta handed Harlan another small giftwrapped box. He opened it and found a plastic disc inside.

"What's this?" he asked.

"My birth control pills. I thought you should have the pleasure of throwing them away."

They made a silly little ceremony of flushing the pills down the toilet, and then drank champagne and went to bed. Harlan made love in a fever of excitement that brought them both to dizzying heights of passion. Afterward, he held her close, caressing her, murmuring love words, and planning aloud for the child he was sure would soon be on its way. She smiled and nodded and agreed with all he said.

"You're the most wonderful wife any man could ask for," he whispered as he drifted off to sleep, never knowing that two weeks before, she had been fitted with an IUD by her gynecologist.

When almost a year went by and she was still not pregnant, Harlan suggested that Marietta ask her doctor to conduct some tests. She agreed, and after a suitable lapse of time reported that the doctor had found nothing amiss. She sat on Harlan's lap and, fondling and cuddling close, whispered, "I guess we're just going to have to work harder."

"It will be a labor of love," he said, and his lips came down on hers.

Though she spent only two days a week at the office, Harlan began to worry that overwork was the cause of her infertility, and he suggested that she take a leave of absence. She agreed on the condition that he keep her informed on all business matters. He assented at once, for he admired her keen mind and considered her his most valued adviser.

Marietta enjoyed her vast wealth and derived much pleasure from indulging herself for the first time in her life, but she was not the type of woman who could make a career of shopping, playing bridge, and visiting hairdressers and cosmetologists. She continued to study business books and periodicals and to help Harlan with the problems he brought home, but she was restless. Harlan had always been quietly philanthropic, but now, with his booming and expanding enterprises—he was buying up women's sportswear companies too—she decided it would be propitious to publicize his good works. She lent her name and even devoted her time to several charitable organizations, and became a prime mover in the Gotham Foundation for the Arts, an organization that supported museums, theater companies, and musicians. Though the other, hereditary, board members of GFA did not exactly welcome a newcomer with open arms, she soon rose to a dominating position among them, thanks to her sharp wit, her innovative ideas, and, of course, her checkbook.

It was at a GFA party that she met Sanford Gourlay, the Broadway producer. He was among the rich and/or famous New Yorkers who, at a hundred dollars a head, had gathered at the Waldorf to drink French champagne and eat Russian caviar and thereby help the old and indigent actors and musicians at the Jenny Lind Home in Buffalo. A dynamic man in his late thirties, with sharp brown eyes, dark wavy hair, and a short, distinguished-looking beard, Sanford gave the impression that he belonged onstage with his actors. Ten years before, *Variety* had called him "The Whiz Kid of Broadway" and "The Man with the Midas Touch" because everything he produced turned into box office gold. Lately, however, his touch had become tarnished and his whiz had washed out. His last two plays had folded within weeks of opening night, and it was common knowledge that he was having difficulty raising money for a third. When he singled her out as the object of his charm, Marietta was aware that it was not because she was the most beautiful woman in that room filled with glamour, which she was, but because she was one of the richest. It amused her to watch him try to manipulate her by playing upon what he evidently thought was every woman's hidden desire to be part of the wonderful world of make-believe. Finally he extolled "the romance of the theater" once too often, and she couldn't refrain from laughing.

"You made a wise choice when you decided to stay on the sidelines rather than be on the stage, Sanford," she said. "You're not much of an actor."

"What do you mean?" he asked ingenuously.

"I mean that if you're trying to interest me in backing your next play, you're going about it in the wrong way. I'm a businesswoman, not a starry-eyed adolescent. I find sound investments to be far more intriguing than romantic dreams. And since, from what I read, the theater is rarely a sound investment these days, you're wasting precious time talking to me."

"But that's where you're wrong. My next play is a sure winner—simple sets, a streamlined cast. You could probably double your investment in practically no time."

"The key words there are *could probably*." Marietta traded her empty champagne glass for a full one and started to walk away.

Sanford put his hand on her arm. "Read the play first before you give me a definite 'no.' It can't do any harm, and you may find you're doing yourself a favor."

She studied his face a moment. "Why me?" she asked. "You have a room filled with potential investors, many who have been in some aspect of the theater most of their lives. Why don't you zero in on one of them? Or have they all turned you down?"

He shrugged. "I'm not going to be devious with you. Three people in this room have turned me down already. But that's because all they have going for them is money. The three of them put together would still come up with less imagination than your run-of-the-mill IRS man. You're very young, but of all the people in this room, I think you have one of the sharpest minds for recognizing a good business deal when you see it."

"Then why did you come on to me with those ridiculous stories obviously intended to leave me stagestruck?"

He laughed. "Force of habit, I guess. Or maybe I was a little stagestruck myself. You know, you're not only one of the most beautiful women in New York, you also have one of the most formidable minds. Everyone knows you're the brains behind Sabrina Enterprises."

"You seem to forget that my husband was long established and doing very well before I married him."

"Doing very well, yes. But now he's doing magnificently."

"Perhaps he was simply inspired by my presence."

He gave a slow, sexy smile, his eyes moving over her. "Your presence must inspire every man who sees you, but not necessarily to thoughts of creative business deals." His gaze came back to hers. "Your mind now—that's something else. Read the script. Then let's talk again."

"I don't see why I should." As she was saying the words, though, her mind began to churn with a new thought. "But send the script over. If I'm interested, we'll talk." Her eyes locked into his. She hadn't liked the look he had given her before. If it hadn't been for the idea that had just come to her, she would have told him to take his play and shove it. "Just remember that that's all we'll do—talk."

"I'll bring it over tomorrow." His voice was soft, his eyes warm. If he had gotten her message about just talking, he didn't believe it. "What would be the best time?"

"Any time. Just leave it with the doorman—he'll see to it that I get it." With a nod, she turned her attention to other guests whose contributions to philanthropy might be more forthcoming.

At three the next afternoon, the doorman informed Marietta over the intercom that a Mr. Sanford Gourlay was downstairs. It didn't surprise her that Sanford had chosen that hour: three o'clock had long been established among the idle rich as sex time. Late risers had had sufficient time to pamper the puffiness from their eyes with cool compresses and the lethargy from their limbs with perfumed baths; they'd had time to buy a suit at Adolfo's, a pair of shoes at Helene Arpels, or a whole new look at Elizabeth Arden's. Husbands who worked, or played, or played at working, wouldn't be home until cocktail time. What better way to pass the languorous period of from three to five than in a lover's arms?

"I'm not seeing anyone today," Marietta informed the doorman. "Tell Mr. Gourlay to leave the package he brought with you. I'll send my maid down to fetch it."

Sanford Gourlay was duly dispatched and his package delivered.

Manuscript in hand, Marietta settled herself on the sofa with a cup of coffee and told her maid that, with the exception of a phone call from Mr. Wylford, she was not to be disturbed.

Titled *Beyond Suspicion,* the play was about a homespun, popular, national-hero-type president of the United States who is quietly and relentlessly planning a coup d'état when his second term expires, and a young half-cynical, half-idealistic reporter who learns what is going on and is faced with the dangerous task of trying to prove it. The play was suspenseful and frighteningly realistic. More than once, the hair on the back of Marietta's neck prickled. When she finished it, she ran to the phone in a burst of excitement and dialed Sanford's number. She kept the excitement from her voice, however, when he answered.

"Make a reservation for us for lunch at Lutèce tomorrow," she said, "and we'll talk."

"I take it that means you're interested in the play?"

"We'll talk tomorrow," she said. "I'll meet you there at twelve-fifteen. Book a table in the downstairs room." She hung up.

As she approached the entrance to Lutèce the next afternoon, she exchanged a few words with a reporter from *Women's Wear Daily* who had once interviewed her, and she knew that note was being taken of her finely tailored brown Norell suit and beige Balenciaga blouse. The editors of that authoritative newspaper had come to regard her among the pacesetters in New York's world of fashion. Eyes were on her also when she entered the restaurant. She nodded and smiled at friends and acquaintances as she was led to a table already occupied by Sanford, who had had the good manners or good business sense to arrive early so that she wouldn't be kept waiting. Spotting her, he rose and assumed a gentlemanly posture beside his chair. Lutèce was one of her favorite restaurants. Though the dining room above the narrow winding staircase was more elegant, she preferred the downstairs room with its casual, gardenlike atmosphere. The brick floor and wicker chairs reminded her of the bistros and sidewalk cafés she and Harlan visited on their occasional jaunts to Paris. The excellent food brought back fond memories of Parisian cuisine too.

Smiling, she extended her hand and allowed Sanford to peck her on the cheek. After ordering drinks, they chatted about their favorite restaurants at home and abroad. Then he leaned forward and said, "I would have thought you'd prefer to lunch upstairs, where it's more private."

"But I want us to be observed. You see, after we leave, I intend to announce, in behalf of the Gotham Foundation for the Arts, that you have volunteered to join our theater committee. That's the purpose of this lunch—to discuss the work you'll be doing."

He looked confused and disappointed. "I thought it was to discuss *Beyond Suspicion*. I really don't have time to be on charity committees, Marietta, and I don't know the first thing about them."

"Oh, you'll make the time, and you'll learn. Because unless you agree to do that, I won't agree to discuss your play." She lifted the glass of Dubonnet that had just been placed before her. "Agreed?"

"Agreed." He sighed.

With a sip of their drinks, they sealed the pact. "May we talk about the play now?" he said eagerly. "How did you like it?"

"I thought it was excellent. I don't understand why you

haven't been able to get backing from your usual sources. Before I agree to put a penny in it, I want to know why." She gave him a shrewd look.

"I would have thought my problems are obvious. As far as the usual angels go, this play has two strikes against it—the playwright and me."

"I assume they have reservations about you because your last two productions flopped."

He nodded. "Theater people, even those who just dabble in it, like angels, are ridiculously superstitious. Three's the lucky— or unlucky—number. They figure I've had two failures; therefore, the next production is bound to be a dog too."

"What's wrong with the playwright?"

"Nothing, aside from the fact that Sara Gracian is a woman and a newcomer, which scares the shit out of the schmucks with the big money. Excuse me," he added, remembering he was with a lady.

"Not at all. Considering the explanation you just gave me, I think your choice of words was particularly appropriate. Since when has sex had anything to do with talent?"

"According to many shitheads who share my gender, since Adam first discovered the necessity for fig leaves."

She was beginning to warm to Sanford Gourlay. "Haven't any of your angel friends ever heard of Lillian Hellman, Jean Kerr, Edna Ferber, Lorraine Hansberry, and Carson McCullers—just to name a few?"

"Sure, but they insist those gals are too few and far between. Besides, Sara's an unknown quantity. She wrote a couple of really good novels, but because her publisher wouldn't put any money into publicity or advertising, they died on the vine, ignored and unreviewed. No one's willing to take a chance on a woman with that kind of background."

"Except you?"

"I'd back something written by a hermaphroditic, one-eyed pygmy if I thought it was good, and this script is one of the best that's ever landed on my desk."

"You're really gung-ho, aren't you?"

"With a sure-fire hit like this, how can I not be? I'm going to pack it with stars—George Tyrone as the president, and Marcia Rose as his wife. I'm going to fly out to the Coast and talk Bob Redford into playing the reporter. I know I can get him; he owes a favor to a friend who owes a favor to me. Women will storm the box office to see him. We'll be making money by the bushel. As soon as I get my stars lined up, we'll hold a press conference and— Why do you keep shaking your head like an Ibsen heroine? You *are* going to back me, aren't you?"

"That depends. How much backing do you have at the moment?"

"I'm putting up twenty-five percent, and I have two parties who have agreed to buy in for an additional thirty. If you take fifteen or twenty, I know we'll be able to scrape up the rest of the money somewhere. Maybe you can get some of your friends to invest."

"I'll take the remaining forty-five percent."

He shook his head slowly. "That's generous of you, but I always find it works better when I have the largest share."

"Forty-five percent or nothing," Marietta said firmly. "You've had a hell of a time raising money for this play. If I walk away now, you'll be back to square one. If you don't go into rehearsal soon, it will be too late to open this season. I'm making you an offer you can't refuse, and there are only two conditions attached to it."

"I assume I already met one when I said I'd serve on your committee."

She shook her head. "That was part of the way in which one of the conditions is to be met."

"And that condition is?"

"That nobody—not one single person in the entire world—is ever to be told that I am backing this play in any way. That's why everyone is to think that this meeting and any subsequent meetings we may have are about your work for the Foundation. Actually, this will prove greatly to your benefit. Everyone will think you've put up seventy percent of the money for the play."

"That's so simple and so good that I'm afraid to hear the other condition."

"It's a very simple one too. I want Craig Campbell to play the reporter."

Sanford frowned. "Who the hell is Craig Campbell? It sounds like a cheap scotch I used to drink."

"He's an extremely promising new actor I saw in an off-off-Broadway production of *Major Barbara* a few months ago." Actually, she hadn't seen the play, but she had spotted Craig's name in the review; he had been the only member of the cast to get a decent notice.

"You've got to be kidding. That production was an absolute flop. It had so little class that it should have been called *Private Barbara.*"

"The production was a flop—Craig Campbell wasn't. The *Times* reviewer said some very nice things about him."

"It's easy to come up smelling like a rose when you're surrounded by stinkweed."

"You told me not to make a judgment until I'd read the script. I'm telling you the same thing about Campbell: don't dismiss him until you've had a chance to audition him. He's damn good."

"Look, maybe he is, but he sure as hell doesn't have the experience for a part like this. George Tyrone is one of the country's most brilliant stage actors. I can't ask him to play against an unknown who won't give off sparks."

"George Tyrone is a great actor, but he hasn't worked since *Uncle Vanya* a couple of seasons ago. There just aren't that many good parts for a man of his age. It's my guess that he'd be happy to play opposite Donald Duck if it meant getting back on the stage. He also has a reputation for liking to help young colleagues."

"His publicity agent spreads that story to counteract the gossip that he's one of the meanest bastards around." Sanford took a deep breath and tried another tactic: "How about we give Campbell the part of the president's assistant or even the editor of the newspaper? With makeup, we can make him look older and—"

"The reporter." Marietta's heart was beginning to pound.

"You caught a single performance. Maybe the third-string reviewer from the *Times* saw him the same night. Maybe it was the only good night this guy ever had."

"Try him out. Let him read the part for you."

"If he stinks, I won't take him."

"That's your prerogative. Mine is to withdraw my backing if you don't take him. But he won't stink."

"What if the director doesn't want him?"

"Fire the director."

Suddenly a light dawned behind Sanford's eyes, and he made a gleaming smile. "You're having an *affair du coeur* with this guy, *n'est-ce pas?*"

She laughed. "Nothing could be further from the truth."

"Then you hope to have an affair with him. It will be your payoff for making him a star."

"You've been reading too many scripts written for aging actresses." She leaned across the table, her face earnest. "Part of this deal is that Campbell is never to know, not under any circumstances, that I have money in this play or that I suggested him for the part. He must believe that the whole thing is your idea—that you saw his performance or heard about it and knew you had to have him for the role."

"I can't figure you out," Sanford said. "If you don't want this guy to know you had anything to do with it, what's in it for you?"

"Personal satisfaction." She smiled benignly. "I read somewhere that we should all do at least one anonymous good deed for a stranger before we die. I want to do mine now and get it over with. Now let's order our lunch. I'm starving."

Over *mignon de boeuf en croute Lutèce,* they talked animatedly about the play and Sanford's other plans for it. Their earlier discussion had brought each of them a new respect for the other, and Marietta began to think that she had won Sanford's friendship as well. He saw her as a whole person now, not just as a gorgeous body with a good mind. Her intuition told her he still lusted after the body, but she would deal with that when the time came.

The time came when they were having their frozen raspberry soufflé and coffee. Casually, Sanford suggested that they continue their discussion at his apartment.

She put down her cup and fixed her eyes on him. "I have the distinct impression that the theater would be the furthest thing from your mind once we arrived at your apartment."

He had a slow, sexy smile that started in his eyes and worked its way down to his lips. His beard was intriguing, dark, with just a fleck of silver here and there, and his shoulders were strong and broad. At thirty-seven he was what most women her age would consider an older man, yet to her he seemed still young. Quite appealing too. But she was Harlan's wife. He loved her and willingly gave her all she had ever longed for and more. He was a good man who would never consciously hurt or betray her, and she had long ago vowed to herself that she would never hurt him either.

"Well," Sanford said with a meaningful look, "now that you mention it…"

"I think we had better get something straight—now that *you* mention it," Marietta said. "I have no intention of allowing our relationship to progress beyond this point—ever. You seem to be aware of the fact that I'm married, but not of the fact that I take my marriage very seriously. This will be the first and last time we ever discuss your play. When you can assure me that Craig Campbell has been signed for the role of the reporter, I will see to it that you get the money you need. When the receipts roll in, you will see to it personally, so that no one else knows, that I get my share of the profits. Occasionally, I will have to be in touch with you about your work on the Foundation committee. We've discovered this afternoon that we like each other and get along well, so no doubt when we meet at Foundation get-togethers or at other social functions we'll enjoy having a drink together and a nice long chat. But it will never go any further than that."

"Never?"

"Never."

He smiled good-naturedly and spread his hands. "You can't blame an all-American boy for trying."

"Not for trying once," she said. "But twice I would find a bloody bore."

He digested her words a moment, then raised his cup in a little salute. "Ever since reading *Candida* in my youth, I've wondered what it would be like to have a strictly platonic relationship with a beautiful, sexy woman."

"It looks as though you're about to find out."

"Yes, damn it!" he said. But his smile was warm and genuine.

Chapter Eight

Sanford Gourlay kept his end of the bargain. He never told anyone how he had managed to come up with the rest of the money for *Beyond Suspicion,* and when he signed Craig Campbell for the part of the reporter, he told him that he had recalled his impressive performance in the short-lived *Major Barbara.* Marietta and Harlan often attended opening nights, so there was nothing unusual about their presence at the first performance of Sanford Gourlay's new play. What was unusual was the way Marietta prolonged their dinner at the Bull and Bear before the performance; she wanted to make sure that they would arrive at the theater just as the house lights dimmed. If Craig should peek out at the audience before the curtain went up, she didn't want him to spot her sitting in the middle of the fourth row.

After a shaky opening scene, Craig quickly hit his stride, and by the end of the first act he was a match for George Tyrone, his antagonist. Between them they kept the audience spellbound. Though less adept in the little nuances, Craig was as professional as Tyrone, and their styles and temperaments fitted together magnificently. Holding Harlan's hand while Craig was menaced by an assassin, Marietta thought of the waste it would have been to let him fritter away his talent in decrepit off-off-Broadway theaters, waiting for years and years perhaps before anyone of importance took notice of him. Just like the other playgoers, she felt her heart pounding at the end of the third act, but in her case, the reaction was caused by pride rather than suspense, and when the audience gave the performers and the author a standing ovation, tears came to her eyes.

Harlan slipped his arm around her as they moved up the aisle toward the exit. "I've never seen you so moved by a play," he said.

"It was excellent." She hoped her cheeks weren't as flaming as they felt. "Maybe I found it particularly exciting because Sanford told me at a Foundation meeting a few weeks ago that he'd had a hard time raising money for it because the author was an unknown woman. I guess I was feeling a little of the thrill she must have experienced when she was called to the stage."

"She was lucky Gourlay was willing to take a chance on her. That handsome young fellow who played the reporter was lucky too. I don't recall ever seeing or hearing of him before. He must be another of Gourlay's discoveries. This play is going to make reputations for them both."

Harlan was right. *Beyond Suspicion* was the hit of the theatrical season. Acclaimed by all the critics, it received both the New York Drama Critics Circle Award and a Tony as the year's best play, and George Tyrone and Craig were awarded Tonys as best actor and best featured actor. Craig's career was on its way. Within two years, the screen version of *Beyond Suspicion* was showing around the country, and with its release he achieved a popularity that rivaled Robert Redford's. He was in great demand both on stage and screen, and he divided his time between both mediums. Away from work, he seemed to live a quiet life, prodding frustrated gossip columnists to speculate that still waters ran deep and sometimes muddy. The one time his private life made headlines was when, a few years after his rise to stardom, he quietly married Susan Antoinne, co-star in his second movie. She was blond and beautiful, a former Olympic skater. When she spotted that story, Marietta told herself she was foolish to keep reading every article printed about Craig, and resolved not to do it anymore. She found, however, that old habits were difficult to break.

Those were busy and eventful years for Marietta and Harlan—happy years too. Harlan was more in love with her than ever, and though disappointed that she hadn't become pregnant, he was convinced that she longed for a child even more than he did. To help her overcome her disappointment, he devoted himself to making her happy, showering her with expensive gifts, vacationing with her in the world's most beautiful cities, entertaining her in New York's best restaurants, theaters, and clubs. It was upon their return from the ballet and late supper at the Russian Tea Room one December Saturday in the fourth year of their marriage that Marietta received the most tragic news she'd had to cope with since the death of her mother. They had changed into their robes, and Harlan was pouring Remy Martin into snifters when the phone rang. Marietta answered, sure it could be only a wrong number at that time of night.

"Oh, Mari! Mari! Thank God you're finally home!" The girl's voice was shrill and hysterical. "Mama—Cynthia—I. . ." There was a choking sound as the voice broke off.

Marietta's heart began to pound. "Melanie? Melanie, is that you? What is it? What's the matter?"

But there was only sobbing. Then the sobbing receded as a second voice asked:

"Marianne? This is Margaret Higgins. Remember me? I live across the street from Shirley at—"

"Yes, of course I remember you." In her mind's eye she saw the heavyset, graying woman who used to stop in and have coffee with Shirley when Marietta was still living there. Margaret and her mother had been friends too. "Please," she urged, her hand trembling, "tell me what happened."

"There was a terrible fire. Shirley and Cynthia—" Margaret's voice broke. "They were trapped in the apartment. They—they're dead." She began to cry.

"Oh, my God!" Marietta burst into tears and collapsed against Harlan, who, realizing that it was bad news on the phone, had walked over and put his arm around her. Holding her close, he took the receiver and spoke softly and comfortingly to Mrs. Higgins. He let go of Marietta for a moment in order to jot something down on the telephone pad. Then he hung up and pulled her close again. His arms were strong and warm, and Marietta buried her head against his chest, surrendering for a moment to the comfort he offered and to the grief raging in her heart.

"My poor darling," he murmured over and over, a hand stroking her hair.

"They can't be dead!" she cried like a disbelieving child. "They can't be!" She'd had lunch with Cynthia only two weeks before, and had dropped in on Shirley a few Sundays before that. Since her marriage, she had seen neither woman as often as she would have liked. Cynthia was always busy with her job and her studies, and their very different lifestyles had created a distance between them, though certainly not an estrangement. Though Marietta and Harlan did everything possible to put her at ease, it had been obvious that Shirley felt awkward and out of place when they invited her to their penthouse or took her out to dinner at fine restaurants. So Marietta had resorted to dropping in on her occasionally. They no longer had a great deal in common, but for Marietta, there was nothing like a cup of coffee and girl talk in Shirley's kitchen. She kept trying, but could never get Shirley to accept any help from her. Now she never would.

"Oh, Harlan!" she said, pulling away a little and looking up at him through frightened eyes. "Cynthia was my best friend, and Shirley—Shirley has been like a mother to me since I was sixteen. I can't imagine life without them. Poor Melanie! It must be even worse for her."

"I told Mrs. Higgins that I'd come for Melanie," Harlan said. "Will you be all right?" He looked off toward their housekeeper's room, then remembered it was her night off. "Do you want me to ask one of the neighbors to stay with you?"

"I don't want to stay here. I'm coming with you. Melanie needs me."

"She'll have you when we get back."

"No, I'm coming with you," Marietta insisted.

Harlan called their garage, and by the time they went downstairs, the Cadillac was waiting for them.

Traffic was light at that time of night, and Harlan sped down the FDR Drive and across the Manhattan Bridge to Brooklyn. Sensing Marietta's need to be left to her own thoughts, he remained silent, occasionally touching her arm or knee when he stopped for a light.

Next to the charred shell of the four-story walkup where Shirley had lived, the other tenements on St. John's Place looked almost homey and appealing. Harlan found a parking spot across the street, and they climbed out of the car, carefully setting the alarm and locking the doors. The acrid stench of ashes and sodden debris stung Marietta's nostrils and brought tears to her eyes. She gazed across the street at the building she had once called her home. Huge streaks of soot were smeared beneath the smashed windows, like mascara staining the weathered cheeks of an old prostitute who has turned one too many brutal tricks. Scorched pieces of furniture and piles of clothing, the refuse of disrupted lives, littered the sidewalk. Protecting the building against looters, a bored cop stamped his feet and swung his arms in an effort to keep warm.

"Don't look," Harlan said gently, taking her arm and leading her toward Margaret Higgins's building.

The glass was cracked and the lock was broken on the vestibule door, and so they entered the building without having to resort to the panel of anonymous buttons. Inside the paint-chipped hallway they were greeted by the stale, sickening odors of cabbage, fried fish, and an ammonia that had never known the inside of a cleaning bottle.

Upstairs, it was easy to spot the Higgins apartment. The floor near its door had been scrubbed clean in a wide semicircle, and in the middle of that area lay a worn but well-brushed welcome mat.

"Shirley kept her entrance the same way," Marietta said, her voice catching.

Harlan squeezed her hand and rang the bell.

Red-eyed and pale, Margaret opened the door and, after giving Marietta a silent, tearful hug, beckoned them to come in.

"I finally got Melanie to lie down on my bed after she talked to you," she said. "The poor child was so exhausted from grief that she fell off to sleep."

She led them out to her kitchen with its old-fashioned free-standing sink-tub, agate stove, and painted table and chairs. There she served coffee and told them what had happened. Cynthia had come home to spend the weekend with Shirley. Melanie had stayed out late because she was attending a friend's sweet-sixteen birthday party.

"I went over about eight and had coffee with Shirley and Cynthia." Margaret's hand trembled as she put down her cup. "I didn't stay long because they both had colds and wanted to go to bed early. Shirley was going to make them hot toddies. I went to bed early myself. Around eleven I woke up hearing those awful sirens and I ran to my window." Her eyes, filled with the terrible memory of what she had seen, met Marietta's. "People were running and screaming. The flames were leaping. The firemen were knocking out windows and carrying people from the house. God, it was awful!" She began to cry.

Her own heart constricting with pain, Marietta reached over and took Margaret's hand.

"What started the fire?" Harlan asked.

Margaret shrugged. "Who knows? I pulled on my coat and ran down, but the cops and firemen wouldn't let anyone get close. You know how they are—they won't tell you what's going on. I heard someone in the crowd say the boiler exploded, and someone else that the wiring short-circuited. Maybe it was both—or something else entirely. What difference does it make? All those poor people lost their homes, and five of them, including Shirley and Cynthia, lost their lives."

"Did they suffer awfully?" It was hard for Marietta to get the words past the lump in her throat. She pictured her friends surrounded by flames, trapped, screaming, terrified. The vision was unbearable, but it stayed before her whether she closed her eyes or opened them, refusing to fade or to be washed away by her tears.

"I think the Good Lord spared them that. I—I was the one who identified them, and they didn't look too awful." She drew a shuddering breath. "The nice fireman who held me when my legs gave out, he told me it looked like they'd just breathed in too much smoke. Maybe Shirley made those hot toddies too strong and they slept too soundly. Neither one of them was used to whiskey. Maybe they'd taken cold medicine too."

A sudden memory of the horrible phone call that brought the news of her own mother's death flashed through Marietta's mind. "Did you call Melanie at the party?"

Margaret shook her head. "I didn't know where the party was. When the fire was just about out, a car with a bunch of teenagers in it drove up—the father of one of the kids was taking the girls home. Melanie nearly fainted when she got out and saw what was going on. The man offered to take her home with him, but I told him I'd look after her. I brought her up here and tried to break the news as gently as I could. But how can you break news like that gently? All she wanted was to talk to you, to be with you. She kept calling and calling…"

A moan came from the other room, and Margaret got to her feet. "She's waking up."

Marietta rose too. "I'll go to her."

With a nod, Margaret sat down.

"Do you want me to come with you?" Harlan asked.

Marietta shook her head. "I think we both need some time alone."

He nodded his understanding, and she pressed his shoulder in gratitude as she left the room.

Melanie's long dark hair spilled over the pillow in a tangled mass, and her pretty party dress was rumpled. She looked like a delicate doll that had been misused by its owner and carelessly tossed aside. In a way, Marietta thought, it was a fitting description. Melanie had been brutally misused by life, but she intended to see that it would never happen again.

Sensing someone in the room, Melanie opened her eyes and turned her head toward Marietta in the doorway. "Mari?" The name trembled on her lips. "Oh, Mari!" She sat up and held out her arms.

Marietta rushed into them, and they cried together for a long time. Gaining control of herself at last, Marietta began to rock Melanie in her arms, smoothing her hair and murmuring, "Hush now, darling. Hush. Everything is going to be all right."

Finally, Melanie quieted, but when she looked up at Marietta, her eyes were haunted with pain. "No, it's not," she said softly. "Nothing is ever going to be all right again."

Gently, Marietta pushed the girl's hair back from her damp cheeks. "It's true," she said, remembering her own tragedies, "that the hurt never goes away. We never get over losing someone we love, but we do learn to live with it."

"But I don't want to live with it!" Melanie's large, dark eyes filled with tears. "I want to be with Mama and Cynthia. I should have died with them. If I hadn't gone to that stupid party, I would have."

"No," Marietta said firmly. "You didn't die, because you weren't supposed to die. You were spared for a purpose."

"I don't believe that." Anger flashed in Melanie's eyes. "You mean God killed Mama and Cynthia and let me live for a reason? If He did, then God's dumb! I'm not half as good as Mama and Cynthia were."

"I don't know if it was God or fate, or what. All I know is that they're dead, and you're not, and you must never allow yourself to feel guilt about that. Sorrow, yes—but never guilt."

"But how can I live without them, Mari?"

For a fleeting second, Marietta had a vision of herself at sixteen, just a year older than Melanie was now, standing at her mother's graveside, as she had stood years before at the gravesides of her sister and her brother. She remembered awakening the morning after her mother's funeral to the awesome silence that told her her father had abandoned her. How her hands had trembled when she had picked up her empty wallet from the floor where he had dropped it. She had known then that she would never see him again. It was as though he had died too. And she had wished that he had died. It was a terrifying feeling to find oneself penniless and utterly alone in the world at the age of fifteen or sixteen.

She pulled Melanie closer to her. "We don't live—we survive." She said it so softly she wasn't sure Melanie had heard it, but perhaps it was better that way. "Come on now." She struggled for the note of optimism and comfort that had never been offered during her own bereavement: "Harlan and I are going to take you home with us. You'd like that, wouldn't you?"

When Melanie nodded absently but didn't rise, Marietta gently but firmly pulled her to her feet and propelled her out of the room. In the kitchen, as Harlan put his arms around Melanie, she suffered a fresh burst of tears. He held her gently until her sobs subsided, then took her face between his hands and looked down at her, his eyes filled with compassion.

"I can't tell you not to cry," he said. "It's right and natural that you grieve for your mother and your sister. But I can tell you not to be frightened and not to worry. Marietta and I are going to take care of everything. We'll try to make this terrible time as easy for you as possible. Let's go home now."

Melanie and Marietta said their tearful good-byes to Margaret and followed Harlan down the dark staircase to the car. He drove in silence, all three of them sitting together for human warmth. Marietta kept her arms around Melanie all the way back to Manhattan.

At home, Harlan stayed out of the way and let Marietta tend to Melanie's needs and put her to bed in the largest guest room. Returning to their own room, she found Harlan in a wing chair by the window, holding a brandy and with an Agatha Christie lying closed on his lap.

"How is she?" he asked, joining her at the wardrobe.

"She fell asleep almost as soon as her head hit the pillow."

"Grief is a powerful sedative. We escape our sorrow for a while in sleep, but it's always there waiting for us in the morning."

Marietta searched his eyes. Was he remembering Jane's death? She turned away and went into the closet for her robe and night-gown. She wasn't sure how to put what she wanted to say into words. She hated asking for things. It had never been necessary. She had carte blanche to gratify any wish that Harlan might not have anticipated. But this was different. She couldn't just move another person into their home and take responsibility for her without his assent.

"About Melanie…" she began, then faltered.

"We'll take care of everything," he said matter-of-factly.

"I didn't mean just the funeral arrangements."

"Neither did I." He put his hands on her shoulders. "Don't hurt me, Mari. Don't look at me as though you're screwing up your courage to ask an impossible favor. Of course, we'll take care of Melanie from now on. She's part of our family now. I want that as much as you do."

Relief washed over her and she went into his arms.

"You don't know how much this means to me. It's like being able to repay Shirley at last for all she did for me."

"I know how much you loved Shirley, and how much she did for you. You've told me that so many times, and Margaret was telling me too. But we mustn't fall into the mistake of thinking that we're doing this only to repay a debt to Shirley." He stroked her hair tenderly. "That wouldn't be fair to Melanie. She's a sweet child. She deserves to be loved for herself."

Marietta kissed his cheek and pressed her face against the warm, comforting expanse of his chest. Then an icy prickle of fear surfaced in her mind and began slowly to spread through her body as five of his words came back to her: *Margaret was telling me too....* How much had Margaret told him?

"You were alone with Margaret for a long time," she said slowly. "What did she tell you about me?"

"Nothing I didn't already know."

"And what was that?"

"Why, that you're beautiful and intelligent and kind."

She pulled out of his arms and looked up into his face. She could read in his eyes that they had talked about more than her appearance and her personality. "Did she say anything about my childhood or my parents?"

"I told you—nothing I didn't already know."

"Like what?" She held her breath.

He shrugged. "We hardly spoke about it. She just mentioned that your father died when you were very young and that your mother was descended from a Russian princess."

Those were the last things Margaret Higgins would have said. Not because she was malicious, but simply because there was no way she could have known the story Marietta had told Harlan about her past. No one knew, not even Cynthia. Her hands began to tremble, and she turned her back to him. She could pretend to believe him, but he would know she was pretending, and forever after, she would be vulnerable to his doubt and suspicion.

"Margaret never said that." She drew a steadying breath. "Do you hate me for lying to you?"

Gently, he turned her around. "I could never hate you. And I've never considered your little story about the Czarina's friend a lie—just an innocent fantasy."

"Do you mean that you knew before tonight that it wasn't true?"

He tried not to smile.

"How long have you known?"

"I suspected from the very beginning. I wasn't exactly a wide-eyed little kid when you told me that tale."

"But you didn't know for sure until tonight?"

"No, I've known for a long time."

Suddenly, she was angry rather than humiliated. "What did you do—hire a detective to snoop into my background?"

Now he looked angry too. "Of course I didn't. It was that bastard Fred Gibbs at the office. He took it upon himself to have you investigated when he heard we were engaged. I tore up the report without reading it and threw him out."

"Why didn't you ever say anything to me? How you must have been laughing at me all this time!"

"Don't you know me better than that?" He took her face in his hands, the anger in his eyes turning to tenderness. "It's you I love, not your family history. I never gave the story another thought—except maybe to hope that someday you might trust me enough to tell me the truth yourself. But if somehow it was important to you to hold on to that fantasy, I'd be the last person in the world to take it away from you—or to let anyone else try to do it."

"Oh, Harlan." The tears shimmering in her eyes spilled over, and she threw herself into his arms. It was the closest she had ever come to loving him.

Chapter Nine

HARLAN TOOK CARE of everything. He arranged a small, quiet funeral that made the last goodbyes as easy as possible for Melanie and Marietta, and through that sad and trying time he offered them the comfort, the compassion, and the strength they needed.

Melanie was installed in the main guest room, which was redecorated in a style more agreeable to a teenager's taste, and she and Marietta spent many pleasant hours shopping in Saks and Bloomingdale's for a wardrobe to replace the one from the discount stores that had been destroyed in the fire. Harlan was willing to send her to a private school, but, an exceptionally bright girl, she had passed an extremely competitive examination and was attending Stuyvesant High, one of the best public schools in the country, and she would not consider leaving it.

At seventeen, graduating at the top of her class, she was accepted at every college she applied to and deluged with offers of scholarships from dozens of others. Harlan, who had grown very close to her, seemed relieved when she chose Barnard College in Manhattan and would, therefore, be able to continue living at home. Marietta was pleased too; Melanie had always been like a younger sister to her, but now, as maturity closed the span between their ages, she was filling the lonely gap in her life that had been created by the death of Cynthia, her best and only real friend.

It was during Melanie's freshman year in college that Marietta began to notice a change in Harlan. His face was a little drawn, his posture wasn't as erect as it used to be, he was quieter than usual. The difference was so subtle that she couldn't be sure how long it had been going on before it came to her attention. She hoped that if she ignored it, it would disappear as gradually as it had arrived, but it didn't. Their life continued on the same high level, but Harlan tired more quickly, seemed to enjoy less the meals at their favorite restaurants, and now preferred antacids to after-dinner liqueurs.

Finally, one evening, when she came upon him sneaking yet another Maalox into his mouth, Marietta suggested that he see his doctor.

"I already have," he said. "I think John's getting senile. He can't even recognize simple indigestion when he sees it. He wanted to put me in the hospital for tests."

A small chill of foreboding shivered down Marietta's spine. "If you don't trust John anymore, why don't you see someone else?"

"There's no need to." For a split second she saw fear flicker in his eyes. "It's just indigestion. These will take care of it."

"Obviously they're not doing such a great job if you have to take so many of them. I'm sure you're right that it's nothing serious, but go to another doctor, anyway—just to make me feel better."

Reluctantly, he agreed. The second doctor, however, did not concur with his self-diagnosis any more than the first one had. And so, reluctantly, Harlan entered Mount Sinai Hospital for tests. He remained there for exploratory surgery. The aloof, frozen-faced surgeon offered them a moderate glimmer of hope: He believed that he had removed all the cancerous tissue, but, he added with a shrug, one could never tell.

Harlan had entered the hospital looking vigorous and ten years younger than his age; he emerged looking a feeble ten years older. It was as though, on its way through his flesh, the surgeon's scalpel had severed some vital, unknown organ that had kept him youthful and dynamic. Marietta had always been able to delude herself that she had married a mature man; now she could no longer ignore the fact that she was the wife of an elderly one. His back was stooped, his gait was slow, his hands had begun to tremble. The grooves that had added strength and character to his face now became mere wrinkles, and the skin on his once-strong legs looked like a thin, shiny sheet of blue-veined marble. Always cold, he needed extra blankets and came to bed dressed like an old maid, in long wool socks and flannel pajamas worn over heavy underwear.

Perhaps it was because he sensed that he repelled her that he stopped making love to Marietta. Or maybe it was because he feared the humiliation of discovering he was unable to perform. She missed sex, but she kept the silent promise she had made to him when they married and never considered having an affair. Instead, she worked off her frustration and her needs by taking over the reins of Sabrina Enterprises. In a way, even without sex, this brought them closer than they had ever been. Since their marriage, Harlan had depended a great deal on Marietta's keen business sense and had often followed her suggestions and sought her advice, but then she had been an outside consultant. Now she was inside, and she thrived on the excitement and the power. Sometimes Harlan would become infused with her enthusiasm as she discussed a merger or merchandising promotion with him, and he would look almost like his old self again. But those times began to to come farther and farther apart. He was losing weight and energy. The doctors insisted that another operation was necessary.

Actually, the operation wasn't necessary. Harlan, the surgeon discovered, was beyond help; the cancer had spread to his vital organs. Marietta wanted to take him home, where she would set up a hospital bed and arrange for nurses around the clock. Harlan refused; he wanted to inflict upon her a minimum of unpleasantness during his deathwatch. They compromised, and Marietta brought as much of home to his private room in the hospital as she could, decorating it with his favorite paintings and knickknacks. All Harlan really cared about, though, was the photograph of her on his nightstand; he would spend hours gazing at it when they were apart.

But not all the beautiful trappings from home or all the expensive medical care he was able to buy for himself could protect Harlan from the unyielding advance of the malignant invader. As he lay in his silk pajamas in his sunny room with its view of New York's elegant Fifth Avenue, his pampered body experienced the same relentless ravages and racking pain as the workworn, johnny-coated bodies of ward patients suffering from the same disease.

Though Harlan tried to endure the pain, it quickly became so intense that he needed stronger and stronger medication to bring him any comfort. Soon there were only short periods of the day when he was awake, but even then, either because of the pain or because of the aftereffects of the drugs, he was not always coherent. Marietta spent hours sitting by his bed while he slept or rambled inarticulately. Sometimes in the middle of rambling, he would become lucid suddenly. It was important to her that she be there for him then.

Once, in the midst of muttering about a dozen things, he stopped abruptly and she had caught him staring at her.

"What is it, darling?" she asked.

"Pull up the blind," he said. "No, don't come back—stay there by the window. I want to see you that way again, with the sunlight in your hair. That's how you looked that first day on the Riviera, when we walked down the steps to the sea." He sighed, and tears came to his eyes. "Oh, how I wish I could see you once again with the Mediterranean sparkling behind you."

She went over to the bed and took his hand. "You will," she promised him. "As soon as you get well, we'll go back to the Villa Claudine."

He smiled like a parent indulging a child's impossible fantasy. "Of course," he said. And then his mind took up its wanderings again.

Later that evening, a nurse who was new to the floor came in to check Harlan while his private nurse was taking her supper break. He had slipped into a deep, drug-induced sleep.

"Why don't you go home?" the nurse suggested solicitously. "Your grandfather doesn't even know you're here."

"He's my husband," Marietta informed her coldly, "and what matters is that I know I'm here."

Her cheeks flaming, the nurse finished her chores and hurried from the room.

From the time he had taken her into his home, Melanie and Harlan had felt a special closeness. For her, he became the father she had never known, and during his illness she spent as much time with him as her studies would allow. When the doctors revealed that the final days had come, she took time off from college and she and Marietta spelled each other at Harlan's side.

It was Marietta who was with Harlan at the end. She had thought that, heavily sedated, he would simply drift off in his sleep, but he suddenly opened his eyes and looked around the room as though searching for someone or something.

"I'm here," she whispered, reaching out to him.

He gripped her hand, but his eyes continued their search, and he died seconds later, calling out for Jane.

Chapter Ten

THOUGH MARIETTA MOURNED for Harlan and missed him, she felt a relief that his body had at last been released from the tortures of his disease. He had been a good man, she had been fond of him, and now she would never see him again. That realization would creep up on her at odd moments and bring with it a sinking feeling of emptiness and the sting of tears. Her tears were motivated by sorrow, however, not guilt or regret; she had worked diligently throughout their marriage to repay Harlan for all he had done for her, and she was convinced that she had succeeded in making him happy. She had misled him in only two ways: in telling him she loved him and in allowing him to believe that she was trying to conceive their child. To her, they were minor infractions—little white lies, really—and she was sure that if there was a heaven, Harlan would look down from it and understand. He had always understood her. Perhaps he was the only person who ever had.

Except for the five-million-dollar trust fund he had set up for Melanie, Harlan left his entire estate to Marietta, and in the usual thoughtful way of the upper-bracketed, he had arranged and rearranged his assets so that she would have to pay only a pittance of tax. At the age of twenty-eight, she found herself as president and chief operating officer of a go-ahead conglomerate. There were alleged market experts, of course, who did not take her, a young and beautiful woman, seriously. They soon discovered that she had all the makings of what, if she had been a man, would have quickly gained her the label of "financial wizard." Because she was a woman, the label was slow in coming, but as long as the money piled up, that did not bother her in the least.

Harlan had been a good businessman but a rather old-fashioned, shortsighted one, and Marietta had never been able to make him see that the real mission of a corporation was not so much to manufacture a product or to provide a service but to make money. Now that he was dead and she was in charge, she turned all her efforts to that one true goal of modern business enterprise. She consolidated and condensed staffs, sold off divisions that lost money or made only marginal profits, and most important of all, diversified. Soon bathing suits and women's wear became only minor subsidiaries of the multimillion-dollar conglomerate she had built, and partly to emphasize that and partly as a tribute to Harlan, she changed the company name to Wylford Enterprises. She diversified into audiovisual aids for schools and industry, computer parts, cosmetics, and plastics. She surrounded herself with the best business minds available—for the right price, they were always available—and ran her empire with a well-manicured iron hand. Divisional presidents quaked in anticipation of the surprise visits that became her characteristic form of communication with them. She was too fair an employer to dismiss anyone capriciously, and too devoted to the profit motive to tolerate disloyalty and inefficiency, which, as many an executive was told when she handed him his statement of resignation for signing, she often found to be one and the same. At Wylford Enterprises there was soon the saying that one either bowed or broke before the will of Marietta Wylford.

Melanie finished college in three and a half years, graduating summa cum laude. She went on to Harvard Law School, where she was graduated in the top ten of her class. Marietta took her into the business immediately, making her her personal assistant and troubleshooter, and giving her an adjoining office that emphasized her powerful position in the hierarchy. Because both women needed privacy, Melanie moved out of Marietta's penthouse and into an apartment of her own on East Sixty-ninth Street.

Even if she had not been young, beautiful, and sexy, Marietta's fortune would have made her seem so to all the available men both inside and outside her circle. She found herself in constant social demand, and she picked her lovers from among New York's handsomest and most desirable men. She valued her independence too much to consider marrying ever again, but she saw no reason to let the men know that. Uninspired lovers she dropped immediately. Others she allowed to court her, indulge her, and shower her with expensive gifts until she found them becoming either too demanding or too boring to be tolerated any longer. There were countless others waiting on the sidelines, eager to take their place.

As the years slipped by, Marietta found that her lovers, even the expert ones, were boring her more and more quickly. Running her empire had become routine too. She was one of the richest, most powerful, and most beautiful women in the country, but suddenly all of those blessings were not enough. She started looking around for a new company to buy, one that would bring new zest and excitement into her life. She found it in Sizzle, Inc.

Because Philip Bailey dreamed up the idea for *Sizzle* at a time when established magazines were faltering and folding all around the country, few bankers and investors had taken him seriously. Rejecting their negative feedback on a magazine devoted to the lives and loves of the rich, the famous, and the infamous, he started his company on a shoestring, risking almost everything he had. *Sizzle* magazine was an instant success, and he was able to go public within a few years. By the time it caught Marietta's eye as an investment (she had been an original subscriber), it was the most popular picture magazine in America, read by the rich, the famous, and the infamous themselves, as well as by the millions who admired, envied, or emulated them.

While Marietta was looking for an exciting new business, Bailey was looking for an exciting new life. He wanted to get out of a long and miserable marriage and begin tasting the pleasures he'd had to forgo all the years he'd had his nose to the grindstone. His company was worth a lot of money on paper, but he could get his hands on that money only if he sold it. He had begun to think seriously of searching for a buyer when Marietta sent her intermediaries to romance him. Word leaked out that exploratory talks were going on, and immediately others became interested in buying the company too, among them Harrison Kendricks, the British publishing magnate who had recently been buying up even more American publications than his Australian rival, Rupert Murdoch. No match for Wylford Enterprises and Kendricks International, the others quickly withdrew from the picture. Bailey did not want to sell to Kendricks, for he wanted to keep his own finger in the pie, something Kendricks would never allow with one of his properties. On Monday, Fogerty, Finley, and Straus, Kendricks's investment bankers, had announced their client's intention of tendering a hostile bid, and the two conglomerates began to square off for a costly takeover battle. Wylford Enterprises, of course, was on the scene as the white knight in this instance, but in the business arena, the white knight needs more than coffers of gold, God, and the love of his lady fair in order to rout the enemy. That was why Marietta had been so pleased when Philip Bailey came to her that Wednesday evening with the news that he had discovered something he could use to blackmail Kendricks into backing off. It was rotten luck that he had died before she had been able to wrench the secret from him.

It had grown late and cold since Marietta had come out into her garden high above the city. Shivering, she drained the last of her martini from her glass. With Philip dead, she had lost the all-important ally in her fight to gain control of *Sizzle*. Abruptly, the rules of the game had changed. Somehow she had to think of a way to keep Bailey's widow from moving into the Kendricks camp. Either that or convince enough other stockholders to sell out to her before Kendricks could get to them. Actually, she would have to try to do both, for as soon as the news of Philip's death broke, Kendricks would move in like a shark smelling blood. The only way to stop him would be to discover Philip's ace in the hole—and she had only seventeen working days left to do it.

She stood up. Suddenly she no longer felt cold, or tired either. She had never been forced out of a takeover before, not even when she had been the hostile raider, and she would be damned if she would be forced out of this one. Just before going through the sliding doors and into her apartment, she paused for another look at the starry sky, for another breath of the cool night air. It had been years since she had felt so alert, so alive. She would beat Kendricks on this deal. One way or another, she would wind up as the new publisher of *Sizzle.*

BOOK TWO

Spring 1988

Chapter Eleven

S EX IN THE MORNING, Clifford Langhton had discovered early in his marriage, was a great way to start the day, just as sex in the evening was a great way to end it. Of course, being married to a vibrant, gorgeous woman like Stephanie had a lot to do with it. They'd met a dozen years ago, in a time Stephanie liked to refer to as "B.K."—"Before Kendricks." He had been an ambitious and well-regarded reporter on the *Wall Street Journal* then and she was an eager, wide-eyed copy girl fresh out of journalism school. The moment their eyes met while she reached for the Lockheed story on his desk, he knew he had to have her—not just physically, but spiritually and emotionally too. There was nothing of the usual one-night stand about his feelings for Stephanie; he wanted her for a lifetime. It had taken a while to convince her of that. He'd had his reputation as a cynic and a Don Juan to live down, but ultimately he had convinced her of his sincerity, perhaps because she had felt the same way about him.

Before the year was over, they were married. Stephanie had wanted to wait awhile, to try out her wings on life a bit, but Cliff, with thirty breathing down his neck, had been eager to settle down. He had been growing bored with playing musical beds, never knowing whose gorgeous face he would wake up opposite in the morning—and not really caring. He had also grown weary of the endless cocktail parties, and their empty talk about emptier plays and books and people. Surely there was more to life than that. And then he discovered that there was Stephanie. Loving her had added a depth and dimension to living that he hadn't dreamed possible.

Now, in the early morning light filtering through the blinds, he propped himself up on an elbow and looked down at Stephanie as she slept beside him. Her golden-brown hair fanned out on her pillow like rays from a halo. Smiling, he brushed a few stray strands back from her face. At thirty-four, she was even more lovely than she had been at twenty-two. Yet he sometimes wondered if he might have been wrong to rush her into marriage. For though she had matured and grown in every other way through the years, there was a tiny recess of her soul that still held fast to the innocent idealism of youth, a recess that would have been obliterated by more exposure to the real world. Still, he would not have her change. It was refreshing to come home to her and their three little boys at the end of a day of wheeling and dealing for Harrison Kendricks. Over the years, though, he had learned that there were certain aspects of his work that were better left unmentioned.

As Stephanie turned toward him in her sleep, the covers slipped from her shoulders, revealing her full luscious breasts. His loins stirring, he began to gently finger her nipple. Awakening with a purr of contentment, she molded her body to his and wound her arms around his neck.

"Good morning," she said, her voice throaty from sleep and rising desire. "Isn't this where we left off last night?"

"Not quite," he whispered, and burrowed his head between her breasts, a hand descending toward the delectable warmth between her thighs. "Let me refresh your memory."

"Oh, yes," she said, her own hand caressing, kneading, sending white-hot shocks of excitement through him. "Please do…"

Each knew every secret place, every magic switch that would release floods of pleasure and delight in the other, and soon they were lost in their own private world of love and passion. When at last they'd enjoyed the ecstasy of fulfillment, they lay quivering and throbbing in each other's arms, sharing tender caresses while waiting for their breathing to return to normal.

Suddenly their bliss was shattered by the shrill ringing of the telephone on Cliff's night table.

"Damn," he said, reaching for it. Stephanie rolled toward the edge of the bed and groped for her robe.

"That s.o.b. Philip Bailey dropped dead on us last night." The words came over the wire in a crisp British accent. Harrison Kendricks never wasted time on salutations or complimentary closings. "It's a whole bloody new ball game. Get into the city as soon as you can. We'll meet at the Regency for breakfast."

Cliff replaced the receiver and swung his legs out of bed.

"That was either Kendricks or a pervert," Stephanie said. "No one else would call before seven in the morning and then hang up without waiting for a reply."

"Right the first time." He gave her behind a playful pat as he headed for the shower.

"What do you want for breakfast?" she called after him.

"Nothing. I'm eating in the city."

Faintly, her "So what else is new?" came through the closed door.

Knowing better than to distract him while he was getting ready for work, Stephanie showered in the other bathroom and he found her downstairs in the breakfast nook later. In her Liz Claiborne jeans and polo shirt, with her face scrubbed and her damp hair pulled back and fastened with a barrette, she looked only a few years older than Billy, who at ten was their oldest child.

She raised her mug in salute as he came into the room. "Ten minutes of peace before the other lights of my life begin flashing around. Have time for coffee?"

He shook his head. "Wish I did." He leaned down and took a sip from her cup, then kissed her. "It looks like it may be a long day."

"They usually are." She smiled and shrugged as if it didn't matter, but he could see in her eyes that it did.

She walked him to the door where he paused to slip his Aquascutum trenchcoat over his blue three-piece Southwick suit.

"We have theater tickets for tonight," she reminded him, handing him his Mark Cross attaché case.

Hell. He had forgotten about that. And she had been looking forward to it. He touched her cheek. "I'll call you this afternoon and let you know if I can make it. If I can't, take your mom or one of your friends."

"Sure."

They kissed, and he hurried out the door and across the lawn toward their garage.

"Cliff."

He turned. "Yes?"

"Try to make it. Okay?"

"You know I will." He blew her a kiss and then continued across the lawn without looking back.

As always, the pale blue Lincoln Continental seemed to drive itself. No matter how bad the traffic, he was always able to relax when he was behind the wheel of his car. He did some of his best thinking there. And thinking was the most important part of his job.

Harrison Kendricks had come into his life almost ten years before. Kendricks had arrived in New York, it was rumored, to buy the *New York Post*. He encouraged the rumor; it made the owners of the *Clarion*, his real target, and the *Post's* only and very weak evening competitor, frightened enough to accept, without elaborate quibbling over, his extremely low offer. After the sale, Cliff had been sent to interview in depth this international publishing magnate who owned newspapers and magazines all over England, Canada, and the United States. Cliff had gotten his story—and a damn good one too—but as he was going about it, Kendricks was doing some interviewing of his own.

Like most self-made men, Kendricks was not easily moved to admiration, but he was impressed by Cliff's sharp mind, grasp of corporate machinations, knowledge of journalism from both the business and editorial angles; Cliff's excellent contacts among the movers and shakers of the American financial establishment were also not to be dismissed lightly. The interview ended with an invitation from Kendricks to an off-the-record dinner in his suite at the Plaza. And the dinner ended with Cliff's agreeing to leave the *Wall Street Journal* and become Kendricks's personal assistant and troubleshooter, with the promise that he would be made the editor of a worthy and prestigious publication when Kendricks acquired such a journalistic gem. The salary offered and quickly accepted was staggering, and Cliff returned exultant to the cramped apartment in Greenwich Village.

But Stephanie did not entirely share his enthusiasm. She

deplored his becoming involved with a man with a reputation for being almost savagely ruthless. It took an enormous effort, but Cliff finally convinced her that Kendricks did nothing that other successful businessmen did not do also, except that Kendricks was honest enough to admit that he didn't aspire to sainthood. Stephanie was never truly happy with Cliff's decision, but she agreed in the end that it was his decision to make. Certainly, over the years that followed, she had enjoyed the fruits of that decision—a beautiful brick home on a full acre in Scarsdale, designer clothes, trips all over the world. Thanks to Kendricks, Cliff had been able to give his wife and three sons the best of everything. No, it was really thanks to himself. He earned every penny of his salary and his many perks and bonuses. And Kendricks knew it. Kendricks would never have tolerated less.

The editorial plum promised Cliff at their first meeting had never materialized. Not that Kendricks hadn't acquired several magazines and newspapers that fitted that description. But somehow Kendricks had deemed them inappropriate for a man of Cliff's talents. Always, he would hint that there was something even more spectacular on the horizon. The trouble with horizons, Cliff had found out, was that they were damned elusive. He had been disappointed at first, but he had never been bitter. He was bright enough to be aware that Kendricks was using him, but he was also perceptive enough to realize that he relished his power as Kendricks's right-hand man. Secretly, he reveled in the fact that influential outsiders considered him indispensable to one of the world's most powerful press lords. It was a sham, of course. From his intimate vantage point, Cliff was in a position to know better than anyone else that absolutely no one was indispensable to a megalomaniac like Harrison Kendricks.

The person who came closest to holding such a coveted position was probably Nick Washburn. Tall and burly, Nick had silver-gray eyes that telegraphed danger like the cold steel of a switchblade knife. He dated back to Kendricks's mercenary days in Africa, perhaps even predated them. He had the same aura of dark power about him that Kendricks did, but while in Kendricks it reminded Cliff of a panther, in Washburn it reminded him of a snake. Since Kendricks had gone legitimate with the takeover of his brother's newspaper, Washburn had been by his side as his chauffeur-bodyguard. Though nothing was ever said about it, Cliff knew that there was a great deal more to Washburn's duties than driving Kendricks around and making sure no one took a sock or a shot at him. To Cliff, Kendricks delegated the socially acceptable cutthroat and underhanded tactics of achieving the goals of Kendricks International; to Washburn, he entrusted the seamier, outside-the-law ones.

Cliff had always been aware that Washburn would be more difficult for Kendricks to replace than he himself would be. Nevertheless, he recognized that as the professional employee Kendricks trusted more than any other, he occupied a more privileged position. He appreciated that, and sometimes even gloried in it, but he was a journalist at heart, and the hope had not yet died that one day Kendricks would fulfill his promise. His secret dream—he had never even confided it to Stephanie—was that Kendricks would present him with the editorship of the *London Times,* but then Rupert Murdoch showed an interest in and finally bought that prestigious prize. Though Kendricks and Murdoch relished being competitors on the newsstands, they always seemed to shy away from competing with each other in bidding for a journalistic property. Like two magnificent lions tacitly agreeing to hunt only in their own territories, each seemed to prefer to select and secure his own prey rather than attack something the other was obviously stalking. If Cliff was the only professional Kendricks truly trusted, Murdoch was the only businessman he truly respected. So Cliff had given up his dream of the *London Times.* And now *Sizzle* was being dangled before him. If that turned out to be his prize, the long wait would have been well worthwhile.

He parked his car in a garage on Sixty-seventh Street and bought a *Times* at a convenience store. Outside, he paused for a moment to scan the obituary of Philip Bailey. Aside from the information that he had died of a heart attack in the home of a friend, it was a standard summary of the life of an important businessman. The article about a discovery of possible Viking artifacts in Maine, which ran beside it, was far more interesting.

Cliff slipped the newspaper under his arm and headed for the Regency Hotel. Walking along Park Avenue always exhilarated him. Out-of-towners mistakenly believed that Fifth Avenue symbolized New York's wealth, but natives like Cliff knew it was Park Avenue that truly epitomized the Good Life; the combined income of the residents of that street would make Fort Knox look like a church collection basket the Sunday after Christmas bills began rolling in.

Dominated by a huge chandelier and a seventeenth-century tapestry of an idyllic country scene, the small foyer of the Regency, with its needlepoint-upholstered furniture and burgundy drapes always reminded Cliff of a European chateau. That, of course, was what it was intended to do. The hotel's register read like a *Who's Who* of the European elite, and it was only natural that the guests be made to feel at home upon crossing the threshold.

Guarding his portals with vigilance and charm, the maître d' greeted Cliff by name and informed him cheerfully that Mr. Kendricks had not yet arrived. Cliff followed him across the thick blue carpet with its intersecting gold rosettes to Kendricks's favorite table. He nodded to the waiter who was standing by with a coffeepot, then, toying with the napkin on the silver plate before him, glanced around the room. He knew most of the men at the other tables—corporate chairmen and presidents, bankers, stockbrokers, lawyers, company finders, acquisition directors. These men were the true movers and shakers of nations. They controlled the purse strings and kept politicians dangling from them. More business activity was initiated beneath the Regency's muted murals of idyllic landscapes and classical villas than in all the boardrooms of the country.

He saw many heads turn toward the entrance, and his own gaze followed them. Harrison Kendricks had a way of commanding attention when he strode into a room. Over six feet tall, he had the rugged build of a football player, but he carried his powerful frame with the grace and ease of a panther, creating the image of a contained force that might at any moment be activated to deliver an instant, fatal blow. It was an accurate reflection of his strength and his character: In his youth, he had been a mercenary, working for the highest bidder, often spying on the very revolutionaries he ran guns for and trained. No one knew how much blood he had spilled directly or indirectly. Those who were aware of isolated cases dared not speak of them, for knowledge of such acts would indicate collusion.

In 1960, Kendricks became "director of special operations" in the Congo, a position he maintained until early 1964, when he contracted a rare tropical disease that weakened his vision and left his eyes oversensitive to light, necessitating the wearing of tinted lenses at all times. After several months of treatment, he left the hospital in Nairobi for a destination unknown, and he did not surface again until December 1964, when, after not having set foot on his native soil since being sent down from Oxford for disciplinary reasons twelve years before, he suddenly reappeared in England. His mother wept tears of joy as she welcomed her prodigal son back to Golden Oaks, the family estate in Buckinghamshire. His older brother, Nigel, who had inherited, and been successfully running since their father's death, the conservative newspaper founded by their great-grandfather, was less enthusiastic. Nevertheless, at their mother's insistence, Nigel created an executive position on the paper for "dear Harry" and even asked him to be best man at his forthcoming marriage.

Kendricks graciously accepted both offices, but the second was never to be fulfilled: Four weeks before the wedding, in a freak accident that later puzzled the authorities, Nigel somehow lost control of his Bentley, drove it over a cliff, and was blown to bits in the explosion that followed. Kendricks, of course, knew where his duty lay. He took over the newspaper that was now his inheritance and quickly changed it from a marginally profitable Manchester daily with objective reporting of national and international news to a wildly lucrative national weekly devoted to the sensational reporting of gossip and gore. With his profits, he bought a foundering London daily and turned it into the city's most lurid and popular tabloid. After that, the search was on. County by county, he went through Britain, buying up expiring papers and reviving them with a lustiness that drove away competition. Having bought all the domestic papers that caught his fancy for the moment, he turned his attention to Canada and the United States, where he purchased periodicals as well as newspapers and occasionally invested in real estate.

In slightly short of twenty-five years Kendricks had elevated himself from a mercenary to a highly successful international entrepreneur. The transformation had not been a difficult one, the tools of the trades being much the same. He made no effort at all to hide or mitigate his past. The revulsion inspired by what was known of him, and the mystery surrounding what was unknown, stimulated a healthy respect and fear, both in competitors and in those who sought his favor. "Money," he had told Cliff more than once, "buys a man power. And power buys him everything else."

Cliff rose as Kendricks neared their table, crossing the floor without looking right or left. It was his policy to gaze directly ahead, thereby never enhancing the prestige of anyone in a room by singling him out with a nod or a greeting. Those who sought his favor or even recognition had to approach him.

"We don't want to be disturbed," he told the maître d' as he slid into the blue-velvet-backed chair being held out for him. "Tell the waiter to bring us our usual breakfast."

Though his digestion had been poor for the past two days and he didn't really feel up to kippers and eggs, Cliff sat down and said nothing.

Kendricks reached into the breast pocket of the blue silk suit custom-made for him by Gieves and Hawkes of Savile Row and withdrew a gold cigarette case bearing his monogram. It was filled with Sobranies, the black European cigarettes with gold filters and crests that he always smoked. He extracted one and lit it, quickly expelling the smoke through his nostrils. "It was a hell of a time for that vile scumbag to pop off," he said, resuming his telephone conversation at the point at which he had dropped it.

Cliff shrugged. "I'm sure he'd agree with you." The waiter appeared with Kendricks's Darjeeling tea and grapefruit juice for both of them.

Upon his first sip, the acid in the juice attacked Cliff's stomach, and he put the glass aside. "I heard a brief radio report on my way in. There was nothing very informative in the *Times*."

"The news was announced too late for the morning papers to cover it adequately. At least we can thank Bailey for that much. We'll beat them with a full story. Snelling called me from the city desk as soon as word reached the *Clarion*. Guess where it happened."

Behind the tinted glasses, Kendricks's brown eyes were bright with amusement.

"The *Times* said it was in the home of a friend. From your expression, I take it that it wasn't his clergyman's rectory."

"Quite the contrary. It was in the apartment of Marietta Wylford."

"Were they screwing?"

"The bitch says they had discussed business and were having cocktails before going out to dinner. When he said he felt ill, she suggested that he have a little lie-down. She went to check on him later, and found him dead."

"They were screwing."

"Of course they were." Kendricks crushed his cigarette in the blue shell-shaped ashtray and reached for his juice. "But we have no proof."

"Since when has the *Clarion* been devoted to proof? It will make a hell of a story for the first edition."

"No. I told Snelling to play down the story and stick strictly to the facts."

Their kippers and eggs were served, and Kendricks attacked them with zest.

"You must be kidding," Cliff said. "You're handing the *Post* this one on a silver platter."

Kendricks smiled. His teeth were large, square, perfect cutting edges. "And can't you just see their headline? It's bound to be something like SIZZLE PUBLISHER FIZZLES IN BEAUTY'S BED. I told Snelling to feature a different story. Maybe we'll get lucky and a terrorist bomb will go off in the Middle East and kill a few dozen Jews or what-have-you. That always boosts circulation by at least fifty thousand."

"But why let this story slip through your fingers? You'd be able to get Marietta Wylford by the tits. With the circumstances of Bailey's death splashed all over the front page of the *Post* and the *Clarion*, there's no way his widow would be willing to sell her shares to Wylford Enterprises, proof or no proof of hanky-panky."

"You're not usually guilty of such foggy thinking, old man. I'm not holding off to protect darling Marietta. I'm doing it out of respect for the dear departed and out of deference for the feelings of the poor grieving widow." With his knife and fork, Kendricks formed a cross over his heart.

"That's not terribly convincing from a man who's hoping for a bomb in the Middle East."

"As long as the poor grieving widow is convinced. I'm depending on you to see to that. Let the *Post* do our dirty work for us. We'll hold her hand and pick up her stocks."

"You seem to be overlooking probate. The stocks won't be in her hands for a while yet."

"Then perhaps you can put a pen in them and get her to agree to sign them over to us when she does get them. I want you to make yourself as helpful as possible to her in her time of need."

"That's not an easy thing for a stranger to do."

"I save the easy assignments for idiots. You'll find a way. You always do. The main thing is that we must go forward at a brisk pace. We've got the advantage now, at least with the family. I don't want that Wylford bitch to gain another inch of ground."

"Under the circumstances, I'd say she's lost a hell of a lot."

"Marietta Wylford never loses ground—she simply shifts position. That's why it's imperative that we make the most of this time while Bailey's stocks are in limbo. Get a list of stockholders and get on to everyone holding one percent of the stock or more. If you can't bribe them into agreeing to sell us their stock when our twenty-day waiting period expires, then scare them into doing it."

"You seem to forget that we're the hostile raider in this case," Cliff reminded him, shoving the kippers around on his plate. "No one's going to cooperate with us. We may have to get a court order. It will take time. Isn't this what you've hired acquisition lawyers for?"

"I hire acquisition lawyers and company finders and investment bankers because they're a bloody necessary evil here in this corrupt land. When things get tough they're as much use to me as a square wheel. You've handled this sort of thing for me countless times. Why are you finding obstacles now?"

"Because Bailey's death makes this case unique. The SEC has probably been watching you closely since your announcement of intent. Surely, you must know that they'd love to get something on you."

Kendricks threw back his head and laughed. "You Americans and your precious, pathetic institutions. All your politicians and businessmen give lip service *ad infinitum* to the great American way—making it on your own by hard work, clean living, honesty, and integrity—and at the same time they've all got their hands out, ready to grab any currency that foreigners are willing to drop into them. In your insatiable greed you've allowed foreign interests to gobble up your real estate and buy controlling shares in essential industries. One of these days, you're going to wake up and find that the only thing American left in the country is the unemployed population of workers, the upper classes having nipped abroad with their spoils. The land and everything on it will be totally controlled by Arabs, Japanese, Chinese, and the rest of us foreigners you regard with such disdain as you eagerly sell us everything you can possibly profit on. In reality, old boy, your countrymen are a bunch of soulless fucks."

"That must be because we've learned our lesson so well from the mother country."

"Touché." Kendricks raised his fork in mock salute. "At any rate, I'm not worried about anyone inside or outside your venerable institutions 'getting something on me,' as you put it. Let them posture all they like. They're not about to bite the hand that feeds or bribes them. Speaking of bribes, I heard that Gregory Walcott, the circulation director of *Sizzle,* recently dropped a bundle at Caesar's Palace while fiddling the tits of a blonde who was definitely not his fat and fortyish wife. He'll be in the market for a few extra dollars. Let him know we're aware of his problems and would be happy to help if he'll cooperate—or to complicate them if he doesn't."

Suddenly a voice above them was saying, "Harrison, how are you? No, no, don't get up."

Kendricks's face said he wouldn't dream of standing. He briefly shook the beefy hand being extended to him by Alwyn Lloyd, a senator who was up for re-election in a Midwestern state where Kendricks owned two influential newspapers. "You know my associate, Mr. Langhton."

"Of course I do. Everybody knows Cliff. How are you doing, fella?"

The hand was now offered to Cliff, who took it with a nod. "Just great, Senator."

"Good to hear it." Lloyd turned back to Kendricks, his chubby cheeks pulled into an ingratiating smile, his small gray eyes measuring. "Just got back from a fact-finding trip. My last stop was your hometown, London."

"I'm from Manchester."

Lloyd gave a hearty laugh. "London, Manchester—'fraid it's all the same to us country boys."

"I know what you mean. I frequently get Washington and Bridgeport mixed up."

"Great sense of humor, your boss." Lloyd gave Cliff a broad wink, then shifted his gaze back to Kendricks. "Heard some nice things about you over there."

"Really? I've heard some things about you too."

Lloyd's eyes grew wary, but his smile brightened. "A cabinet member I had dinner with one night said the Queen's going to make you one of her knights soon. Guess we'll all have to be calling you 'Sir Harry,' eh?"

"'Sir Harrison' would do nicely. And let's wait and see if it happens first. It's only a rumor at the moment."

"You British are all alike—too damn modest by far. Of course it's going to happen, probably sooner than my Uncle Ed can cut up a pork belly. If anyone deserves it, it's you. And I want to be the first to congratulate you."

"Thanks awfully, old man."

"Don't mention it. Well, see you around Buckingham Palace."

"Ass-licking shit," Kendricks said as he watched Lloyd return to his table. "He's peeing in his pants because I spotted him feeling up a very pretty lad in the men's room of a Washington nightclub recently. Of course, they both claimed that the chap's zipper was stuck and Lloyd was being a good public servant and trying to help him fix it. I have no intention of printing the story at the moment, though. Schmuck that he is, he suits me better than his opponent, who wants to pile taxes on corporations so that public works programs can be started and welfare benefits increased."

"Is it true about the knighthood?"

"It's true that it's rumored."

"How do you feel about it?"

"Vastly amused, old boy. I used to think it was all what you Americans picturesquely refer to as a crock of shit. But now that I've hit my middle years, I'm not so sure. My money and position, of course, have brought—and bought—me respectability, but I must say that I find the idea of having it conferred on me directly by the Queen herself quite delicious. My dear mother would be most gratified to see her prodigal son legitimatized in the eyes of the world by Her Majesty. She's past eighty now with not much to look forward to except her sherry and soap operas on the telly. The poor thing has become too senile for bridge. I'd rather like her to be able to boast about her son the KBE at tea with her few surviving cronies." He heaved a sigh and then resumed caustically, "And then, of course, there are all those people who would shudder to see me get it. Their chagrin would be most gratifying of all."

"I hate to show my ignorance, but what would you be given a knighthood for? I always thought it was an honor rather like the Nobel Prize, conferred for a distinguished life's work in the arts or science or for some great discovery. How do businessmen get it?"

"The same way we have always gotten it—by adding gold to the royal coffers, or in our own times, to the country's coffers. God knows, I've done enough of that. In fact, it's quite likely that, since my enterprises will be bringing more and more money into Elizabeth's shrinking realm, I may even be given a peerage one day." With mock gravity Kendricks brushed imaginary specks from his shoulders. "Can you picture the faces of the peers when I don my robes and take my place among them in the House of Lords? I'd rather like that."

Yes, he would, Cliff realized, studying Kendricks's face, suddenly seeing a new side of him. Kendricks was trying to make it appear that a knighthood or a peerage would be a lark, but obviously it meant a great deal to him. Kendricks the marauder was beginning to long for legitimate respectability, which added a surprising new dimension to Cliff's perception of the man.

"I hope it comes through for you," Cliff said.

"We'll see." Kendricks dismissed the matter and became all business once more. "In the meantime, there's a great deal to be done right here, and very little time to do it in. I suggest you get on it immediately. Make your first stop the bank. Those sons of bitches are too complacent by far. Remind them that the half million they'll pick up is nothing compared with what they'll get if we win, and tell them to get off their asses. Drop in on those lawyers we're paying a fortune to, and tell them I expect them to ferret out any skeletons Marietta Wylford may have buried in her corporate or personal closets. And don't forget the grieving widow and lecherous circulation director, and anything or anyone else you may think of."

Kendricks signaled for the bill, then turned back to Cliff. "I'm flying to Boston to sack that idiot Daley. He's had six months to build up the circulation of the *World*. His excuses bore me. I don't consider a rise of ten thousand as signifying anything but sheer laziness. I'd intended to send you to take care of the matter, but upon second thought, I believe that my presence will tone up the rest of the staff. Remember, as you go about your work, that you're doing this one for yourself as well as for me."

In spite of his many disappointments, Cliff felt his heart quicken. He had heard the words before, of course, but maybe *Sizzle* really would be his.

When the waiter arrived with their bill, Kendricks glanced at it, then gestured across the room. "Give it to Senator Lloyd," he said. "He very kindly asked us to be his guests." He rose and preceded Cliff from the room, looking, as usual, neither left nor right.

Chapter Twelve

MELANIE DANIELLE sat back in her chair at the long polished table in the *Sizzle* executive conference room and relaxed for the first time since receiving Marietta's call the night before. Her own telephone calls had produced the desired results: so far, no word had leaked out about the activity engaging Philip Bailey's attention when he expired. The tabloids, of course, would make the most of the situation, but no one could stonewall better than Marietta, and in a few days they would soon have fresh scandals to exploit. By the time she arrived in her office that morning, she had everything under control and had even arranged to call on Bailey's widow, Louise, in the late afternoon.

During their regular nine-thirty coffeebreak in Marietta's office, Marietta had come up with the idea of addressing a meeting of *Sizzle*'s management. Melanie went into action immediately, and when they arrived at the magazine at eleven o'clock, the executives were awaiting them in the conference room. Ranging in age from about thirty-five to a youthful sixty, they were all males, all, except one, impeccably dressed in three-piece suits from Brooks Brothers or Paul Stuart, all with the polished, comfortable look of men who have been educated in the best schools and have entrée to the best circles. And all, Melanie sensed, were decidedly nervous. Marietta sensed it too, Melanie knew, for she was reacting as she always did in such tense situations; to her, the smell of a sweating antagonist or subordinate was both challenging and invigorating.

Only one man among them didn't fit the general picture, Melanie noted as she looked around the table, and that was David

Belmont, the editor of *Sizzle*. He was about thirty-seven, and wore his brown tweed sports jacket with the relaxed air of a man who shaped his own life and thoughts. But, of course, that was the image most editors liked to project.

He felt her gaze on him and turned. His eyes were brown, beneath strong, well-shaped dark brows. His hair was thick and dark, but cut in the no-nonsense style of a man who has neither the desire nor the patience to preen before mirrors. A little too thin to be called sensuous, his lips curved gently into a sensitive mouth. He did not smile at her, as any of the other men at the table would have done in the same situation. Instead, he returned her gaze frankly for a moment, then shifted his eyes back to Marietta, who was still addressing the group.

Marietta had begun by reminding them that, whether they liked it or not, the company was soon to be taken over by a conglomerate, in accordance with the wishes of Philip Bailey.

"It's been no secret that Wylford Enterprises is interested in buying," Marietta was saying now. "I'm sure Philip discussed my offer with many of you gentlemen. However, the situation became complicated Monday when Kendricks International tendered a hostile bid. It has become even more complicated now that Philip is dead. He would have fought a Kendricks takeover with all his strength. In fact, we were about to discuss our joint strategy at dinner last night when he took ill. His fight is now yours. If you lose it, gentlemen, you will very soon discover that you have lost a great deal more than a simple stock skirmish."

She nodded at Melanie, who opened the folder before her and said in a forceful tone, "What you are about to hear comes from recent editions of *Editor and Publisher.*" She began to read aloud:

"In 1975, Harrison Kendricks bought the *Tacoma Register.* Within the first three months, he had replaced thirty percent of top management with outsiders imported from Great Britain. By the end of the first six months, eighty percent of the top management had been either terminated or reassigned to subordinate positions. By the end of the first year, only one of the original managers remained on staff, and in the area of middle management, half had been terminated with no replacements hired. Of the fifty percent middle managerial positions that remained, only two were filled by original employees.

"In 1977, Kendricks International emerged the victor in a bitter takeover battle with Continental Pharmaceuticals for the control of *The Good Life*. Though the then-current management had elevated that magazine into the most popular and lucrative general publication in the Midwest, the editor-in-chief and publisher were replaced by Englishmen within the first six weeks of the Kendricks ownership. At the end of five months, seventy-five percent of top management had been replaced—half by outsiders and half by persons moved up from middle management at a fraction of the salaries paid to the original officers. One manager, who had been reassigned to middle management with a sixty-percent slash in salary, resigned, but had to sue in court for his severance benefits, of which he finally received forty-five percent. After one year in the Kendricks conglomerate, the entire staff of *The Good Life* had been cut fifty-three point seven percent. Only one original top manager remained—the founder of the magazine, who, according to the takeover agreement, collected a large salary as a vice president of the Good Life Division of Kendricks International, but who performed no official duties.

"Also in 1977, Kendricks International took over the Toronto *Observer*. Within—"

"Thank you," Marietta broke in. "I think you've made our point quite clear." She continued, "We have similar depressing statistics for all the Kendricks takeovers, including those in Great Britain, where he has been equally brutal. The figures can easily be verified, and we'll be happy to supply copies to any of you who wish to see them." Marietta glanced around the table. "All of you are bright, or you wouldn't be holding your present positions. I'm sure you don't need anyone to spell out the only conclusion that can be drawn from the figures that have just been read. But in case they have left you too stunned to think clearly, I'll do it for you: If Kendricks International wins the takeover battle for *Sizzle*, each and every one of you can kiss your job good-bye."

"And if Wylford Enterprises wins?" David Belmont was the only one bold enough to voice the question in the minds of all the men at the table.

"It is the policy of Wylford Enterprises never to relieve an executive of his or her duties without sufficient reason."

"I'm sure Harrison Kendricks would make the same statement," Belmont persisted.

"Yes, but in the view of the data just presented, any such statement from the mouth of Harrison Kendricks would be highly suspect. At Wylford, our policy is: 'If it works, don't fix it.' We acquire only companies that we are sure will make a strong bottom-line contribution. And as long as those companies and their officers fulfill their potential, we can see no reason to institute shifts in personnel."

"That 'fulfill their potential' sounds like a catch-all escape clause." Emboldened by Belmont's example, Gregory Walcott, the circulation director, was the next to speak.

"Wylford Enterprises did not join the Fortune Five Hundred by sheltering nonperformers. I can't imagine that anyone here has not made inquiries into our policy since learning of our interest in your organization. You will have discovered that our record for retaining in-position officers is far better than Kendricks's."

"What guarantee do we have that it won't change now?" Mike Conway, the advertising director, asked.

Marietta returned his sharp gaze. "Absolutely none. There are three factors, however, that you should keep in mind. The first is the past record of Wylford Enterprises. The second is that *Sizzle* would represent our first venture into publishing, and, therefore, it would not be pragmatic for us to make personnel and policy changes before becoming more familiar with the industry. The third, Ms. Danielle will outline briefly for you now."

Once again, Melanie opened the folder before her. "We know from our meetings with Philip Bailey that there are no golden-parachute clauses in any of your contracts. The lack of such a termination agreement leaves all of you vulnerable in the event of a takeover, and especially vulnerable in the event of a takeover by a hostile raider, such as Kendricks. We promise you only blood, sweat, and tears and suchlike British goodies if Kendricks wins, but we can offer you more positive insurance in the event of a Wylford takeover. We are prepared to sign an agreement with each of you providing that anyone who is dropped within eighteen months of a Wylford takeover will be given a cash settlement equal to twenty percent of his annual salary plus bonuses and be guaranteed full salary for two years."

"The top brass at Conoco, Phillips Petroleum, and AMF have been covered for a hell of a lot more in termination agreements," Conway said.

"Those agreements were made with their own companies as insurance against the consequences of a takeover," Melanie reminded him. "Philip Bailey had no intention of providing any kind of parachute for you, and coming from us as bidders, the offer is most unusual and perhaps not really in our own interest. Nevertheless, we have engaged Howard Roth, an executive-compensation lawyer with Fenner, Hartwell and Roth, to draw up the agreements. They'll be available for any of you who wish to sign them."

"Will they cover resignation as well as termination?" Walcott asked.

"We're generous, not foolish," Melanie said. "The agreements will cover only termination for reasons other than neglect of duty, dishonesty, and gross insubordination."

From somewhere along the table came a barely audible mutter: "Big deal."

"Of course," Melanie went on, as though she had not heard the remark, "you are free to sign or not, as you choose."

"A year and a half isn't a very long time," Fred Watkins, the vice president in charge of personnel, pointed out. "What's to keep Wylford from stringing us along for that period and then terminating us all the moment the agreement runs out?"

"Good business sense," Marietta said crisply. "My charity work is directed toward philanthropic organizations; it is never extended to the subsidiaries in my conglomerate. When it is determined that an executive is no longer giving his all to the team, he is dismissed. In the long run, the cost of cushioning his exit by activating the provisions of a termination clause is a great deal less than the cost of keeping such a millstone around the neck of a whole division." She looked around the table, meeting each pair of eyes. "And now, gentlemen, I think we have made the position of Wylford Enterprises clear. It will be greatly to your advantage to work with us in our takeover bid. Of course, note will be taken of those who are friendly to us as well as of those who are not."

Marietta rose, and the men sprang up to their feet too. "Thank you for coming, gentlemen. The next time a meeting is called in this room, I intend to be presiding as chief executive officer—with or without your cooperation."

Melanie stood beside Marietta as the men filed out, shaking her hand, offering words of encouragement on her bid. Each was such an accomplished executive that it was impossible to judge whether the sincerity in his eyes and voice was genuine or phony.

As did the others, Gregory Walcott reached for Melanie's hand after he had paid homage to her boss. He was a tall man of about fifty whose brawn was beginning to run to fat. A rather weak mouth detracted from any impression of strength his wide, angular face and jaw might have evoked. He held her hand and gazed into her eyes much longer than propriety called for.

"I hope we'll be able to discuss some of these matters, just the two of us," he said, his voice low and sexy.

Male chauvinist jerk, Melanie thought, but she smiled sweetly and said, "I'll be happy to answer any questions you may have. Just phone my office. If I'm not there, my assistant will help you."

"I'm sure she can't possibly be as well"—his eyes traveled over her bosom—"supplied with data as you are. I'd much rather deal directly with you."

"He's exceptionally well informed and capable; otherwise, I wouldn't keep him on my staff." Still smiling, she extricated her hand and turned her attention to the next man in line.

Marietta had asked David Belmont to remain, and when the others had finally left, she informed him and Melanie that she had booked a table for the three of them for lunch at Le Perigord.

He raised an eyebrow. "I wish you had told me earlier. I'm scheduled to attend the mayor's luncheon for President Mitterrand."

Marietta threw him a sharp glance. "What did France ever do for you?"

Melanie liked his smile—ironic yet warm.

"Give me a moment to arrange for a stand-in. Or, if you prefer, I can meet you there."

"We'll wait," Marietta said. She watched him leave the room, then turned to Melanie. "He's going to make a strong ally. At any rate, he's the only one of this whole bunch whom I'm willing to trust. I think he has more brains than the rest of them put together."

"He has to," Melanie reminded her. "He puts together the product they sell."

GEORGE BRIGUET, one of Le Perigord's founders and owners, knew all three of them by name, of course, and as was his custom, he gave them a peek at the day's special, veal in a piquant herb sauce, and a brief encomium on its delights before leading the way to the choice table he had reserved for them. Actually, every table at his establishment was choice, as is *de rigueur* in a restaurant frequented by gourmets, diplomats, politicians, celebrities, and the cream of society. They passed two United Nations ambassadors from opposite sides of the Iron Curtain, washing down the day's special with glasses of Volnay-Santenots 1959, and smiling so affably that Melanie looked twice to make sure they were the same men who had last week scathingly denounced the outrageous territorial ambitions of each other's nation. In a banquette nearby, Laura Grinelle, one of the country's most powerful literary agents, was holding court with Jonathan Reynolds, a writer she had elevated from hard-core porn to the top of the best-seller lists. No doubt they were celebrating the million-dollar deal with escalator clauses she had recently negotiated for his latest novel, about a pope who falls in love with a Russian spy. Holding her glass of Perrier as though it were a scepter in her emerald-and-diamond-beringed hand, she seemed to be delivering a dissertation from a lofty peak, and he listened with the rapt attention and respect due such a modern alchemist who could change mere words into pure gold.

Their drinks were quickly served, and Marietta raised her Dubonnet.

"To friends and allies," she said.

"I'm flattered that you number me among them upon such short acquaintance," David said after a sip of his Johnny Walker Black on the rocks. "May I ask why?"

"First, because I think you are the cleverest and most intelligent of all the *Sizzle* executives. And second, a Kendricks takeover would be more devastating to you than to any of them."

He looked amused by her assessment of him and his situation. "You see me as a desperate man?"

Marietta laughed. "Far from it. I'm well aware of your professional standing both before you were appointed editor of *Sizzle* and after. If Kendricks gave you the boot, you'd land on your feet very quickly someplace else."

He sipped his drink, waiting for her to go on. Melanie, as she studied him, noticed the long dark lashes that swept over his brown eyes. His eyes were wary now, waiting, measuring Marietta and her words, just as they'd measured Melanie herself in the conference room. Melanie wondered what they'd look like if they were filled with warmth and laughter. And then she wondered why she was having such frivolous and uncharacteristic thoughts. She, too, turned her attention to Marietta, who continued:

"It's not your future or your career I see you most concerned about—it's the magazine itself. Even if you were making twice your salary someplace else, it would rankle you to see Kendricks take something you had built into a prestigious publication and turn it into one of his shit sheets."

"He might not, you know. Like you, he's a businessman who knows a good thing when he sees it. It's quite possible that he'd adopt a hands-off policy."

"Anything is possible," Melanie pointed out, "but we have Kendricks's record, which helps us forecast probability. Not even his most lucrative publications have gone unchanged. He delights in putting his stamp on them all."

"Exactly," Marietta said. "*Sizzle* would never be the same."

"And why do you think that would bother me more than the others?"

"Because they're strictly businessmen. All they're interested in is profits. The few Kendricks may keep on staff for a while won't care what he does with the magazine as long as they continue to get their salaries, bonuses, and perks. Those he fires won't give a backward glance once they latch on to other positions. You're a different breed—you're a journalist, not a businessman."

"I hate to disillusion you, but any journalist who wants to get to the top and stay there had damn well better have the mind of a businessman. Periodicals aren't peddled in a vacuum. An editor has to create a product that will sell, or he's dead."

"The mind of a businessman, yes—but not the soul."

"I didn't know businessmen had them."

Marietta's teeth flashed in a smile. "I'll pretend I didn't hear that."

"Are you also going to pretend that you won't take an interest in running *Sizzle* if it becomes a part of Wylford Enterprises?"

"Of course not. I take an interest in the running of all my companies. If I didn't, I wouldn't be where I am today. But this is my first venture into publishing, and though I'm fascinated by this new challenge, I know I have a great deal to learn about it. I'm prepared to rely on trusted employees, such as you. You can check my record in every case in which Wylford Enterprises has branched out into a new field."

"I already have."

"Then I haven't underestimated you, and you know that it's imperative to get *Sizzle* into our camp. That's your only insurance that it will remain unchanged and that you will remain at the helm."

"I take it you want me to go on record and let stockholders know via the media that I think a Kendricks takeover would be dangerous and detrimental, and that, no matter how attractive a stock option he offers, I think they should all sell to you." He spread his hands, then picked up his drink. "I can see no problem with that."

"I'm gratified that you feel that way," Marietta said, "but for the time being, I'd prefer that you play your cards a little closer to your chest. You'd be much more helpful to us if you didn't antagonize the Kendricks contingent in public."

"You mean you want me to appear open to their approaches so that I can report back to you."

"Why not? Duplicity is part of a journalist's stock in trade, isn't it? And certainly, what's at stake here is every bit as important as the biggest scoop you ever got by devious means. More so, probably."

"And just what do you have in mind?"

"First, let's order lunch," Marietta said. "And then we'll get down to business." She turned and signaled for their waiter.

Over lunch—scallops from Dieppe for Marietta and baby trouts sautéed in shallots, lemon, and white wine for Melanie and David—they discussed battle plans.

Marietta told David what Philip Bailey had said about getting information on Kendricks that would make him back off, but he hadn't taken David into his confidence or even hinted that he had such information.

"I want you and Melanie to track it down as soon as possible," she said. "Tear his office apart if you have to, but don't let anyone know what you're after. I also want you to get a list of stockholders. Bring it to my place this evening, and the three of us will go over it."

"I don't know if that can be done so quickly."

"You'll find a way." Marietta dismissed any possible problems with a wave of her hand.

When they left the restaurant, Melanie agreed to join David at the *Sizzle* offices after her visit with Louise Bailey. Then she took a taxi home to pick up Philip Bailey's briefcase, which was her entrée to the widow.

As BEFITTED THE MAN who was founder, publisher, and editor-in-chief of *Sizzle*, Philip Bailey had resided with his wife in a duplex on Park Avenue in the Seventies. The door of their apartment was opened by a tall, thin, dour-faced, gray-haired woman wearing a plain navy-blue dress that might or might not have been a uniform.

Melanie identified herself and said she was expected.

"She can't see anyone right now." The woman's authoritative tone made Melanie dismiss the idea that the dress was a uniform.

"Yes, she can. Who is it, Nora?"

The tall woman turned, and Melanie followed her annoyed glance to the far end of the foyer, where a plump woman in a long blue silk robe had just appeared. Though in disarray at the moment, as if she had been tearing at it with her hands, her hair had obviously been expensively coiffed, from its artistic reddish-blond color to its elaborate waves. Her eyes were bright, as though she had been crying.

"I'm Melanie Danielle, Mrs. Bailey," Melanie answered for herself. "We spoke briefly this morning, and you said I might come over this afternoon."

Louise Bailey swayed a little, and put a hand on the wall to steady herself. "Oh, yes. The emissary from the widow Wylford."

"You're supposed to be resting." Nora's voice was stern.

Looking at Louise Bailey's puffy and overly bright eyes, Melanie felt a moment of self-revulsion for intruding at such a private time. She longed to say that she would come again in a week or two, when Louise was feeling more herself. But she knew that postponement of even a day might be detrimental, and she couldn't let Marietta down that way. She assumed a sympathetic expression and remained silent.

"Go back upstairs, Louise," Nora said.

"Stop ordering me around. I'm forty-three years old. I'm not your baby sister anymore." Louise turned to Melanie. "Come this way, Miss Danielle."

Melanie followed Louise along a hall hung with pop art paintings of bottles of Pepsi Cola and packages of Wrigley's chewing gum, of Paul Newman seen through a strip of orange celluloid. Nora brought up the rear, mumbling under her breath, "You'll always be my baby sister."

The decorator of the living room must have been inspired by a visit to the beach. The furnishings were mostly Scandinavian—large, angular sofas and chairs in muted shades of beige and blue nestled in cozy groupings like picnickers on the sand-colored rug. Tables of Lucite slabs on chrome legs added to the watery motif, which was furthered by the pale-blue walls, whose only decoration was a single, huge, chrome-framed painting of three blue equilateral triangles crowding the lower right-hand corner of a tan canvas.

Louise motioned Melanie toward a beige velvet sofa, and then headed for the elaborate bar that was over near a window.

"Will you join me in a martini?" she asked, already sloshing a huge quantity of gin into a pitcher.

"Don't you think you've had enough of those?" Nora asked.

"I think," Louise said with a strained calm, "that I've had enough of your interference. If you're so interested in naps, why don't you take one yourself?"

"I'm not tired," Nora said petulantly.

"Then go run around the block ten times until you are. I want to talk to Miss Danielle alone."

Her cheeks flaming, Nora left the room. Louise watched her retreat, then added more gin to the pitcher.

"Nothing for me, thanks," Melanie said.

Louise shrugged, brought the pitcher and a glass over and sat down on the other end of the sofa. After downing one martini she immediately poured another, and Melanie began to wonder if the brightness in her eyes had been caused by gin rather than by tears.

"So how is the dear widow Wylford?" Louise asked brightly. "She really is a *femme fatale,* isn't she? Men literally drop dead from the sheer joy of screwing her. Or is it that she's such a nymphomaniac she works them to death?"

"I assure you, Mrs. Bailey, that nothing like that took place," Melanie said. "Marietta Wylford and your husband were strictly business associates. They were about to go out to dinner when he took ill. She's really distraught about it, and she has asked me to extend her sincerest condolences to you."

Louise took a swallow of her martini. "The only thing sincere about that bitch is her lust for money and for power and for men."

Melanie shook her head rather sadly. "You could never say that if you knew her as I do. She's a wonderful woman."

"You really believe that garbage, don't you?" Louise leaned closer to inspect her face, and Melanie could smell the day's consumption of alcohol on her breath.

"It's not garbage. Marietta Wylford's not only my boss, she's my best friend. If anyone knows what she's really like, it's me. I've known her since I was a child."

"Well, it's time you stopped seeing her through the eyes of a child. She's a bitch."

If the woman next to her hadn't been drunk and grief-stricken, Melanie would have been angered by her words. But she of all people knew how heartbreaking and confusing it was to lose loved ones. Louise was looking for a scapegoat to hate and blame, and she had latched on to Marietta.

"Marietta is aware that gossips and papers like the *Post* and the *Clarion* and the *News* will read all kinds of unpleasant things into the fact that your husband died in her apartment, but you mustn't let them influence you. She sent me here particularly to assure you that—"

"She's wrong," Louise broke in.

"Wrong? About what?"

"About the *Clarion*. They're not going to print any dirty stories. They assured me of that in person."

"Has Harrison Kendricks been here to see you?" Melanie tried not to sound surprised.

"No, not him. A man who works for him. Clifford Langhton. He's a nice man. A very understanding man." Louise finished her drink and gazed off into space.

"What did he say?" Melanie prodded gently.

"That Harrison Kendricks had sent word to his editors that Philip's death was to be treated with respect out of deference to him and to me. He said Mr. Kendricks was a great admirer of Philip's."

"Surely, you know that your husband didn't return the compliment."

Louise shrugged. "What difference does it make? The main thing is I'm grateful that our dirty laundry won't be spread all over the pages of at least one tabloid."

"The key word there is 'grateful.' That's exactly what Harrison Kendricks wants you to be. He may have sent a nice, understanding man to see you, but Kendricks himself is no gentleman. If he's passing up a chance to increase the *Clarion*'s circulation by not printing the same type of story as the other tabloids, it's because he thinks he can make more profit on you in another way." Melanie studied Louise's puffy face, wondering if the woman had drunk herself beyond the point of comprehension. "Mrs. Bailey, Harrison Kendricks was trying to buy *Sizzle* out from under your husband, and your husband was fighting him every inch of the way. He must have mentioned it to you."

Louise's mouth pulled down in bitterness. "Philip wasn't

in the habit of confiding in me. I know only what I read in the newspapers."

"I'm sure he was only trying to protect you from the tension and unpleasantness he was experiencing, which is all the more reason for you to become aware of it now. He was fighting desperately to keep from being swallowed up by Harrison Kendricks. He'd want you to continue his battle and not allow yourself to be manipulated by such a man."

"Do you think I'm too drunk to know that what you're really saying is that I should allow myself to be manipulated by Marietta Wylford?"

Melanie was beginning to wish she had accepted the offer of a drink. It might have made her feel more comfortable about her mission. She drew a breath and shook her head. "Wylford Enterprises never has to resort to manipulation. Companies are always eager to become part of its family. Your husband wanted very much to join, as you must know if you've been reading the papers. When I arrived, I had no intention of discussing business with you. It came up when you mentioned that Harrison Kendricks had the bad taste to send someone around to see you. Your husband's death has put you in a vulnerable position. I'm only trying to help you see that you shouldn't allow people who don't have your best interests in mind to take advantage of it."

"You know," Louise said, refilling her glass, "if all this wasn't so distasteful, it might almost be funny. Two huge conglomerates are sucking up to me, and neither can be sure how Philip disposed of his various holdings. Even I won't know for sure until his lawyer comes over tonight."

"Philip was an honorable man. He would have seen to it that you were well provided for in his will."

"Not because he was honorable but because he had a guilt complex. No doubt he has divided everything smack down the middle between me and that psychotic son-of-a-bitch son of his. You look surprised. Didn't you know that Philip had a son?"

"Yes, but I thought he was your son too."

"God forbid that that creep should have any of my blood in him. Are you married, Miss Danielle?" As Melanie shook her head, Louise nodded approval of her single state and resumed:

"Take my advice—never settle for being a second wife if it means taking a man away from his present one. Stick with being his mistress—you'll save yourself a lot of heartache." She poured herself another drink. "I wasn't really a homewrecker, you know. Or do all of us homewreckers say that?" She shrugged and took a sip. "It's true. Philip's marriage was all but over when we met. It was when he started *Sizzle*. He'd hocked everything to launch that magazine. She was one of those former society girls—or at least she pretended to be—and pinching pennies stuck in her craw. She bitched and nagged every inch of the way. I'd gone to work for him as his secretary or assistant or whatever you'd call someone who was always there and did whatever had to be done. I think I was one of the few people in town who truly believed he could pull it off with that magazine. I was barely more than a kid then—and, God, he was wonderful. The word 'dynamic' hardly describes the way Philip was back then...."

Her voice trailed off, and a faraway look came into her eyes, giving Melanie a glimpse of what she must have looked like as a young woman filled with hero worship and love. She took a long swallow of her drink, and her eyes clouded over once more.

"We became lovers, but I couldn't stand the sneaking around. I come from a very proper family. You saw Nora." She nodded her head in the direction her sister had taken when she had left the room. "She's only a shadow of what my parents were like. I didn't have to twist Philip's arm. He was crazy about me too. I guess it's hard for a man not to be crazy about a sexy young thing who worships the ground he walks on. His wife didn't give a damn. She gave him a divorce, and we got married. She was glad to be rid of him until *Sizzle* began to take off. Then she changed her mind and tried to get him back. Philip wasn't interested. One night she took an overdose of pills. There was no note, and the doctor was sure it was an accident, but Philip never believed that. He blamed himself, and he tried to make up for it by overindulging his kid and closing me out of his life. Actually, I think he wanted to blame me even more than himself. Maybe he did."

"He must have still loved you," Melanie said gently. "After all, he stayed with you all these years."

"I think he was afraid I'd commit suicide too if he left me.

He didn't want two deaths on his conscience." Her mouth twisted with bitterness again. "He blamed me, all right. He shut me out of his life, out of his bedroom. He never tried to hide his affairs. That was part of his punishment. He knew I had no right to complain. Wasn't I the first one to give him the idea that marriage vows weren't to be taken seriously?"

Melanie was feeling increasingly uncomfortable. She didn't want to hear these revelations, yet didn't know how to cut off Louise without appearing rude and antagonizing her.

"I tried to win him back," Louise went on, running a hand over her wild hair. "I kept my figure, kept up my appearance. Do you think he noticed? Not on your life. All he ever noticed was how much I drank. He said I had a drinking problem. He was right. *He* was my drinking problem." She raised her glass as though in a toast and downed its contents. "Never trust men. There's a bit of Dracula in all of them—except instead of a woman's blood, they drain out her youth, and then toss her aside to wander like a zombie in the Land of the Loveless."

Melanie's heart went out to the pathetic woman before her. "That's no longer the case," she said, thinking of the men who panted after Marietta. "Today men find women of all ages desirable."

"Some men have always found certain women of all ages desirable," Louise said, "but they're the exceptions. Besides, those women have made their own private pacts with the devil for their eternal power over others."

"I think—"

"How old are you?" Louise snapped, peering at Melanie through her bloodshot eyes.

"Twenty-eight."

"No, really—how old are you?"

Melanie smiled. "Twenty-eight."

Louise shook her head in amazement. "I've never known a woman to admit to twenty-eight until she's at least five years past it."

"Not anymore," Melanie said. "That's what I've been trying to tell you. This is 1988. Things have changed."

Louise gave her a long, pitying, almost sober look. "The only thing that has changed," she said, "is that young women like you *think* things have changed. Come back when you've found it necessary to celebrate your twenty-eighth birthday for the fourth or fifth time, and we'll talk about it then."

Melanie smiled and shook her head. "I'd like to see you long before then, because you'll be having problems over the next few weeks that I can help you with."

"Would you be coming for yourself, or for Marietta Wylford?"

"I'd be coming for you."

Louise shook her head. "I really don't think so. And that's too bad. I rather like you. You seem to have a soul in addition to a brain. Why don't you get out from under that bitch's thumb before she destroys you and turns you into a greedy, conniving imitation of herself? Start your own business—or buy one, like everybody else seems to be doing these days." Her eyes lit up with a better idea. "Why don't you buy *Sizzle*? If you made it a three-way fight, you could win. I sure as hell would prefer to sell you any stock Philip may have left me—if I decided to sell it to anybody."

Melanie's heart caught. It was the perfect answer. All she had to do was say that she thought it was a great idea, get Louise to sign an agreement to sell her all the *Sizzle* shares she inherited as soon as Philip's will had been through probate—and then Melanie, in turn, would sell the shares to Wylford Enterprises. In Melanie's place, Marietta would have jumped at the chance without wasting a blink of an eye or a second thought on the deception. It wouldn't be the first time Melanie had involved herself in hypocrisy to advance the interests of Wylford Enterprises. But in the past, it had been corporate duplicity. Now, looking into Louise Bailey's glazed eyes, she knew she could never bring herself to employ such tactics on the personal level.

"I can't do that," she said.

"You don't have the means?"

Certainly she didn't have at her disposal the vast wealth that Marietta and Kendricks had, but the money Harlan had left her had been wisely invested by Ronald Bennett, her trustee, and had increased considerably by the time she came in to it at twenty-one. She enjoyed the excitement of the stock market, and once the money was her own responsibility, she had been a little more adventurous in her investments than the conservative trustee, and her capital had grown even more. She even owned stock in *Sizzle,* maybe as much as one percent. Though she rarely thought about it, she was a wealthy woman. In addition, she knew the ways of business and had connections with fast-track investment bankers. The idea had never before entered her mind, but she realized at that moment that if she ever wanted to take over a company, she could probably do it.

"Perhaps the more appropriate word in this case is 'won't,'" she said. "I won't be disloyal to my friend."

"Pity. She'd chop *you* up and sell you for dog food if she thought she could make a profit on it." Louise sighed and reached for the martini pitcher, then drew back her hand. "You said on the telephone that you had something of Philip's."

With a nod, Melanie reached over the side of the sofa for the briefcase she had placed there. "He had this with him last evening. You see—it really was a business meeting."

Slowly, Louise stretched out her hands, as though reaching for something fragile. Taking the briefcase, she placed it on her lap and drew a hand over it tenderly. "Thank you for bringing it over." She looked up hesitantly, her eyes filling with tears. "I'm really very tired."

"I understand," Melanie said. She rose and picked up her purse. "I can see myself out."

Louise turned her attention back to the briefcase, continuing to stroke it.

Melanie was almost out of the room when Louise called her name. She turned and saw the other woman gazing at her.

"You can tell Marietta Wylford for me that I intend to go along with her version of Philip's death for my sake, not for hers," Louise said. "She can make a condolence call, come to the funeral—I'll even face the press with her if she'd like."

Melanie's pulse quickened. She hadn't expected such a stroke of luck. And then she saw the resentment that had leaped into Louise's eyes.

"And," she went on, "you can tell that goddamn bitch that I'll never forgive her, because my husband died in her arms and not in mine." She picked up the briefcase, leaned her forehead against its rim, and cradled it to her bosom as though it were a child.

Melanie stood motionless for a moment, unable to fulfill her function with the denial that Marietta would have expected. She had intruded on the woman's grief and privacy long enough. Perhaps another day.... Quietly, she turned and continued to the door.

THE AIR WAS COOL and clear despite the fumes of rush-hour traffic. Melanie considered taking a cab downtown to the *Sizzle* offices, and then decided it might be faster to walk the fifteen short blocks. Besides, work took up so much of her time these days that walking was about the only exercise she was able to get. She missed tennis and swimming. Maybe, after they won *Sizzle,* she would be able to take them up again, even get away for a vacation. But she doubted it. Marietta would soon be off on another project, and then another....

It gave her a creepy feeling to think that she was probably taking the same route Philip Bailey had followed every day. Or had he taxied to work? Once in a while, maybe, but not often. He'd had the athletic build of a man who liked to keep fit. She had heard somewhere that he was an excellent squash player. He had excelled at everything he put his mind to—except marriage. But maybe he hadn't put his mind to that. She thought of the many other marriages she saw in her corporate world. More often than not, it appeared, persons who were proficient in business were lousy in life. But that wasn't a valid observation. After all, business *was* life, wasn't it? At least, it had begun to seem that way to her more and more. And yet, as exciting and stimulating as her work was, she always felt that there was something big missing in her life.

She had thought she'd found that something three years before, when Ted Hastings came into her world. He was tall, muscular, and movie-actor handsome, and had a charm that went straight to her heart. She had joined The Racquets, a posh tennis club on Madison Avenue, and they met when, through a mix-up, he had appeared an hour earlier than his scheduled time on the court, which was assigned to her and a friend. The half year with him had been the most beautiful of her life—all those evenings they'd danced pressed together, the walks hand in hand, the gazes across candlelit tables. Never had she felt so loved, so wanted. Never had she loved so much.

They were only a month away from their wedding when, as in a soap opera, she found out about Lenore. Beautiful, sexy, and ambitious, Lenore was the real love in Ted's life. She worked at The Racquets, and it was she who had arranged the "accident" that brought Melanie and Ted together. Their plan was to have Melanie fall in love with Ted and marry him, then use her influence with Marietta to get him a cushy executive position at one of the subsidiaries in the Wylford Group. Once he was securely entrenched, there would be a divorce. The scheme would have worked too, if Lenore's jealous older sister hadn't gotten drunk one night and come to Melanie's place to spill the beans. Of course, Ted tried to deny it, but even if she hadn't been able to see the truth in his eyes, Melanie would never have been able to ignore the many little things that suddenly fell into place once she knew the truth about him. His denials failing to convince her, he had switched tactics, swearing that though he had started out to deceive her, he had soon fallen hopelessly in love with her but had been blackmailed by the vicious Lenore into continuing his affair with her. The denials had been less of an insult to her intelligence.

She still got a sinking feeling—half anger, half self-recrimination—in the pit of her stomach whenever she thought of Ted. How could she have allowed herself to be taken in that way? But she knew how. Despite her intelligence and excellent education, despite the position of power and prestige she occupied in Marietta's sparkling world at such a young age, she had been lonely and vulnerable. On the rare occasions when she paused to think about it, she admitted to herself that she was still lonely. But she would never again allow herself to be vulnerable.

There had been few men in her life since then. She didn't delude herself that she was the type of woman who stunned men like a bolt of lightning from the sky. She had been endowed with neither a beautiful face nor a breathtaking figure to take the edge off the fact that she was an intelligent woman in a powerful position. The men who followed Ted into her life had, like him, been mainly interested in currying her favor for their own advancement or gain. The difference had been that she had known it, and hadn't allowed them to use her. In fact, it had been the other way around. She had tried to use them to alleviate the loneliness and fill the gap she felt in her life. But she had quickly discovered that, for her, casual sex was a turn-off, not a turn-on. If she had to choose between meaningless relationships or no relationships at all, she would opt for the latter.

She had made her peace with the likelihood that she would never really know love. What she'd had with Ted, after all, had been only an illusion. Maybe love didn't exist anymore. It had once. She had seen it in Harlan's eyes whenever he looked at Marietta. And though she hardly remembered her father, she had seen it in her mother's eyes every time she had spoken of him. But Harlan and her father were products of times gone by. Perhaps the men of her own generation were incapable of such emotions. Maybe the women were too. And so she had filled her life with her work, devoting herself to Wylford Enterprises and to Marietta, who, after all, was her family and best friend rolled up into one. And on those occasions when she awoke in the middle of the night feeling as though she was floating in an endless, throbbing void, she would turn on her lamp, drink a glass of chardonnay, and read a book on corporate law until the wine or the dull words lulled her back to the comfort of sleep once more.

She arrived at *Sizzle* well after five, and a security guard in the lobby insisted upon announcing her to David.

"I thought you'd forgotten," David said when she stepped out of the elevator on the editorial floor.

"I never forget a business appointment."

"And what about personal ones?"

"Only when business appointments get in the way. Any luck with your search?"

"No, but I'm hoping that your fresh eyes will pick up something my tired, jaded ones have missed."

He turned and led the way through the reception area to the offices inside. Only one bank of overhead lights was on, and they cast long shadows as they walked along the floor filled with desks and lined with cubicles for higher-ranking staff. In the eerie silence it was difficult to believe that the area had been bustling with activity only a short time before.

At the end of the room they entered a thickly carpeted alcove with a secretary's desk, a leather sofa with two matching chairs, and a coffee table on which recent issues of *Sizzle* were displayed. On the wall hung blowups of covers featuring the public's favorite celebrities in recent years—Paul Newman, Ronald and Nancy Reagan, Princess Di, E.T., Dustin Hoffman, Craig Campbell, Meryl Streep. Beyond the secretary's desk was a closed door with Philip's name in gilded letters on a plaque.

"Where's your office?" Melanie asked.

David pointed toward the opposite end of the floor. "Upon the expensive advice of a professor at the Harvard School of Business, Philip used the pincer method with the hired hands." His smile was as nice as she remembered it.

"I'd have thought he would have wanted his office on the executive floor."

David took a ring of keys from his pocket and inserted one in the lock. "You forget that he was also editor-in-chief. He very much liked to keep a hand in things here."

"Was that a problem for you?"

"Occasionally—when he'd forgotten to tell me about a story he'd assigned. But for the most part, we worked together extremely well."

He opened the door, flipped on the overheads, and waited for her to precede him inside.

It was a fitting office for the creator of the nation's most popular and widely imitated magazine, and Philip had ruled over it from a thronelike brown leather swivel chair behind an oversized mahogany desk. The huge expanse of floor was covered with a rust-colored carpet much thicker and richer than the one in the secretary's alcove. Matching drapes hung from corner windows that overlooked the East River and midtown Manhattan. The furnishings were in art deco. A long, fully stocked bar stood on the left, and near it, arranged in a comfortable grouping to inspire conviviality, were a large tweed sofa, two armchairs, and a cocktail table. On the right, no doubt reserved for less convivial occasions and certainly for less important people, was a long table to which six tall-backed chairs were drawn up like sentries on guard. Low bookcases were filled with books, magazines, and bound volumes of *Sizzle.* Above them and throughout the room hung photographs of Philip in the company of national and international celebrities whose activities he had chronicled to their mutual profit.

Though she knew there were more important things to do, Melanie could not resist looking at the pictures. She had met Philip Bailey only recently, and there had been nothing to distinguish him from other tall, good-looking men in their fifties who were running to fat. Now, in the earlier photographs, she saw what Louise had meant when she said that the word *dynamic* hardly described Philip. Flanked by John and Robert Kennedy, he looked every bit as charismatic as those two brothers. Shaking hands with Robert Redford, he made the viewer pause a moment to remember which of the two was the movie idol. As the years progressed, his hair thinned and his waist thickened. Creases etched their way into his face and his strong jawline began to dip into jowls. The most recent photo showed him in full evening dress either making a presentation to or receiving one from President Reagan. Both were smiling energetically into the camera. Melanie paused a moment, looking at Philip's beaming face, his eyes so bright and intelligent, so full of life, his body adorned in his tuxedo, and a sudden image of him in Marietta's bed the night before, lying naked and staring blindly, flashed before her. No matter what the trappings we surrounded and protected ourselves with along the way, that was the end which awaited us—we went naked and blind from this life. In spite of herself, she shuddered a little. David's voice came from behind her, softly putting her thoughts into words:

"*Memento mori.*"

She sighed and glanced around the room. "All this—and now nothing."

"Don't feel sorry for him. Most people die without possessing a fraction of what he had." He gave a little shrug. "But then, a great many people wouldn't want it."

"That I find hard to believe."

"Do you?"

He was watching her closely, and as she returned his gaze, she had a sudden vision of her mother as she looked dressed for church on Sunday mornings. No, Shirley would not have coveted Philip's wealth and life-style. She might have liked an easier life for herself, perhaps, and certainly for her daughters, but she had never longed for wealth or power or glamour; in fact, she had always been rather suspect of them. And what about Cynthia? If she had lived and earned her law degree, would she have used it to achieve a fancy layout like this? Melanie doubted it; more likely, Cynthia would have joined a legal services group in a poverty area.

"Well," she said finally, "I guess we all know a few exceptions."

"Obviously we're not among them," David said, his tone suddenly brisk and businesslike, "or we wouldn't be here now. We'd better get to work if we're going to get to your boss's place before the evening is over."

"Where do you suggest we start?"

He shrugged. "I've already covered what ground I could. I talked to his secretary. She remembers no mail marked *Personal,* no mysterious phone calls, no appointments with anyone who was a stranger to her. He had lunch yesterday with Michael Briggs, the president of Briggs, Wombley, and Ritter, the advertising agency. I phoned Briggs and asked him the details of the lunch, saying we were gathering the facts on Philip's last day for a retrospective we'll be running on him. According to Briggs, when the luncheon conversation didn't center around advertising contracts it was strictly small talk. No friends or strangers joined them or even stopped by their table to pass the time of day. Leaving the restaurant, they shared a cab, Briggs dropping Philip off here on his way to his own office. I know he came directly back here, because I ran into him as he was getting out of the cab and we rode up in the elevator together."

"What time was that?"

"About three."

"That means he got whatever it was sometime between then and the time he arrived at Marietta's at six."

"Not necessarily. He could have gotten it in the morning, or the night, or even the day before."

Melanie nodded. "If it was the day before, I think he would have told her earlier. But, of course, that wouldn't have been the case if it had been during the night."

"It's doubtful that he got it after five. His secretary left at five-fifteen, and the security guy in the lobby says he didn't see any outsiders come in between then and five forty-five, when Philip left."

"There's the fifteen minutes between then and the time he arrived at Marietta's."

"Most of which was probably spent in a taxi stuck in traffic."

"Still, a lot can happen in fifteen minutes."

"But he didn't have anything with him," David reminded her. "And it was too late to stop off and hide it in a bank vault."

"So it must be here." Melanie looked around, feeling helpless. "God. I don't know where to start—or even what to look for. It could be anything—a scrap of paper, a photograph, a letter, a tape…"

"Just pray it isn't a microdot. I've already been through his desk, but I'd like you to take a look there too. I may have missed something. I've covered the bookcases on the right wall. I'll hit the ones on the left now."

Melanie walked over to the huge desk and ran her hand along the thick, highly polished wood. "I think I saw Edward Everett Horton sitting behind a desk like this in a rerun of an old Fred Astaire-Ginger Rogers movie."

David laughed. "I'm not surprised. Philip once told me that as a poor kid during the Depression, his only escape from misery was the movies, which cost all of a dime back then. He said he swore that when he grew up he'd have a fancy office like the ones he saw depicted on the screen."

"His was even better. It was real, not make-believe."

Appropriately for an executive's desk, the top was bare except for a gleaming gold-and-crystal quartz clock bearing a Tiffany logo, a handsome gold desk set, and an appointment calendar, which was still turned to the day before. Melanie picked it up and studied the initials and names Philip had jotted down next to the hours.

"Who's 'M.C.'?" Melanie asked, pointing to the first notation, for 10 a.m.

David came over and glanced over her shoulder. "Mike Conway, our advertising director. He'd just gotten back from the Coast and was filling Philip in on the activity out there—strictly business. 'Trautman, eleven-thirty' is the assistant personnel director. She came up to discuss a personality problem that's surfaced in the accounting department. Philip was a real stretcher. He wanted to be sure his authority was felt everywhere in the company and insisted on being consulted on everything."

Melanie moved her finger down past the next notation, jotted beside noon—*Lunch-Christ Cella-Briggs*—to the following entry, written next to three-thirty: *Maxwell.* "Who's that?"

"Gus Maxwell, a photographer. He and Philip go back a long way—they met in the old days at *Look* magazine. Maxwell has been down on his luck in the past few years—he's been sick and drinking too much because of it. Or maybe it's the other way around. Anyway, on and off, Philip would throw him an assignment for old times' sake, and once in a while he'd stumble in with some shots he'd taken on speculation that Philip would buy. That's what it was yesterday: Maxwell had gotten some shots of a reception Mayor Koch threw recently, and Philip bought them. He sent them down to me with the notation that if I couldn't use them, I should just write them off. That's what I intend to do. Poor old Gus is really slipping. I don't know what he'll do now that Philip's gone. He was probably the last of the soft touches. The 'M. Shoper' listed for four-thirty is one of the principals in the personality problem that Beth Trautman had consulted with Philip about in the morning. He's a very bright and competent guy, but he has a touch of paranoia. He wanted to make sure his side of the story had been represented fairly. Philip's secretary says Shoper left about five minutes before she did."

With a sigh, Melanie pushed the calendar back in place. "So much for that. Now down to work."

David walked over to the bookcases and began methodically removing books and riffling through them. An examination of the desk drawers revealed nothing to Melanie beyond the usual contents of an executive's desk—business papers, personalized memo pads, pencils, ballpoint pens, a calculator, Maalox, Alka-Seltzer, aspirin. When she came across a package of condoms, she glanced at the sofa more closely and realized that it opened into a bed. She wondered how many aspiring starlets had paid for a mention in the magazine on it. Having removed their contents, she checked the drawers for secret compartments and for material taped to their undersides—all with no success. There was nothing taped beneath the desk or desk chair, nothing hidden beneath the chair or sofa cushions, nothing secreted between the folds of the sofa bed.

"Philip sometimes spent the night after working late," David said when she opened the bed.

"My innocence doesn't need protecting," Melanie said, getting down on her knees and leaning over to inspect the bottom of the mattress. "I've already spotted the rubbers."

"Oops, I forgot about them."

"Do you have a casting couch in your office too, or do you prefer to take publicity-hungry young women home?"

"I have a couch in my office, but I use it only for sleeping when I've been up all night on a grueling deadline."

"Really." It was an ironic comment, not a question.

"Really." David's voice remained cool. "Philip Bailey was my boss. One of the reasons he held on to the title of editor-in-chief was that he liked what he regarded as the sexual perks of the office. That was his business. Mine is to put together a high-quality magazine. I'd fail miserably if I based my decision on who made good copy by who made good lays." His eyes held hers. "The trouble with you women is that you lump all men together and tar us with the same brush."

She returned his gaze a moment, not sure why she felt so pleased and relieved that she could believe him. "The trouble with you men," she said, mocking his rather smug tone, "is that you set yourselves up as qualified to judge the trouble with us women."

He raised an eyebrow and smiled. "Score one for your side."

She closed the bed and replaced the pillows. "Shall I help you with the books?"

"There's just one shelf left. Why don't you check the bathroom?"

None of the pale-blue bathroom tiles concealed a secret

compartment, nor did anything fall out when she shook the thick, rich monogrammed towels that hung from the racks. Philip had hidden nothing in the stall shower, or beneath the monogrammed lid of the toilet seat, or in the whirlpool footbath. Remembering David's remark about microdots, Melanie opened every bottle and box behind the sliding mirrored doors of the medicine chest, but found they contained only the tranquilizers and prescriptions and over-the-counter remedies for colds and indigestion that their labels identified. There was nothing in the pockets of the brown silk robe on the hook behind the door or beneath the thick navy-blue rug. The toilet paper roll contained only toilet paper, and the only things that fluttered out of the magazines piled on the Lucite table beside the john were those annoying little tip-in subscription cards. Melanie gathered the cards and put them into the wastebasket, but not before turning it upside down to check whether anything had been taped to its bottom.

"Nothing in the bathroom," she said, returning to the office.

David was on a chair, checking the contents of the closet shelves. "Nothing up here, either," he said, climbing down.

Together, they went through the pockets and checked the linings of the clothes hanging in the closet—a Burberry raincoat, several sports jackets and pairs of pants, ties and custom-made shirts from Sulka. There was nothing hidden beneath the inner soles of the Bally shoes or in the folds of the Pierre Cardin umbrellas.

"Shit," David said, tossing back a pair of Totes.

"Does he have a safe in here?" Melanie asked.

David shook his head. "There's one in the comptroller's office, of course, and Philip had access to it. I checked this afternoon, telling the comptroller I was expecting some top-secret material on a forthcoming story and I had a hunch Philip had received it yesterday and put it in the safe. He opened it, but there was nothing there he didn't know about."

All that remained were the pictures. Working together, they removed them from the wall and checked them inside and out.

"Well, that's it," Melanie said as David rehung the last photograph. "We'd better get over to Marietta's. She's not going to be thrilled with our news."

"How does she accept failure?"

"She doesn't."

"I thought as much. Come on. My briefcase is in my office. We'll pick it up on our way out."

At the door, they turned for one last look around the room. David went back to straighten a lamp shade. Aside from that, everything was in its place. They'd done a thorough but tidy job. Not even a master spy would guess the room had been searched.

David closed the door and locked it. "If your boss's deal falls through and we both find ourselves out on the street, we can go into business as private eyes."

"Sounds exciting, but I doubt it will come to that."

Once again, Melanie followed him through the silent offices. The setup at the other end was like Philip's area, but not as posh. The secretaries' desks were identical, but the sofa and chair in the surrounding area were a little smaller and upholstered in velour rather than leather.

David's office was smaller than Philip's, and its furnishings, though expensive and in excellent taste, were far less elegant. There was an executive swivel chair behind a large walnut desk, the top of which was covered with piles of paper—manuscripts, galleys, proofs, photographs—all arranged with a neatness that implied David knew exactly where everything was. Next to the desk stood an ancient Royal typewriter on an elegant walnut stand. Two armchairs faced the desk, and the sofa that didn't convert to a casting couch was over near a bookcase-lined wall. In the area occupied by a bar in Philip's office stood a long walnut table upon which were what appeared to be three huge pads. Each bore a photostat of a *Sizzle* cover, and, David explained when he saw Melanie looking at them, they were dummies of forthcoming issues in different stages of production. Above the table and extending far beyond it on the wall was a huge bulletin board. Tacked to it were color proofs of the current and upcoming covers, memos, proofs of layouts, and a huge chart divided into squares representing every page in the magazine, with careful notations of everything that would appear on those pages.

"This is quite different from Philip's quarters," Melanie said.

"I'm a reactionary. I believe an office should be designed for working."

Melanie laughed. "That sounds more like a revolutionary idea to me."

"Depends on which angle you look at it from," he said, taking a rather battered-looking attaché case out of his closet, "management or labor."

He locked the door to his office behind them, and they waited for the elevator in a comfortable silence.

It was a little after eight when they signed the night watchman's log and left the building. Melanie and David looked up at the few stars that had penetrated the haze of city lights and pollution.

"A pleasant reminder that there is more dazzle in heaven and on earth than may be recorded in the pages of a popular magazine," he observed.

Melanie turned to look at him, surprised, because the same thought had just passed through her own mind.

Their eyes met and held a few seconds until he said: "I don't suppose there's time for a cup of coffee before we meet with your boss."

She shook her head. "I don't suppose there is. Marietta is probably pacing by now. She doesn't like to be kept waiting."

David seemed about to say something else, but then changed his mind and hurried across the curb for an approaching taxicab. They didn't speak on their way to Sutton Place. Melanie sensed a strain to their silence, and felt rather awkward about it.

IMPATIENT FOR THEIR NEWS, and furious when she heard it, Marietta quickly ushered them into the living room where her housekeeper had set up a cold supper from Zabar's before leaving.

Over wine, roast beef, Westphalian ham, and assorted cheeses and salads, Melanie and David filled in Marietta on the details of their unsuccessful search.

"If he received it the day or night before," David said, "he could have placed it in a bank vault on his way to work."

Marietta shook her head vehemently. "I'm positive he received it yesterday. I can't remember his exact words, but he definitely said something that led me to believe that."

"Maybe he sent it to his lawyer," Melanie suggested.

"No, because he insisted that he was the only one who was going to know about it or handle it until he got to Kendricks."

Melanie had another thought. "He could have mailed it to himself. A lot of people do that when they want to keep something out of the hands of others for a while."

The idea appealed to both Marietta and David as a strong possibility.

"I'll watch his mail at the office," David said.

"We'll have to watch it at his home too," Marietta pointed out.

"That's going to prove a little harder." Melanie put down her wineglass and told them about her visit with Louise Bailey. "She's as bitter as hell about Philip's dying here, Mari," she finished. "To save face, she's willing to pretend to the press and the world that the three of you were friends, and that you and Philip were having a strictly business meeting, which is why she didn't attend. In private, though, you're not going to be able to approach her with a ten-foot pole. And that goes for me too, because she considers me just your stooge."

"Damn!" Marietta said. Then she brightened. "But there's David. How well do you know her, David?"

He shrugged. "Not very. We've met at a few company dinners and cocktail parties. She tends to drink too much and get a little teary. I can't say that I blame her. Philip used to bring her and then totally ignore her. I felt sorry for her and let her cry on my shoulder a few times. Once, when Philip actually forgot she was there and left with a strong contender for our next Miss Sizzle contest, I took her home."

"Did you make love to her?" Marietta asked.

"Of course not—not that it's any of your business."

"At the moment I think it is very much my business. And why 'of course not'? I think it would have been the gentlemanly thing to do."

"That," David said, pouring himself more wine, "depends on your definition of a gentleman. Obviously it differs from mine."

Though she could think of no reason why she should be, Melanie was rather pleased by both his answer and his tone of proud indignation. She slipped off her shoes and tucked her legs under her on the sofa. "There's more about Louise, Mari," she said. "Kendricks had managed to insinuate himself before I got there. Clifford Langhton had been to see her earlier."

"That son of a bitch." Marietta's eyes flashed. "Did he get her to sign anything?"

"Kendricks is too smooth an operator for that. What he did was ingratiate himself by letting it be known that the *Clarion* wouldn't sensationalize Philip's death."

"So that's why they featured a fire in Brooklyn on the front page. Did you see the *Post?*" Marietta walked out of the room and returned displaying a copy of the *Post,* its headline blaring: SIZZLE PUBLISHER FIZZLES IN BEAUTY'S BED. "Touching, isn't it? They even managed to dredge up a photo of me as Lady Sabrina for their centerfold feature."

"Kendricks must be eating his heart out over having to pass up the story, if that's any satisfaction to you," David said.

"Talk about cold comfort." Marietta tossed the newspaper on the coffee table, front page down, and turned to Melanie. "What else did Langhton tell Louise Bailey?"

"She didn't say. He seems to have made a good impression on her, though, which isn't surprising. I've met him. He's a handsome, charming guy. Louise strikes me as a woman who'd be supremely vulnerable to him. I think we have a problem."

"I don't." Marietta curled up in an armchair and looked over at David. "We have our own handsome, charming, devastating guy, and he has the advantage of already having her confidence."

"If you're implying what I think you are—" David began.

"I'm implying exactly what you think I am." Marietta leaned forward and gave him a penetrating look. "Cultivate the lady, make yourself indispensable to her. She'll trust you and your judgment because you're not affiliated with Kendricks or with me. Make her see that she should tender her shares to Wylford Enterprises. You've got sixteen days—or should I say nights?—to convince her."

"You seem to think I can outdo Casanova."

"As long as you make *her* think that you can."

"I'm not sure that I like this idea."

"I don't really give a damn whether you like it or not. It's your assignment to see it through—if you want to keep your job. And any time you get squeamish about your chores, just remember that under a Wylford ownership you'll have no editor-in-chief put over you—*Sizzle* will be yours and yours alone. You'll have absolute editorial authority."

Every man has his price, and Melanie realized as she watched David's face that Marietta had just found his. But then, Marietta always found everyone's price. Looking away from them, Melanie poured herself some more wine. She took a large swallow of it, then said to Marietta:

"It's quite possible that you're sending David on a wild-goose chase. Louise told me she didn't know whether Philip had left her his shares in the company. Since the marriage wasn't a good one, it's possible he didn't. He might have left them all to his son by his first marriage. Or he may have divided the shares between the two of them. Or arranged for their immediate sale. She won't know for sure until Philip's lawyer visits her this evening."

"She's his wife—Philip had to leave her most of his estate, didn't he?" Marietta asked.

"According to law, his wife is entitled to two thousand dollars and one-half of the rest of his property—that's what she can claim if he left her less than that. Philip was a wealthy man—there are ways he could have met that provision and still have deprived her of his stocks."

Marietta turned to David. "Do you think he would have done something like that?"

He shrugged. "I guess we'll know soon enough."

"Certainly, you'll know soon enough," Marietta said crisply. "Get to that woman and find out the terms of the will as soon as possible." She leaned forward. "This could be an added complication, but nothing we can't handle. We'll just have to work faster and harder. Did you get the list of stockholders?"

David opened his attaché case and took it out. "I made three copies," he said, handing one to her, one to Melanie, and keeping one for himself.

Conversation stopped as they studied the list. Bailey, of course, had maintained his control of the company by owning the largest block, thirty-five percent. He had gone public with *Sizzle* at a time when it was doing well but when Wall Street was not bullish on periodicals. As a result, Melanie noted, there were only a few institutional investors, most of which had bought large blocks of stock in more recent years. Making a quick mental calculation, Melanie estimated that those insurance companies, trust funds, and so on, currently owned close to twenty-five percent of the shares. The remaining forty percent or so were owned by individual investors, ranging from those with only a few shares to those with an actual percentage of the company, but those numbers never appeared to run more than three or four percent, and most were lower. She herself was listed with one percent, as was David. The other *Sizzle* officers owned about three percent among them. The rest of the names on the list read like a roster of notables in society and the art and entertainment worlds. Melanie suspected that some had bought stock because they thought it was the "in" thing to do, others because they hoped, mistakenly, that owning a small piece of the magazine would assure them good—or protect them from bad—publicity in it, and a few simply because they thought, correctly, that it was a wise investment.

At first her eyes had passed over, but later they came back to rest on, the name of one investor, who, at four percent, owned one of the largest blocks of stock—Craig Campbell. She glanced at Marietta, who, impassively, was still studying her own list. By now she must have noticed Craig's name too, but it appeared to have evoked not even the slightest reaction.

Melanie returned to her list, but instead of traveling farther along, her gaze remained on Craig's name. In her mind, she saw him as he had looked at their first and only meeting, the Thanksgiving Marietta brought him home to dinner, which, incredibly, must have been about seventeen years ago! He had probably been in his mid-twenties then, but remembering the day, she still saw him through the eyes of a worshipful eleven-year-old. He had seemed so tall and handsome to her, so mature, so warm and full of laughter. There had been none of the awkwardness one usually sensed with a stranger; he had fit right into Shirley's little family. He had been so kind to Melanie, too, not ignoring her or patronizing her as friends of Cynthia and Marietta often did, but talking to her as though she were a grown-up whose opinion he respected. He had played three games of checkers with her, winning one and perhaps allowing her to win the other two, but if he had contrived his own defeats, he had done it so artfully that she had been unable to detect it—and she had been a bright and perceptive child. Even now, she could remember the delicious, pungent aroma of the cider he had mulled in her mother's battered old soup pot; she had never tasted anything like it before or since. What she remembered most about that warm, happy, long-ago Thanksgiving, though, was the way Craig had looked at Marietta, the way she had seen him tenderly brush her hair back from her face or telegraph a kiss to her from across the room. If a woman can look back and pinpoint her first conscious, trembling step on the shaky ladder to maturity, Melanie knew that for her it had been upon that day. Until then, she had thought of love and romance as silly and sappy, an absolute waste of a girl's time. But when she saw Craig looking at Marietta, a seed suddenly came to life in her heart and began to flourish in the glow surrounding the two visitors. Someday, when she grew up, she had found herself thinking, she wanted a handsome, tall, wonderful man to look at her in exactly the same way.

She had never again met Craig, though she had seen him in many movies and plays. Regarded as box-office gold, he was never in a play or movie that was not a hit. His success could be attributed to a great extent to his enormous and versatile talent—critics had dubbed him an American Laurence Olivier—and also to the fact that he chose his roles with care; his dark good looks and the sex appeal that seemed to increase with maturity hadn't hurt either. There was never any scandal or gossip about him in the papers, for he led a very private life with his wife and three children and was apparently devoted to them. An excellent businessman, he handled his own investments and had built up a fortune for himself. His name was also linked with many charities and philanthropic organizations. It was impossible for Melanie to believe that Marietta hadn't been following his career too, but over the years his name had never been mentioned between them.

Marietta's voice broke in on her thoughts: "Melanie, you're a million miles away."

"Sorry," Melanie said. "I was figuring out share percentages in my head. You were saying?"

"I was saying," Marietta repeated a little impatiently, "that you and David are the only people on this list we can count on as definitely committed, and together you have only two percent. I'll get a copy of this to our bankers, but I don't intend to leave everything up to them and our lawyers. You can never really depend on people who get paid fat fees, win or lose. I want a personal touch here. We'll divide the list among us. I'll take the institutional investors. Many of them do business with some of our subsidiaries or hope to. I'll exert pressure and twist arms. You two take the rest of the list. Absolutely no one should be overlooked, no matter how few shares he or she owns; we want the options tendered on every share possible. Naturally, time is of the utmost importance. I know you can't get to everyone here and abroad personally in less than three weeks." She turned to Melanie. "You'll send out letters to everyone who owns less than one percent."

Melanie nodded. "That leaves a great many others."

"I want personal contact with all of them," Marietta repeated. "Divide the list between you as you see fit. David, you're in an excellent position to know something about all these people—their weaknesses, their vulnerabilities. Fill Melanie in. I want you both to use every tool at your disposal."

"You seem to have overlooked one very important factor," David said. "My time is extremely limited. I have a magazine to put out."

"You won't if this isn't handled properly," Marietta reminded him crisply. "Delegate your duties, as any other good executive would do. See to it that—"

Interrupted by the intercom, she dashed out of the room to answer it. David's eyes followed her, and then he said to Melanie:

"Is she always such a martinet?"

It was a judgment rather than a question, and a put-down at that. Melanie felt disappointed in him. "No," she said. "she's always such a businesswoman. If she weren't, she wouldn't be where she is today. You wouldn't have made a crack like that about a man, would you?"

He looked surprised, and then, as her meaning penetrated,

he shook his head and said, "Don't try to pin a male-chauvinist label on me—it won't stick. I'd have said the same thing about a man. If I have any prejudices, they're aimed at destructive conglomerates, no matter what the sex of their führers." He sighed. "I guess I've used it as a defense mechanism to disassociate myself even though I've had to play ball with hard-nosed business types throughout my career." He looked down at the list in his hand. "It's time I admitted I'm a part of it too."

"Don't look so glum. Big business makes the world go round. It's exciting to be a part of it."

He smiled wanly. "I hadn't thought about it that way."

"Maybe it's time you did."

From outside the room came the sound of Marietta opening a door and greeting someone. The answering voice was male, deep, and confident. In another moment, she returned with Mark Winston, the handsome and dynamic vice president of Phillips, Stein, and Winston, the public relations firm that had started with a popcorn account and now handled Presidents and the oil industry. Mark was one of the many men in the Marietta menagerie, but Melanie doubted that he was there on a purely social call. She was right; after introducing the two men, Marietta revealed that she had hired Mark's firm for the duration of the takeover battle.

"He's going to make me come out looking like the white knight I am," she said.

"And Kendricks, of course, like the diabolical villain he is," Mark said, going to the bar.

"That shouldn't be very difficult, considering his reputation," David said.

"On the contrary." Mark poured some Drambuie over ice. "His reputation makes it more difficult. People aren't surprised or outraged by anything that's written or said about him. If we revealed that his favorite exercise is kicking old ladies on the street, the public would only sigh and say that the old ladies should have been home knitting. We have to come up with a new approach. We're thinking of hitting the stockholders through their patriotism. A 'don't let a damn foreigner dictate what will be published in America's foremost periodical' theme."

David shook his head. "That sounds a little naive to me. I think most investors would sell their grandmothers to the Russians for the right cash and stock transfer offer."

"Of course they would—unless you know exactly how to condition and manipulate them to do otherwise." Mark lifted his drink in silent salute, then took a satisfying sip. "That's what my job is all about. You have to discover the sensitive nerve—then hit it hard." He turned to Marietta. "I heard this afternoon that Kendricks has hired Norton and Norton to handle his publicity. No sweat. Our boys clobbered them when Global Oil was stalking Sunrise Foods, and we can do it again."

"You'd damn well better," Marietta said.

Mark retrieved his attaché case from a table and, sinking into a chair, opened it on his lap. "I've got a plenitude of knockout ideas here and more on the back burner," he said, shuffling through stacks of paper.

Marietta glanced at her watch. "We can go over that ourselves. Melanie and David have a lot to discuss, and I don't want to hold them up."

Elated to be dismissed at last, Melanie sprang to her feet. It had been a long day, preceded by what had seemed an even longer night, and it was far from over. David closed his attaché case and stood up also. They exchanged good nights with Mark and then followed Marietta out of the room.

"Does Mark know about Philip's mysterious discovery?" Melanie asked softly.

"No, and I don't intend him to. Absolutely no one is to know except the three of us. If Philip mailed it to himself, it should be at his home or on his desk tomorrow. If his lawyer has it, David should be able to find out by then too. A safe-deposit box will take longer, and there's no time to lose if it turns out to be a dead end. We can't spare either of you to go nosing around in Dallas, and even if we could, you wouldn't know how to go about an investigation without calling attention to yourselves. I want you to hire a private detective tomorrow. Get Burt Dutton. From what I've heard, he's discreet and the best. If he's on another case, tell him we'll double his fee to put it on hold." She opened the door. "Divide your list and get started on it tomorrow. I want you to keep in touch with Melanie at all times, David, so that she's always up to date on what's happening on your end, especially with Louise. And, Melanie, I want you to get to Philip's son as soon as possible. If he inherited stock, we want him on our side."

They had said good night and started through the door when she called them back.

"Cross Craig Campbell off your list. I'll take care of him."

"Maybe you should leave him to me," David said. "We're friends. I've known him for years."

Marietta's eyes hardened as they did whenever anyone dared question an order or decision. "I said I'd take care of him. Can you find out for me where he is?"

"No problem. I'll call his agent tomorrow."

Marietta nodded and sent them off. In the hallway, Melanie stood still a moment, looking at the door. So the name had stirred up memories in Marietta too.

"An old fan?" David asked.

"No, an old friend," she replied, and started along the corridor.

"Can I interest you in a quiet restaurant and a cup of coffee? We've got a list to go over."

"My place is nearby. Let's take care of it there. It's not the kind of thing Marietta would want us to be seen doing in public."

"You make it sound like sex," he said with a teasing smile.

Melanie smiled too. "People involved in this kind of transaction often think of it as the next best thing."

By one a.m., David had filled her in on the fancies and foibles of everyone on the list, and they had divided it evenly between them.

Melanie smothered a yawn. "How can you remember so much about so many people?"

"It's my business," David said. "I'm sure you can quote chapter and verse from business law texts."

She stood up and walked over to the coffeemaker, holding up the pot in an offering gesture.

"No, thanks. If I have any more, I'll never get to sleep tonight."

"Do you really think anything will keep you awake after the day you've put in?"

Smiling, he pushed his cup over to her. She filled it and hers and sat down again, saying, "I know he's Marietta's prospect, not ours, but just out of curiosity, what are Craig Campbell's weaknesses?"

"I'm not sure he has any."

"Come on."

"Where have you been all these years? Don't you know he's Hollywood's great enigma? He seems to have no vices, only virtues."

She smiled, wanting to believe it, but then she remembered David's face before, when Marietta told him that a Wylford takeover would mean his full editorial control of *Sizzle.* "Everyone has his price," she said, stirring her coffee.

"Then I'm sure your boss will find Campbell's. What was yours?"

She looked up abruptly. "Was?"

"You're young and bright and sensitive. It seems to me you're not really the type to go in for these machinations." He nodded toward the table and her list with all the personal notations beside each name. "It just follows naturally that if you are involved in it, it's because Marietta Wylford saw your price and named it."

"Well, you're wrong," she said coldly. "I work for Marietta because it's what I want to do and what I like doing. Marietta wouldn't use bribery or blackmail on me. We're good friends."

"How long have you known her?"

"All my life, I think."

"You think?"

She shrugged. "When I look back, it's hard to remember a time when she wasn't there. She came to live with us when she was alone and still in her teens and needed help. And then, years later, when I was alone and in my teens and needed help, she took me to live with her. So you see, I know a side of her most people are unaware of. I admire what she has done with her life, and I appreciate what she has done for mine."

"I see."

"No, I don't think you do. But I really don't care."

He reached across the table and touched her hand. "Don't be angry at me. It's late and I'm tired, and I said something I didn't mean. Or maybe I did mean it. At one point back at Marietta's place, I saw you watching me. I sensed what you were thinking, and I felt I was standing naked and vulnerable before you. I didn't like the feeling. I guess I was trying to see you naked and vulnerable too. It wasn't very gallant, and I apologize."

She smiled, warming to him again. "There's no need. Where have you been the last few years? Women don't expect men to be gallant anymore."

"We do still owe each other common courtesy as human beings—with or without the sexual revolution." He picked up his list, folded it, and slipped it into the inside pocket of his jacket. "I suppose I would have felt less naked if my motive for going along with Marietta's demands had been more admirable—if I'd been willing to do all I'm obviously going to have to do for the sake of a beloved wife and a houseful of adorable and helpless little children. But my beloved wife walked out on me eight years ago and I have no children. I realized back then that the work we do is all we can count on in life and all that makes it worthwhile, or at least bearable. I've pursued that goal too long to turn my back on it now."

"There's no reason why you should."

"No," he said, "I guess there isn't. It's just business. And business, when you get down to it, is just life." He stood up. "I'd better let you get to bed. We both have some very long days and nights ahead of us."

She walked him to the door. "If you look at it positively, it can be a very exciting time."

"I don't know about exciting," he said, smiling down at her, "but I think it may have some pleasant moments. I'll be in touch tomorrow."

Melanie locked the door after him. Too exhausted to clean up, she left their cups on the kitchen table, undressed, and climbed into bed. But the sleep she had expected was a long time in coming.

Chapter Thirteen

THE ORGANIST WAS playing "Jesu, Joy of Man's Desiring" by Bach. Marietta shifted impatiently in her pew and looked around. The church was filled with the well-dressed people who had come to see Philip Bailey off on his final earthly journey. Most, she supposed, had come simply for reasons of propriety; the only thing they truly mourned was having to sacrifice a few precious hours of sleep on a Sunday morning. There were politicians, ranging from a cabinet member through a few senators and congressmen to a sprinkling of state assemblymen and members of the city council. There were stars and superstars from Broadway and Hollywood, best-selling authors, and renowned journalists. Outside the church, TV news crews had set up their equipment, and reporters held quick, poignant interviews with celebrities as they entered. Marietta had arrived in time to see Jenlyn Westcott, TV's preeminent sex goddess for the past two seasons, who had tried unsuccessfully to sue *Sizzle* for libel a few years before, actually shed a tear, which she wiped away with a French lace hankie while she told a reporter from ABC that Philip Bailey had been "an inspiring friend to everyone in show business, superstars and bit players alike." Since all cameras were focused on Jenlyn's chest, in eager anticipation of a benevolent wind that would blow open her mink, Marietta had hoped to slip into the church unnoticed, but a sharp-eyed newswoman from Channel Five spotted her and quickly zeroed in with her crew.

"And here is the beautiful Marietta Wylford in whose arms Philip Bailey died," the reporter said into her microphone.

As the reporter had expected, Marietta was unwilling to let

such a comment go uncorrected. She looked into the camera, her lovely face filled with concern and regret, her eyes with sincerity, and said, "How I wish that were true—that I'd been able to give some comfort to Philip in his last moments—but that's not the way it happened. When he arrived to escort me to a business dinner, he took ill, and I suggested that he lie down for a while. Later, when I went to check on him—Well, we all know what I found." She sighed sadly. "I've lost a good friend, and the world has lost a great journalist."

She headed once again for the church, but the reporter pursued, asking, "Are you still interested in buying *Sizzle?*"

"More than ever," Marietta told her. "It was Philip's last wish that I and no one else should carry it forward, and I think last wishes should be respected, don't you?" She turned and swept regally inside.

She had handled that very well, she thought. Just as she had handled her first public meeting with Louise, which had immediately followed. Of course, Louise had collaborated. The two women had greeted each other as true old friends, with a kiss and an emotional embrace. They'd even managed to shed a few tears in each other's arms. Marietta had been pleased to notice a reporter from the *Daily News* witnessing the tender encounter. Louise had smelled like the distillery she and Harlan had once visited in Scotland, and she made a mental note to ask Mark Winston for the name of the PR genius who created the myth that vodka had no odor.

Louise had been even less sober on Friday, when Marietta made her official call at the Bailey residence. There had been several others in the room then, and their presence had been a restraining influence. The conversation had been almost uncomfortably cordial, the liquor, perhaps, inspiring Louise to play her role to the hilt. She kept slipping her arm around Marietta and telling everyone what a dear friend she was to both Baileys. Marietta would pat her hand and smile, answering in kind, all the time fearing that the liquor might suddenly reverse its effect and send Louise into a rage. When the proper amount of time had elapsed, Marietta got up to take her leave, feeling an immense relief that nothing untoward had happened. Louise rose from the armchair where she had been languishing in her grief and took Marietta in her arms. "Dear, dear Marietta," she said for all the company to hear. Then, her lips close to Marietta's ear, she whispered, "You goddamn whore. I hate your stinking guts." They withdrew from each other's arms, eyes filled with sadness, and, gently, Marietta brushed a loose strand of hair back from Louise's forehead. "Do take care of yourself, dear," she said as Louise gave her a teary widow's smile.

She wasn't looking forward to going back to Louise's place after the funeral, but it had to be done. There would be more people then. Maybe she could lose herself in the crowd.

Melanie slipped into the pew and sat down beside her. "It's all set," she said. "I have a reservation on the seven o'clock flight."

Marietta nodded. Mark Bailey had complicated her plans by refusing to return to New York for his father's funeral. No doubt he was sulking over the terms of Philip's will. David had learned that Philip had left Mark a generous trust fund and ten percent out of his own thirty-five percent share in the company. The remaining twenty-five percent and the rest of his estate he had left to Louise. Philip had further complicated things for Marietta—not to mention for his profligate son—by naming Louise as Mark's trustee: Only the interest on the trust fund and the dividends on the stocks were to be paid directly to his son. Mark could neither sell the stock nor touch a penny of the principal without Louise's consent. Though it would use up precious time, it was imperative that Melanie visit Mark Bailey in Amsterdam and get his signature on a letter of intent stating that he wanted to sell his *Sizzle* shares to Wylford Enterprises. It would then be David's responsibility to convince Louise to approve the transaction, as well as to sell her own stock in the company to Wylford.

"I spoke to Dutton's secretary a little while ago," Melanie continued. "She said he's due in the city early this evening. He'll be at your place by ten."

"I'm not sure I want to hire him now," Marietta said. "I don't like the idea that he wouldn't drop his current case and come immediately when you contacted him."

"You said yourself that he's the best there is. I checked around, and everyone agrees with you. The fact that Dutton has professional ethics and won't drop a case for a more lucrative one says something for him."

"Not a hell of a lot."

"Well, he has obviously solved the case he was working on, or he wouldn't be coming back. That says something for him too."

"We'll see."

"It's your decision. There's not much time to look around for someone else."

A stirring at the back of the church caused Marietta to turn her head and witness the solemn entrance of Harrison Kendricks. Eyes straight ahead, as if in search of the Holy Grail, he made his way down the aisle, closely followed by Clifford Langhton. They slipped into a pew a few rows behind. She wondered if he had seen her.

"How much do you think he sees behind those tinted glasses of his?" she asked Melanie.

"Probably a great deal more than the rest of us."

As the service began, Marietta's mind slipped back to her mother's funeral. There had been no organist, no flowers. She remembered how the funeral director had sneered when she chose the simple pine coffin rather than the gleamingly polished, brass-handled, satin-lined one he had tried to con her into buying by playing on her sorrow and appealing to her devotion and sense of responsibility. She had wanted to tell him that Jesus Himself had been laid to rest in less, but, of course, she had been only a kid then and too grief-stricken and frightened to speak up. Later, she had wanted to tell the minister that he could have done better by her mother too. With bowed head and suppressed rage, she had listened to him rush through the service, eager to get on to what he considered more important activities. The closest he came to a eulogy was when he referred to her mother as a "good, hardworking woman." It was such a brief and inadequate dismissal of a woman who had unquestioningly and selflessly devoted her wretched, poverty-ridden life to her family and to God, staunchly refusing to admit that she had been disappointed by both.

Now, in a vast church filled with the fragrance of elaborate wreaths and reverberating with the golden tones of a magnificent organ, she heard a man who had devoted his self-seeking life to the pursuit of money and power and sexual gratification being eloquently eulogized by his minister, a congressman, and David Belmont. Of the three, David's eulogy was the least offensive, for he did not, like his predecessors, attempt to depict Philip as a saint and valiant champion of the American way of life. Instead, he spoke about Philip's career and contributions to journalism, and he lightened his talk with amusing anecdotes that revealed the warm and touchingly human side of the departed. Having known Philip Bailey rather well, Marietta was sure that David had made up every one of the stories.

The widow had requested that the graveside ceremony be private, which greatly pleased Marietta; funeral services tended to invigorate her, making her aware of the blessing of her own life and its exciting challenges; cemeteries, on the other hand, depressed her, every tombstone being an aching reminder of her mortality.

Outside the church, as the cortege lined up, she observed with satisfaction that Louise had asked David to join her in the lead limousine, where he was holding her hand and comforting her.

As the cortege slowly began to wend its way down Park Avenue, it was followed by another procession—that of long, sleek, gleamingly polished, chauffeur-driven Cadillacs, Rolls-Royces, Bentleys, and Lincoln Continentals pulling up to the curb to collect their owners.

"I'll drop you at your place," Marietta said to Melanie as her cream-colored Rolls pulled up. Harlan had disdained the use of a chauffeur, and during his lifetime, they had both driven their own cars, he always a Cadillac, she a Porsche or Jaguar or whatever took her fancy. After his death, Marietta had sold his Cadillac and, indulging one of her childhood fantasies, ordered a Rolls with pale-blue leather upholstery, a mobile phone, and a bar. For those times when she longed to feel the wind in her hair and get away from it all by herself—or with a choice lover—she kept a bright-red Alfa-Romeo Spider in the garage.

With a fine sense of the occasion, Fred, her chauffeur, looked properly solemn as he opened the door for her. Tall and heavy, he was the nephew of Bernice, her housekeeper-cook, and when

Bernice had confided one day that his parole would be assured and expedited considerably if he had a job awaiting him, Marietta had offered to engage him as her chauffeur. As with most of her generosity, the offer was not entirely altruistic. She was aware that, indebted to her for his freedom, he would work hard and be loyal. The fact that he was serving time for having been at the wheel of a getaway car was also a positive factor in her eyes, for it indicated that he was a skillful driver, though less skillful in disposing of loot from his bank robbery. With his physical bulk and his prison record, she was sure, too, that he would be an excellent body-guard if the need ever arose. He had proved a great asset over the years.

Once they were settled in the car and on their way, Marietta poured a little Harvey's cream sherry for herself and Melanie.

"You look like you can use this," Marietta said. "Why so glum? Philip Bailey meant nothing to you or to most of those people back there. You should have emerged from the church feeling as renewed and happy to be alive as they did. Funerals are a barbaric ritual for the living rather than for the dead. They're an effort to cover up the fact that nine-tenths of the people who attend are sitting there and really thinking: 'Ha, ha! He got zapped, and I didn't.'"

Melanie took the sherry. "I was watching William Justin being helped into his car by his chauffeur. God! That man must weigh a ton. Suddenly I had a mental image of him sitting on a camel and trying to get through a needle's eye, and it depressed me."

Marietta laughed so hard that she had to put down her drink. "That's quite an image. I should have thought it would have given you a fit of giggles. You don't believe that camel-and-needle's-eye business, do you? I'm convinced that a smart ancient prototype of a Howard Hughes slipped it into the Bible to discourage the poor from stealing from him. There's no such thing as heaven and hell. They're the imaginary product of a very lucrative big business called religion. Don't tell me you think that God exists?"

"I can't be sure that He doesn't."

"I can. All I have to do is look at the front page of a news-paper or drive down a street in our old neighborhood." She studied Melanie's face a moment. "This is an extremely peculiar conversation to be having with a pragmatic person with a law degree from Harvard. What's gotten into you?"

Melanie turned her head to the window. "It's either spring fever or the fact that I was up most of the night planning this trip and making sure that everything will run smoothly here while I'm away. I guess I'm a little punchy."

"You must be to have come up with that vision of a three-hundred-pound banker sitting on a camel. Did it have one hump or two?"

"Two, but it's highly possible that it was one before Justin got on his back."

Marietta burst out laughing again, and Melanie joined in, her dark mood obviously gone.

After dropping off Melanie, Marietta had Fred drive her home. There, she ate a salad, relaxed in a bath, changed into a chic but sedate navy-blue Givenchy dress, and then departed upon what she hoped would be her final call on Louise Bailey.

Her first sight in the crowded living room was of Louise and Harrison Kendricks off in a corner having a cozy tête-à-tête. Though a suitable obscenity crossed her mind, there was no trace of it on her face or in her eyes as she crossed the room to pay her respects to the widow. Kendricks wore the dark gray suit he had worn in church. Exquisitely cut by his Savile Row tailor, it somehow made him look churchly and infinitely compassionate.

"Marietta dear," Louise said. "I knew you'd come. Wasn't the funeral beautiful? Philip would have loved it."

The idea of anyone loving his own funeral always seemed outrageously ludicrous to Marietta, but she solemnly agreed, taking the hand Louise held out to her and bending to kiss the tilted cheek.

Louise kept hold of her left hand. "I suppose you've met Harrison Kendricks."

"No," Marietta said, "I haven't."

"Had the pleasure," Kendricks added, as though she hadn't completed her admission of social negligence or deprivation. Though he might not have done it under other circumstances, he was standing. "How do you do, Mrs. Wylford?"

"Very well, thank you," she said coolly. She did not extend her hand, and simply nodded toward him, a movement he reciprocated before resuming his seat.

She waited until he was completely settled, then said sweetly, "Do sit down."

Unperturbed, he responded with another nod.

"Have you heard?" Louise bubbled. "It will soon be *Sir* Harrison. The Queen is going to make Mr. Kendricks a knight."

This was news to Marietta, but before she could say anything, Kendricks twisted his lips into something like a modest smile and said, "Now, wherever did you hear that, Mrs. Bailey?"

Louise smiled coquettishly and patted his arm. If she'd had a feather fan, she would have tapped him with it, Marietta thought. "A little bird told me. A very reliable little bird."

"A cuckoo bird, I assure you," Kendricks said. But his face, Marietta noted, said just the opposite. No doubt his name had been mentioned in connection with honors and he was expecting a knighthood to come through. No doubt, too, that he had ordered Clifford Langhton to slip the news to Louise, aware that, like most Americans, who profess devotion to the national ideal of a classless society, she would be impressed to the point of gullibility concerning her stocks.

"We'll see," Louise said with a giggle.

"I'm very thirsty," Marietta said, hoping Kendricks would take the hint and get up to bring her a drink. She could then usurp his seat and his access to Louise's ear. The eyes behind his tinted glasses were brown, she noted as they locked with hers. With a smile that exposed his white, square teeth he said helpfully, "There's a bounteous refreshment table across the room."

"Really? How very kind of you to point it out." She turned to Louise. "Will you excuse me, dear?"

"Of course, dear."

"By all means," Kendricks added.

Seething, she walked across the room. How long had Kendricks been insinuating himself with Louise this afternoon? They made quite a cozy twosome, didn't they? Where the hell was David? He should have been in that chair, holding Louise's trembling little hand. Damn!

She finally spotted David off in a corner, sipping a drink.

"I'll take one of whatever that is," she said before he even had a chance to greet her. He nodded and went over to the bar. When he returned, she discovered she had ordered a scotch and soda, which she hated, but she drank it anyway. She was so angry that she almost enjoyed the unpleasant taste.

"What's he doing here?" she asked, glaring in Kendricks's direction.

"The same thing you are, I imagine."

"If you were sitting next to her, he wouldn't have been able to claim that chair."

"Come on. He'd have found a way. I've been sticking to her like glue. I went to the john, and when I returned, he was there."

"Well, find a way to get rid of him."

"I'm fresh out of bombs. Relax. Her spending a few minutes with him isn't going to hurt our side."

"Don't be so sure." She watched Louise smiling up at Kendricks. "Women find a man like him very exciting."

"Do you include yourself in that generalization?"

"Of course not," she said. But her eyes went to Kendricks. To his broad shoulders, to the taut, strong muscles beneath his custom-made suit, to his tanned face, strong jawline, straight dark hair with just a sprinkling of gray. And to those dangerous eyes behind those mysterious tinted lenses. If he wasn't exciting, he was certainly very much a challenge. "What do you know of a rumor that he's up for knighthood?"

"If there is one, it hasn't crossed the Atlantic yet to my knowledge."

"As of today, it has. He admits to the rumor and seems damned pleased about it. The Queen must really be scraping the bottom of the garbage barrel."

"Maybe she's just grateful. The taxes he pays must be enough to keep all the royal horses in grade-A oats."

"God! How I wish we knew what Bailey had on him."

"If anyone can find out, it will be Dutton. When I spoke to Melanie early this morning, she said he was coming in tonight. Did she get reservations for today?"

"She's booked on KLM's seven o'clock flight."

"Is she going to stop over in Paris?"

"Why should she do that?"

"I told her that's where Craig Campbell is on location for his next movie, remember? I thought you'd have her see him while she's on the Continent."

"And I told you that I'm taking care of him. I leave for Paris a week from tomorrow." She looked around the room. "I think we'd better mingle and ignore each other from now on. I don't want Louise or Kendricks to decide we're a little too chummy. Get back to her as soon as you can."

"Until I can think of an opening, I'll go butter up her sister. It may come in handy to have her on my side."

She watched him work his way over to Nora, who was standing off to one side of the room, overseeing the gathering with a disapproving eye. Nora's expression softened, though, when David approached. Obviously she had a weak spot for handsome, charming, intellectual young men.

Smiling, Marietta turned and began to mingle too. She knew almost everyone in the room—certainly everyone worth knowing—and the time passed quickly, almost pleasantly, until she was able to take her leave. By then, she was relieved to see, David was once again installed in his rightful chair beside Louise. Kendricks was no longer in the room. She had no idea when he had left. But, of course, he wouldn't have considered it necessary to say good-bye to her.

DINNER AT 21 with Mark Winston added a bright touch to a long, dull day. First they had martinis standing at the crowded bar, where Marietta's shimmering plum-colored matte-satin Oscar de la Renta dress brought admiring glances from the women, and the figure inside it from the men. Though he had begun to bore her in bed, Mark was still an amusing companion as well as a desirable escort, and he kept her entertained with anecdotes inspired by the memorabilia in miniature of famous patrons—baseballs, footballs, trucks, airplanes—suspended from the ceiling above the sixty-foot mahogany bar.

"I see that they admit Rudolf Nureyev without a jacket," Mark said later as they made their way to the spacious upstairs dining room. "If I tried that, Michael and Harry wouldn't let me past the front door."

"Don't be jealous, darling," Marietta advised. "You can easily remedy that. Take a few years of ballet lessons. When you have all the world at your feet, there are things even Michael and Harry will overlook."

Because Marietta was not only well known and powerful but also more decorative than any of the furnishings, they were seated at one of the most visible tables at the top of the stairs. They dined on cold salmon with pressed cucumbers and green sauce, followed by *escalopes de veau Charleroi,* with palm soufflé and the house's famous potato puffs. All this was, of course, beautifully washed down with glasses of Taittinger Comtes de Champagne. When at 21, Marietta would never consider any dessert other than chocolate pots de crème, which they had with their demitasse. As they ate, Mark told her about the publicity campaign he was tuning up.

"First of all, we'll plant ultra-positive stories about you and Wylford Enterprises in all the dailies, mags, and TV business reports," he said. "Naturally, we won't be able to get a line in the *Clarion,* despite the fact that Ron Forster and I were classmates at Princeton."

"Screw the *Clarion.*"

"That, my dear, is what they're trying to do to you. We don't need them, though. We'll have quite enough impact with the other media."

He sketched out some of his ideas, and she was pleased at the abundance of clever stratagems, including the presentation of Lady Sabrina's collection of memorable bathing suits to the Smithsonian.

"You haven't forgotten that I'm paying you to besmirch Kendricks, I hope," she said when he finished.

Blithely he flicked the ash from his cigarette. "I have a special genius assigned to that—Ralph Sonders. He's the guy responsible for getting Craine International Lasers to bow out of that North Sector Oil takeover skirmish last year."

Marietta raised her snifter of Grand Marnier. "Here's to your Mr. Sonders."

Mark had expected, of course, that they would top off the evening at her apartment, and was disappointed when he stopped his Mercedes in front of her building and she pecked his cheek, telling him she was exhausted and he shouldn't bother to look for a parking space.

As she unlocked her door upstairs, she shook her head, thinking of Mark's hangdog expression. When this *Sizzle* business was over, she was going to have to ease him out of her life. He was a delightful escort and she would miss his quick wit and easy conversation, but she had no patience with bedroom bores. How predictable he had turned out to be in bed! Adept at public relations, he was sadly deficient in sexual relations—four strokes, three pats, seven kisses (sloppy, wet ones at that), and then—bang!—the big thrust. No wonder his wife had walked out on him. She was sorry she had let him stay Thursday night, and was still feeling frustrated and unfulfilled from that brief encounter. What she needed was a glorious roll in the hay with Victor Bronson, currently her best lover, but he was away on one of his periodic trips to Paris, perhaps adding to his expertise. She sighed. She had been through intervals like this before. Upon second thought, what she needed even more than Victor was the excitement of someone new.

She was hanging up her white and ivory dyed mink when William announced over the intercom that a Mr. Burt Dutton was downstairs.

"Send him up, William," she said.

She had heard of Burt Dutton, but she had never met him or seen a picture of him, so she didn't know what to expect when she opened the door. Certainly it wasn't the huge man, bursting with vitality, who seemed to fill the entranceway. Well over six feet tall, he had the broad shoulders and the dark, rugged good looks that women pray for in a lover. His thick, dark brown hair was cut stylishly long, falling almost to the collar of his tan Harris tweed jacket. He wore a brown turtleneck, brown slacks, and brown loafers. He couldn't have been more than in his early thirties.

Marietta wasn't aware that she had been staring until he said:

"If you were expecting Humphrey Bogart, I'm sorry to disappoint you."

The hint of irony in his deep, rich voice was reflected in his eyes, and it told Marietta that he was damn well sure that she wasn't in the least disappointed.

"Sorry," she said. "I'm just tired. It's been a long day. Come in, please."

She had intended to give him his instructions in the study, but immediately changed her mind and led the way to the living room. Maybe it was because she had been thinking about sex just before his arrival, but the air seemed to vibrate with his maleness as he followed her, and she felt responding vibrations within herself. She was aware, too, of his eyes on the expanse of smooth, glowing neck and shoulders revealed by the low-cut back of her dress, and she smiled to herself.

At the entrance to the living room she paused and indicated the bar inside. "Why don't you fix yourself a drink and relax for a moment? I just got home, and I've been longing to get into something more comfortable all evening. You can pour me a brandy while you're at it."

In her bedroom she lingered for a moment at her mirror, wondering about his first reaction to her. No doubt he had known what to expect—her pictures were in enough newspapers and magazines. Still, she was sure he had felt the same pleasant surprise and strong attraction.

She opened her closet and walked inside, looking at the long row of robes and negligees. She didn't want to wear anything too blatant, and chose an emerald-green silk robe. She draped it across the bed, then removed her dress and hung it up, took off her black French-lace half slip and strapless bra, peeled off her pantyhose and bikini panties. Naked, she padded to her vanity and applied fresh dabs of Opium on all strategic body areas. She slipped on the robe, tightly fastening its belt around her slender waist. The robe's full length and severe tailoring were intriguingly deceptive, for the soft, shimmering material hugged every curve of her body in a way that contradicted the no-nonsense message of its style. She removed the pins from her hair, which she had been wearing in an upsweep, and let it cascade provocatively over her shoulders. Before leaving the room, she removed the bedspread from the bed, turned back the covers, and switched on the soft pink nightlight.

As she walked into the living room, the cool silk of the robe caressed her breasts, making her nipples firm and erect and, judging by the gleam in Burt Dutton's eyes, eminently visible. He rose from an armchair and extended a snifter.

"More comfortable now?" he asked.

"Much."

She sat down on the sofa, and when he started back to the chair she patted the other cushion. "Sit here. There's no need for us to shout across the room."

Nodding, he retrieved his glass from an occasional table and complied, though he didn't sit as close as she would have liked.

She raised her glass. "To success in your search."

He raised his glass too and took a sip. The liquid in it looked extremely pale.

"What are you drinking?" she asked.

"Ginger ale. I don't drink booze."

She raised an eyebrow. "Don't—or can't?"

"Don't." The word was brusque and emphatic.

"Do you smoke?"

"No. And as for your next question—it's none of your goddamn business."

She gave a breezy laugh. "Ah, but that answers my next question. I was wondering whether you cursed."

He smiled and put down his glass. "Now, about the search we just drank to. It would help if you told me what you want me to look for."

"If I knew that, I wouldn't have to hire you."

At last he looked intrigued, and she told him about her takeover battle with Kendricks and Philip Bailey's unknown evidence, about the unlikelihood of Bailey's having entrusted it to anyone, and about the search already made by Melanie and David.

"For all we know," she ended, "he may have dug a hole and hidden it beneath a tree in Central Park."

Burt nodded a couple of times, as if he foresaw no great problems. "Before I start digging up the trees, I want to go through his office. I don't care how thorough you think your people were, they're not professionals. And I want to do his apartment too."

"The office can be arranged. His apartment is a different story. His wife will never let you in."

"Just manage to get her out of there. Have someone take her shopping for a new hat or a poodle. I'll find a way to get in and she'll never know I've been around."

"All right, but I think it's a waste of time. You won't find anything in either place."

"There's an old rule of thumb in my profession—never overlook the obvious. Later, if nothing turns up here, I'll take off for Dallas and do my thing there. Personally, I can't imagine anything Bailey could dig up that would embarrass a guy with a reputation like Kendricks's."

"Philip had something. I know it."

"You mean he thought he had something. Desperate people sometimes get crazy ideas."

"Far from being desperate, Philip was euphoric when I saw him."

"Any doctor will tell you that a lot of people who are about to die are euphoric. But if there's anything to find, I'll find it—and in plenty of time for you to get Kendricks off your back."

As if already relaxed by his efforts, she curled up on the sofa, careful to ensure that the robe fell away sufficiently to reveal an enticing curve of calf. "You're pretty self-confident, aren't you?"

"I know my capabilities. You seem to be confident that I'm capable on several fronts too."

"Really? What makes you think that?" Her heart beat faster as he subjected her to a slow, long look.

"First, you hired me sight unseen. Second, when sight was seen, you came out dressed like that."

She draped her arm over the back of the sofa and gave him an ingenuous smile. "You might be jumping to conclusions. As I told you, I just wanted to get comfortable."

"And as I told you," he said, drawing so close that she could smell the exciting scent of his after-shave, "in my profession we never overlook the obvious."

Though inside she was trembling with excitement, she remained perfectly still as he reached out and untied her belt.

Slowly, prolonging his anticipation, he parted the sides of the robe until her body was exposed in all its lush delectability.

"What a pair of tits!" he said, reaching for them.

"Must you be so coarse?" she asked, but her voice was caressing, and she wound her arms around his neck.

"They're tits," he said, his voice as seductive as hers, "and you couldn't wait to show them to me." He slipped her arms from around his neck, put one at her side and draped the other over the sofa as she'd had it before. "Don't move. I want to look at you that way while I undress."

She watched him, fascinated as he removed his jacket and his turtleneck and tossed them on the table. His chest was broad and muscular with an intriguing patch of short dark hair. He stepped out of his shoes, pulled off his socks, then straightened to unfasten his fly, never taking his eyes off her. His gaze was like a white-hot caress that left her whole body trembling. "You're a natural redhead, I see," he said. "That's nice. I like that."

She knew he meant it as a compliment, and she glowed in his pleasure. Her eyes went to his jockey briefs, and the considerable bulge inside, and she gasped in delight when he removed them.

For a moment, they remained that way, he standing, she sitting, gazing at each other's nakedness. Then he held out his arms and said softly, as though intoning an endearment, "Bring that gorgeous pair of tits over here, you beautiful little whore."

She rose from the sofa, letting her robe fall to the floor, and went to him. "Let's go into my room. The bed's all ready."

"I'll bet it is," he said. He grabbed her hips and crushed her to him. "Baby, why waste precious moments walking when we can be screwing?" His lips came down on hers in a kiss that left her head spinning. Then they sank to the carpet in a frenzy of kisses and caresses.

Marietta couldn't remember the last time she had been so excited, so aroused. She thought she would burst with passion and drown in fulfillment as they made love four times, each time in a wilder, more exotic position.

Finally, breathless from passion and exhaustion, she nestled her head on his chest and whispered, "Come to bed." She had visions of sleeping in his arms and then awakening to more torrid sessions of lovemaking. She would go to the office late tomorrow. Maybe she wouldn't go at all....

"Sorry, babe." He slipped out from beneath her and began putting on his clothes. "I always sleep in my own bed."

She sighed, brushed off his jacket, and handed it to him. "It's probably just as well. I doubt that we'd get much sleep the other way."

He gave her a slow sexy smile as he stepped into his shoes and shrugged into his jacket. She reached for her robe, but he shook his head. "No, leave it where it is. I want you to walk me to the door the way you are."

She smiled and went to him, slipping her arm around his waist. He slipped his arm around her too, his hand cupping her buttock. They walked that way to the door. There, they paused.

"When will I see you again?" It was the first time in her life that she had ever asked a man that question.

He squeezed her buttock. "Well, now, babe, that's entirely up to you," he said. "You give me a call whenever you want me. I'll come. Unless, of course, I'm in Dallas. Then you may have to wait a day or two."

She smiled and turned to him, putting her arms around his neck. "It'll be worth the wait."

He raised his eyebrows. "You can always get someone to fill in for me while I'm gone."

"But no one could fill in as well."

"That sure as hell is true." He cupped his hands over her breasts. "Don't forget to arrange things about Bailey's office and apartment tomorrow."

"I won't." It was difficult to keep her mind on business while he was gently squeezing her breasts.

His hands still working their magic, he leaned down and kissed her, leaving her head spinning. Then, sending tantalizing little shocks of ecstasy through her, he said softly, "About my bill. You know it's a thousand dollars a day, plus expenses. Five thousand minimum. But after what happened tonight—"

"Oh, no!" She cut him off with a kiss. "Business is business. The deal still stands. I don't expect you to give me any breaks because we've become lovers."

"Babe, you've got me all wrong," he said. "What I was about to tell you is that overtime like that is extra. It's a thousand bucks a screw."

It took a moment for his words to penetrate. And then she felt as if every drop of blood had been drained from her and replaced by ice water. She stepped back and slapped his face as hard as she could. "Get the hell out of here—and forget about the case."

He shook his head. "You're not going to take me off the case. You love that idiotic magazine more than you hate me. Anyhow, I've always had a soft spot for a lady in distress, and I think I'm the only one who can help you."

She flung open the door. "All right. But after this, you deal directly with Melanie Danielle. From now on it's strictly business."

"That's what it's been from the moment I walked in," he said, and added with a smile, "When you were still working your way up the ladder of success, I bet you didn't give away your goodies either."

She slammed the door behind him, then ran into the bathroom and stood for a long time under a hot shower. It didn't make her feel better.

Chapter Fourteen

THOUGH IT WAS unlikely that the Wylford bitch would go anywhere after two in the morning, Nick Wentworth waited across the street from her apartment house for thirty minutes after the departure of Burt Dutton. Then he slipped out of the shadows and walked briskly to the black Dodge he had parked three blocks away. He had access to Harry Kendricks's three cars—the Rolls, The Aston Martin, the Alfa-Romeo—and could drive them any time he wanted. The Dodge was his own, purchased for him by Harry, and preferable for errands that required a low profile.

He drove to the garage where all the Kendricks cars were kept, then walked the few short blocks to the Kendricks townhouse. The streets were dim and deserted, but he felt no sense of danger. What was the worst that could happen? If attacked by a mugger, he could dispose of the armed or unarmed creep in ten seconds flat. It would be as simple and as easy as brushing off a fly or swatting a mosquito, and worthy of no more thought than such actions took. The dangers of New York City's streets were child's play compared to what he had known in the old days with Harry. Those had been good times, exciting times. Guns, explosives, rockets—they had smuggled a complete line of weaponry to such clients as the IRA and PLO. And Africa—God, how he missed Africa! Those dark, steamy jungles where they never knew what was stalking them—animal or human. The thrill of torching a village or blowing up a sleeping battalion. There was no one else in the world who could play one side against the other, who could plan a job and carry it out the way Harry could.

Nick wanted to laugh—or to spit—every time he read about

a terrorist act. Those creeps were rank amateurs, publicity-crazy fanatics who were interested only in their idiotic causes. The only real cause, Harry used to say, was money, and the best way to pile it up was to do your work quickly and secretly. It sure as hell had worked like a charm for them. What was suspected about Harry's past was only a fraction of what he had actually done. The history books all said that Lumumba was captured by Congolese troops. But who had arranged for his capture? Only Nick and Harry knew that. And who had paid for it? That, only Harry knew. And later there was that plane crash. The whole world still thought it was an accident. Nick himself probably would have too, if Harry hadn't brought him along as a lookout while he tampered with the engine. There were probably things even Nick didn't know about. Harry wasn't the type to brag or answer questions—and they weren't together every single day.

There was that time in '63, too, when Harry got laid up with that damn eye business. It was the longest they'd ever been apart. It was also the first time Nick had ever tried to plan a job and carry it out on his own. He sure as hell came to appreciate Harry's brains then. He wound up getting caught and thrown into a stinking Ugandan prison. The only thing that kept him alive was his promise to his corrupt guards that Harry would show up one day with big bribes for them. When the prison grapevine reported that Harry was out of the hospital, and weeks and then months began to pass, it became more and more difficult for Nick to put off the trigger-happy guards. He managed to, though, and just before Christmas Harry showed up, as Nick had known he would—with plenty of money for the guards, and even a substitute body for them to bury.

Harry had changed, though. Well, not exactly changed. He was the same Harry, but his goals were different. He told Nick he had become bored with sweating in the jungle. He wanted to have a go at being legitimate. From then on he wanted to earn his money by stealing it legally, the way businessmen and gentlemen did. Harry thought it would be a lark. Nick wasn't so sure—he thought he would miss the old excitement. But Harry assured him that there would be plenty of exciting things for Nick to do if he stuck with him. Business was just guerrilla war fought in offices instead of jungles, and there would be many skirmishes Harry would need Nick to carry out for him. There was no way Nick could refuse. After all, the one time he had attempted to function without benefit of Harry's brains, he had wound up owing Harry his life.

In a way, Harry had been right—there were some thrills, some risks, some danger. Like the time he'd been sent to sabotage that real estate deal in California, or that union business he'd taken care of in Texas. But meaty jobs like that were few and far between. Mostly it was routine stuff—breaking a few heads, or tailing someone to get the goods on him....

Nick sighed and walked up the steps of the townhouse, reaching for his keys. He wondered if Harry ever missed the old days, or even thought of them. Certainly, Harry never referred to them, and Nick was wise enough not to say anything about a subject Harry hadn't introduced first. Even after all these years, Nick never knew what Harry was really thinking.

The brooding sound of Schumann's *Fantasia in C Major* told Nick that Kendricks was still awake and awaiting his report. He paused for a moment at the huge double doors that stood open, giving access to the drawing room with its authentic Georgian furniture. He always thought the rooms in Harry's homes should be roped off with a velvet cord, like in a museum. The furniture in every one of them was worth hundreds of thousands of dollars—millions, probably, if you added the paintings and the doodads. Nick would have traded it all for the huts with straw-strewn floors that they had shared in the old days. And Harry—as aristocratic as he looked in his velvet lounging jacket and yellow silk shirt had looked better still in old army fatigues and camouflage suits soaked with sweat and sometimes blood.

Quietly, Nick slipped into the room and sat down on a Georgian wing chair. At the gleaming old Bösendorfer, Kendricks continued to play, his head never turning, his fingers never missing a note. But Nick knew that Kendricks was aware of his presence. All those years in Africa, stalking and being stalked, had honed the hearing of both men to the perfection of jungle beasts.

Nick didn't go for classical music, but he knew better than to fidget. He sat with the same immobility as when waiting for an unsuspecting victim to walk into a trap. Kendricks did not stop at the end of the movement, but played the long piece all the way through. Then he reached for the brandy glass atop the piano, stood up, and turned to face Nick.

"What's she up to?" he asked, walking over to the settee and sitting down.

"Dinner at 21 with Mark Winston."

Kendricks looked amused. "Obviously she's hired the swine to depict her in the media as a combination Mother Teresa and Warren Buffett. Did they go to beddy-bye at his place or hers?"

"Neither. She wouldn't even let the guy walk her to the door when he dropped her off."

"Winston must be slipping. I thought he was one of her preferred lovers."

"He may be, but it was no go for him tonight, unless they did it under the table at 21."

"That woman has the hottest pants in town, but I think she'd keep them on in 21. Maybe the poor darling had a headache."

"If she did, the cure arrived about ten-thirty in the shape of Burt Dutton, the private dick."

"In more ways than one. It's a big apartment house. Are you sure he went to see *her?*"

"Of course I'm sure. I managed to be in earshot when the doorman called up to announce him."

"What time did he leave?"

"About two. It couldn't have been all business. They must have been screwing their brains out." A vision of Marietta as she had looked that evening flashed before Nick, and he licked his lips. "God, that bitch is something else."

"She is indeed" Kendricks swirled the brandy in the snifter, then took a sip.

"Do you think she hired Dutton to get something on you?"

"I think she's much too smart for that. She knows that people are so accustomed to suspecting the worst about me that additional dirt would only enhance my reputation. There's nothing he could uncover that could harm me."

Nick's mind raced back to the old days. "But—"

"Nothing." Behind his glasses, Kendricks's eyes were as steely as his voice.

"Then why did she hire him?"

"No doubt to get information on some of the stockholders so that she can blackmail them into selling her their options. She's a shrewd businesswoman. She'd certainly want to explore that angle." He leaned forward, another thought obviously occurring to him. He held his brandy up to the light and studied it, mulling over what was on his mind. "Or maybe," he said at last, "the sweet thing is getting a little nervous about some of the information that must appear in the coroner's report on Bailey. Maybe she wants Dutton to get hold of it and alter it."

"He wouldn't change it. He's got a reputation for being straight."

"Nothing is straight forever. Even parallel lines meet in space, Einstein tells us."

Nick regretted his naive gaff, and tried to remedy it by saying, "Sure, he'd probably take the money, but I don't think he'd take the risk. He'd just tell her everything was taken care of—show her some phony proof."

"Possibly. But we can't take a chance on his perhaps coming through for her. I want you to get a copy of that report, down to every last gory detail. It may come in very handy."

Nick smiled. "It's as good as done. I know who to go to. It will cost us, though."

Kendricks smiled too. He reached into his pocket and tossed Nick a key. "Take it out of petty cash."

"What about the Wylford bitch? Do you want me to keep tailing her?"

"It would be a waste of your talents. So far, she's made all the obvious moves. It's easy enough to predict the rest."

"I take it she doesn't have much imagination."

"Then you take it wrong. It's because I don't underestimate her that I can predict her moves. She's one of the few real challenges I've come across on this pathetic battlefield called Wall Street. She's in my league—we think alike. That's what makes the prospect of defeating her so much more delicious." He drained his glass and stood up. "I breakfast at the Regency at nine."

"The limo will be ready."

As usual, Kendricks did not bother to say good night.

Tired, Nick had been looking forward to drinking a Bud and relaxing with a Ludlum novel until it put him to sleep. But now there was a contact to make, work to be done.

He went through the house, checking that the alarms were active and all the windows and doors were secure. Satisfied, he left by the front door, locking it behind him. On the front steps, he paused for a moment, taking a deep breath. It wasn't the cool night air that invigorated him, though. It was the thought of the job that lay ahead. Whistling softly, he jogged down the steps. It was going to be a real pleasure, getting Harry something he could use to cut that clever bitch down to size.

Chapter Fifteen

Glistening in the early morning sunlight, Amsterdam's forty canals circled the ancient city like golden rings bestowed upon her hundred islands by a lavish, doting lover. Melanie looked out the window of the taxi she had taken at Schiphol Airport and wondered why, on her few trips to Europe, she had ignored Holland and spent all her time in England and on the Mediterranean. Of course, aside from whirlwind business trips to Paris, London, Rome, Athens, and Madrid, she'd had only two European vacations, both cut short by transatlantic appeals from Marietta to rush home and help her resolve a business crisis.

The taxi driver maneuvered expertly over the bridges and through the narrow streets filled with well-dressed bicyclists on their way to work, and finally pulled up before the stately Amstel Hotel on the Professor Tulpplein overlooking the Amstel River. Inside the luxurious lobby dominated by a magnificent central staircase, she crossed the plush red carpet to the desk. As she registered, she suddenly realized how exhausted she was. Though the city was coming alive at the start of a new day, as far as her body was concerned it was the end of an old one, and she had been unable to sleep on the flight over.

When the bellhop had delivered her and her suitcase to her room, she looked around, not sure what tempted her more—the gleaming bath or the luxurious bed. The bed, she decided. She sifted through the contents of her purse and pulled out the slip of paper on which David had written the name and phone number of the hotel where Mark Bailey maintained a suite. She dialed and asked to be connected to him.

The phone was picked up on the second ring by a sleepy woman who shouted a few words in Dutch.

"May I speak to Mr. Bailey, please?" Melanie asked.

The woman switched to English, and said rather suspiciously, "Who is calling?"

"Melanie Danielle. I'm here from America on business."

There was a pause and the sounds of a muffled discussion. Then a male voice came over the wire. "Who the hell is this?"

"Melanie Danielle, Mr. Bailey. I just flew in from New York with a business proposition that I think you'll find very interesting."

"You've got the wrong guy. I'm not interested in business. Pleasure's my game. Anna here will confirm that."

Anna complied with a giggle followed by a lewd moan.

"Pleasure takes money, Mr. Bailey. I came over to tell you how you can make a great deal of it with no effort at all. Interested?"

"Maybe."

"I think you'll have a much more enthusiastic answer when I tell you what I have in mind. I have to get a little sleep. Then I thought perhaps we could meet for lunch in your hotel or mine."

"Where are you staying?"

"The Amstel."

"Too many social climbers. They make me want to puke."

"All right. Your hotel then."

"No. In the first place, I'm not sure I want to have lunch with you. I think we can discuss whatever it is over a drink. Business, even when it means making money, bores the hell out of me. Meet me in the Apollo's Poisson Rouge Bar at two. I'll give you fifteen minutes."

She wanted to slam down the phone, but kept her voice calm and pleasant. "I'll see you then. I'll be wearing a green dress and—"

"Lady, you don't have to tell me how you'll be dressed. I can spot an American businesswoman a mile away. You all look alike," he said, and hung up.

Not bothering to open her suitcase for pajamas, she undressed and slipped into the bed naked. The sheets felt silky and cool on her body. She turned on her side and nestled her face in the huge, fluffy pillow. Closing her eyes, she welcomed drowsiness and sleep, but they were dispelled by the image of David Belmont. He had shown up at five the evening before and had offered to accompany her to the airport, saying he needed a break from widow-watching. She didn't tell him, but she was glad he arrived just then. Five minutes later and he would have missed her. On the drive out to Kennedy in the limousine she had hired, she wondered why he had come, for he sat beside her in brooding silence. Sensing his reluctance to discuss business and having run out of subjects that evoked more than grunt or a nod from him, she had, in the end, remained silent too.

At the airport, after she had checked in with KLM, they went up to the cocktail lounge for a drink. There, as she nursed a gin and tonic and he a Scotch at a table overlooking the waiting area, he gazed down on the bright scene below and seemed to relax finally. People of all races and in all attires—students in dungarees and vivid backpacks, women in everything from saris to slacks, men in hats from turbans to skullcaps—were milling about, chattering in different languages. Some looked happy to be leaving and others sad to be left behind or perhaps it was the other way around. Her attention caught by a child's squeal of excitement, Melanie turned toward the direction of the sound and saw a little boy jumping up and down in front of the huge picture window as he watched a jet nosing into the sky.

"I'm with him," she said. "Modern technology never ceases to amaze me."

She was still watching the child, but though David didn't answer, she was aware that he had switched his gaze from the window to her. She turned. There was something disturbing in his clear brown eyes. She sensed puzzlement there, and wariness. He was observing her as though trying to read her innermost thoughts. It made her uncomfortable, but she refused to look away. She took a sip of her drink, and asked the question that had been nagging her since her doorman had announced his arrival:

"Why did you come?"

He shrugged. "I think everyone who's traveling across the stormy sea should have a friend to see her off, even if she'll be gone only a day or two. If I'm not mistaken, the ancient Greeks made a ritual of it. I knew Marietta sure as hell wouldn't perform such a little civility for you."

"Why don't you like her?"

"What I've been trying to figure out is why you do."

"I wish you'd give her a chance. I've told you—she's a warm, loving person when you get to know her."

"So I've heard. And you've known and idolized her since you were a kid. I think you're still seeing her through the eyes of a kid."

"You're the second person who has said that to me in the last few days."

"Two people in a few days? That may mean it has some validity."

She shook her head. "Not when both of them had been drinking."

He smiled and lifted his drink as though for a toast. "*In vino veritas.*"

"Remind me of that the next time I have a hangover."

"I don't see you as the hangover type."

He was right, but she didn't tell him that. "What type do you see me as?"

"No type. That's what puzzles me."

"Because you like to file away people in neat little compartments? Sorry I don't fit."

He studied her a moment. "What you don't fit is the dirty little game you're involved in with Marietta Wylford."

"When are you going to understand that the 'dirty little game' you refer to is accepted as good, clean business throughout the world? Besides, you're involved in it too—up to your ears."

"That doesn't mean I have to like it. Do you like it?"

"I like my job, and I do what must be done."

"But do you like doing what must be done?"

Her eyes met his. "Not always."

"I've met Mark Bailey. He's a creep. He's in his thirties, but he'll always be a parasitic, pampered, perennial rich kid. He's never worked and never will. From the time he was thrown out of Yale, he has been indulging himself with the best booze, drugs, and girls his father's money can buy. Are you going to sleep with him for his letter of intent?"

There were some things she had never done and didn't think

she would ever do, even for Marietta, but she was too insulted and infuriated by his question to tell David that. "That's none of your business."

"Maybe not. But are you?"

"Why do you care?"

"*Care* is too strong a word. I'm curious, that's all."

"I'm not curious about what's going on between you and his stepmother."

His face hardened. "That's because you think you know what's going on between us."

Yes, she did, and she didn't understand why it bothered her.

He finished his drink and signaled for another. "This is a revolting conversation. Let's change the subject."

"With pleasure. It was your choice, not mine."

He smiled, the warm smile that she liked. "You're right. You choose the subject."

"Tell me something about Amsterdam. Have you ever been there?"

"A few times. It's a beautiful city, built up by the sweat of its inhabitants from little more than a sandbank a thousand years ago into one of the most important trading centers of the fifteenth-century world. Do yourself a favor and take a little time off from wooing that creep to see some of it." He reached into a pocket for his pipe and pouch of tobacco. "Take a canal boat ride, stroll the streets. And be sure to look at the buildings when you do. Before Napoleon, the houses were all identified by gable stones carved with reliefs depicting the occupation of the owner. A lot of them still have the original stones." He laughed. "On one of the business streets, I spotted a bank with a gable stone showing Santa Claus, the city's patron saint, taking care of three little children in a tub. Talk about trying to project a favorable public image!"

Melanie laughed too. "If I see it, I'll stop in and find out if they're giving any money away."

"Don't count on it." He lit his pipe and drew on it. "The Rijksmuseum is a must, of course. And get to the Keukenhof Gardens in Lisse, about an hour outside Amsterdam."

"Slow down," Melanie begged. "I'm going to be there only

about a day and a half, not allowing for jet lag." She enjoyed talking to him when he was relaxed and forthcoming. She wished their conversation could go on even longer, but it was time to board her plane.

He insisted on carrying her small suitcase, and walked her to the preboarding area. Before getting on line she held out her hand and said, "Thanks for the travel tips. Wish me luck on my mission."

Instead, he said, "Have a good trip."

Their eyes held. His grip was warm and firm, and she withdrew her hand slowly, reluctantly.

"Thanks for coming to see me off."

He gave a deprecating shrug and nod.

She was still reluctant to join the line. "Dutton's going to see Marietta tonight. If he finds out what Philip knew about Kendricks, give me a call. I'm staying at the Amstel."

His eyes took on that half-amused, half-knowing look. "I assumed that's where you'd be. Nothing but the best for Wylford women."

"Is there anything wrong with that?" She hated it when he put her on the defensive.

"How can there be anything wrong with having the best?" He nodded toward the lengthening line. "You'd better take your place."

Instead of accompanying her, he remained where he was, and she had the uncomfortable awareness of his eyes upon her as she advanced toward the metal detector. When there were only a few people ahead of her, he suddenly rushed over and touched her arm.

"I just remembered two musts," he said. "Even if you have time for nothing else, don't leave Amsterdam without seeing Anne Frank's house and Our Dear Lord in the Attic. They're more important for people like us to see than all the art treasures in the museums."

"Why 'people like us'?"

"You'll know when you see them."

The middle-aged man behind her prodded impatiently: "Lady, the attendant just called you. You're next."

"Oh. Sorry." Melanie moved up and placed her suitcase and purse on the counter and walked through the metal detector. Turning, she saw David disappear into the crowd. She collected her things and began her long walk out to the plane, feeling an unaccustomed, childlike disappointment that he hadn't stayed to wave good-bye.

Even now, as she snuggled under the covers in a hotel room half a world away, the mere memory of the incident was enough to revive the feeling of being lonely and bereft. Telling herself that jet lag had addled her brain and her emotions, she eventually drifted off to sleep.

Her Cartier travel alarm had been a gift from Marietta, and when it awoke her at eleven-thirty, she felt refreshed and excited at the prospect of seeing some of the city before her meeting with Mark Bailey. She showered, slipped into a pale green Chanel blouse, her russet Irish tweed suit from Rodier's in London, and comfortable brown Ferragamo pumps just made for walking. An hour later, map in hand, she was strolling the stone-paved streets of Amsterdam beneath a Delft-blue sky.

She found the city as charming as David had assured her it would be. The narrow houses on the canals stood side by side like tall, thin soldiers in closed formation, ever vigilant in their determination not to allow the sea an inch more than its allotted space. Many had been built centuries ago by traders and merchants who used them as homes as well as offices and warehouses, and their facades of brick and white stone sparkled like buildings never did back in New York City. With a thrill of discovery she spotted a few with the gable stones David had mentioned. Projecting from the topmost gable on every house was a broad, sturdy beam with a hook attached. Melanie wondered if it had some symbolic significance, then realized it was simply a form of Dutch ingenuity when she saw a sofa being hoisted to the upper floor of a building by means of a rope attached to the contraption.

The city's many carillons were ringing out one o'clock when Melanie was walking along the Prins Hendrikkade. She paused where the Geldersekade met the Oudezijds Kolk before a building shaped rather like an irregularly cut wedge of Edam cheese and topped by a steeple. It was the Schreierstoren, or Weeping

Tower, where, since 1487, women had gathered to bid farewell and a safe and prosperous return to their seafaring men. Among the bronze plaques affixed to the ancient building was one noting that on April 4, 1609, Henry Hudson had sailed past the tower in his ship, the *Half Moon,* en route to what was now Melanie's hometown.

Not far behind the tower, Melanie found the Amstelkring Museum. Inscribed on its facade were the words *Ons' Lieve Heer Op Solder;* it was the Our Dear Lord in the Attic that David had spoken about, which turned out to be one of the sixty-two clandestine Catholic chapels that the city fathers closed their eyes to when Romanism was outlawed in the country in the late sixteenth century. In 1664 the sanctuary had been created in the attics of three adjoining houses, and Melanie mounted the narrow stairs that the devout had climbed surreptitiously for more than two centuries, and then stood in awe before its baroque altar. As she looked at the revolving tabernacle and swinging pulpit that could quickly be concealed at the approach of intruders, she thought of the tenacity with which the faithful of all religions had clung to their beliefs throughout the ages, willing—and all too often forced—to die for the right to worship God in their own way. How ironic it was that they were oppressed and murdered in the name of that same God by others who believed that they alone had the true faith. Shaking her head, Melanie wondered what God made of it all. She would have liked to linger over the display cases in the adjoining rooms, but time was running short, and she hurried down the stairs and out into the street, on her way from the sublime to the lascivious in the person of Mark Bailey.

At the Apollo Hotel, Le Poisson Rouge turned out to be an underwater bar with an elaborate aquarium filled with golden, glittering fish that, if they were not living creatures, might have been created by Amsterdam's great jewelry designers at the house of Bonebakker. It was not crowded at that early hour, and Melanie looked over the well-dressed patrons drinking either alone or with others. Seeing no one who fit her preconceived, and possibly totally wrong, idea of Philip Bailey's erring son, she told the bartender whom she had come to meet. Cordial and helpful, he said that everyone knew that gentleman, and if she would make herself comfortable, he would direct him to her as soon as he arrived. Grateful for his help, she sat down at a table, ordered a gin and tonic, and amused herself by watching the fish. None of the men who arrived were directed to her table, and after twenty minutes she began to suspect that she was being stood up. She assumed the bartender thought so too and was saying as much in Dutch to a beautiful young woman who had just entered, for they were looking in her direction as they spoke. Melanie turned her attention back to the fish, deciding to give Bailey five more minutes before calling his hotel.

"*Neem me niet kwalijk, Mevrouw.* You are waiting for Mark Bailey?" The voice was soft and melodious.

Melanie looked up to see the woman who had been speaking to the bartender. Eyes the color of the Amsterdam sky peered at her from below long, silky blond bangs. Makeup would have been a desecration on her smooth complexion.

"Yes," Melanie said. "Has he been delayed?" The young woman looked blank.

"Is he going to be late?"

Understanding dawned in the woman's eyes. "Ah, late. No. He will not be here. I have come to tell you not to wait."

"Did he send you?"

Her long, straight hair moved in a silken arc as she shook her head, and the thought crossed Melanie's mind that back in New York women paid fortunes to duplicate its color, without success, more often than not. "No. I came because I did not think it was nice to make you wait. Mark sometimes does things that are not nice."

Something in the woman's face told Melanie that she was motivated by more than simple good manners. "It was very good of you to come. Won't you join me for a drink?" She extended her hand. "My name is Melanie Danielle."

"Anna Baaker." She slipped her hand loosely into Melanie's, then sat down and ordered a Pernod.

"I think you answered my call this morning," Melanie said.

Anna nodded. "Mark does not like to be awakened so early."

"Is that why he decided not to come?" Melanie asked with a smile.

"No, no. Not at all. After he spoke to you, he telephoned

to someone in America and told that person what you had said. That person told him not to see you."

"Do you know who that person was?"

Anna shrugged and sipped her Pernod. "I forget his name."

"An old friend, perhaps?"

"No. It was a man who had come to see him Friday. A businessman who had flown in from New York."

Damn! Melanie thought, but she managed to sound only mildly curious as she asked, "Did you see this man?"

"Yes. He came to the hotel. Mark made me stay in the bedroom while they talked."

"Was he tall and blond?"

Anna nodded.

"Was his name Clifford Langhton?"

"It could have been. I am not good at remembering foreign names. Do you know him too?"

"Yes, he's an old friend." Melanie smiled. "I can't imagine why he told Mark not to see me. Maybe it's some kind of a joke."

Anna had a lovely smile. "That is possible. Mark likes jokes." Her smile faded and her look hardened. "But sometimes his jokes are cruel."

"Well, if you can help me see Mark, maybe I can get the last laugh in this joke."

"Last laugh?"

"I mean, I can make the joke be on my friend instead of on me." She gave Anna a between-us-girls smile and felt heartened when Anna returned it. "Did Mark sign any papers for my friend? Do you know if my friend gave him any money?" She was still smiling and casual, but inside she was seething because Kendricks had beaten them to Mark Bailey. Her only hope was that Bailey sounded like a manipulator who would bide his time and play both sides against the middle.

Anna gave a little gesture of despair. "Mark does not talk to me about his business. But I came out of the bedroom as your friend was leaving. He did not look very happy. He was telling Mark to think about what he had said. He gave Mark his card and told him he would contact him again soon."

So Langhton hadn't clinched a deal. Melanie's spirits began

to rise. "Anna, it's very important that I see Mark. Is he still at his hotel?"

"No. He left Amsterdam soon after he talked to your friend."

"Where did he go?"

"I do not know."

"When will he be back?"

"I do not know."

"Really?"

"I cannot be certain."

As the bright blue eyes executed a flutter, Melanie was suddenly aware that Anna wanted her to know she was lying. She understood then: The grubbing s.o.b. had sent his mistress to exact a bribe in exchange for information on his whereabouts. She smiled to herself. He didn't know whom he was dealing with. She would change that bribe into insurance.

"I think you can be certain, Anna. Won't you tell me, please?"

"Mark would be very angry if I did. He might hurt me." She touched her cheek, perhaps indicating the future site of a scar or other disfigurement.

Playing along, Melanie said with infinite compassion, "I promise I won't tell him you told me. And, of course, I'll give you a present to make up for any difficulties it might cause. It would be only fair."

"A present?"

"Yes. We'll go to a shop and buy whatever you like. Or perhaps you'd rather have a check so you can pick out something at your own convenience."

"I think that would be much better. I do not have time to shop right now. There is a fur coat that I saw in De Bijenkorf. It would cost only ten thousand of your American dollars." Bailey had no doubt rehearsed her. Her lines were rather stilted, but she had them letter perfect.

"Well, I certainly don't want it on my conscience that you'll suffer frostbite next winter," Melanie said, withdrawing a company checkbook from her purse.

"My name is spelled B-a-a-k-e-r," Anna said helpfully as Melanie took out her pen. "The banks, you know, always discount foreign checks."

"I'll allow for that," Melanie said, filling in the figure. "Now, where can I find Mark?"

Anna's eyes watched Melanie's hand move across the paper. "He really is away for the day. He will be back tonight, though. He spends every night in the Wilde Eend. It is a bar on Zeedijk, in the *rosse buurt*. It is not really dangerous there. Just be careful not to stray near the Oudezijds Achterburgwal at night and you will be all right."

"Will you be with him?"

She shook her head. "He does not like me to come out with him at night. I am his at-home friend." She shrugged. "For now."

"And for later?"

She shrugged again. "Did you make a mistake?" she asked, because Melanie had ripped out the check and was writing another.

"No." Melanie handed her the first check.

"But it is dated more than ten days from now."

"I think you can understand that. I want to make sure that I meet Mark tonight."

"But why not date it for tomorrow?"

"Because," Melanie said, handing her the other check, which she had made out for five thousand dollars, "I also want to make sure that Mark Bailey agrees to my business offer. If he does, in ten days both checks can be cashed. If he doesn't…" She shrugged. "I'm counting on you to be very persuasive when he returns to his hotel suite. Can you be persuasive, Anna?"

Anna smiled knowingly and looked at the second check—the one Mark Bailey would never know existed. "Very persuasive." She took a deep breath that swelled her bosom.

Melanie passed a pad and her pen across the table. "Please write down the name and address of that bar for me."

She jotted down the information and passed the paper back across the table. "He is usually there by twenty-two hours. The district is just a few blocks from the Oude Kerk. You cannot miss it."

"Thank you," Melanie said, putting the pad into her purse. "You're sure he won't be back in the city before then?"

"It is very doubtful. He went to Haarlem." She stood up, slipping the checks into her large shoulder purse. "It will give you a chance to see some of our beautiful city. *Tot ziens.*" She hurried out of the bar.

With a sigh, Melanie leaned back and finished her drink. Then she signaled for the bill and left too. She had a choice: She could spend the hours until 10 p.m. back in her hotel worrying about whether Mark Bailey would be at the Wilde Eend, or she could spend them enjoying herself. She decided on the latter.

Outside, she experienced an unexpected lightheadedness from her drink, and realized that she had not eaten anything since breakfast on the plane. She stopped at the first sidewalk café she came to and ordered an *uitsmijter,* a Dutch specialty that the waiter assured her was light and delicious. It turned out to be fried eggs and cold beef on buttered bread. She ate it while watching the colorful canal boats glide by, and nothing had ever tasted better.

Her strength renewed, she walked back to the Dam, the hub of the city, where, on the Amstel River in the year 1000, Dutchmen had built the wooden dam that gave Amsterdam its name. There, after a look at the vast and magnificent Royal Palace, the Nieuwe Kerk, which was, indeed, new in 1408 when it was built, and at the monument to Dutch victims of World War II with its twelve simple urns containing soil from the eleven provinces and Indonesia, she boarded a glass-enclosed boat for a tour of the city's waterways. A rather bored tour guide announced the sights in several different languages, and she soon stopped listening and surrendered herself to the enchanting vista of Amsterdam past and present. The floating flower market, its barges almost overflowing with blossoms of every color of the rainbow, took her breath away, and she longed to reach out and pet the occupants of the cat barge.

Pleasantly weary by the end of the tour, she returned to her hotel and decided to take a brief nap before dinner. But she fell into a deep sleep and didn't awake until after eight, which scotched her plans for dinner at the famous Five Flies. As she changed into a tailored but delicate blue silk dress by Donna Karan, she decided to save time and eat at the hotel, not that dining in the Amstel's La Rive could ever be considered a comedown for a girl from Brooklyn. There, in the warm, elegant, librarylike room overlooking the canal, she had one of the most delicious meals of her life. Afterward, she returned to her room and changed back into her suit, a safer, more sensible choice of clothing for a foray into the town's red-light district.

Downstairs, she waited until the doorman had closed the door of her taxi before telling the driver her destination.

He turned around, surprised. "You are sure that is where you want to go?" he asked in English, shaking his head.

"I'm sure," she said.

"But that is—"

"I know exactly what it is and where it is," she told him.

With a shrug, he faced front and started the car.

Amsterdam by day had been fascinating, but by night, she discovered, as the taxi made its way through the narrow streets, it was enchanting. The lights on the bridges transformed the canals into shimmering ribbons of gold, and spotlights turned the houses along the main streets into sparkling and mysterious storybook domains.

As the taxi turned into the Oudezijds Voorburgwal, she saw another side of Amsterdam. In the stately houses that had once belonged to respected burghers, sex shops and sex theaters now blatantly displayed their wares. Prostitutes wearing more makeup than clothes strolled and strutted the streets, or sat, sometimes topless, in huge picture windows, living advertisements for their own special services.

The driver turned to her once more. "You are sure…?"

"I'm sure," she said wearily.

In another moment he pulled up before a narrow building with a hanging sign that depicted a mallard in flight behind the words *Wilde Eend.* She tipped him generously for his solicitude, then strode to the door with the firm, determined step with which she always approached business meetings.

Inside, it took a moment for her eyes to adjust to the thick haze of tobacco and marijuana. The slate floor was littered with butts, and the walls were tiled with what might have been factory rejects from Delft. Above the bar, the large canvas, depicting a duck hunt, was a bit of a disgrace in a city noted for its Dutch masters, but perhaps it had been tossed off by an inebriated artist in exchange for his bill. Some of the men sitting at the bar looked no less respectable than guests in her four-star hotel. The flashy women draping themselves around them were obviously prostitutes. Two rows of booths occupied the back of the small room. A woman's moans emanated from the booth closest to the bar.

As Melanie approached the bartender, all eyes at the bar turned on her, the women's filled with disdain, the men's with lewd evaluation. Both sexes quickly dismissed her as an object of immediate interest, and they returned to their drinks, drugs, and petting.

"Do you speak English?" she asked the man.

"*Ja*," he said, and added with pride, "Some of our best customers are English."

"I was told I could find an American named Mark Bailey here."

"*Ja*," he said, and pointed to the last booth on the right.

"Thank you." She started off in that direction, but stopped when the bartender called after, her, his voice challenging and authoritative:

"You did not yet order your drink."

"Oh. Sorry." She returned to the bar and ordered a *genever.* He filled a tiny glass with Dutch gin and plopped it down in front of her, returning neither her change nor her courteous smile, but she hadn't really expected either.

She picked up the glass and made her way carefully to the back of the room, averting her eyes from the first booth, where the moans now mingled with the high-pitched giggles of another female and the groans of a male.

Mark Bailey was sitting beside a prostitute of amazonian proportions wearing a tight scoop-necked pink jersey over her huge braless breasts. His mouth was engulfing hers and his hand was well under her short black leather skirt. Her legs were spread apart to facilitate his forages. Melanie's approach over the slate floor had not been a particularly quiet one, but if he was aware that she was standing over him, he gave no sign of it.

"Mr. Bailey?" she said, her voice and face showing no sign of her revulsion.

He waited a full thirty seconds before withdrawing his mouth from the woman's. He left his hand where it was. "Yeah?" There was disinterest in his glazed blue eyes as he looked up, but recognition too.

"I'm Melanie Danielle. We have an appointment to talk business."

"Had," he said. "It's been and gone. Didn't you get the message that I'm not interested?"

"On the contrary. I got a very different message. I think you're most interested. Otherwise, you wouldn't have been here when I walked in, would you?"

"I don't know what you're talking about," he said, his eyes shifting away. But he didn't object when she sat down opposite him.

"It might be better if we discussed this alone," she said, nodding toward his companion, who was scowling at her for interrupting a woman at work.

"Don't worry about Wilhelmina," he said, winking. "She speaks only Dutch and the language of love." He leaned over and patted the prostitute's breast.

Melanie watched him with disgust, thinking that David's description of him had been precise and appropriate. Mark Bailey was a creep. He had a suite in a luxurious hotel, yet it was obvious that he made little use of its bathing facilities, for his dishwater-blond hair was stringy and greasy and his fingernails were lined with dirt. His cashmere jacket could be called expensive, but certainly not clean. Dissipation had taken its toll, and he looked much older than his thirty years.

"If you don't mind," Melanie said, "I'd like to get down to business. I have a plane to catch tomorrow."

"Run, run, run. That's the trouble with you business people. You never take time to enjoy the simple pleasures of life." He whispered something into Wilhelmina's ear, and she laughed and snuggled closer.

"It's because people like me run, run, run that people like you can spend their lives in leisure."

"How nice for people like me."

"Yes. And I'm here to make it even nicer. I represent Wylford Enterprises. Before he died, your father agreed to sell us his stock in *Sizzle.* All that remained to be done was the simple signing of the papers. Since he died before that could take place, the stock went to you and to his wife instead of directly to us. But that's a matter that can be remedied. I know that, according to the terms of the will, you can't sell your shares without Louise Bailey's approval, but I'm sure that if you sign a letter of intent to sell those stocks to Wylford, she'll grant that approval."

His face hardened. "Why the hell should she?"

"Because she'd want your father's last wishes to be carried out."

"You're dreaming. She hated his guts as much as she hates mine. She would never do anything either of us wanted."

"I have no idea what kind of relationship you have with your stepmother, but I can tell you that you're wrong about her relationship with your father. She loved him, and she would want to see his wishes for the magazine fulfilled."

"Maybe she does, but I don't. It will give me great pleasure to screw the old man in death the way he screwed me in life, not letting me get my hands on my money. Go peddle your papers someplace else, baby."

"If you send me away, it's yourself you'll be screwing, not your father. Wylford Enterprises is prepared to offer you fifteen dollars a share above the market price if you sign a letter of intent now."

"I've been offered twenty by another source."

"Harrison Kendricks is a shrewd businessman, not a foolish one. I doubt that he offered you more than twelve dollars above the current market value, with a promise to match and top by a dollar or two any offer that Wylford made."

"So then why should I take fifteen if he'll give me seventeen? I'm a smart businessman too."

"If you intend to pass up our offer for a deal like that, I'd say you're a very naive one. Kendricks is the hostile bidder. Wylford has rounded up almost enough shares for a peaceful takeover. Yours, of course, would give us a nice cushion, but we can get by without them. Our offer to you is strictly a courtesy."

"Sure. That's why you came all the way across the Atlantic to make it."

"I'm not denying that we'd like your shares. I'm just pointing out that we can score without them. For the sake of argument, let's say that your stepmother agreed to allow you to tender those shares to Harrison Kendricks, and then we routed him—which we certainly will. He'll no longer have any interest in buying them."

"So then I'll get her to agree to let me sell them to you."

"At that point, I doubt that we'd be interested in purchasing them. Certainly not at the bonus price I'm offering you now. What's your answer, Mr. Bailey?"

"You're not fooling me for one minute. Wylford is panting after my shares. You should be willing to do a hell of a lot more for me."

"Our money offer remains firm. We would, however, be willing to offer you a chance to buy stock in Wylford Enterprises at an attractive rate."

"Don't make me laugh. There are other inducements."

"What did you have in mind?"

He looked her up and down through half-lidded eyes. "What if I said a week in bed with you?"

Her stomach turned, but she managed not to gag. She raised one eyebrow and said coolly, "I'd say you were kidding."

"Why?"

"Because I'm obviously not your type."

"Maybe I like variety."

"I know your type, Mr. Bailey. Not only do you despise women like me, down deep you find us threatening and intimidating. Frankly, I think we both know that you wouldn't be able to get it up with me."

Anger flashed in his eyes. "Don't be so damn sure."

"Do you really want to waste your time trying to prove me wrong?"

"I could throw you down on that seat and screw the hell out of you right this minute, and no one here would raise an eyebrow. But it wouldn't be worth the effort. You're right about one thing and one thing only—titless bitches like you turn me off. I bet you've never outgrown your training bra."

"Mr. Bailey, a woman like me takes it as a compliment when she's told that she can't possibly attract a man like you." She reached into her purse and took out some papers. "Now, if you'll just sign this letter of intent, I'll be able to take my offensive face and figure out of your sight."

"We haven't finished yet. I still haven't told you what else I want." He leaned across the table. "I want a week in bed with Jami Wells."

"Jami Wells? She's a baby! I can't arrange such a thing. I'm not a pimp."

"Get your act together, lady. Dear old dad used to say that the key to his success was procuring the right whore at the right time. Jami's eighteen and the biggest whore in Hollywood. She's been screwing around with everything in pants since she was fourteen. Everyone knows she broke up her last director's marriage—and that guy's sixty if he's a day."

"If you know so much about her sex life, why don't you arrange to get in on the action yourself?"

"I'm too lazy to write letters or try to arrange for introductions. Besides," he added, stroking Wilhelmina, "I'm used to a whore coming to me. But I get hot nuts every time I see one of Jami's movies. Did you see *Young Lovers?* Total frontal nudity. God, what a piece! And those tits—so firm and round just begging to be bitten. You get me a week with her, and I'll sign your piece of paper."

"It's out of the question. Anyhow, I read somewhere that she's rehearsing for her first Broadway play."

"All right then, a weekend. I don't want to screw her career— only her body. We'll just stay in bed for the entire forty-eight hours." His smile showed an abundance of stained teeth. "Do this for me and we're in business. It isn't as if you're taking advantage of a virgin."

"I can't guarantee that she'll agree to come."

"You make it attractive enough for her, and she'll agree."

Melanie sighed, sick of him, sick of herself. "All right." She passed the papers across the table.

"Are you kidding?" He pushed the papers back. "Have Jami bring them when she comes. Don't worry. I'm a man of honor. I'll sign them then."

"Why don't you sign a letter of intent for half the stocks now, and one for the other half when she comes?"

"Because I'm not stupid. And now I suggest that if you embarrass easily, you'd better leave. Because I got such a hard-on just talking about that sexy little bitch that I'm going to have to have Willie here give me one of her special blow jobs." He said something in Dutch to Wilhelmina, who laughed throatily and slipped down to the floor on her knees.

Keeping her face impassive, Melanie snatched up the papers and her purse and strode away with all the dignity she could muster.

"Have her here this weekend," Bailey called after her. "Tell her I've got the biggest pecker this side of the Atlantic. That'll get her." Then he groaned to Wilhelmina, "Oh, baby, baby, *yes!*"

Once outside, Melanie ran across the road to the canal and vomited. Bent over, she let the night breeze cool her hot, damp face. Hearing footsteps, she spun around and saw a man who had been sitting at the bar in the Wilde Eend. As he staggered closer, he smiled and put a hand to his crotch. She began to run, along the street and across the first bridge she came to. On the other side she spotted a cab and hailed it. She had had a surfeit of Amsterdam at night, and didn't look through the window until she reached the Amstel.

Back in her room, she found her bed turned down for the night, and she thought that she had never seen anything that looked more inviting. First, though, she took a shower, trying to wash away the crawly feeling that being with Mark Bailey had evoked.

The next morning she called her assistant in New York and told him to set up a lunch date with Jami Wells.

"It has to be tomorrow," she said. "Be insistent. Make her realize that I'll be offering a once-in-a-lifetime opportunity. Then get every bit of information on her you can dig up, from gossip to reviews, and have it on my desk first thing in the morning, along with a summary and a listing of cogent points."

"Jesus, Melanie! It's one o'clock in the morning. Everything's closed. I know I have a well-deserved reputation for being a whiz, but there's no way on earth that I can do all that by nine."

"Nine tomorrow, Ben, not today. I won't be back in New York until this evening."

"Oh, right. I forgot about the time difference. Don't worry. I'll take care of everything. I'll leave the information with your doorman this evening. You'll be juggling with jet lag and won't want to come to the office before lunch. I'll have Jami at Sardi's at noon Wednesday, with a red ribbon on her million-dollar ass."

"Bless your efficient little heart. See you soon."

She had a leisurely breakfast on the terrace, leafing through a guidebook while she wondered what to see before her plane took off at three. The Rijksmuseum, she decided. After her experience the night before, what better way to spend her last few hours in Amsterdam than in the uplifting company of Rembrandt, Vermeer, and the other Dutch masters?

But later, when her taxi pulled up before the imposing towered building on Stadhouderskade, she made no move to get out. All the way there, she had been trying to ignore David's parting words to her, but she couldn't get them out of her mind.

"Rijksmuseum," the driver said, turning to face her. "Rembrandt, Vermeer, Hals—"

She shook her head that she had changed her mind. "*Prinsengracht twee-zes-drie,*" she said.

He shrugged and drove on, announcing a little later as he stopped, "Anne Frankhuis."

Before entering, she gazed up at the four-story brick building that looked so like its neighbors, and yet, because of what had happened inside it forty years before, was so very different from them. It was a warehouse that had stored not only goods, but also, for just over two years, preserved the lives of eight Jews from the Nazi invaders who had conquered Holland.

Inside, Melanie climbed the steep stairs and walked the long corridor leading to the hinged bookcase that hid the entrance to the small quarters shared by the four Franks, the three Van Daans, and the dentist, Albert Dussel. As a high-spirited child of thirteen, Anne Frank had followed her parents and her older sister, Margot, in the same direction, fleeing the madness of anti-Semitism that was tearing apart her once-secure world. Two years and one month later, as a sensitive and perceptive young woman of fifteen, she was marched back along it by the Gestapo, on a journey to her death in one of Hitler's concentration camps.

Back in her own teens, Melanie had read through tears the diary Anne Frank wrote during those two years of hiding. She thought she had forgotten it, but now the gray cover of her mother's paperback, and the picture of Anne in the upper right corner, came rushing back. Everything she saw triggered another poignant memory: the marks on the wall recording Anne's growth, the map of Normandy depicting the Allies' progress, the little table where Anne had labored over her studies and then recorded all the hopes, fears, and petty quarrels of her housemates along with her private thoughts in her beloved little red-checkered diary.

In Peter Van Daan's tiny room. Melanie stood at the foot of the ladder to the attic, wishing it was open to visitors. She longed to look through the one safe window in the hideout, allowing the inhabitants a breath of fresh air and a sliverlike view of the world outside, a world forbidden them because they were Jews. It was to that window, with its glimpse of sky, that Anne went time and again to bolster her courage and renew her hope, unshaken in her belief that a person cannot be lonely, unhappy, or afraid for long when she is alone for a while with nature, heaven, and God. Standing side by side at that window and sharing its magic, she and the sixteen-year-old Peter had felt the first tender stirrings of love. And then came the August night when, for a reward of a dollar and forty cents a head, an informer led the SS to their hiding place....

With a shiver, Melanie turned away from the ladder and left the room.

Back on the street, she felt no desire to see works of art. She wanted to spend the rest of her day walking through Anne's beloved city, seeing the everyday sights that Anne had longed to be a part of once more, inhaling the cool, fresh air that Anne had yearned to breathe again in freedom.

Longing for another look at the flower market with its profusion of colors and blooms, she headed toward the Singel canal. When she heard the haunting strains of a lively waltz, she hurried in its direction and discovered a huge calliope being pushed by a troupe of burly men. It was a magnificent, whimsical instrument—all curlicues, statues, and flowers. The music that came tumbling forth from its cymbals and pipes and drums called out to the child that lingers so longingly in every grown-up's soul, and Melanie found her eyes misting as she remembered Coney Island and the carousel rides with her mother and Cynthia. When one of the men approached her, she smiled and dropped two *kwartjes* in his cup, then continued on her way, the lovely melody following her on the breeze.

The flower market was ablaze with color, and she felt almost heady from the confirmation of life shouted by each petal. Everywhere she looked she saw flowers—displayed in the stalls and on the barges moored along the cobbled quay, in the arms of pedestrians, in the baskets of bicyclists. She bought an armload of tulips though she knew she probably couldn't take them home, but what she wanted for the moment was the luxury of carrying them, looking at their brilliant colors, and rubbing her cheek against their shiny starched-satin petals. Catching a glimpse in a shop window of a happy young woman with a similar bouquet, she turned for a better look and found no one behind her. She turned back to the window and realized with a little shock of pleased surprise that she was looking at herself. The shop she had stopped before, she saw, was J.D. Berkman, and displayed in its window were old Dutch pipes. An image of David lighting his pipe flashed across her mind, and on impulse, she opened the door and entered. She was greeted by the pungent, tangy smell of tobacco, and by a pleasant clerk who patiently showed her pipe after pipe as she struggled to make a decision.

The bells of the Mint Tower were striking noon as she emerged from Berkman's; her time in Amsterdam was running out. After a quick lunch of *rijsttafel* at an Indonesian café, she taxied back to the Amstel and packed. Before leaving her room for the last time, she placed her flowers on the dressing table, along with a lavish tip for the chambermaid.

It was after eight when she cleared customs in New York. Exhausted from the long flight, she carried her suitcase into the International Arrivals Terminal at Kennedy Airport, telling herself that she longed only for home, a warm bath, and bed. Still, she found her eyes straying half hopefully toward the faces of the people gathered behind the barriers, waiting to greet the new arrivals. Almost enviously, she watched the hugs and kisses and handshakes all around her. Had she really expected David to be there? She was more tired than she thought, she told herself as she stepped into a taxi; otherwise, she could never have regressed to such adolescent fantasy.

At her apartment house, the doorman handed her the thick manila envelope that Ben had dropped off earlier. Upstairs, she dropped the packet on the hall table, kicked off her shoes, and headed for the leisurely bath she had promised herself.

Later, revived a little by the bath and wrapped in her favorite old terrycloth robe, with a comfortable pair of scuffs on her feet, she padded into the kitchen and put the kettle on to boil. Then she dialed Marietta's number. She was rather relieved when there was no answer, for she didn't really feel like talking.

While she brewed a cup of tea, she foraged in the refrigerator for a snack that might tempt her, settling on a bunch of grapes and a wedge of Bonbelle cheese. Though she rarely pampered herself that way, she arranged everything on a lap tray and then carried it into her bedroom. There, she curled up in bed, nibbling the cheese and fruit and sipping her tea while she read the information Ben had gathered on Jami Wells.

Many women who had lived long, full lives would go to their graves without accumulating half the experience eighteen-year-old Jami already had, both figuratively and literally, under her belt. The indulged daughter of a wealthy, ambitious widow, Jami had been groomed for a singing career from the time she could lisp "I'm a Little Teapot" without prompting. Her big break came when, at thirteen, she seductively wiggled her fanny through a TV commercial for Golden End's new line of leather pants for juniors, nibbled at a hot dog extended by a teenage boy in similar attire, and said over her shoulder into the camera, "When a girl wears Golden Ends, she know it's only the beginning..." The commercial ended with a close-up of the two behinds undulating into the sunset. As a result of the public outcry that followed the first showings, the commercial was withdrawn from TV, Golden Ends pants became the hottest-selling item on the market, and Jami Wells was signed to star in *Disco Dreamer,* a critical flop but a roaring box-office success.

Jami's next two films enjoyed the same fate: rotten reviews and rollicking revenues. Like Brooke Shields before her, Jami became one of the most publicized and photographed girls in the country, with her face on the cover of every magazine except the likes of *Popular Mechanics* and the *National Review*. Though her dancing and singing were as amateurish as her acting, no TV special worthy of its network would dream of shooting before it had signed her as one of its headliners. Rarely a day went by without mention of her name by Hollywood commentators and newspaper columnists. Then she began to slip, for the public had been offered fresher teenage idols—the members of the Brat Pack. Jami's fourth film, *Love Rebel,* cleared only a mere million above cost, and *Young Lovers,* despite the total frontal nudity that had appealed to Mark Bailey, barely broke even. When another movie role was not immediately forthcoming, Jami's mother prodded her to announce that she wanted to get away from Hollywood for a while to pursue more serious acting, and they left for New York and a Broadway musical, for which, it was rumored, they were providing more than half the backing. To heighten public interest, everything about the play was being cloaked in great secrecy, but though this tactic evoked at least some of the desired publicity, theater people were predicting that the play wouldn't run past opening night—if it managed to get that far.

In her private life, Jami seemed to be a combination of Lolita and Moll Flanders. Ben listed affairs with two rock stars, four of her leading men (the fifth was gay), three of her directors (two of whom were old enough to be her father, the third, her grandfather), one hairdresser, two married actors, and an intern who had treated her when she was brought to a Los Angeles hospital with a piece of coal dust in her eye. *And those are only the affairs that can be documented!* Ben wrote. *They're just the tip of the iceberg—or should I say volcano? That kid must have the hottest pants in Hollywood.*

In Hollywood? Melanie thought. *What about in the country?* She slipped the material back into the envelope, put her tray on the floor, and switched off the light. She felt repelled by what she had just read, but at least she no longer felt squeamish about asking Jami Wells to spend the weekend with Mark Bailey.

Her telephone rang before her clock-radio switched on the next morning.

"Welcome back," Marietta said. "Did you get him to sign?"

Melanie squeezed her eyes together a few times to focus them and her mind. "Not quite. He's holding out for a weekend with Jami Wells."

"Damn. Do you think the little tramp will come across with her charms?"

"I'm having lunch with her today. I plan to make it well worth her while."

"What guarantee do we have that he'll sign after the weekend?"

"The fact that it won't be worth Jami's while if he doesn't. What's been happening at this end?"

"David's off to San Francisco to see Laura Leslie and a couple of others."

Would he have been at the airport last night if it hadn't been for that? No, of course not. She gave herself a mental shake. "When will he be back?"

"Tomorrow, I hope. I don't like him being away from Louise too long. Kendricks is after her too."

"Naturally. How's our private eye doing?"

There was the briefest of pauses before Marietta's voice came over in its cool, sharp, most businesslike tone. "He found nothing in Philip's office and nothing at the apartment. He left for Dallas last night."

"Too bad he couldn't turn up Philip's evidence. I'm sure he'll be able to uncover what it was based on down there, though."

"He'd better. I just got word that Halpern and Oberon tendered their three percent to Kendricks's bank. Those sons of bitches. I've ordered our subsidiaries to stop doing business with them."

"They can still withdraw before the deadline."

"They had damn well better."

"Let me know what Dutton finds out."

"*You* let me know. He'll be reporting directly to you. I want nothing to do with that lowlife."

"What's wrong with him?"

"He's a creep." Her tone forbade further inquiry. "I have to run now. I'm breakfasting at the Regency with our investment bankers. They seem to need a not-so-gentle reminder that they'll wind up with only a piddling seven hundred thousand bucks unless they put some muscle into this deal."

"Good luck. I'll see you in the office after my lunch with Lolita."

She hung up the phone and slipped back under the covers, but sleep wouldn't come again. With a sigh, she got out of bed and went into the kitchen for a cup of coffee and to catch up on the *Times* and *Wall Street Journal,* always left at her door whether she was at home or away. After a call to Ben to check on things at the office, she reluctantly began to get ready for her luncheon appointment.

MELANIE HAD FORGOTTEN it would be a matinee day when she had told Ben to book her a table at Sardi's, and she arrived to find the restaurant crowded with suburban matrons. Their animated chatter became hushed, and their jeweled hands paused en route to their drinks or mouths as they watched George greet Melanie and lead her to the choice table that had been reserved for her. But when they realized that her face had not provoked any of the caricatures of show-business greats on the walls, they sighed and returned to their gossip and refreshment.

Wanting her mind to be absolutely clear, Melanie ordered a Perrier and lime. Then she waited for her guest. And waited.

In the tradition of sex goddesses who favor mortals with their company, Jami Wells made her entrance a half hour late. Filled with disdainful envy, every pair of matinee-bound eyes was glued to her celebrated little behind as she followed George to Melanie's table. Her form-fitting Golden End leather pants were so tight in the crotch that Melanie winced, almost able to feel their pinch in her own nether region. Braless breasts undulated merrily beneath a low-cut cranberry-colored jersey that clung tightly enough to have been painted on them.

With a smile, Melanie rose and extended her hand across the table. "I'm Melanie Danielle, Miss Wells. I'm glad you could make it."

"Jami." Her cool blue gaze met Melanie's and slid away as quickly as her fingers slid in and out of her hand. She plopped down on the banquette with practiced exuberance. "I'm glad I could make it too. I'm starving." She turned her big blue eyes on the waiter who had just come over to their table. "My friend will have a Kahlúa and cream, and I'll have a Coke." Her voice dropped to little-girl coy. "And don't you dare tell my mother I didn't order Diet Coke the next time you see her."

After sharing a conspiratorial smile, the waiter went off with her order. As soon as his back was turned, the smile disappeared from Jami's face. She reached for a roll and bit into it savagely. "That bitch counts every goddamn calorie I eat."

"With excellent results, evidently." Melanie smiled approvingly at her figure, assuming correctly that, like most vain people, Jami thrived on flattery.

Jami smiled as she preened lovingly. "Yeah. Well. Anyway, I'm a woman now. I can take care of myself. I wish I could get that through my mother's thick skull."

"Mothers are like that. They mean well."

"Is your mother a pain in the ass too?"

"My mother died when I was fifteen."

"I hope you realize how lucky you are."

The waiter appeared with the drinks. Jami sipped the Coke until he was halfway across the room. Then, as Melanie had known she would, Jami reached for the Kahlúa. "Have you seen my movies?" she asked, raising the glass to her lips.

"Not all of them," Melanie said diplomatically. "I'm out of the country a lot."

"You should get a VCR. Then you can buy prints and see my movies as often as you like." She finished the drink and placed the empty glass in front of Melanie. "Order another one of these for me, will you? Those shitheads in government give me a royal pain. Why the hell did they have to move the drinking age up in New York? I agree with George Washington: 'No taxation without intoxication.'"

Melanie signaled the waiter for a refill, which was promptly supplied.

"Are you a producer or something?" Jami asked. "The guy who called yesterday didn't say."

"I'm a corporation lawyer."

"Hey, that's great! I'm a corporation. My mother runs that end of things, though, so I can concentrate on my art. Have you bought tickets for the opening night of my play?"

"I told my secretary to pick them up," Melanie lied. "He probably has them at the office."

"*He?* Oh, wow. A guy secretary? Do you screw around?"

Melanie shook her head.

"He's gay, huh?"

"I'm sure he's not, but it's none of my business."

The appraising look that came to Jami's eyes was one of disdainful superiority. "You probably just don't know how to turn him on." She downed the second drink and had Melanie order another. "Try porn films. I bet that will do the trick. Especially the kind with monsters in them. Guys really go for that. Me and Mickey—Michael Davenport, you know, my leading man in *Dreams of Love*—anyway, me and Mickey once thought it would be fun to see how Frankenstein did it, so we rented this flick called *Frankenstein Meets the Wolfwoman.* I laughed so hard I nearly pissed on the floor. Then Mickey said we should pretend we were monsters. He got so excited we wound up busting the bed and having to pay for it. It was worth it, though. God, that was some night. Mickey had never been able to keep it up for so long. After that, Mickey always wanted to watch that flick first. I finally told him to go to hell. I mean, when I have guys in crazy costumes in the room, I don't want them on some goddamn screen. I want them to be live guys who'll take their turn screwing me, right?"

It was the wrong time for the waiter to appear with the menus; Melanie had just lost her appetite. Nevertheless, she ordered her favorite—crabmeat-stuffed avocado—and Jami joined her, explaining that it would make her feel less guilty about having Sardi's irresistible frozen cake with zabaglione sauce afterward.

Throughout the meal, Jami kept up a monologue about her hyperactive sex life, making Melanie wonder how she found time to act between orgies.

"Did you ever do it on top of an elephant? Me and this guy I know sneaked onto one of the sets for *Jungle Fever* one night and climbed up on this humongous stuffed elephant. Far out." Jami began wolfing down her frozen cake as though she were afraid her mother might show up and whisk it away from her. "I don't think there's anything I haven't tried."

"How about a canal boat in Amsterdam?"

Jami thought a moment, then gave a shrug of dismissal. "I've screwed in yachts, motorboats, canoes, even a submarine. A canal boat doesn't sound so special."

"It would be if it was with the man I have in mind."

There was a flicker of interest in her eyes. "Who's that?"

"His name's Mark Bailey."

"Never heard of him."

"That's because he's an expatriate."

"What kind of pervert is that?"

"It's not a pervert. It's a man who chooses to live abroad because of his life-style. He has quite a reputation in Europe as an international playboy. He's very choosy, though. He sleeps with only the most beautiful women in France and Italy. There's only one American he's ever expressed an interest in—and that's you. He's seen all of your movies—and now he wants to see all of you in person."

Smiling with pleasure, Jami writhed in her seat as though she was already feeling Mark Bailey's fastidious hands on her body. "And he asked you to tell me that?"

Melanie nodded gravely. "He asked me to arrange for you to fly to Amsterdam this weekend."

"Jeez, I can't this weekend. The play—"

"Whatever your plans for the weekend, cancel them," Melanie cut her off, leaning across the table, trying to look earnest and dramatic. "Mark Bailey lets a woman say no to him only once, and then he drops her forever."

"I don't know. What if he turns out to be a creep?"

"He has devoted his life to enjoying all the pleasures his truckloads of money can buy. Does that sound like a creep?"

"No, but I don't know... I mean, if I'm going to go running off to spend the weekend with some guy I've never seen before, I think I should have some kind of guarantee that it's going to be fun, you know?"

Jami was definitely her grasping mother's daughter. "What you want, I think, is insurance, not a guarantee," Melanie said.

Jami shrugged. "Well, whatever."

"I'm prepared to offer you that. How do two covers on *Sizzle* magazine and three feature stories over the next twelve months sound?"

Jami's eyes glowed, but then she shook her head, trying to look unimpressed. "Like shit," she said. "I get my face on magazines all the time."

"Not recently you haven't."

"It's going to be on *Cosmo* soon. And *People* and *Us* are going to run it. Then—"

"Come on, Jami. Don't try to snow me. I've done my homework. You haven't had a cover in eighteen months. And the newsstand sales of your last one were in the pits. You need publicity, and you need it badly."

"I get plenty of publicity. Covers aren't everything, you know. Newspapers and magazines are always printing stories about me. The *National Star* had a full page about my being a reincarnation of Clara Bow. And Rona Barrett mentions me all the time on TV."

"The only publicity you've had lately is a couple of ho-hum lines in the New York papers about your new play. And Rona Barrett hasn't said a word about you since she mentioned in passing that you were leaving Hollywood for rehearsals in New York—and predicted your play would be a dog. Your biggest story in months was the write-up in the *Enquirer* about the scream-a-thon you had with your mother in Saks Fifth Avenue. Those things aren't exactly a publicity bonanza. You're a fading star, Jami."

Jami's eyes hardened. "It's those wimpy Brat Packers. Why did they have to come along and spoil everything?"

"When you're in show business—or any business, for that matter—there's always someone younger or prettier or more talented who comes along and captures everyone's attention. But there's no reason why those fresh new faces have to have all the attention. There's plenty of room at the top for all of you, and

I'm here to offer you a chance to start climbing up the ladder again."

"What's the catch?"

"No catch. You help me, and I'll help you. All you have to do is spend this weekend in Amsterdam with Mark Bailey and come back with his signature on some papers I'll give you."

"That's all?"

"That's all. It'll be the easiest publicity package you've ever earned. I'm sure this won't be your first deal of the sort."

"You can say that again." She still looked skeptical. "There's something fishy about these papers, right?"

"Nothing fishy. It's all perfectly legal."

"Yeah. But I'll have to get him drunk, or something, and slip them to him when he's not thinking straight, is that it?"

Melanie laughed. "You've been reading too many spy stories. Mark Bailey knows all about the papers and has agreed to sign them—provided that you're the one who presents them."

"In other words, I'm the price he asked."

"Is that so bad? You've got nothing to lose, and a great publicity package plus a wonderful weekend to gain."

"What if I forget to have him sign the papers?"

"Then you'll have gained the weekend, but you can kiss the publicity package good-bye. Well, what do you say?"

Jami shrugged. "Why not?"

"Great." Melanie reached into her purse and brought out the papers. "I'll arrange everything for your trip and have your flight tickets and expense money delivered to you. Just make sure you don't forget to bring these along. You have a lot riding on them."

Jami slipped the papers into her purse. "This guy better turn out to be good in bed."

Melanie patted her hand. "Honey, he'll screw your brains out. Just be sure you get his signature on those papers before you drop your pants."

Looking reassured and happily expectant, Jami polished off a second piece of frozen cake.

When they left the restaurant, Melanie hailed a cab and dropped Jami off at the theater where she was rehearsing. As Jami was standing at the cab door, Melanie gave voice to a worry that had been eating away at the back of her mind:

"Will your mother have any objections to your going off for the weekend?"

"Are you kidding?" Jami asked with a derisive smile. For just a fleeting moment hurt flashed in her eyes, making her look like a lost little girl. Then her features quickly hardened again. "All that bitch worries about is how many calories I eat and whether I show up for rehearsals on time. She'll be pleased as hell about this. For a cover on *Sizzle,* she'd arrange for me to sleep with King Kong." Jami laughed. "Actually, I've always thought that would be kind of kinky. I can never understand why Fay Wray screamed all through the picture. Did I tell you about the time I did it on top of an elephant? Oh, yeah—I did. Well, so long. I'll see you soon—with your precious papers." She slammed the car door and strutted toward the theater.

It was a moment before the driver started the cab again, and Melanie didn't have the heart to prod him; his eyes had been glued to Jami's behind.

Chapter Sixteen

PROBABLY BECAUSE IT was where he and Stephanie had spent their honeymoon, San Francisco was one of Clifford Langhton's favorite cities. Every street and landmark seemed to trigger another love-filled memory as his taxi wound its way from the airport to California and Mason Streets. The palatial Fairmont with its gleaming tower was a world apart from the homey and modest Hotel Grant, at the foot of Nob Hill, where he and Stephanie had stayed twelve years before. Still, as he trod the plush carpeting through the gold and marble lobby to the Fairmont's registration desk, it was a vision of the Grant's cheerful lobby with its huge fireplace that filled his mind.

Upstairs in his luxurious room, he hung up the clothes he had brought along for his overnight stay. Occupying only three hangers, they looked rather desolate in the huge walk-in closet, and he found himself wishing, as he had been ever since boarding the plane at JFK, that he could have brought Stephanie along. But their time together would have been brief, and she would never have understood some of the things he might have to do in town. They were both better off with her staying home in Scarsdale with the boys.

It was already noon, which didn't give him much time if he wanted to arrive before Brent Allen for their luncheon appointment. He washed up quickly in the gleaming bathroom, changed his shirt, and hurried off to Trader Vic's.

EVEN MORE MONUMENTAL than his image on the screen, Brent Allen swung through Trader Vic's in his custom-made cowboy boots, hat, jeans, and shirt looking as though he had arrived on his favorite stallion instead of in a chauffeured Rolls-Royce. As he extended his huge hand toward Cliff, his tanned cheeks creased into the smile that had been winning fans all over the world since he first thundered across the screen in 1948 as the star of *Westward the Wagons*. From that moment on, like George Washington, he had been first in the hearts of his countrymen—women adoring him as the perfect lover, outdoor style, and men admiring him as the perfect specimen of a "real man."

"Howdy," he said, crushing Cliff's hand. "You must be Clifford Langhton. You've come a long way just to get some good vittles, boy. Sit down, sit down," he added as he swept off his hat.

"I can't tell you how glad I am to meet you. Like everyone else in this country, I've been a fan of yours for years." Actually, Cliff enjoyed a simple Western upon occasion, but not the epics in which Allen annihilated the Mexican army and whole tribes of Indians.

Brent grinned, showing rows of bright, even, well-capped teeth, and then feinted a jab at Cliff's shoulder. "Now don't go telling me how many years. You'll make me feel like an old-timer."

"Brent Allen will never be old. There's a law against it."

"Well, if there ain't, there sure ought to be." He laughed and puffed out his broad chest. "The secret is to keep fit and keep going. Never let up. You got to ride as hard and live as hard as you always did. That way there ain't nothing and nobody in the world can catch up with you."

"It sure seems to work for you."

"Damn right it does." He looked at Cliff's gin and tonic as the waiter presented himself for drink orders. "What are you drinking, boy? That ain't that sissy French seltzer water, is it?"

Cliff laughed. "Far from it. It's gin and tonic."

Brent looked unimpressed. "Better, but not much. Why don't you join me in a Scorpion? It's so wicked it'll put hair on your chest."

"Thanks, but I think I'd better stick to this while I wait for jet lag to catch up with me."

The Scorpion was served, complete with gardenia garland. Brent sniffed the flower. "These always remind me of Laura Leslie.

Remember her? She was in a couple of my pictures. Lousy actress, but what a pair of tits. She loved gardenias. Demanded a bouquet of them every time we screwed. For all that she had a gorgeous ass and tits, she was a lousy lay. Saw her at a party about a month ago. She's fat and sixty now. God, what a mess! They should take women out and drown them the minute they hit thirty. They're sure as hell no good for anything after that." He raised his glass. "Well, cheers."

He downed the drink quickly in the best cowboy tradition, wiped the back of his hand over his mouth, and ordered another. And another. And another. By the time the waiter brought their Indonesian rack of lamb with peanut-butter sauce, Brent fit in extremely well with the restaurant's nautical decor—he was sailing. Throughout the meal, he treated Cliff to stories of his adventures, sexual and otherwise, both on and off the screen. Since many of them were recognizable movie plots, Cliff doubted their veracity, but he listened intently and reacted with the proper amount of awe and admiration. In the meantime, he wondered when Brent would give him an opportunity to bring up business matters. Or if Brent would be sober enough to know what he was talking about when he did.

Suddenly, Brent leaned across the table, took Cliff's chin in his huge hand, and turned his face as though trying to view it in a better light. "Did anyone ever tell you you've got a great profile? With that blond hair and those blue eyes, you could give Robert Redford a run for his money. How would you like to get into movies? I could arrange a screen test for you."

Cliff pulled back and laughed. "Redford's safe—at least from me. I don't have any interest in an acting career or any talent for it."

"Talent's the least of it. It's having friends in the right places that counts. You ever change your mind, you let me know, hear? With a face like that, you could go places. What the hell is it that you do again? It seems to have slipped my mind."

"I work for Kendricks International," he reminded Brent. "I came out here to talk to you about your stock in *Sizzle*."

"Oh, yeah. You and that feller who was here yesterday. He's the editor. Took me to lunch at Jack's. Wanted me to sell all my shares to some dame with a fancy name."

Cliff was delighted to hear that Belmont had moved into the Wylford camp; one less impediment to his command of *Sizzle* when Kendricks won his stock battle. He kept his voice casual as he asked, "What did you tell him?"

"That I wanted to study all the angles and talk to my business manager first. Hell, I may be a cowboy, but I didn't get to be a rich cowboy by being dumb."

"And have you talked to your business manager?"

"Not yet." Brent polished off his drink, then leaned across the table. "Why don't you tell me about it, old buddy?"

It was the damnedest thing. It had to be an accident, but suddenly, Cliff felt Brent Allen's knee rubbing against his thigh. He smiled and shifted in his seat. The knee retreated, but Brent didn't acknowledge the accidental contact by as much as an "excuse me" or the flicker of an eyelash.

"When you talk to your manager," Cliff said, as though nothing had happened, "tell him that Harrison Kendricks has authorized me to offer you a full ten percent above any offer you get from Wylford Enterprises if you tender your shares to Fogerty, Finley and Straus, our investment bankers, within the next ten days."

"Feller that was here yesterday said something about *Sizzle* running some stories on me if I played it his way."

"That's a promise he can't come across with. Kendricks is going to massacre those varmints, and then that guy's going to be out on his ass. If you want stories in *Sizzle,* the smart thing to do is sell to Kendricks."

The knee was back again, moving slowly from side to side. Then it retreated. "I dunno…" Brent's eyes held Cliff's. "You one of these editor fellers too?"

"I started out as a reporter before I went to work for Kendricks, and it looks like I'll wind up being the editor of *Sizzle.*"

"How'd you like to wind up being a speech writer and press secretary for a very important senator?"

"Which one?"

"Why, me, boy! *Me!* I'm not going to be a cowboy all my life, you know. I got me some good friends. Some very important friends. They want to send me to Washington to straighten out the mess this country is in. They say it's time for a third party, and

I think they're right. The Republicans pretend they're for what we believe in, but when it gets down to the nitty-gritty, to really getting tough with the freeloaders in our society, they always sell out in the end."

"And you won't."

"You can bet your bottom dollar I won't. I'll stick it to those freeloaders all the way. When I get through with them, they'll be begging to be taken off the welfare rolls."

"First you have to get elected," Cliff pointed out.

"Do you think I wouldn't be?" Brent's features took on the look of a belligerent drunk. "The people of this state love me. They see me as their macho image and father figure rolled into one. Hell, I'm ten times more popular than that old has-been Ronnie. My name on the ballot would guarantee a landslide. And once I got to the Senate, there'd be no stopping this old cowpoke. I always did think 'Hail to the Chief' was a hell of a lot more catchy than 'The Streets of Laredo.'"

"Did you tell the fellow you had lunch with yesterday that you're going to run for the Senate?"

"Naw. He struck me as sort of a cold fish. Not like you." His bleary eyes took on an intimate look, and he patted Cliff's right hand, letting his fingers linger. "I can tell you're a warm, friendly fella. The kind that can keep a secret." He looked around quickly, then lowered his voice. "And it is a secret, you know. My friends— the guys who want me to run—they don't want me to talk about it yet. You'll keep it under your hat, okay?"

"Absolutely." Cliff withdrew his hand from beneath Brent's and raised it in a Boy Scout's pledge. "But in the meantime, just between us, let me point out how important it could be to you to get your *Sizzle* shares into the hands of Fogerty, Finley and Straus. Harrison Kendricks owns four very influential newspapers in the state of California and twenty-seven throughout the United States. You play ball with him, and sure as shooting, he'll back your campaign—or campaigns—two hundred percent. He'd be a powerful ally to have in your corner."

"Makes sense," Brent said, nodding his head sagely. "Makes a lot of sense. And what about you? Are you interested in my offer?" The knee was back again, slowly jostling.

Though it sickened him, Cliff did not move his thigh away. "I'll be back in California in a few weeks after the takeover battle has ended. If Kendricks has won it with the help of friends like you—why, then, I'd be glad to go out to your spread and talk about a future association."

The two men exchanged a meaningful smile. Brent's eyes lit up and he moistened his lips. "Now that's the kind of talk I like to hear. We can go places together, boy. Big places."

Cliff pulled back his leg and signaled for the bill. "It seems to me that the first place you have to go is to see your business manager."

"You've got yourself a deal, pardner," Brent said, holding out his hand.

Cliff submitted to the cowboy star's crushing grip. Afterward, he managed to refrain from wiping his palm on his napkin.

It was almost five by the time Cliff got back to his hotel room. He longed to rest for a while, but was due to pick up Laura Leslie at six-thirty for drinks and dinner. He shaved off his day's growth of beard, then took a long hot shower, which revived him a bit and washed away some of the crawly feeling from his meeting with Brent Allen. After toweling himself, he slipped on the silk Andrew Fezza robe Stephanie had given him for Christmas and stretched out on the vast bed. He knew what he needed to make him feel better. He reached for the phone and called home.

Billy was breathless when he answered the phone, and Cliff smiled, imagining the race with his brothers when it began to ring. "Is it him, is it Daddy?" he heard chorused in the background by Chris and Jon and Stephanie, and he could see Billy nodding his handsome blond head, trying to look grown-up and important as he said, "Hi, Dad. How's the weather out there?"

"Gorgeous, I think. I've been so busy I've hardly had time to notice. Besides, I'd much rather be back home with you—even if it was raining rocks there. How was school today?"

For the next ten minutes, he spoke to each of his sons, discussing schoolwork, hockey and basketball scores, the time difference between New York and California, and the best kind of glue to use on a model car. Then he heard Stephanie complaining to them good-naturedly, "It's my turn, you guys," and at last her lovely voice was saying, "Hi, darling," as only she could say it.

"Hi, yourself. Are the boys being good for you?"

"They're being perfect angels, as always," she said, no doubt making a face, for he could hear giggling. "Get lost, fellas," she told the boys. "It's time for grown-up talk."

"You mean mushy talk," Billy said, and his observation was followed by the sound of receding laughter.

"Alone at last," Stephanie said, "for whatever good it will do us with three thousand miles in between."

"Those miles will have turned into millimeters by tomorrow night. Then I promise you there will be nothing between us, not even a sheet."

"That might prove a little chilly."

"Wanna bet?"

She laughed. "How has your day been?"

"Lousy, and it's only half over."

"Poor baby. What did you do?"

"I had lunch with two boring acquisition lawyers who were so old they looked as though they should have been eating gruel instead of sipping martinis."

"And tonight?"

"Dinner with a bunch of boring stockbrokers."

"Maybe it won't be so boring. When we took the kids on a tour of the New York Stock Exchange, I saw some in skirts."

"Unfortunately, there won't be any of that type among the ones I'm dining with tonight. They're all male, middle-aged, and deadly dull. I know, because I've had the displeasure of their company before."

"Well, cheer up. How long can one dinner last?"

"Forever when you're being bored out of your skull. How has your evening been?"

"Same old thing. I had cocktails with Prince Charles, dinner with an oil sheik whose name slips my mind, and later on, after the boys are tucked in bed, Mikhail Baryshnikov is going to stop by and take me dancing. Dull, dull, dull."

"Don't let Mikhail keep you up too late. I don't want you all tuckered out when I get home tomorrow."

"Um," she purred. "I have big plans for you too."

"Tell me about them."

"I wouldn't want to melt the cross-country telephone wires." There was a muffled sound in the background. "Oh, hell. The boys are at it again. I'd better go referee before blood is spilled. I'll see you tomorrow, honey."

"I love you."

"You too. Gotta go. Be good."

"What else?" he said, but she had already hung up.

As he was dressing for dinner with Laura Leslie, a passing remark by Brent Allen came back to him, and he phoned the hotel florist, requesting that a bouquet of gardenias be boxed and sent to his room. While he was waiting, he shined his shoes with the electric shoe polisher the hotel provided. He always got a kick out of that.

BEFITTING THE STAR who had been Marilyn Monroe's greatest rival, Laura Leslie would consider only a suite in the Hyatt Regency when she was spending more than a day in San Francisco. Perhaps she felt most at home there because the hotel's somewhat pyramid shape reminded her of the happy time she played Cleopatra in *Queen of the Nile,* or because the sumptuous lobby with its ivy-festooned balconies, high sky-lighted roof, caged birds, and abundance of flowers brought back memories of her greatest motion picture triumph, *Scheherazade.* Or maybe, Cliff thought as he stood before the door to her suite, it was simply that after knowing hunger in the Great Depression, she loved living in luxury.

Also as befitted a movie queen, Laura's door was opened by an authentic French maid complete with black stockings, high heels, and little white apron and cap. "Monsieur Langhton? Come this way, please," she said in a charming accent. Though the accent and uniform matched the role, the woman herself did not; she was middle-aged and neither pretty nor curvaceous. But, Cliff thought as he followed her, what former sex goddess would want a glamorous French maid around?

The maid led him into the spacious, dimly lit living room, where her employer, having gracefully arranged herself on the couch, was waiting to greet him.

"Monsieur Langhton," the maid announced, and retreated.

Brent Allen had been bitchy. Though the age was probably correct, there was no way Laura Leslie could be dismissed simply as being "fat and sixty." The years had enriched her voluptuous figure, but the extra weight was distributed evenly in all the best places. Her shimmering silk gown, of an electric shade of aqua, clung to her body as though the designer had sewn her into it. Her shapely legs, which were propped up on the sofa, peeped seductively out of a slit that reached mid-thigh, as did her breasts from the neckline that seemed to be plunging to meet the slit. Long, snug sleeves gave the gown a touch of stateliness. It mattered not at all that the dark hair that had been transformed to blond forty years ago was now probably gray at the roots; it fell in golden waves to her shoulders just as in her days of glory. And if the face it framed was perhaps puffier than it used to be, it still held traces of its original beauty.

Her right arm was draped along the back of the sofa, and she offered her left hand, palm down, in the regal gesture of a sovereign granting a courtier permission to approach. "How nice to meet you, Mr. Langhton," she said. It was the same sultry voice that, in his teens, had made his underwear tight in dark movie houses.

"And to meet you," Cliff said, taking her hand in both of his, and hoping that she hadn't expected him to kiss it. "You're even more beautiful than on the screen—but I suppose everybody tells you that."

"Not everybody," she said with a rather wistful smile.

Up close, the thick makeup was more apparent, but it had been applied with care, and the result was a work of art rather than garishness. But there was no way to hide the signs of age on her hand. The brightly lacquered nails and diamond-encircled sapphire ring could not long distract Cliff from the jutting blue veins and the little brown spots, tiny footprints left behind by time on its relentless advance.

Suddenly the plump hand stiffened, and Cliff wondered if Laura had sensed his thoughts. Quickly he said, "That's a magnificent ring."

Laura smiled and withdrew her hand, admiring the ring

too. "It was a gift from my fourth husband, Sir Hugh Hunting-ton-Crawford. I was really sorry we couldn't get along and had to divorce. I rather fancied being called Lady Huntington-Crawford. Did you bring along sandwiches—or is that box for me?" she said archly.

"For you," Cliff said, presenting it to her.

"How exciting."

"Not as exciting as that ring, I'm afraid."

"I'll be the judge of that." She opened the box. "Gardenias!" She looked up at Cliff, her face filled with unpretended pleasure. "How ever did you know that they're my favorite?"

"I guess I just hoped they would be, because you're my favorite actress and they've always reminded me of you."

She studied his face as though trying to determine whether he was giving her a line. He did his best to look boyish and sincere. Evidently he succeeded, for she smiled and buried her cheek in the blossoms.

"They're magnificent," she said, and extended the box to him. "Be a dear. Find Marie and ask her to arrange them for me."

"I was hoping," he said, trying for a shy note, "that you might wear one. I'll never forget how you looked when you played that Civil War heroine in *The Colonel's Daughter* and you went to the ball with magnolias in your hair."

"You have a good memory."

"Some things are impossible to forget."

She removed a flower and fingered the petals. "My hair was arranged in the style of the period then. I'm afraid this gardenia wouldn't look right in it tonight." She snapped off the stem and slipped the blossom into the V of her plunging neckline. "How does it look here?"

"Very beautiful," Cliff said, "and ecstatically happy."

She laughed at his melodramatic gaze of unrequited longing.

He found Marie in the dining room, reading a copy of *Sizzle*. Laura was just as he had left her back in the living room, holding her position like an artist's model.

"Why don't you make us a drink?" she suggested. "How are your martinis?"

"I have a reputation for making the best in the East. But I

was hoping to take you to the Top of the Mark for drinks before dinner."

"Fans make such a fuss over me there," she said. "Let's have our drinks here, where we can talk in peace and I can get to know you."

He went over to the huge wet bar and mixed a large pitcher of martinis. And then another. Laura tossed them down as though they were water and she had just returned from a week in the desert. Her desire to "get to know" Cliff appeared to be limited to discovering how many of her movies he had seen and to hearing how much he admired her in them. He was lavish in his praise.

"Those were *real* movies," she sighed. "They don't make them like that anymore. They just make garbage. All they want to put on the screen now is a woman's tits and ass and pussy and show her in bed screwing. You don't have to be an actress these days—you have to be a goddamn whore. Well, if I want to see two people screwing, I just look in the mirror I had installed in my ceiling at home—I sure as hell don't have to go to a movie to see it. And I'm sure as hell not going to flaunt myself naked or screw on a giant screen for any director."

Cliff doubted very much that she would ever been asked to. Brent Allen had said women should be drowned after thirty. Hollywood was crueler to its sex goddesses. When the glow of youth began to fade and was no longer considered worth recreating with makeup and special lighting, it didn't take them out and drown them—it simply turned its back on them. It was almost twenty years since Laura's last film, an Italian production about a woman gladiator in ancient Rome. It was such a disaster that it was never shown in America.

"And I'm not playing any goddamn thirty-year-old tramp's mother, either," she added, no doubt alluding to her only job offer in recent years.

She held out her glass, and Cliff refilled it, shaking his head sympathetically. "I can't imagine that any producer in his right mind would ask you to do such a thing."

"The goddamn sons of bitches are all out of their minds." She tossed off the drink, and extended her glass again.

Cliff poured the last few drops into it. "How about dinner now? I have reservations at Ernie's."

With a shrug, she finished her drink, put down the glass, and then held out a hand in the same imperious gesture as when he had entered the room. He took it and helped her to her feet, amazed that she could stand after all that alcohol.

"Dinner sounds good," she said. "I can never get enough of Ernie's cream of lobster soup."

Marie brought her purse and wrap, and as they left the hotel, Laura's gait was as steady as a temperance worker's.

Walking into Ernie's was a return in time to San Francisco's "Bonanza Era." The mahogany and stained-glass bar was a museum piece from a less reputable establishment on the Barbary Coast, and the flamboyant furnishings had once graced the mansions of social climbers who had amassed their fortunes in Gold Rush days. Seated at an intimate table near an elegant red-flocked wall, Cliff and Laura ate the *bisque de hombard* Laura had been longing for, and also partook of *canard roll aux oranges*. Laura drank most of the two bottles of Dom Perignon.

Laura had only two topics of conversation—her movies and her husbands and lovers. There had been five husbands, and Cliff lost count of the lovers. Evidently, she was as demanding in bed as she was reputed to have once been on the movie set, for she had little praise for the men in her life, and described in detail and with great scorn their sexual shortcomings. There was the macho singer, heartthrob of millions, who couldn't maintain an erection for more than sixty seconds. The world-famous psychiatrist, author of a best-selling marriage manual, who was unable to perform unless they staged a mock rape. The suave French actor, renowned for his playboy roles, who reeked from body odor because he never bathed, believing that water would wash away his natural oils and cause premature wrinkles (perhaps he didn't really count as a lover, because when he refused to shower, she refused to let him in her bed). The celebrated quarterback who liked to prance around in her panties and negligees. The highly respected former cabinet member who could copulate only from behind while barking like a dog. The distinguished judge who could get an erection only if, wearing his black robe, she put him over her knees and spanked him. On a scale of one to ten, most of the men in her life came in with negative numbers.

"I never married a man unless I tried him out in bed first," she said, "and in my whole life, there were only five who could pass the test. They all slowed down after we were married, though, and I wound up having to kick them out too." She laughed. "You know, Brent Allen wanted to marry me back when he was in some of my movies. My press agent thought it was a great idea. The sex goddess and the all-American hero. All-American crock of shit is more like it. I told them both to go to hell." Her eyes hardened. "Christ! That shit is still starring in movies, making love on the screen to kids young enough to be his granddaughters. I'd like to see some director make him drop his pants for full-frontal nudity. He'd be laughed right out of the country. He's got a dick no bigger than a cocktail frank. The few times I let him screw me, he had to bring along a dildo to help him out."

Though she hadn't ordered it, the waiter came over and placed a brandy Alexander in front of her. She looked up at him and smiled. "You never forget, do you?"

He was a fortyish man with kind eyes and a nice smile. "Of course not, Miss Leslie."

Laura took the waiter's hand and turned to Cliff. "Years ago, I told Joe that my mother used to say a real lady always ended a meal with a brandy Alexander. Ever since then, he has always remembered to bring me one."

"That's because he knows a real lady when he sees one," Cliff said.

"Can I get you something, sir?" Joe asked.

"Bring him a Rémy Martin," Laura answered for Cliff. "That's how real gentlemen end their meal."

When Joe returned with a brandy snifter, Cliff warmed it in his hand a moment, then tilted it toward Laura. "To a real lady," he said in adoration.

A little teary-eyed, she lifted her glass and took a genteel sip. "Mama died when I was still playing bit parts. I wish to God she could see me now. She'd be so proud."

Cliff looked across the table at the fading star. Alcohol had turned her eyes pink and glassy, their lids puffy. In her hotel suite she had dimmed the lights and spread out on the sofa, forcing him to take the chair placed a comfortable distance away. Here, at an intimate table for two, he was better able to see the thickness of her makeup and the wrinkles it could no longer hide. The creases in her neck were more obvious, as were the little loose pouches of flesh at her jawline. He had begun to suspect, too, that that golden mane of hair was not her own. It seemed to him that it was Mother Leslie's good fortune that she had not lived to see her daughter now. He smiled and tried for a pious look as he intoned the platitude he knew would comfort the soddenly sentimental woman across from him: "I'm sure that, in heaven, your mother knows and is proud."

"Do you really think so?" she asked, gazing up to the ceiling where, perhaps, the spirit of her mother was hovering, a ghostly brandy Alexander in hand.

"Absolutely," he assured her solemnly, signaling Joe for their bill.

With a sigh of satisfaction, she polished off her drink in a single gulp that left a frothy halo around her mouth.

While Joe went off with Cliff's credit card, Laura made a trip to the women's room. By now her gait was wobbly, and she paused occasionally to grasp the back of a chair. Cliff wondered how the hell he was going to get her to talk business.

Laura returned just as Joe was giving Cliff his customer's receipt.

"Good night, Miss Leslie," he said.

"Good night, Joe. Thank you for taking such good care of us." She watched the waiter leave, then turned to Cliff, still smiling. "I've toyed with the thought of sending my chauffeur around to pick up Joe one night and bring him back to my place. It would be a real treat for him, don't you think?"

"It would change everything between you, though, whenever you came in here."

She shrugged and sighed. "I suppose you're right. Besides, he's not very handsome and too old for me anyway."

If anything, Joe was at least ten years her junior—probably closer to twenty—but Cliff was diplomatic enough not to mention it.

"Still," she said rather wistfully, "I bet he'd know how to make love to a woman. You may not believe this—" She leaned closer, obviously forgetting her principal topic of conversation through-out dinner "—but I've been around a lot. I mean *a lot.* And I've found that the best lovers aren't the actors or the politicians or the big, macho sports stars. They're all too goddamn in love with themselves. The best lovers are the *real* guys—guys like Joe there, or you, or the guy I was with last night. Now, *he* knows how to treat a woman."

Suddenly Cliff had a dread feeling of calamity. "What was the name of the lucky guy?"

"Don't remember. Donald Something. Or was it Daniel? Hey, maybe you know him. You said something before about working for *Sizzle.* He works for *Sizzle* too."

"Was it David Belmont?"

"That's right. David Belmont. Is he your boss?"

"No, he's not my boss. I'm going to be his boss soon, and I'd like to talk to you about that. Why don't we go to the Starlite Roof or the Venetian Room?"

"I have a better idea," she said, dropping her voice to an intimate hush. "Why don't we go back to my suite?"

Riding back to the Regency, Cliff ascertained that though David greatly impressed Laura and promised her cover stories in *Sizzle* that would guarantee a comeback, she had not yet tendered her shares to the Wylford bankers; her business manager had advised her that morning that a better offer might be forthcoming from other quarters.

"He was darned right," Cliff said. "I'm about to make you a much better offer."

Later, in the living room of her suite, over snifters of Rémy Martin, he outlined for her the same money and publicity package he had presented to Brent Allen that afternoon. She, too, found it irresistible, especially when he promised that Harrison Kendricks would use his considerable influence with Hollywood producers and bankers to get her comeback off the ground with a sequel to *Scheherazade.*

"It's the deal of a lifetime," he told her. "And the only work you have to do for it is pick up the phone and call your manager or broker."

"I don't want this to be just another movie," she said. "I want the best producer, the best director, the best screenplay."

"They're yours," he assured her. "Just make that phone call in the morning, and the wheels will be set in motion."

"What if Kendricks Enterprises doesn't get the magazine?"

Cliff laughed. "That's like asking, 'What if the sun doesn't come up tomorrow?' Harrison Kendricks never loses."

She rose to her feet rather unsteadily. "This calls for a celebration."

He stood up too; even cockeyed drunk, a woman like Laura Leslie would notice and appreciate the courtesy. "Shall I order champagne?"

Slowly, she walked her fingers up his chest and wound her arms around his neck. "I have a much more enjoyable celebration in mind."

She tilted her face up to his, her eyes closed, her lips parted. Her eye shadow had liquefied and then congealed in streaks along the creases of her lids. As he brought his lips down to hers, her tongue shot out eagerly to meet his, and her hand left his neck and darted down to grasp his crotch. The surprise move sent a shock of pain rather than pleasure through him, but she interpreted his gasp as a sign of passion. Pulling away, she murmured in a sultry tone, "Let's go into the bedroom, where we can seal our bargain properly." She took his hand and led the way.

Laura Leslie did not employ a French maid for assistance with irregular verbs. Dim, romantic lighting and a turned-down bed with perfumed sheets awaited them.

"Sit there, honey," Laura said, gently pushing Cliff into an easy chair. Then she walked over to a bedside table and switched on a tape recorder. Instantly, the room was filled with the mellow strains of violins playing the theme song from *Queen of the Nile*. Trying without success to move in time to the music, she began a drunken striptease.

Cliff watched the pathetic performance, glad he'd had so much to drink, wishing he had finished the brandy he left behind in the living room.

After kicking off her shoes, Laura removed the wilted gardenia from between her breasts, waved it under his nose, then, with a coquettish giggle, placed it behind his ear. She turned her back to him, wiggling her buttocks while she waited for him to unzip her gown. When he had complied, she faced him again and slowly slipped the gown from her shoulders, undulating her hips while it slipped to the floor. Her breasts sagged and were surprisingly small. It was a disappointment to discover that the voluptuous figure he had lusted for in his teens had been the product of clever dressmaking and creative photography. Beneath the dress, she had been wearing only pantyhose, and she hooked her thumbs under the waistband and slipped them down to her thighs. Then she lay on the bed, extended her legs overhead, toes pointed so that he could appreciate the shapely curve of her calves, and slowly peeled off the pantyhose.

Once naked, she rose clumsily and performed a few bumps and grinds. The skin where her arms met her torso creased in tiny accordianlike folds. The flesh of her inner thighs was flabby, and her dark pubic hair was sprinkled with gray. As she beckoned Cliff to rise, he wished that he could make his penis as well as his legs respond, bringing his evening's work to a successful conclusion. While she undressed him, he found the secret. If he half-closed his eyes, he could pretend she still looked like his childhood image of her. It worked, and by the time she had him stepping out of his trousers and shorts, he was ready and willing. He pulled her close and kissed her.

She slipped from his arms and lay down on the bed, a leg propped up, arms stretched over her head. "Come sit beside me," she whispered, "and tell me how beautiful I am."

"You're beautiful," he complied, running his hands over her. "You're the most gorgeous woman in the world."

"Again. Tell me again."

"You're beautiful… gorgeous… magnificent."

"You've never seen a more beautiful woman, have you?"

"Never."

"No, say the whole thing."

"I've never seen a more beautiful woman, and I never will."

"Now tell me how beautiful my tits are," she said, pulling his head down to suckle.

"You have beautiful breasts, so soft, so—"

"No, no! Tits. Call them tits."

"You have beautiful tits. Gorgeous tits."

"The most beautiful tits in the whole world."

"The most beautiful tits in the whole world."

They completed the ritual all the way down to her ankles and back up again.

"Now!" she gasped finally. "Mount me now! Keep saying it. Keep telling me."

"You're beautiful," he said with every thrust. "You're gorgeous. Beautiful. Gorgeous..."

Her whole body shuddered in a massive orgasm, and then the alcohol finally got the better of her and she passed out.

Cliff lay beside her awhile, catching his breath. Exhausted from his long day and the drinking and the sex, he was tempted to go to sleep. But he knew he should get back to his hotel in case Stephanie called. Besides, if Laura found him in bed with her when she woke up, she would want a repeat performance, and he had already paid her more than enough for her goddamn stocks.

Knowing that Laura would be dead to the world for hours, he turned the lights up as he searched for his shoes. She lay there breathing heavily—almost snoring—blowing out each breath with a little puffing sound. Her wig was slightly crooked, her false eyelashes missing. He had read somewhere that she rarely went out during the day. Looking at her in the bright light, he realized why. The makeup had not yet been invented that would hide those wrinkles from the unpitying brilliance of the sun's strong rays. Sadly he shook his head and pulled the covers up around her shoulders. Why couldn't sex goddesses be allowed to age gracefully and in peace?

Early the next morning Cliff sent two dozen gardenias to Laura Leslie, enclosing a card with the message: *To the most beautiful woman in the world for the most beautiful night of my life. Clifford Langhton.* That done, he decided he deserved the treat of breakfast at Sears, even if it did mean waiting on the queue that seemed to be a permanent fixture before its door.

On their honeymoon, he and Stephanie had eaten breakfast there several times, and the moment he walked into the brown and gold room with its bright, cheerful paintings, his spirits began to lift. The little table that had been their favorite was occupied, but it didn't matter. For him, the whole place was filled with loving memories. He sat at the counter and ordered Swedish pancakes and bacon, feeling in heaven as he ate all eighteen of the delectable light, golden discs smothered in whipped butter and warm maple syrup. Revived, he went off in search of presents for Stephanie and the boys.

He never tired of climbing the roller-coaster hills with their gingerbread houses, cable cars, street-corner flower stalls, and sudden, surprising glimpses of the sparkling bay. He knew that Stephanie longed to settle in San Francisco one day. Well, maybe they would. Someday.

As he walked to the Pearl Empire on Geary Street, he couldn't help thinking that when he and Stephanie had paused to admire its display twelve years before, it had not occurred to either of them that someday they'd be able to shop there without trepidation. He selected a gold and jade bracelet for her, and ordered it gift wrapped before even alluding to its price. He had come a long way in twelve years.

Farther along the street, a sweet, luscious aroma began to tickle his nostrils. He followed it to its source, Findley's Fabulous Fudge, where he found it difficult to narrow his selection from the twelve tempting varieties down to a pound each of three.

From Findley's he taxied to Pier 39, where, feeling like a kid again, he wandered around in The Kitemakers, trying to decide on gifts for the boys. It was easy in Billy's case—he was on a prehistoric kick, the walls of his room covered with drawings of dinosaurs—so for him Cliff chose a pterodactyl kite. He finally bought an octopus for Chris and an eagle for Jon. As he was paying for his purchases, his eye kept going back to the beautiful rainbow kite. Stephanie would love to see its vivid colors rippling and soaring through the sky. He told the clerk to wrap it with the others, and laughed when he was given buttons that read *Go fly a kite* along with his receipt.

Time was running short, and he taxied back to the Fairmont, in a hurry to pack, check out, and get to the airport. At the desk he was given a package that had been delivered. Upstairs he unwrapped a framed photograph of Laura Leslie as she had looked thirty-five years ago. She had inscribed in a childlike hand: *To my darling Clifford—With all my love, Laura.* The last thing he needed was to bring that souvenir of San Francisco home to Stephanie! He slipped the photograph out of the frame, tore it into little pieces, and flushed it down the john. "Sorry," he murmured as he deposited the frame in the wastepaper basket.

After packing, he sat down on the bed and telephoned Laura. Obviously, despite all her drinking, she remembered their night in bed, but he wanted to make sure she remembered the business deal it had consummated.

Marie answered the phone, and there was a brief pause before Laura's voice came over the wire:

"Clifford darling! The gardenias are absolutely beautiful. I'm simply surrounded by them—and I adore them. When will I be seeing you again?"

"Not for a while, I'm afraid. I'm leaving for New York this afternoon."

"It was very naughty of you to leave in the middle of the night."

"I knew if we woke up together in the morning, I'd never be able to tear myself away. And that wouldn't be fair to you. I want to get back to New York so we can start the ball rolling on your next movie. Did you call your business manager?"

"It was the first thing I did this morning. Everything is being taken care of. When will you be back?"

"I don't know. I have a lot of business to take care of in New York. Besides, you're going to be so busy with your new movie you won't have time for anything but work."

She gave a throaty laugh. "I always make time for fun with the proper playmates."

"I'll keep that in mind when I get back to town. Thank you for the picture. I'll treasure it always."

"I wanted you to have something to remember me by."

"With or without it, I'll always remember you."

As soon as he was able to get Laura off the phone, he called Kendricks in New York. "Mission accomplished," he said. "Brent Allen and Laura Leslie are tendering their stocks to our bank."

"What precious plums did you have to render to convince them?"

"Cover stories in *Sizzle* and publicity in your papers. Allen, it seems, has political ambitions and is eager for all the publicity he can get."

"I've heard rumblings of that nature. Allen's a shithead, of course, but he has some good people behind him—people who would be looking out for our interests. A man with a public image like Brent Allen's would be very valuable for their cause. If he'll just keep his own bloody mouth shut and say and do what they tell him to, it could work out very well indeed."

"Unless the country finds out first that he's a flaming fairy. The son of a bitch made a pass at me."

Kendricks laughed. "I'm sure you managed to hang on to your virtue."

"Not only hold on to it, but to get his shares as well." Cliff laughed too. "I simply batted my eyes at him and told him I'd look him up in the future when, with his help, we'd accomplished our mission."

"Good man. You've learned to play the game well."

"I've had the best possible coach."

"I hope things were a little more pleasant for you with Laura Leslie."

"If you mean you hope I wound up in bed with her—I did. But it was strictly business and no pleasure. She's a far cry from the sexpot of thirty years ago."

"All in an honest night's work, my boy."

"To sweeten the pot, I told her you'd use your influence to get the wheels in motion for a movie comeback for her." Suddenly, with a shiver, he saw Laura as she had looked in the glare of the light when he had pulled the covers over her the night before. "Actually, maybe you could do something. She's really rather pathetic, and needs a helping hand."

"Screw the old bag. At her age, she should know better than to believe a man's promises."

A cold knot began to form in Cliff's chest. Was Kendricks telling him that he should know better than to trust in promises too? But the knot quickly disappeared as Kendricks went on:

"Good job, old man. Every day you're bringing us both closer to our goals."

"I know one guy who's trying to keep us from them—David Belmont. The bastard has joined the Wylford camp. He was out here the other day trying to persuade Allen and Leslie to sell to them."

"It's to be expected. He knows he'll be out out on his ass the minute we take over."

"I hope he hasn't done a better job of convincing others I haven't been able to get to yet. He's in pretty thick with Bailey's widow."

"So are you, old boy. Not to worry. We're going to win. If things start looking sticky toward the deadline, I have other cards to play."

As usual, Kendricks hung up without saying good-bye.

THE STARS WERE shining brightly overhead when Cliff got out of the taxi, but it was the lights of his home that attracted him. From behind the curtained windows they beckoned to him like warm, welcoming arms. He paid the driver and started up the path to the porch. Before he had reached the halfway point, the door opened and two small figures in pajamas and robes came bursting out to meet him.

"Come back here! You'll catch cold!" Stephanie called after their two younger sons, but her tone was one of fond indulgence, not command, and the boys continued into his outstretched arms.

Their small, firm bodies felt so good and clean! He hugged them both, then scooped up Jon in his right arm and, with Chris's "help," carried his suitcase in his left hand. Billy, who at ten considered himself too mature for such overt outbursts of affection, was jiggling with excitement beside his mother in the doorway. Forgetting that he had forsworn hugs and kisses, he threw himself into his father's arms on the porch.

"Maybe I should go away more often," Cliff said, disengaging himself from the boys.

"The hell you should." Stephanie's eyes were filled with love, her smile with mischief.

"Miss me?" he asked, pulling her close.

Her lips were soft and yielding, and he kissed them hungrily, as though it had been years since he had possessed them.

Jon tugged his jacket. "What did you buy us?"

Reluctantly, Cliff let Stephanie slip out of his arms. "I can't remember," he teased. "I think it was some socks and underwear."

"No, *really*, Daddy—what did you buy for us?"

"Why don't you fellas bring my suitcase into the den, and we'll see."

While the boys lugged the suitcase, he and Stephanie followed, their arms around each other. Though he loved every room of their house, the den, with its pine-paneled walls, colorful hooked rug, wide fireplace, and cozy early American furniture, was Cliff's favorite. Stephanie had arranged a tray of cheese and crackers on the coffee table, and beside it stood a bottle of Lochan Ora and two cocktail glasses from the set they had bought on their last trip to Venice.

"Are you hungry?" she asked. "I'll fix you a roast beef sandwich."

"Not for food," he said, pulling her a little closer. "I ate on the plane." He sat down on the couch, and the boys placed the suitcase at his feet. While he opened it, Stephanie poured their drinks. "Funny," he said, removing the parcel from Findley's. "This doesn't smell like socks at all. They must have given me the wrong package."

"Fudge!" the boys cried, tearing open the boxes.

"Just what the dentist ordered," Stephanie said, laughing.

"Careful with that stuff," Cliff said as everyone reached for a piece. "It's addictive."

Stephanie cut off a slice with the little plastic knife that was enclosed in the box. "Yum!" she sighed, biting into it. "It's wicked. Thank heaven this place is in San Francisco and not around the corner. My figure would be shot in a week."

Cliff reached into the suitcase and distributed the kites, along with promises to help everyone with them. "Including you," he said, handing Stephanie hers. "Wait till you see this beauty against the sky."

"Maybe it will show you where there's a pot of gold," Jon said.

"You and your brothers are my pot of gold." Stephanie

hugged him, then took his hand. "Come on. It's way past your bedtime."

Cliff sank back on the sofa and sipped his drink contentedly. Home, with Stephanie and the kids—that was his pot of gold.

Later, when the children were asleep and they were in their own room, Cliff stretched out on the bed in his robe, watching Stephanie brush her long brown hair. She was wearing the vermilion silk kimono he had given her for Christmas, and his eyes followed in the mirror the tantalizing jiggle of her breasts as her arm stroked vigorously. Unable to resist any longer, he went over and put his arms around her from behind, his hands slipping inside the kimono to caress the luscious softness.

Putting the brush down, she leaned back and nestled her head against him. Their eyes met in the mirror, and her lips telegraphed a kiss. "I'm so glad you're back," she said.

"So am I. I missed you like hell." He kissed her cheek, then straightened up and reached into his pocket. "I have something for you."

She swung around on the bench to face him. "But you already gave me a rainbow kite. What more could a girl ask?"

"Well, if you don't want it…" he teased.

Laughing, she held out her hand. "I said I couldn't ask for more. That doesn't mean I won't take more. What is it—a model airplane?"

"Actually, I was going to get you the Golden Gate Bridge, but I wasn't sure what you'd do with it."

"Wear it as a tiara, of course. Though it might be a little awkward getting through narrow doorways."

"My thought exactly. So I bought you this instead." He handed her his purchase from the Pearl Empire.

As she always did, she removed the paper carefully and slowly, relishing every second. When she finally opened the box, her eyes sparkled as brightly as the gold of the bracelet. "Oh, Cliff! It's beautiful," she cried. She held out her hand and he fastened the bracelet around her wrist, then he drew her to her feet.

"*You're* beautiful," he said, taking her in his arms. Their lips met in a long, dizzying kiss. When it ended, he unfastened her kimono, and she let it drop to the floor. Then she reached out and unfastened his robe. For a moment they stood there gazing at each other. Finally, she slipped her hand into his and they walked over to the bed. Side by side they lay there, kissing, caressing, exploring, stroking secret places, building their passion until it became an exquisite pain that was at last released and relieved in the joyful burst of consummation. Afterward, tenderly, gently, they brought each other back to earth again.

For a long time they lay in each other's arms, basking quietly in the warm afterglow of love. Then Stephanie propped herself on her elbow and looked down at him. "Tell me again that you love me," she said, a slight quaver in her voice.

He reached up and brushed her hair back from her face. "You know I love you."

"Sometimes," she said, "I get scared." She shrugged, unable to put her feelings into words. But he knew what she meant.

"Sometimes," he said, "we all get scared. It's a normal reaction to happiness. We're afraid it will be whisked away. But that can never happen to us. We'll always have each other. We'll always have our love." He pulled her down for a gentle kiss.

"Tell me again, anyway," she said, nestling her head on his chest contentedly.

"I love you," he whispered, stroking her hair. "I'll always love you…"

After Stephanie drifted off to sleep, Cliff lay awake for a long time, staring into the dark, stroking her hair, feeling the welcome pressure of her head on his chest. It was true: he would always love her; she would always be the best part of his life.

Chapter Seventeen

DINNER HAD BEEN delicious, from the caviar and *terrine de foie gras* through the light-as-air, cream-filled hazelnut roll. But then, Melanie reflected as she strolled with the other guests into the living room, Marietta's formal dinners were always nothing less than perfection. They were works of art planned and prepared by one of the best chefs in New York, served on Spode china by an impeccable staff, and complemented by vintage French wines in delicate Massena crystal stemware by Baccarat.

Except for Melanie and David Belmont, the guests had been limited to nine, all of whom owned or controlled a considerable amount of *Sizzle* stock. Melanie had been seated next to Ronald Bennett, her old trustee, now a Citibank vice president in charge of estate planning for the well-to-do who had no desire to dabble in business. It was her mission to convince him to sell the shares of *Sizzle* in their portfolios to Wylford Enterprises. He was a balding, paunchy man in his late fifties, with heavy-lidded eyes that may have given him a very sexy appearance twenty or thirty years ago but now simply made him look sleepy. Melanie kept in mind, however, that the eyes beneath those misleading lids were quick and astute, missing nothing. By the end of the meal, she knew her own agile mind still held his admiration, as it had through the years, and she was reasonably sure that, as a result, Wylford Enterprises would gain the shares he controlled, which added up to about four percent.

Across the table, looking suave and handsome in a tuxedo, David had been seated between Mrs. Bennett and Martha Asquith, the plump, silver-haired widow of Thomas Asquith, who had risen from hamburgers to hotels to insurance companies. Quiet and shy, Martha had none of her late husband's conviviality and adventurousness, but she did possess all of his stocks. David's assignment was to charm her shares of *Sizzle* into the Wylford camp.

Marietta, of course, charmed everyone. In her Givenchy hostess gown of sea-green crepe de chine with its long sleeves and high Victorian neckline, she looked sexy and alluring to the men and elegantly wholesome to their wives. The conversation around her was always stimulating and never lagged, and whenever her delightful laugh rang out, everyone smiled. She herself avoided all mention of business; she was simply giving an intimate dinner for friends. Her well-publicized activities were sufficient reminders of what was currently expected of those friends if they entertained hopes of being invited to future intimate dinners.

In the living room, Cuban cigars were available for the gentlemen, and brandy and cordials were served to all. Marietta walked among her guests, keeping the talk as bright and lively as the sparkle of her emeralds and diamonds every time she moved a hand to emphasize a point.

After a while, sure she wouldn't be missed, Melanie picked up her Irish Mist and slipped out to the roof garden. It was a cool April night, but her black silk gown had a matching jacket that protected her from the breeze. Too restless to sit down, she strolled through the garden, but found that not even the fragrance or the beauty of the blossoms soothed the strange stirrings within her. Perhaps she'd had too much wine. Or too much Ronald Bennett. Or too much of an evening surrounded by persons whom, for the most part, she didn't care for. She rested her arms on the brick wall and gazed out over the city. The skyscrapers in the distance looked like elaborate models fashioned for a pampered child's train set.

"We New Yorkers are a very chauvinistic lot. We never tire of looking at our city, do we?"

Her heartbeats seemed to skid, and she took a deep breath, willing them to become normal again. She hadn't been aware of David's presence until he spoke.

"Is it chauvinism or the kind of fascination that the monster held for Frankenstein?"

He shrugged. "Maybe a little of both. Or a lot. It's not like you to sound so cynical about the hub of the great world of business. Don't tell me you've had a change of heart."

She laughed. "Never. I guess I'm just a little out of sorts tonight."

"A touch of spring fever?"

"Maybe."

He leaned his elbows on the wall and looked out over the city too. "I don't blame you. No matter how charming our hostess and how delicious the dinner, it's much too beautiful a night to spend locked up with the likes of Ronald Bennett and Martha Asquith. What would you really like to be doing?"

"I hadn't thought about it." It was true. So much of her social life had revolved around business for so long that she wasn't sure what she would do, given a choice. "What about you? If you had your druthers, what would you be doing now?"

"What I'd really like is a stroll through Central Park, but since I'm not foolhardy enough for that, I'd opt for my second choice—a pepperoni pizza in my living room with the TV tuned to an old horror movie."

"Can you eat a whole pizza by yourself?"

"I hadn't intended to eat it by myself."

"Ah, a dream girl to go with the dream pizza. Did you have someone specific in mind?"

"I had someone very specific in mind."

Though she wanted to look away, her eyes seemed riveted to his. "Anyone I know?" Why did she find it so difficult to keep her voice casual?

For a moment, he studied her face. "You should know her," he said at last. "Unfortunately, I don't think you do."

His swift, sharp reply left her feeling bewildered and angry. Quickly, she changed the subject. "Did you enjoy your trip to San Francisco?"

"Not in the least. Do you think I enjoy playing the sycophant to the likes of Brent Allen and Laura Leslie?"

"Laura Leslie is a very beautiful woman. Most men wouldn't mind making love to her."

"I'm sorry that you haven't noticed yet that I'm not most

men," he said. "Anyway, I managed to extricate myself gracefully from the sexual tribute she seems to demand from every male who comes within ten feet. I told her she had always been my ideal, the perfect woman, a virginal goddess against whom I measured all other females, much to their detriment. Meeting her had been a dream come true. All I asked was one kiss to treasure for the rest of my days. With eyes bleared by whiskey and tears, she granted my request and assured me she'd deposit her shares with the Wylford bankers. I wish all these extracurricular jobs I've had to undertake for your boss could be discharged so easily and so well."

"It wasn't discharged so well. Laura Leslie turned her shares over to the Kendricks bank yesterday."

"Damn!" he said, shaking his head. "I was sure we had her shares in the bag. The next morning she sent me a photo of herself with a glowing inscription. When I called to thank her, she told me I was the first real gentleman she'd met in her life. She promised the stocks would be ours. I don't know what went wrong."

"Obviously, one of Kendricks's people followed you with a better offer—one that was made to Brent Allen too. His stocks have also moved over to their side."

"I guess I'm too much of an amateur at this kind of chicanery."

"Don't blame yourself. You've been at it only a little over a week. In that time, you've brought in a hell of a lot of shares from show biz people. The most urgent thing right now is that you hold on to that inside track with Louise Bailey."

"That's really important to you, isn't it?"

"It's important to us all."

His jaw tightened. "Maybe you'd like to give me a few pointers. I assume your trip to Amsterdam was more successful than my excursion to the Coast."

"It looks that way."

"Congratulations," he said, his tone far from felicitous.

Uncomfortable under his gaze, she forced herself to shrug casually and turned to look out over the city. In the awkward silence that followed, she could still feel his eyes on her.

"That's a nice gown," he said finally.

"Thank you," she said, pleased.

"But it should be worn by a woman twice your age," he went

on, taking the joy out of the compliment. "Why do you wear such drab colors, such plain designs? You should wear bright and interesting styles, like Marietta."

"Marietta was made for colorful, interesting clothes. I wasn't."

"You have a strange image of yourself. You're a very attractive woman and you've got something Marietta, with all her beauty, no longer has—youth. Don't let it slip away without making the most of it. Do something with your hair—have it cut and styled, wear bright colors. You could do so much more with what you've got. There's no reason why you should always shrink behind Marietta's shadow."

"And you think copying Marietta would be better?"

"Of course not. I'm not suggesting that you imitate her. I'm encouraging you to let loose and be yourself."

She glanced down at her gown. "Did it ever occur to you that I am being myself?"

"No. What has occurred to me is that you've never given yourself a chance to discover who you really are."

"I understand myself better than you think," she said, anger creeping into her voice. "What I don't understand is why you're always picking at me."

"If you really understood yourself, you'd know why."

She hated it when he looked at her that way, as though he could see inside her, read her thoughts. She wanted to tell him exactly what she thought of his arrogance. No, better simply to turn and walk away. But she couldn't bring herself to do either.

"So this is where you two have been hiding." Marietta's voice came from behind them, light, charming, and yet reproachful.

"Not hiding," David said as they both turned. "Just getting a little air."

"And enjoying a tête-à-tête while the guests you're supposed to be looking after are left unattended?"

"I was filling in David on Burt Dutton's progress in Dallas," Melanie said, wondering why she felt the need to make excuses.

"Lack of progress, you mean. I'm beginning to think that man's a complete phony."

"There's that real estate deal he's looking into," Melanie reminded her.

Marietta dismissed the real estate deal with a wave of her hand. "*Everybody's* involved in shady real estate deals." She turned to David. "Martha Asquith has been hinting that she'd like to leave. The poor dear is out way past her bedtime. She seems quite taken with you. When you see her home, I'm certain she'll invite you in. Be sure you accept her coffee—and whatever else she offers. Don't bungle her the way you did Laura Leslie."

"I didn't bungle Laura."

"I'm not interested in excuses."

"I wasn't about to offer one. If you'll excuse me, I'll see to Mrs. Asquith."

"The night is young," Marietta reminded him as he started toward the sliding doors. "When you've finished with Mrs. Asquith, look in on Mrs. Bailey. Every minute counts."

"You must think I'm Superman."

"Men who work for me have to be."

Flexing a bicep, he continued on his way.

"There was no need to come down on him so hard," Melanie said.

Marietta looked surprised. "Hard? You've seen me when I come down hard. We both know I was being a pussycat."

"Sure," Melanie said, making her right hand into a claw and sweeping it through the air. "A purrfect pussycat."

Laughing, they rejoined the party.

About an hour after David had left with a beaming Martha Asquith, the rest of the party called it a night too. Melanie accepted a ride home from Wallace Carlyle, a portly stockbroker of sixty-eight who fancied himself a ladies' man. Happily, he'd had too much to drink, and almost as soon as his chauffeur settled him in the Cadillac, he closed his eyes. With a sigh of relief, Melanie gave the chauffeur her address. By the time they reached it, Wallace was snoring gently, perhaps dreaming of past or future assignations.

Upstairs, she changed into a pair of silk pajamas and climbed into bed, not feeling the least bit sleepy. She turned on the television, but all the late movies seemed to be light romantic comedies from the fifties. Every time a love scene came on, she impatiently switched channels. Finally, she turned the TV off in disgust, telling herself she wasn't in the mood for comedies. She wasn't in the mood for sleep, either, and after tossing and turning awhile, she put on her bedside lamp and began to read an article on Swiss incorporation statutes in the *Harvard Law Review*. That did the trick. Before long she was nodding. The journal fell to the floor with a little plop that startled her awake just long enough to turn off her lamp and curl up under the covers before slipping into a deep sleep.

THE ALARM WAS ringing. Melanie reached for it, but it wouldn't turn off. Of course it wouldn't turn off. She didn't have an alarm clock; she was always awakened by music on her clock-radio. Sleepily, she looked at the illuminated digits. It was only three-thirty. What was making that damned buzzing sound? And then with a jolt of apprehension she realized that it must be the doorman ringing her on the intercom. She threw back the covers and jumped from the bed, tripping over the law journal on the floor. Her right knee throbbing, she scrambled to her feet and raced to the intercom in the foyer.

"Yes?" she said, her heart pounding. "What is it?"

"Sorry, Miss Danielle." The doorman's voice was hesitant, apologetic. "But there's a friend of yours here who insists on seeing you. I told him it was much too late, that you must be asleep, but he refuses to leave until I inform you he is here."

"Who is it, George?"

"He says his name is David Belmont." George lowered his voice. "He's pretty drunk, miss, but I think he'll go quietly when I tell him you want him to leave."

What in the world was David doing on her doorstep, drunk, at half past three in the morning? "No, it's all right, George. You can let him come up."

"Are you sure, Miss Danielle? I'd be happy to see him safely into a cab."

"He's not falling-down drunk, is he?"

"No, not that bad, but—"

"Just head him in the direction of the elevator then, George, and send him up."

"Well, okay. But if there's any trouble, ring down. I was a

bouncer in a bar once, and I know how to handle guys who get out of line."

"I'm sure that won't be necessary, George, but thank you." Melanie replaced the receiver, then looked down at her pajamas and bare feet. She hurried into the bedroom, pulled on her old terry robe and slipped on her scuffs. No sense dressing for company.

The bell, when it rang, sounded like an emergency alarm.

"Oh, for crying out loud!" Melanie muttered, and rushed to open the door.

David stood slumped against the doorpost, his jacket open, his black bow tie askew, his eyes bleary. He gave her a silly, drunken smile. In his left hand he held an unwrapped bottle of champagne. "I was right," he said. "I told old What's-his-name you'd be up."

"If you don't stop leaning on my doorbell, you'll have the entire floor up."

"Oh. Sorry." Looking surprised to find his right hand still on her bell, he removed it, then staggered back a bit.

Melanie took his arm and pulled him inside, closing and locking the door behind him. "And you were wrong: I was asleep—the doorman woke me when he rang the intercom. Didn't anyone ever tell you that three-thirty in the morning is a hell of a time to drop in on people?"

He waved the bottle of champagne expansively. "Never too early or too late to party. Had a very productive evening. Very productive. Two women are eating right out of the palm of my hand. After I left Louise, I stopped off in a bar near her place to celebrate. Then I said to myself: 'David, old man, it's selfish to make merry all by yourself. Melanie will be so proud of your progress. It's only fair to let her celebrate too.' So I bought this bottle from the bartender and took a cab straight here." He looked around. "Where are your glasses? We need glasses for our celebration."

There was no trace of high spirits in his tone, and his eyes were dark and brooding. His words didn't fool her; he had been drinking to eradicate the evening's events, not to exalt them.

"We need cups, not glasses," she said, taking the bottle from him and leading the way to her kitchen. "Follow me."

In the kitchen, she put the champagne into her refrigerator and closed the door on it firmly.

"Want champagne," David said, slumping down in a chair at the little table.

"You'll get black coffee and like it," she told him, putting the kettle on to boil. She sat down opposite him. "Now, what are we celebrating?"

"The fact that I'm irresistible," he said. "Old women want to mother me—and middle-aged ones want to marry me."

So that was it. Louise Bailey wanted more than sex and sympathy in return for her share of the company.

"That *is* something to be pleased about," she said, pretending not to notice the self-disgust in his eyes. "And I'm sure it's nothing you can't handle."

"Sure, I can handle it. I've had a quickie course in the Marietta Wylford School of Business. Poor old Martha doesn't lean too much toward the incestuous in her motherly feelings—a few kisses and fond pats on the derriere will keep her happy. She's calling her stockbroker Monday morning. Then I'm to report to her place for an intimate lunch to celebrate the transaction. And as for Louise—well, if she's falling in love with me, that's her own lookout. All I have to do is keep lying to her until she does what we want. Right?"

Melanie looked away from the misery in his eyes. "Right," she said brightly.

"Sure. Who told her to go and fall in love? Woman of her age should know better than to trust a guy like me." His attempt to sound belligerent was pathetic. Unsteadily, he rose to his feet. "I'm going to go back and tell her that. Set her straight about the whole thing."

"No," Melanie said firmly, turning off the jet beneath the now-whistling kettle. "You're going to sit down and have some coffee. It'll make you feel better."

"Feel fine," David insisted, taking a step and lurching against the refrigerator, making its contents rattle. "Got to see Louise. Got to tell her not to fall in love with me. Know what it's like to love someone who can't love you back. Got to tell her..." His voice trailed off, and his eyes focused on Melanie in her old robe and slippers, her hair tangled from sleep. "How come you're in your robe?"

"I was asleep when you came. I told you, remember?"

He blinked. "Oh. Shouldn't have made you get up. Sorry. You go back to bed. I'm going to see Louise." He staggered toward the kitchen doorway.

"Wait." She had to think of some way to stop him. "You look tired. Why don't you lie down for a few minutes? Then you'll feel fresh and rested when you go to see Louise."

He thought it over for a few seconds, then raised his hand, index finger pointed toward the ceiling. "Good idea. Just for a few minutes, though."

"Absolutely. Just for a few minutes. Come on." She preceded him out of the kitchen and started toward her bedroom because he was too tall for her sofa. Suddenly sensing that she had made the short trip down the hall alone, she turned and saw him clinging to the kitchen door frame.

"Your floors are tilting," he said.

"I'll have them fixed first thing in the morning," she assured him, returning to his side. "Now, come on." She slipped her left arm around his waist and pulled his right arm over her shoulder. He leaned on her all the way to her room, but it felt good.

After helping him shrug out of his jacket, she gave him a gentle push, and he sat down on the bed. She squatted down to remove his shoes.

"You look very pretty," he said. "You should have worn that outfit tonight instead of your grim black dress."

She laughed as she looked up at him. "Can you imagine anyone going to one of Marietta's parties in a ratty old robe?"

With a shaky hand he reached out and touched her cheek. "You look very pretty when you laugh too."

His touch was warm and gentle, and she had to fight the urge to grasp his hand and press it even closer. But she knew that the tenderness in his eyes was inspired only by alcohol. Quickly, she got to her feet. "Lie down." Her tone was more abrupt than she had intended it to be.

He looked around, as though realizing for the first time that he was in her bedroom, sitting on her bed. "Are you coming to bed too?"

"Not with you, I'm not. I think you've had quite enough women for one evening, don't you?"

"Marietta says I have to be Superman. Do you want to sleep with Superman?"

"Not when he's drunk, thank you."

He looked around again and made an unsuccessful effort to stand. "Shouldn't stay here. Should go home."

"Don't be ridiculous. You're in no condition to get yourself home. Lie down."

"Guess it's okay. I mean, with me playing kissy-kissy with the stepmother and you the stepson, that makes us practically related, doesn't it?" The hurt and anger were back in his eyes.

"You're very drunk," she said, trying not to show how his tone cut through her. "Lie down."

With a shrug, he obeyed, saying, "Just for a few minutes."

He passed out the second his head hit the pillow.

For a moment, Melanie stood there looking down at him. She had been so strong until he had come into her life. Did he have any idea what happened inside her every time he made one of his biting comments or casual compliments? God, she must be getting soft in the head.

She opened his tie and collar. She knew nothing would happen if she stretched out beside him. But that thought depressed her even more than the thought of his making drunken love to her simply because she was a body and she was there. She took a pillow and blanket from the closet and turned out the light.

In the living room, she curled up on the sofa, willing herself to go to sleep and forget that David was in the next room. But her whole body tingled with the knowledge of his nearness.

AWAKENED BY THE delicious aroma of coffee, Melanie sat up on the sofa and looked around in confusion. Then she remembered David's unexpected visit the night before. She pulled on her robe and padded out to the kitchen. While coffee perked on the stove, David stood at the counter, a dish towel tucked into the waistband of his trousers, surrounded by the ingredients for pancakes, which he was mixing in a large bowl. His stiff white dress shirt was rolled up at the sleeves and open at the throat, his hair was damp, and there were two scratches on his face where he must have nicked himself with her Gillette Daisy. He turned and gave her a sheepish smile.

"Good morning. Since I had the gall to force the rather questionable pleasure of my company on you last night, I decided to go whole hog and avail myself of your shower and your razor." He nodded toward the bowl. "It's not much, but I hope I can make some amends with my sour-milk pancakes."

Melanie smiled. "I'm amazed you could find the ingredients. I love to cook, but rarely have a chance to. Do I have time for a shower?"

"Sure. Just give a holler when you're almost ready."

She showered and pulled on a pair of jeans and her old Barnard sweatshirt. About to head for the kitchen, she turned back and added a touch of mascara and a little lip gloss.

"In that getup, you don't look old enough for college," David said, handing her a plate piled high with golden-brown pancakes.

"This is the best breakfast I've had in years," she told him through a delicious mouthful.

"It seemed the least I could do after barging in on you and making an ass of myself. Thanks not only for putting up with me but also for putting me up." Looking mock serious, he placed his hand on top of his head. "The pounding inside my skull gives me some idea of how drunk I was last night. What happened isn't exactly as clear as crystal, but I remember enough to know that you didn't take advantage of my condition and compromise my virtue."

"I hope, sir," she said, adopting the same tone and making a mock bow, "that you are suitably impressed."

"Gravely disappointed might be a better description of my feelings."

They both laughed, but Melanie found herself wishing that it wasn't just a gallant joke.

Conversation remained light during breakfast, but when they moved into the living room with second cups of coffee, the talk became more serious.

"I owe you an apology for my conduct last night," David said. "At the risk of sounding like a professional virgin—I don't usually do things like that."

"I'm aware of that, which is why I let you come up. You seem to have had quite a night after leaving Marietta's."

"A nightmare of a night. I don't have much stomach for playing a corporate Casanova to women I care nothing about. I've managed so far for the sake of our great cause, but last night Louise said something about getting married, and I don't think it was just the liquor talking." He shook his head, his eyes darkening. "She'll be hurt when this is over. I hadn't counted on that. It isn't fair to her. She's been through enough."

With all her heart, Melanie wished she could tell him to break off the affair, but she couldn't be so disloyal to Marietta. Too much was riding on what happened between Louise Bailey and David. When she remained silent, David got up and went to the window.

"I've got to stop seeing her," he said, staring down at the street.

"You can't do that. Walking out on Louise would be walking out on everything we've been working so hard to achieve."

He turned around to face her. "It might be the smartest walk I ever took."

"More likely the dumbest." She got up and joined him. "David, Louise Bailey is fantasizing when she says she's in love with you. She's an alcoholic who loves only herself and her bottle. She's setting herself up for you to leave her, so that when you do, she'll have one more excuse to turn to drink."

"Are you sure of that?"

No, she wasn't sure. What she was sure of was that she didn't want David to wreck Marietta's hopes or his own career. "Yes," she said, her eyes never leaving his. "I am. There's too much at stake, David. We can't stop now. In less than two weeks, this will all be over, and if things go well, we will have won. Then you can go back to being the editor of the hottest property in the country and never have to worry about being connected with this end of the business again."

"And you?"

She shrugged. "I'll go on helping Marietta collect more businesses and run the ones she has."

"And doing the things that, as Marietta would put it, 'have to be done'?"

She nodded, wishing he wouldn't look at her that way. It made her feel so full of doubts about matters she rarely permitted herself to question.

"You slept with Mark Bailey for his stock, didn't you?"

"No, I didn't." It was strange, how pleased she was to be able to say that without averting her eyes. But then she became uncomfortable under his gaze, and she knew that she couldn't leave it at such a half truth. She turned away and stared down at the street. "I didn't sleep with Mark Bailey, but I pimped for him."

"And you hated it as much as I hate what I'm doing, didn't you?"

She shrugged.

Gently, he turned her toward him. "Why are we letting Marietta do this to us?"

"You're reading too much into it, David. It's business, pure and simple. It's as necessary a part of the corporate scene as Xerox machines and computers. And we're doing it because we want what Marietta wants. Maybe not on as large a scale, but we want it nevertheless. And for you there's the added incentive of knowing that if we win, you'll not only keep your position, but be able to retain your editorial integrity and independence. That makes it all worthwhile, doesn't it?"

With a sigh, he dropped his hands to his sides. "Yes, I suppose it does."

But from the look in his eyes, she knew that for him the end would never entirely justify the means. Still, she had brought his thinking back along positive lines. It was time to change the subject. She gave him a bright smile. "I almost forgot—I bought you a present while I was in Amsterdam. I'll be right back."

She went into her bedroom and dug the box out of her drawer. Returning to the living room, she found him still at the window.

He took the pipe from the box and held it up to the light, then squinted into the stem and balanced it in his hand. "It's a beauty," he said, running his fingers over the bowl. "Thank you. I'm really touched."

She could tell he meant it, and she suddenly felt embarrassed, almost tongue-tied. "I'm glad you like it."

"Why did you do it?" He asked the question softly, studying her face in that maddening way he had, as though he were trying to read her innermost thoughts.

"Just a wild flight of impetuosity. When I passed the store, I thought of you and couldn't resist going in."

"I like that," he said.

"That I'm given to wild flights of impetuosity?"

"No—that you thought of me."

They were standing so close that she could see a tiny scar just below his lower lip. She had never noticed it before. She wondered if he had gotten it in a fight as a child. No, he'd probably gotten it breaking up a fight. She longed to reach up and touch it. Even more, she longed to reach up and touch his lips. They looked so firm, so smooth. What would it feel like to have them pressed against hers? Maybe if she gave the right signal, he would kiss her. Or maybe he would pretend not to notice. After all, there was that woman he had mentioned last night. Better to shift her position, move back, not give out any signals that might be studiously ignored. Why leave herself wide open only to be repulsed? Besides, she was beginning to suspect that what she wanted from David Belmont was a great deal more than a kiss or even one wild, tumultuous bout in bed. It was a terrifying thought.

With a shrug and a laugh of dismissal, she stepped back. "Of course I thought of you," she said lightly. "It's only natural to think of a business acquaintance when one's on a business trip, isn't it?"

"Only natural," David agreed. A shade seemed to slip down behind his eyes and his tone became more formal. He put the pipe back into its box. "Did you get any sightseeing in?"

He said the words as though he were passing the time of day with a stranger, and a chill slipped through her.

She wondered if she had imagined the warmth they had seemed to share earlier. Copying his cool detachment, she began telling him about a few of the sights she had seen. For some reason, she couldn't bring herself to mention the two places he had especially recommended and which had moved her most—Our Lady in the Attic and the Anne Frank House. When the phone interrupted her reminiscences, she wanted to kiss the caller.

It was Marietta. She was leaving for Paris late tomorrow, and she had some last-minute chores for Melanie. They were on the phone for almost fifteen minutes.

When Melanie hung up, she found that David had tidied the kitchen and was ready to leave. He was standing at her door in his jacket, the pipe box sticking out of its pocket.

"Thanks again for last night," he said. "I'm sorry I put you out of your bed."

"No problem." As she walked him to the elevator, she tried unsuccessfully to recapture some of their earlier warmth. Damn it, what had happened? Why had he come to her if he disliked her so much?

"Well, so long," he said when the elevator arrived. "I promise—no more middle-of-the-night crying jags."

"Just one question," Melanie said. "Not that I minded in the least, but why did you come to me with your woes? Shouldn't you have gone to your pepperoni pizza girl?"

"I thought I had," he said. "I guess I was wrong."

The elevator door closed, and Melanie was left standing alone in the hallway.

Chapter Eighteen

AS FAR AS MARIETTA was concerned, nothing could compare with the luxury of flying to Paris first class on Air France. It was like being in a fine hotel that had gently detached itself from the earth and begun to float without allowing a drop of Dom Perignon to splash out of a single guest's glass. Naturally, she had arranged to be met at the airport by a Cadillac rented from Bernard Durant *et Cie.* As always, she had requested Jean Larre to be behind its wheel. Jean, a silver-haired man in his fifties with the fine looks of an aging matinee idol and the exquisite manners of a diplomat, was fluent in five languages and had been chauffeuring her around Paris ever since her first trip with Harlan.

"*Bienvenu,* Mme. Wylford," Jean said with a little bow. "How good it is to see you again." He held the door for her while she climbed into the car, then placed her Bottega Veneta luggage in the trunk. "The Ritz, as usual?" he asked, taking his seat.

"As usual," Marietta said, leaning her head back against the plush upholstery. She had left New York at seven p.m. on Monday and it was now seven a.m. Tuesday in Paris. Unable to sleep on the plane, she was suddenly very tired. She didn't realize that she had dozed off until she heard Jean saying, "We have arrived, madame."

Opening her eyes, she found herself in the magnificent Place Vendôme. Though the sun was shining, it had rained during the night, and the sidewalks and eighteenth-century limestone houses with their sloping roofs had a freshly washed look. Like its neighbors in the elegant octagon, the Ritz had been designed to look impressive in all kinds of weather, and the Rollses, Cadillacs,

Bentleys, and Ferraris pulled up before its entrance seemed no more than interchangeable medals on a sash of honor.

After informing Jean that she would require his services again at noon, Marietta crossed the carpet of the lobby whose gilt and satin chaises had comforted the derrieres of royalty, aristocrats, and just plain ordinary millionaires, and registered at the desk. Everyone knew her by name, of course, and she was quickly shown to her favorite suite.

A restful nap and stimulating shower later, she was dressed in a black Givenchy pants suit and soft white silk blouse with romantic, almost demure, lace ruffles at the end of its long sleeves and around its high, yoked neckline. She limited her jewelry to a pearl and emerald ring she hadn't been able to resist the last time she was in Harry Winston's and a pair of pearl earrings one of her lovers had given to her for Christmas. She had planned to drop in casually on Craig's film set, but a call to the production company elicited that background footage was being shot and Craig was not on call for the next few days. At first she considered that a setback. Then she realized it might be an advantage: She could have Craig all to herself for a few days—time enough to win his stock options. Time enough, perhaps, to win even more than that. If only he hadn't decided to spend his break from filming away from Paris....

Before leaving New York, she had ascertained that Craig was staying at the Lancaster, alone; his wife almost always remained home with the children when he was on location. A quick phone call confirmed that he was in. No, she told the clerk, she did not wish to be connected to his suite.

A final inspection before a full-length mirror revealed what she already knew—that she looked smashing. The flush on her cheeks, however, was not entirely thanks to her cosmetologist behind Elizabeth Arden's Red Door. Her fingers trembling a little, she applied a few additional drops of Opium behind her ears and to the pulse points on her temples and throat. Then, her heart pounding and her mind whispering, *Let him still be in...* she picked up her Hermes shoulder strap purse and hurried out of her suite.

Despite the frustrations of Paris traffic, Jean delivered her to the Lancaster in no time at all. Unlike the Ritz, which was in the middle of perhaps the most beautiful square in Paris, the Lancaster was on the Rue de Berri, an unpretentious little street just off the Champs-Elysêes, the perfect place to hide away a luxury hotel for millionaires and celebrities who prefer privacy to limelight. Because the management always guarded that privacy tenaciously, Marietta was not permitted to present herself at Monsieur Campbell's door unannounced. After the desk clerk had made the necessary phone call, she was told she might go up; Monsieur Campbell was staying in number seventy-two, the penthouse suite.

Not until she had emerged from the elevator and had begun climbing the flight of stairs to the penthouse did Marietta admit to herself that there had been a moment in the lobby when she had held her breath, actually afraid Craig would refuse to see her. It was an unprecedented slip of self-confidence, and she was glad to shake free of it.

Craig was waiting for her at the door. As filled with anticipation as she had been about their meeting, she wasn't completely prepared for the sweet, sensuous ache that shot from the back of her throat down to her groin at the sight of him. Of course, she had known from his movies and his photographs in magazines and newspapers that the years had been kind to him; the boyish good looks had matured into a strong, rugged handsomeness, and his body had remained muscular and trim. Still, seeing him framed in the doorway in his gray flannel slacks and blue turtleneck shirt was very different from the one-dimensional images she was used to. She was aware that the years had worked the same magic on her, but if he was as moved by her appearance as she was by his, his face gave no sign of it. He did smile, though. Not a warm, hearty smile of welcome—just a polite upturning of the lips.

"This is a surprise," he said, giving no hint by his tone whether he meant a pleasant one or otherwise.

"I just arrived in Paris, heard you were here, and decided to take you to lunch," she said, as though it had been weeks, not nearly two decades, since their previous meeting.

He stepped aside so that she could enter. "That's very nice. But didn't it occur to you that I might have plans?"

"None you couldn't break for a very old friend. I've reserved a table at Ledoyen."

"That's pretty tempting."

"I was hoping *I'd* be."

At last the smile reached his eyes. "That, too," he said. "Can I get you a drink?"

"Dubonnet would be nice if you have it."

"Like a Boy Scout, I'm prepared for almost everyone's tastes." He went over to the bar and poured her drink. For himself, he opened a bottle of Perrier and poured it over ice. "Cheers."

"To old friends," she toasted.

He nodded, but didn't repeat the words. "Excuse me for a minute. I have to phone someone. Make yourself comfortable."

While Craig was on the telephone in the other room, Marietta looked around. The suite was elegantly furnished with antiques and beautiful paintings. There were mirrored screens and a wood-burning fireplace, and a terrace overlooked a lovely courtyard garden. An open screenplay lay on a table near one of the overstuffed velvet chairs, and Marietta realized that she had probably interrupted Craig in the studying of his lines or the examination of a future role.

On the table near a vase of flowers stood a silver-framed photograph of a wholesome-looking blonde in her mid-thirties and three children ranging in age from about six through ten and all bearing a striking resemblance to Craig. A shadow fell over the picture, and she realized that Craig had come up behind her.

"Lovely family," she said automatically, turning to look at him.

His eyes, on the photograph, were filled with love. "I have a wonderful wife and three great kids." He looked at her. "Do you have any children?"

She shook her head.

"No, I didn't think you would have."

She wasn't about to walk into that one. Instead, she nodded toward the flowers and changed the subject: "A bouquet from one of your admirers?"

He laughed. "I don't know whether they're fans, but the management here delivers fresh-cut flowers to every guest daily. Would you like to pin one on your jacket?"

She shook her head. "No, thanks. I wouldn't want to mar the lovely arrangement." Actually, she didn't want a flower on her lapel to detract from the total effect she had worked so hard to achieve when she was dressing. She finished her drink. "My car's waiting. Shall we go?"

"Why not?" He had already put on a blue cashmere jacket that had a decidedly custom-made fit.

AT THE LEDOYEN, the foyer was dominated by a grand staircase that must have been designed for the dramatic entrances of beautiful women in shimmering gowns and glittering jewels. It had always seemed to Marietta that the lovers from *La Traviata* would have felt quite at home singing "Un Di, Felice, Eterea" among the brocaded silk armchairs, candelabra, red satin table linens beneath white lace overlays, vermeil tableware, and bowls of fresh flowers.

Marietta and Craig were seated at a table with an excellent view of the garden and its fountains, flower borders, willows, and chestnut trees. Their wine was poured into crystal glasses, their courses dispensed from Louis XV serving carts. In such an atmosphere, it was difficult not to be warm and cordial, and Marietta sensed Craig's reserve yielding a little with every sip of wine and every bite of *les rognons flambés*.

She kept the conversation sprightly and flowing, and saw to it that they spoke a great deal about Craig's career and not at all about hers, and she managed to keep the talk from touching upon his wife and children. By the time they were savoring their *crêpes soufflées flambées au Cointreau* and sipping their demitasse, the years seemed to have slipped away, and they were once again sharing special looks and laughter.

Before they left, Marietta put down her lace-edged napkin and turned for a last look at the garden. Craig's gaze followed hers, and he said:

"Everything they say about April in Paris is true, isn't it?"

"Suddenly I have a terrific yen for more chestnuts in blossom. Let's take a walk in the Bois de Boulogne."

Craig smiled indulgently. "Sounds like a pleasant way to work off some of our excess calories."

It had been ages since Marietta had been in the Bois. For years, Paris trips for her had meant board meetings and boutiques by day and café society by night, but her intuition told her that a stroll together through the park might awaken in Craig's mind fond memories of similar strolls through Central Park. Perhaps it did; he seemed even more relaxed and happy in the sun-dappled woods than he had been in the restaurant. It was his idea to hire a horse-drawn carriage so that they could view in style the lakes and waterfalls and the charming Parc de Bagatelle with its little castle that was built in sixty-four days for Charles X on a bet, and its lovely gardens ablaze with tulips, hyacinths, and narcissi. As they passed the nearby children's playground, Craig turned to Marietta and asked, "Have you ever been to the Jardin d'Acclimation?"

She shook her head.

"You don't know what you've been missing," he said, and he told the driver in perfect French to take them there.

Marietta had expected—or hoped—that they were heading for romantic gardens where he would suggest a stroll beneath shady trees beside a sparkling lake, and she was surprised and disappointed when the driver reined his horse before the entrance to a combination children's zoo and amusement park.

Craig paid the driver and helped her from the carriage. "You're going to love this," he said.

She doubted that very much.

She was wrong. The Jardin d'Acclimation was designed to charm both child and adult alike. Perhaps adults enjoyed it most of all, for the true joys of childhood, like so many of life's delights, are never really appreciated until they are forever lost. Marietta and Craig watched children clambering over logs and whimsical structures just made for climbing, and listened to them shouting with joy atop ponies and pint-sized rides. They paddled a boat across a clear lagoon, complete with mill and working water wheel. They laughed in the house of funny mirrors, tried their luck on the archery range and at miniature golf, ate warm waffles, and fed the animals. The puppet theater was closed, but they watched the dolphins perform at five. Marietta couldn't remember when she'd had so much fun. Or perhaps she could: seventeen years before, bundled up against the cold, strolling hand in hand with Craig, tasting New York City's delights.

Later, Craig whisked her in a cab to the Porte Dauphine at the end of the Avenue Foch. "You've never seen Paris until you've seen this," he said, and gestured toward the Place d'Étoile, painted gold and pink in the light of the setting sun.

Marietta caught her breath at the spectacle. "It's beautiful!" she said. But even as the words were leaving her mouth, even as her eyes continued to take in the scene before her, she was aware of a subtle change in Craig. He was no longer gazing in awe at the Étoile. He was looking at her; she could feel it. And she could feel, too, that if she turned to look at him, she would find the awe still in his eyes, but directed toward her. Sunsets enhanced her charms, silhouetting her fine profile and voluptuous figure, deepening the coppery tone of her hair. Slowly, her heart pounding, she turned to him. She was right. In his eyes she saw the same desire that had been there seventeen years before.

"I don't want this day to end," she said.

He didn't kiss her, as she had hoped he would, but his gaze slipped down and caressed her lips, then returned to meet hers. "Neither do I," he said huskily. "I'll pick you up for dinner at eight-thirty."

Though they neither spoke nor touched as they left the park, Marietta wasn't offended or concerned. For she knew that Craig's thoughts were of her.

Back at the Ritz, Marietta informed the concierge that she would probably be retaining her suite through the weekend. Time was running out in her fight for *Sizzle*, but she knew that she could depend on Melanie to take care of everything in her absence. She had come to Paris to get the option on Craig's stock, hoping, perhaps, for a little more. Now she was hoping for a great deal more. All through the years she had managed to hide from herself how much Craig had continued to mean to her. One afternoon with him had changed all that. She wanted him back. Not just for a night or a week or a month, but forever. And she would have him. He was there for the taking—she had seen it in his eyes as he had looked at her bathed in the golden light of the setting sun.

Curled up on her bed like a contented cat, she telephoned Melanie in New York to tell her of her change in plans.

"Is Craig giving you a hard time?" Melanie asked.

"On the contrary," Marietta said, practically purring. "Everything you've heard about the magic of April in Paris is true."

"I have a suspicion it's more like the magic of Marietta Wylford."

Marietta laughed and changed the subject. "What's happening on the home front?"

"Little Miss Hot Pants is having so much fun that she hasn't been able to drag herself from Mark Bailey's bed. I called her doting mama and told her that her daughter can screw Bailey as long as she likes, but if she screws us in the process, there'll be no publicity in *Sizzle*. Mama took off like a shot for Amsterdam, promising to be back soon with the papers. Alfred Bonner came through with the shares he controls, but it looks like we've lost Rosner and Goodwin to Kendricks."

"Ralph Goodwin is a bastard. He and Kendricks deserve each other. What else?"

"We got a report and a bill from Burt Dutton. Aside from that real estate deal, all he's been able to find in Dallas is evidence of some strong-arm union-busting techniques at Kendricks's newspaper, none of which, of course, can be traced back to Kendricks himself. Even if it could be, Kendricks wouldn't blink an eye, so it sure as hell wouldn't embarrass him into pulling out of the running for *Sizzle*. Dutton is sure that Bailey named another city, not Dallas, and you misunderstood."

"There's nothing wrong with my ears—just with Dutton's competence. Pay him and tell him he's off the case."

"There's a problem with the bill, Mari. Dutton has listed an additional four thousand dollars under the heading 'personal services.' When I questioned him about it, he said to ask you."

Marietta's cheeks burned, and her knuckles turned white as she grasped the receiver as tightly as she longed to wring Burt Dutton's neck. But her voice was cool and controlled as she said, "Pay it—and let him be damned." She took a long, steadying breath. "We'll find Philip's information without that bastard's help. I want you and David to keep going over everything. Somewhere there's bound to be a clue."

Marietta hung up and stretched out on the bed, but it was impossible to rest. Not that she allowed thoughts of Burt Dutton's slimy behavior to disturb her. It was just that she couldn't keep her mind from reliving every moment of the afternoon with Craig. Finally, she gave up on the idea of a nap and relaxed in a warm perfumed bath.

By the time she stepped out of the marble tub, Marietta had their future completely planned: Her business and Craig's career would make it impossible for them to be together all the time, but in addition to her Sutton Place penthouse and summer home in the Hamptons, she had her apartment in London, and if he wanted to give his California ranch to his wife as part of a divorce settlement, they could buy another place on the Coast. Of course, there were fine hotels all over the world too. They'd find plenty of opportunities to be together. Maybe after everything was settled with *Sizzle* she should look into buying a film production company....

After applying precious drops of Chanel to all the strategic places, she slipped into a royal-blue silk crepe Oscar de la Renta gown that left one shoulder bare and ended in an intriguing draped knot over the other. She chose sapphires and diamonds, of course, to complement it. As she was stepping into her silver Gucci sandals, it occurred to her that if she was to remain in Paris a few more days, she would need more clothes than she had brought along. Tomorrow morning she would drop in at Dior's.

At precisely eight-thirty Craig arrived and escorted her to his own chauffeured Mercedes. In the car, on their way to La Tour d'Argent on the Left Bank, he delicately touched the sapphire pendant that gleamed at her throat. "You really don't need that," he said. "You look like a jewel yourself."

At the restaurant, Claude Terrail, wearing the omnipresent cornflower in his buttonhole, greeted them cordially and informed Craig that he had succeeded in reserving the King's table for him. First, though, they had the obligatory predinner drink in the Petit Salon de la Gastronomique, famous for its eighteenth-century-carriage phone booth, the vermeil plates and silverware which Napoleon III bestowed upon Cora Pearl, his beautiful English mistress, and other gastronomical memorabilia. After all, as Craig said with a smile, what better place for a museum devoted to gourmanderie than a restaurant that has been serving royalty since 1582?

Later, they were ushered to the choicest window table in the dining room. There, looking out over the Seine to the flood-lit apse of Notre-Dame and the sparkling lights of Paris, they studied the sterling-silver-plated menus. Marietta started the meal with *potage* Claude Burdel, and then, from the twenty-five delectable duck entrées, decided to stay with her old favorite, *caneton Tour d'Argent.* During their dinner they drank an 1865 Chambertin, and they ended their meal with the wickedly delicious *poires en soufflé charpini.*

Craig smiled and shook his head when they were presented with their certificate, bearing their duck's exclusive number and a description of its pedigree. "Would you have believed seventeen years ago that one night we'd be sitting in one of the world's finest and most expensive restaurants?"

Actually, seventeen years before, Marietta had strongly believed that one day she would eat in all the world's finest restaurants—it was what she had worked so hard to achieve. What she had not foreseen was that one day Craig would be able to take her as his guest. She didn't say any of that, of course. She simply smiled in answer.

His eyes grew wistful. "How I longed to give you the best back then."

"And now your wish has finally come true, hasn't it?" she asked softly.

He didn't answer, but his blue eyes studied her face in a way that thrilled and yet disquieted her.

It was almost midnight when they left the restaurant, the hour when after-dark Paris is just coming alive. Much too early to call it a night, they agreed. Craig told his driver to take them to Castel's.

Only the cognoscenti know how to pick out Castel's on the Rue Princesse, for there is no sign or marking to distinguish it from the other buildings on the dim, rather nondescript street.

But that, of course, was exactly how Jean Castel wanted it. As always, Jean was seated at his little table near the gleaming aluminum bar, bathed in the soft light from the art nouveau lamps. He chatted with Craig in French about the movie he was making, and with Marietta about the weather back in New York. The other three tables were already filled with Jean's friends, but Marietta and Craig hadn't intended to stay in the bar. Their destination was the *cave*, with its warm, provincial atmosphere and dancing to records. They were given a choice table near the dancing area, just to the right of the door, and they ordered drinks and sat in a comfortable silence, watching the couples on the floor.

"I hope you're going to ask me to dance," Marietta said finally.

"It's pretty crowded. You might get crushed."

"I don't crush easily." She stood up.

He rose too. "I should have remembered that." His smile softened the words.

At the edge of the dance floor, she turned and waited for him to take her hand and slip his arm around her waist. It was the first time he had touched her that day, and she shivered with pleasure, feeling as though his flesh was searing hers.

As the night wore on, they danced several times, and each time Marietta managed to get him to hold her just a little closer. Finally, she rested her cheek against his chest.

"Tired?" he whispered, his lips brushing her hair as they formed the word.

She would never tire of being held that way, but she longed to get him alone. She nodded. "I think jet lag is finally catching up with me."

"I'm amazed it hasn't before now. It's time I got you back to your hotel."

On the drive back she rested her head on his shoulder, pretending to sleep, but feeling deliciously aware of every sensation pulsating through her body. As the chauffeur turned into the Place Vendôme, she raised her head and looked at Craig.

"This afternoon, I said I didn't want the day to end. Now I don't want the night to end. Come up to my suite."

"I don't think that would be such a good idea."

His voice throbbed with yearning, but she didn't like the

married-man look that had suddenly come over his face. Alone in her suite with the lights turned down, she knew she could make it disappear.

"I think," she said, touching his cheek, "that it's the best idea I've had all evening."

He didn't answer, but his hand reached up and covered hers. And when the car stopped and the doorman was helping her out, he leaned over and said a few words to the chauffeur before following her inside.

The radio in her suite played in four different languages, but she switched it on to soft music, which speaks in every tongue.

"Call room service for a bottle of Mums, will you?" she said, heading toward the bedroom. "I have to get out of these shoes."

It was a great deal more than her shoes she got out of when she closed the door behind her. All she was wearing when she reopened it was a gold-embroidered emerald-green silk kimono, gold mules, and a fresh application of perfume.

The champagne had arrived, been uncorked and poured. Craig was standing at the window, and in his tuxedo, his fine features outlined in the soft lamplight, surrounded by Louis XV decor, he looked completely at home. Hearing her enter, he turned, and she heard him catch his breath at the sight of her.

"I thought I might just as well get comfortable while I was at it." She tried to sound offhand and casual.

"I was afraid you might be doing something like that."

"Afraid?" She walked over and slipped her arms around his neck. The soft strains of "Petite Fleur" were coming from the radio. "Dance with me."

He put his hands on her waist and looked down into her eyes. "Do you know what you're doing to me?"

"I know what I hope I'm doing to you," she said, tightening her arms around him and swaying to the music. "Dance with me."

He didn't dance with her. He kissed her instead.

It was as though she had suddenly been caught in a gigantic whirlpool that sent her swirling slowly downward. First her brain was caught in it, then her throat, then her heart, her stomach, her groin. Down, down she went in a spiral of joy and desire. With sex so much a part of her life, how could she have forgotten that a kiss could be like this? She pressed closer, never wanting it to end.

Finally, he raised his lips from hers. Tenderly, he took her head between he hands and looked into her face as though he was trying to memorize every detail of it. His eyes were unreadable. They seemed filled with desire, yet tortured by pain. "Oh, God, Mari!" he said, his voice catching on her name. And then he was kissing her again—her lips, her eyelids, her cheeks, the hollow at the base of her throat.

"The bedroom," she whispered, trailing her lips down his neck. "Come into the bedroom…" She took his hand and led the way.

Once there, she reclined on the bed and watched him undress, growing more excited with the removal of each garment. His body was just as she remembered it. No, more beautiful than she remembered it. It seemed fuller and firmer, stronger now.

Standing, she unfastened the kimono and let it slip to the floor. She was exquisitely aware of every inch of her flesh as his gaze traveled slowly down her body, then back up again to meet her own.

"You're even more beautiful than I remembered," he said, his eyes shining with wonder, and perhaps tears.

And then they were in each other's arms again, kissing, moaning with desire. Gently, he lowered her to the bed. Even after all those years he remembered every touch, every caress that would send her pulses racing in a fury of passion that kept building, building, until she thought that she could stand no more, until that final, crucial, exquisite moment when they were at last united in the ecstasy of release.

Later, they made love again, slowly, more leisurely, but with no less joy. And then they drifted off to sleep in each other's arms.

She couldn't be sure how long she had been sleeping when she awoke. She reached out for Craig, but he wasn't beside her. Turning her head, she saw him sitting on the chair upon which he had dropped his clothes earlier. Already in his trousers and shirt, he was reaching for his shoes.

"Hi," she said sleepily, switching on the bedside lamp. "What are you doing?"

"Getting ready to leave." He put on his shoes and stood up. "I didn't want to disturb you."

Sitting up so that the covers would slide down and reveal her breasts, she smiled and shook her head. "Don't tell me the years have made you so conventional." She pulled back the covers on the other side and held out her arms. "Come back here. We have all those lovely hours till nine, when we'll have croissants in bed."

"I think you've seen too many of my movies," he said with a wistful smile. "It's only on the screen that I'm a super sex god. I'm not twenty-one anymore, you know."

"Neither am I, thank God. Come hold me, and we'll talk."

"I didn't mean to imply I'm over the hill. Do you really think we'd just talk if I got back into that bed?"

"Well…" She gave him a slow smile. "In between, we could talk. There's a lot we have to talk about."

He raised his eyebrows but made no move to join her. "Like what?"

"Like how I'm going to make you a very rich man."

"Apparently you haven't noticed that I already am a very rich man."

"But no one is ever rich enough. I can make you even richer."

"And how do you propose to do that?"

"By making you an extremely attractive offer on your shares in *Sizzle.* All you have to do is tender them to my bank."

For a few moments, he just stood there, studying her. When he spoke at last, his voice sounded weary, disappointed. "I've been waiting all day for you to say that, and I'm glad you finally did. It makes leaving here much easier."

An icy trickle of fear slipped slowly down her spine. "What do you mean?"

"I mean," he said, reaching for his jacket, "that I was aware from the beginning that you didn't 'just happen to hear' that I was in Paris and then impulsively decide to drop in on me after seventeen years. Did you really think I'd fall for that line? My God, Mari! In the space of seventeen years, we must have been in the same city on the same day dozens of times, yet never before did you decide to look me up. I knew you had an ulterior motive, and I knew exactly what that motive was. I'm not just a dumb actor—I'm a businessman too. I read the *Wall Street Journal* more carefully than I do *Variety*. I'm well aware of the battle you and Harrison Kendricks are waging over *Sizzle*. In fact, a guy named Clifford Langhton, an emissary from Kendricks, was just over here wining and dining me at Maxim's, offering me a very attractive money and publicity deal. I figured that you, or someone from your camp, would be bound to surface soon."

God damn that son of a bitch Kendricks! Must he always be one step ahead of her? "What did you tell Langhton?" she asked, straightening up, pulling the covers around her, suddenly all business.

"Exactly what I'm about to tell you except to Langhton, I put it a little more politely: You can take your offer and shove it." He put on his jacket and buttoned it. "I had lunch with you because I wanted to see how you'd go about broaching the subject. As the afternoon passed and you never brought up the matter, I began to think that you'd changed your mind, that you were beginning to feel some of the old magic too. But it was all an act, wasn't it?" He gestured angrily toward the bed. "You figured all you had to do was let me make love to you, and you could get anything you wanted out of me."

The fear was back again, sharper, colder than before. She grabbed her kimono and put it on as she rushed over to him. "You're wrong. What happened here tonight wasn't some kind of bribe. It happened because I wanted it to, because I—"

"Forget it, Mari," he cut her off. "You're not getting the shares. But don't worry. Neither is Kendricks. I'm sick to death of people like the two of you playing havoc with the economy, making only investments that will create more wealth at the top instead of creating jobs where they're needed and—"

"Will you listen to yourself!" she broke in. "You sound like a bleeding-heart editorial in the *New York Times,* written no doubt by someone who has invested in Japanese cars and computers up to his eyeballs. I don't see you hurting from the money you've made through your investments. For God's sake! People never went into business to create jobs—they went into business to make money—the more the better. And today's economy offers a unique opportunity—"

She broke off, aware of the cold, hard look in his eyes. What was she doing? This was no time to give him a lesson in economics. She was fighting for a lot more than his stock. She forced a smile. "This is ridiculous. I don't want to argue with you. I don't even care anymore whether you give me your stock option." She slid her arms around his neck. "It's true that that's what I came to Paris for. But what you said earlier is also true. I did feel the magic, Craig. I want it to go on and on. We don't have the awful hurdles we had years ago. Now there's nothing to stop us from being together."

He didn't put his arms around her too, as she was hoping he would. "You mean now we're both over the hurdle of poverty."

She nodded.

"And what about the hurdle of my wife and children?"

"That's no hurdle that we couldn't easily clear."

Reaching up, he removed her arms from around his neck and placed them at her sides. "That *you* couldn't easily clear, you mean. You haven't changed at all, have you? You still go directly after what you want and the hell with who gets hurt in the process. Once it was me. Now it's Susan and the kids."

"I didn't mean we'd just leave them high and dry, darling. We'll take care of them. We'll do everything we can to make them comfortable." She wished he would stop looking at her that way. "Of course you'll let Susan have any homes and property you own together, anything she wants."

"Just as long as you get what you want." He shook his head. "You have it all figured out, don't you? But what about what I want?"

"But you want *me!*" She couldn't understand why he was being so difficult.

"Not anymore I don't."

She smiled and nodded toward the bed. "You certainly had me fooled back there."

"No," he said, "I had myself fooled." He ran his hand over his face, and when he looked at her again, the coldness in his eyes had turned to pain. "I can't believe that I just took twelve years of love and threw it out the window for one night of trying to recapture something that never existed in the first place."

"Are you telling me that you never slept with another woman since you got married?"

"I not only never slept with another woman since I married Susan, I never wanted to sleep with another woman—until tonight."

"I can't believe that."

"No, I guess you can't." He gave her a pitying look. "That's because you don't understand the first thing about love. You think of a relationship only in terms of how much gratification, sexual or otherwise, it can bring to you. That's self-indulgence, not love. Love is putting another person at the very core of your life, devoting yourself to making that person as happy as he or she makes you."

She laughed, trying to bring the conversation down to a lighter, safer plane. "You make it sound like some kind of dreary drudgery. I seem to recall reading somewhere that love is simply never having to say you're sorry."

"That's simplistic bullshit. Real love is trying never to do things you'd have to say you're sorry for. Things like we did here tonight."

"I don't regret a thing," she said huskily, moving a little closer.

"But I regret everything." He ignored the hand she held out to him. "Look, Mari, I love Susan. She's more than my lover, my wife, the mother of my children. She's my best friend, the one person in the world I can share every thought, every feeling with. I'm never really whole or complete without her. What I did tonight was a rotten betrayal. She may be able to forgive me for it, but I'll never forgive myself."

"You've been acting too long," Marietta said, becoming impatient. "You're getting melodramatic. We're good together. We belong together. You wanted what happened tonight as much as I did."

"God knows I can't deny that. But it was—I don't know—" He shrugged, searching for the right words. "—April madness, an aberration." Shoulders slumping, he walked over to the window.

"It was real!" she insisted, following him, forcing him to face her.

"No, Mari. What's real is my wife, twelve beautiful years of marriage, and three wonderful kids. Today—today was some kind of crazy dream, a futile exercise in trying to recapture something from the past."

"But we did! We recaptured something precious and beautiful. Something we should never let go of again."

"We recaptured nothing. What we did was reenact something that I'm beginning to think never really existed in the first place."

A band seemed to be tightening around her heart, radiating pain to the back of her throat. It was a new and frightening sensation, and she found it difficult to speak above it. "I don't know what you mean."

"I mean that the girl I fell in love with seventeen years ago never really existed except in my imagination. You can't recapture what was never real."

"That's ridiculous! I'm the same person today that I was back then."

"Yes, you are. I finally woke up to that tonight." His eyes were sad. "There's really nothing more to say. It's time I got back to my hotel."

"There's a lot more to say!" she cried, frightened by his look, impatient with his stubbornness. "You can't turn your back on everything we could have and be together. You're rich, but I'm richer. I could give you so much. We can produce movies together. We can—"

"Forget it, Mari. You can't buy me."

"Goddamn it! I'm not trying to buy you. I'm trying to show you how wonderful life with me could be."

"Wonderful?" He shook his head. "Not for me. Even if Susan didn't exist, we could never make it together, Mari. We're too different now." He looked out the window. The first rays of dawn were streaking the sky with pink, bathing the Place Vendôme in a rosy hue. Atop the huge column molded from cannon he had captured in battle, a toga-clad statue of Napoleon oversaw the spectacular sunrise.

Craig gestured toward the statue. "You're rather like him, you know. Both of you set out to conquer the world, and in your separate ways, you both managed to do it. The problem is that you both concentrated too much on conquering the outside world. It's what we do with the world within us that counts. You lost sight of that world long ago, Mari." He glanced at the statue again. "That toga no more makes Napoleon a genuine Roman emperor than all your jewels and power and money can turn you back into the kind of woman I can love. You're a taker, Mari. Even when you give, it's really only as a means of taking something you want more. If you weren't such a dangerous woman, you'd be a pathetic one." He walked back to the chair and picked up his tie. "Good-bye, Mari."

Trembling with rage, she stood there, watching him leave the room. How dare he throw her offer in her face! How dare he say such things! It was because of her he was where he was today. If she hadn't gotten him his break, he would still be playing bit parts, or else be back on the farm, squeezing a living out of the dirt. *Tell him!* a voice inside her urged, and she rushed out of the room after him. It would be the perfect revenge. It would turn everything to ashes in his mouth. He was about to open the door when she reached him.

"Who do you think you are to talk to me that way?" she cried. "If it weren't for me, you'd be nobody, nothing!"

He whirled round to face her, his eyes blazing. "What the hell are you talking about?"

Tell him! the voice cried. *He'll never be able to live with it. It will serve the sanctimonious bastard right.*

"Well?" There was more than anger in his eyes now. There was a flicker of fear too.

"Your precious career," she began, and she saw the fear flicker brighter. "If I hadn't—" Her voice caught at the look in his eyes. She swallowed, then forced herself to go on: "If I hadn't walked out on you seventeen years ago, you never would have thrown yourself into acting the way you did, never would have gotten your career off the ground."

There was a flash of relief, and then his eyes became cold and hard. He inclined his head in a mock bow. "You'll forgive me for never sending you a thank-you note."

As he reached for the doorknob once more, fear ripped through her. If he left now, like this, she would never see him again.

And then she did something she had never before done in her life—she begged. "I don't want to fight with you, Craig," she said. "I don't want us to hurt each other. Don't go. Please."

He must have known how much that cost her. He looked at her for a long moment. Maybe it was because of something he saw in her expression, or maybe it was because of something her words stirred deep inside him, but suddenly his face softened. His eyes took on a faraway look and seemed to fill with memories. Slowly he reached out and touched her cheek. "Oh, Mari," he said, and there was a world of sadness in his voice. "If only you had said those words seventeen years ago. There are too many years between us now. Too many people. We can't go back. No one can ever go back."

His hand dropped to his side, and she longed to reach out and grasp it, but she knew she didn't dare.

Their eyes held, locked in sweet visions of a past that could never be recaptured.

"You can have the stock, Mari," he said huskily.

Her tears made his face shimmer and grow blurred. "It's not your stock that I want," she whispered.

The tenderness in his eyes told her that he understood, but still he shook his head.

"Don't you see?" he said. "It's the only part of me that I can ever give you now. I'll call my broker in the morning."

He drew back a step, took a deep breath, and then opened the door and closed it softly behind him. For a while, Marietta stood there staring at the closed door. Her whole body trembled, and she felt drained and empty. Finally, she turned and walked slowly over to the phone. She picked up the receiver and called the desk. "I've had a change of plans," she said dully. "I'll be leaving today after all."

She climbed back into bed and pulled the covers up to her chin. Suddenly she felt cold. So very, very cold.

Chapter Nineteen

Returning home from Europe Friday evening, Clifford Langhton was more confident than ever that Kendricks International would triumph yet again. Craig Campbell had gone over to the Wylford bitch, it was true, and so had Mark Bailey, but Cliff had won more than enough options from others to compensate for their loss. Besides, Mark Bailey couldn't really be counted out—after all, his stepmother had to approve any sale of his stocks, and she was still sitting on the fence. David Belmont appeared to have a strong influence on her, but she hadn't jumped over to his side yet. No battle could ever be counted as lost until the opposition had actually won it.

It was what had happened in London that cheered Cliff the most. Rumors of a knighthood or possible peerage for Kendricks were getting stronger—so strong, in fact, that even men who despised Kendricks believed them and were preparing to accept him into their homes, if not yet their clubs. Lord Sedridge, who headed one of the greatest financial empires in Great Britain and who always cut Kendricks in public, had welcomed Cliff into his oak-paneled office on Threadneedle Street, given him a cigar, and agreed that the British must stick together when it came to overseas investments. He had promised to place his *Sizzle* shares with the Kendricks bank immediately.

As his plane touched down at Kennedy, Cliff patted the un-smoked cigar in his pocket. He had brought it back for Kendricks as a symbol of Lord Sedridge's newfound esteem. His suitcases were bulging with gifts for Stephanie and the kids—something from every city on his itinerary. Five long days away from home.

He would be glad when this business was over. The extensive traveling was taking its toll. He was exhausted, and his stomach wasn't right—too much rich foreign food. He had even been having some trouble in the bathroom the last day or two. Though he was always scrupulously careful not to drink the water, something had obviously hit his kidneys or his bladder the wrong way. He would watch his diet for the next few days. Just being home with Stephanie and the boys was probably all he needed to get himself back in top shape. Once Kendricks made him the editor of *Sizzle,* this kind of crap would be behind him. It would be good to be a journalist again. He had so many plans for that magazine. He would bring in a new art director too. A lot more could be done with the layouts....

Customs cleared, Cliff carried his suitcases through the sliding doors that led into the waiting area of the International Arrivals Building. His heart beating a little faster, he looked around expectantly. No plans had been made, but he was half hoping that Stephanie and the boys might have decided to meet him. They would all go out to dinner on the way home. It was Friday evening, so the kids could stay up late. Or maybe Stephanie had hired a sitter and come alone. That would be even better. Five days was a long time to be apart. Especially when he hadn't even heard her voice for the last three of those days. Each time he had called, the boys had told him she was out or unable to get to the phone. It would be so good to have her all to himself for a little while....

But the feeling of happy expectancy drained as he scanned the faces of the people standing behind the barriers. No one among them was smiling and waving and calling to him. With a sigh, he headed for the taxi stand.

He dozed a bit on the long ride home, awaking as the taxi turned into his tree-lined street. His brief moment of disappointment forgotten, once again his heart began to beat in sweet anticipation. His heartbeat slowed, though, when the driver pulled up before a darkened house. Quickly he paid the fare and hurried up the walk.

Though it was obvious no one was there, once inside the house he switched on the lights and called out, "Anybody home?"

There were no happy squeals or footsteps thundering down the stairs. There was no note on the telephone table in the hall or on the Charlie Brown bulletin board in the kitchen.

He brought his suitcases upstairs and left them in the bedroom, feeling too let down to unpack. He had told the boys when he would be home. No doubt they had fouled up the message when they repeated it to Stephanie. She had probably taken them out to dinner, maybe even to a movie. She wouldn't keep them out too late, though, even on a Friday night. Before long, they would come home, see the lights on, and race into his arms in a rush of excitement. Smiling to himself, he went back downstairs. Their happy surprise at finding him waiting would more than cancel out his disappointment at coming home to an empty house.

In the kitchen he puttered around, fixing a tray of cheese and crackers, mixing his own special garlic-and-onion dip. He brought the food into the family room and placed it on the cocktail table, then got out the Harvey's and two sherry glasses. He put Chopin's *Prelude* on the stereo, poured himself a glass of sherry, and sat down on the reclining chair to wait. The combination of Chopin, sherry, the reclining chair and jet lag was too much. Within minutes he was asleep.

He couldn't be sure what finally woke him. Certainly he hadn't heard the car pull up or anyone enter the house. But suddenly he was aware he was being watched. Groggy from sleep, he opened his eyes and turned his head slowly.

Stephanie stood in the doorway. Wearing gray slacks and a pale-yellow top, her hair tumbling to her shoulders in soft waves, she looked every bit as beautiful as if she had been dressed in one of her expensive designer gowns. But there was something about her rigid posture that sent a chill through him as he elevated his chair.

"So you're back," she said, no trace of welcome in her voice.

"The boys?" he asked. "Are they all right?"

"They're with my folks for the weekend." Her eyes didn't sparkle as they usually did when she revealed that they were about to have some time alone. "I've just been upstairs. I'm glad you haven't unpacked your bags. I want you to take them and get out."

He had already covered half the distance between them,

but he froze, unable to proceed. It was as though her words and icy stare had put up an invisible barrier, one he could not cross. Maybe, he thought hopefully, he was dreaming. But he knew he had never been so agonizingly awake.

"What the hell are you talking about?" he asked, forcing the words out between lips stiff with fear.

"Don't put on an innocent act, Cliff. Under the circumstances, it's outrageously out of place." She walked into the room, brushing past him as she headed for the cocktail table. He reached out and touched her arm, but she shook his hand off and poured herself some sherry.

"Is this some kind of joke?" he demanded.

"If it is, it's a particularly obscene one and it's being played on me." She took a long swallow of her drink, her back still turned to him.

He longed to grab her by the shoulders and shake her until she stopped talking in riddles, but he kept his trembling hands at his sides. "I seem to have been tried and judged in absentia," he said, now more angry than afraid, the coldness in his voice matching hers. "It would be only common decency on your part to inform me of the charges."

"Common decency," she repeated. "An interesting choice of words in light of our situation." She put down her glass and whirled to face him. "Let's divide them between us. I'll take *decency*. You sure as hell deserve *common*." The fire blazing in her eyes was quickly extinguished by the tears that suddenly brimmed there. "God damn you, Clifford Langhton! You've given me herpes!"

"Oh, my God!" He felt as though a gigantic fist had punched him in the gut, sending all his righteous indignation whooshing out of him, and leaving only revulsion and self-disgust in its place. That problem in the bathroom, those painful little blisters that had suddenly appeared—it wasn't just a bladder infection. Where had he picked it up? His mind raced back. Laura Leslie. God damn that bitch! Why hadn't she told him she was infected? He'd like to kill the dried-up old whore. He'd like to get his hands on her—

"Stop looking so shocked," Stephanie interrupted his dark thoughts. "Surely you knew."

He shook his head, unable to speak.

"Oh, God. The doctor said sometimes people are hardly aware of the symptoms." She closed her eyes, then opened them, rage blazing out. "But me—I nearly scream with pain every time I go to the john. I feel like my flesh is being burned off by the blisters that cover it. And there's no cure. It will go away, but it will keep coming back. Again and again. Forever. I feel so filthy. So used. God damn you, Cliff! What have you done to me?" Tears spilled down her cheeks and she began pounding on his chest. "Damn you, damn you, *damn you!*"

The pain from her fists was nothing compared to the pain he felt inside. His own eyes filling with tears, he slipped his arms around her and held her close as she collapsed against him, sobbing. "Honey, honey," he whispered. "I'm so sorry, so very sorry. Don't cry. Please don't cry." He rubbed his cheek against her hair. "Everything will be all right. We'll see this through together."

Suddenly she drew a shuddering breath and jerked away from him. "Not together. Never again together." The fury was back in her eyes. "What do you think this is—a lifetime case of consumption? This is VD, Cliff. You didn't catch it by sitting next to someone who neglected to cover a cough. The doctor can ease my symptoms until they disappear, and later he can help me over all the recurrences. But when it comes to our marriage, the infection is fatal."

"There's no reason why it has to be."

"I can think of a very good reason in the shape of the woman you couldn't resist, the one who gave you the present you so generously passed along to me. Go back to her—and good riddance." She walked over to the window and stood there, staring out into the night.

"Honey, you don't understand," he said, going over and touching her shoulder. "It was nothing. She meant nothing to me."

Shrinking away from his touch, she turned to look at him, her face filled with disgusted disbelief. "Is that supposed to make me feel better—that you take our marriage so lightly you could be unfaithful with someone who means nothing to you?"

"I wasn't being unfaithful to you, not really." Cliff ran his hand through his hair in exasperation. "Our marriage had nothing to do with this. It was strictly business."

"Strictly business? Since when does Harrison Kendricks pay you to screw whores?"

"Since the whores have stocks he wants to get his hands on!" he yelled. Why was she being so difficult? Surely she knew she was the only woman he could ever love. "For God's sake, Stephie, grow up! Big business is a lot more than keeping ledgers. More deals are made in the bedroom than the boardroom. And it doesn't have a goddamn thing to do with marriage!"

"It has every damn thing to do with *our* marriage! I don't recall anything in the vows we took about 'forsaking all others except business associates.'"

"You're being deliberately naive. I've never forsaken you, not in my heart."

"Bullshit! You're the one who's naive if you actually believe such unadulterated crap. Like a little boy telling a lie, did you cross your fingers while you were screwing that whore and think it made everything all right? If you did, then you've got a lot of growing up to do. Because the important things in life can't be measured by degrees. There's no such thing as 'a little screw' or being 'a little bit unfaithful.' You're either faithful or you're not. I don't think there's anything more to say, Cliff. Why don't you just get your bags and go?"

"Damn it! There's a lot more to say! I love you. You can't just throw everything we have out the window over a simple business deal."

"Why not? You did. And it probably wasn't the first time, was it?"

He wanted to lie and say it was, but he knew she wouldn't believe him.

"Never mind," she said with a sigh. "I can see the answer in your eyes."

She started to turn away again, but he grabbed her shoulders and forced her to face him. "I won't let you do this to us, Stephie. I love you. Nothing has ever changed that, and nothing ever will change that. And I know you love me too."

She shook her head, tears glistening in her eyes. When she

spoke, her voice was thick with emotion. "I don't love you. I loved the man I thought you were. But I just found out that that man doesn't exist. At least, he hasn't existed for a long, long time. Please, Cliff, leave now. There's no sense in prolonging this awful agony."

The tears in his eyes turned her face to a shimmering blur. "Everything I've done," he said, his voice breaking, "I've done for you."

A look of incredible sadness came over her face, and it hurt Cliff more than all her tears, all her fury. "Knowing me as you do, you can't possibly believe that," she said softly. "Everything you did, you did for yourself—for your own ambition, your own ego."

"You were happy enough to live off the fruits of my labor," he couldn't resist saying.

"If you really think that, then you've been blind to my feelings for a very long time." With a sigh, she turned back to the window. "I'll give you five minutes, Cliff. If you don't go, I will."

For a moment, he stood there looking at the rigid set of her shoulders. His heart felt as though it was being slowly, relentlessly squeezed in a hammerlock. He longed to reach out and touch her, but he couldn't bear to see her shrink away from him again. Finally he turned and went upstairs for his bags.

She was still at the window when he came down. He paused on the threshold. "I'm sorry, Stephie," he said. "You'll never know how very sorry I am."

She turned to face him. "I think I do know. But it doesn't change a thing."

"Will you keep in touch?"

"Only through our lawyers. I've already spoken to Tom Bradford. I assume you can get one of the many lawyers you know to handle your end."

"But my things—" he said, grabbing at any straw that might make it possible to see her again.

"Our lawyers will arrange for all that."

"The boys..." It was hard to get those two words out over the lump in his throat.

"They love you, Cliff. I'd never make them suffer for what you've done to me. We'll work something out so that you can spend plenty of time with them."

"Thank you." That hammerlock was tightening, making it difficult to breathe, to think over the pain. "Stephie, I—"

"Good-bye, Cliff." Resolutely, she turned back to the window.

There was nothing left to do but leave.

EVERY COMPANY WORTH its tax deductions owns or rents apartments. Ostensibly, they're homes away from home where overworked out-of-town executives can rest their weary heads. More often than not, they're government-subsidized *pieds-à-terre* where raunchy VIPs, visiting or local, can entertain themselves and clients with classy call girls and opulent orgies. Kendricks International had such an accommodation in a high-rise condominium on Third Avenue in the Sixties. Unable to bear the thought of a hotel, it was to this haven that Cliff retreated on Friday night.

Appropriately enough for a building financed by Arab petrodollars, the doorman had the physique of a fierce harem guard, and it occurred to Cliff that the man would come in handy if he had trouble ejecting any carousers who might be using the apartment. Pausing before the door, however, he heard no sounds from within, and once inside, all that met him was silence and darkness. With a sigh of relief, he bolted the door behind him.

His sigh was premature. When he flipped on the light in the larger of the two bedrooms, he found Jack Hatfield, the circulation director of the *Clarion,* having his own circulation stimulated by an elaborate blow job administered by a call girl clad only in high black boots and a nurse's cap. Hatfield was lying on the bed in ecstasy, wearing nothing but a silly grin and a stethoscope.

Unperturbed, the call girl paused only long enough to say to Cliff, "It's a hundred bucks if you just watch—double if you want to play." She was made up to look older, but she couldn't have been more than eighteen.

Cliff swallowed back the bile rising in his throat. "No playing and no watching. Get your clothes on. The party's over."

"I still get paid."

"No one's going to cheat you," Cliff assured her.

With a shrug, she got to her feet and sauntered over to a pile of clothes on a velvet-upholstered wing chair. Slowly she reached for her black-lace bikini bra.

"Not here," Cliff said impatiently. "Dress in the john."

She shrugged again, picked up her clothes, and left the room.

Cliff turned to Hatfield, who was huddled in the king-size bed like a shy virgin, the covers pulled up to his chin. The pose was particularly ludicrous for a man in his late fifties with thinning gray hair and a jawline that was turning to jowl.

"What the hell do you think you're doing?" Cliff demanded. "You know this place isn't to be used for casual screws." Then he blanched as Stephanie's words suddenly came back to him: *There's no such thing as a little screw....*

Hatfield sat up straighter, his embarrassment turning to bluster. "Hell, I'm here with permission. I was given the key for the night."

"This place is to be used strictly for the sweetening of business deals. Are you going to tell me that that little whore is a client?"

"All right. So I hired her for Bob Gibbs—that was strictly legitimate—I had Kendricks's blessings. But Gibbs canceled out at the last minute. His wife called—their kid was rushed to the hospital with appendicitis. There I was with a perfectly good whore all lined up. It seemed a shame to waste her talents."

Cliff picked up Hatfield's clothes from the floor and tossed them on the bed. "You're a dumb schmuck. You know Kendricks wants the rules observed."

"What he doesn't know won't hurt him." Hatfield got out of bed and reached for his briefs. With his bulging belly and sagging pectorals, he looked like a pregnant old woman with hair on her chest. Cliff turned away in disgust. Would he look like that in ten or twelve years? No, of course not. Stephanie always watched out for his health, making sure he ate right, exercised and kept in shape. And then he remembered that Stephanie wouldn't be around anymore.

"Come on, Cliff. You're a man of the world. What are you looking so grim about?" Each piece of clothing he put on seemed to restore a little more of Hatfield's self-confidence.

His mind a jumble of conflicting images, Cliff hardly heard the question. Thoughts of Stephanie led to thoughts of his sons, then to thoughts of the beautiful wife and teenaged daughters Hatfield had introduced him to recently.

"That girl's probably younger than your daughter—the one who's up at Vassar," he heard himself saying. "Doesn't that bother you?"

Hatfield gave him a lewd smile. "Only in the nicest possible way." He walked over to the mirror and began putting on his tie. "In case you haven't noticed, they don't make call girls our age—thank God!"

"What do you want with whores? You've got a gorgeous wife."

Hatfield nodded toward the bed. "Do you think I could get my wife to play doctor with me like that?" He turned to the mirror, admiring himself as he carefully combed his sparse hairs across his bald skull. "Let's face it—variety's the spice of life. We all need a little young blood now and then to keep the old juices flowing. Know what I mean?" He gave Cliff an elaborate wink in the mirror.

"Well, get the juices flowing somewhere else. This place is off limits for your private parties." Cliff's head was pounding and that awful vise was tightening around his heart again. All he wanted was to be alone. Thinking that if he had to talk to Hatfield any longer, he might take a swing at him or throw up, he rushed out of the room.

"All right. I'm going, I'm going." Pulling his jacket on, Hatfield followed on his heels.

Fully dressed in a suede jacket and black slacks, the girl was standing in the hallway, looking every bit the model she no doubt claimed to be whenever asked her profession.

"Come on, baby," Hatfield said in the tone of one more sinned against than sinning. "We're moving up to the Waldorf." He opened the door and turned to Cliff, a hint of fear in his eyes. "This will stay just between us guys, won't it?"

"As long as the Waldorf doesn't show up on your expense account."

The spark of fear turned to a flash of anger. "What the hell is it with you and this holier-than-thou crap? I know for a fact that you screw around plenty."

"Not for my own pleasure."

"Sure. Tell me about it."

The girl began to giggle. "Boys will be boys," she observed.

"With me, it has always been strictly business," Cliff said, anger burning a trail from his neck to his cheeks.

"What do you think that makes you—some kind of a goddamn saint? Tell your wife you do it strictly for business, and see if she'll think it's hardly worth a mention. In case you haven't noticed, buddy, a fuck is a fuck is a fuck. Don't kid yourself that you're better than me. We're two of a kind."

Hatfield slipped his arm around the girl and walked out. Cliff could still hear her giggles as he locked the door behind them.

Within a few minutes he was calm enough to telephone Kendricks at his town house. Kendricks was out for the evening, and he informed the butler that Kendricks could reach him at the East Side apartment if he was needed during the weekend. Next, he went up to the bar in the living room and picked out a nice full bottle of Cutty Sark and a glass. He proceeded to drink until he passed out.

On Saturday he sobered himself up for a visit to a doctor whose office was in the same building. An affable middle-aged man with a cherubic face, Dr. Goulden tentatively, but almost conclusively, diagnosed his condition as a relatively mild case of herpes. With a casualness that no doubt came from constant repetition of his discourse, Dr. Goulden explained that only the symptoms could be treated; the disease itself could not be cured. In two or three weeks, the symptoms would abate, and it would be safe to resume sexual intercourse; future partners, of course, should always be informed that he is a carrier, for though the disease cannot be passed along during its latent stage, one can never be sure at exactly what point a flare-up has been triggered.

"There's no need to look like it's the end of the world," the doctor said as Cliff rose to leave, clutching his prescription for an ointment called Zovirax. "You're not alone in this, you know. There are about fourteen million people in this country who have the disease. They've learned to live with it—you will too. It isn't pleasant, but it's no great tragedy."

"That," Cliff said, "is what you think, doctor."

At the nearest drugstore he waited in a chair while the prescription was filled. Then he returned to the apartment and drank himself into a stupor again.

Sunday was hell. He woke up with his head pounding, his mouth full of cotton and his mind filled with the achingly sweet memory of how he had spent the day just one week before. He and Stephanie had awakened early, made long, leisurely love, then showered together before the boys began stirring. After breakfast they all went off to the park, where he helped Stephanie and the boys launch the bright, colorful kites he had bought for them in San Francisco. It was a clear, crisp, beautiful day with a perfect updraft, and the kites took to the sky like fantastic creatures suddenly set free. Every detail of that day was engraved upon his mind: the trees with their bright new leaves and blossoms; sunlight skipping across the pond, leaving a wake of golden ripples; the boys' rosy cheeks and delighted laughter, Stephanie's sparkling eyes and windswept hair. It was easy to believe in heaven on days like that. Easy to believe in jealous gods, too, when one looked back upon them. Had some malevolent spirit been lurking about, watching that joyful scene with envy in its heart and destruction on its mind? Cliff sat up and reached for the bottle of Scotch he had left on the bedside table the night before....

SOMEWHERE, CLIFF HAD read that there are at least ten million alcoholics in the United States. He wondered how they got started on Monday mornings. His head pounding, he groped his way into the shower and stood beneath its hot, stinging spray for a full five minutes. It washed away a little of the fog that engulfed his mind and blurred his vision, but none of the pain. Having dried himself, he stepped over to the mirror, hoping he had revived sufficiently to shave without slitting his throat—not the worst of calamities in his present state of mind. His hand shook so much that the procedure took three times as long as usual, and as he applied a styptic pencil to the nicks and scratches, it occurred to him too late that he should have gone to a barber for a professional job. Dressing, he fought down nausea, and was thankful that he didn't have a breakfast meeting scheduled. His stomach protesting all the way, he did manage to force down a cup of black coffee before he left for the office.

As always when he returned from a trip, his desk was piled high with papers. Martha Wilmont, his efficient and loyal middle-aged secretary, was a whiz at keeping things moving during his absence, but matters that needed his personal attention she always arranged for him in neat piles in order of descending importance, marking them *URGENT!!!*, *urgent!!*, *urgent,* and *pending.* While waiting for word that Kendricks had arrived after breakfast at the Regency with a senator who was currying his favor, Cliff sifted through the *URGENT!!!* pile. Glad for the opportunity they offered to take his mind off his personal problems, he tackled the complex business issues with a zeal unusual in one suffering from a colossal hangover.

At ten forty-three Martha came in to announce that she had just heard from the receptionist that Kendricks had arrived. After waiting ten minutes for Kendricks to get settled, Cliff gathered up some papers and headed for his office.

The entrance to Harrison Kendricks's office was guarded by two British secretaries of indeterminate age, both forgettably attractive in an efficient, intelligent way. They sat behind twin gray steel desks and seemed to be eternally typing some Sisyphean assignment on their IBMs, pausing only to answer the telephone, to announce callers, and to scurry into their boss's office at the sound of a buzzer. Even with their eyes glued to their work, they were always immediately aware of visitors, and as Cliff came into view, one of them interrupted her typing to announce his arrival to Kendricks. "Go right in, Mr. Langhton," she said with a smile as impersonal as it was bright. Approaching the door, Cliff wondered as he often had whether the two ever went to the john or to lunch. Maybe they were humanoid robots.

"Good morning," he said, opening the door. He tried to imitate the secretary's smile, at least in brightness.

"You look like bloody hell." Kendricks was seated at a large nineteenth-century cherrywood writing table. Reflected on its gleaming surface were its only ornaments: two telephones, a solid-gold pen set, and a gold Tiffany desk clock that was turned toward visitors to remind them that they were taking up the time of its owner. The rest of the room displayed the same spare yet elegant simplicity. The eggshell-colored walls bore gold-framed maps of the United States, Great Britain, and Canada, little red flags indicating locations of the many subsidiaries of Kendricks

International. Against one wall stood a long bar, its gleaming top bare; against the opposite one, a long, low bookcase, its volumes lined up as precisely as Her Majesty's palace guards. The coffee-colored designer blind on the huge window behind Kendricks matched the carpet upon the floor and was at the moment open to reveal a panoramic view of Manhattan.

"I feel like bloody hell," Cliff admitted, sinking down on one of the high-backed upholstered chairs that had been designed to be just uncomfortable enough to keep visitors from overstaying their welcome. "Stephanie threw me out. She wants a divorce." It was the first time he had said the words out loud, and they seemed to grate against his throat as they emerged, then hang suspended in the air, his lifeblood dripping from them. That awful pain returned behind his eyes, and his vision blurring, he fought back tears, knowing Kendricks would view them as a disgusting sign of weakness. Still, he felt relieved to have it out in the open. He was gripped by an almost desperate need to talk about it, to confide in someone who would listen sympathetically, offer comfort and advice. Who better than Harrison Kendricks? All those years of pursuing common goals made Kendricks the nearest thing he had to a real friend. Once he'd had many trusted friends, but his work for Kendricks had left no time for nonbusiness associates, and one by one they had drifted away.

It was impossible to tell Kendricks's reaction from behind his tinted glasses, but there was no hint of sympathy in his voice as he said, "I assumed as much when Williams told me you were staying at the apartment for the weekend. Damned inconvenient time for it to happen. But no doubt it's for the best. You'll find you're better off without her. Wives can be a bloody nuisance. That's why I have never married."

"It's not just Stephanie I've lost—it's my sons too."

"You say that as though you've been careless and mislaid them somewhere. They'll still be around, old boy, but now it will be at your convenience, which is as it should be for a man with your responsibilities. How did the trip go?"

Realizing that that was all the sympathy and understanding he would get from Kendricks, Cliff pulled himself together and delivered an oral report on his trip. The change of subject was therapeutic, and he found his depression lifting a little as he enumerated his successes and told anecdotes connected with them. He was even smiling when he reached into his breast pocket for Lord Sedridge's cigar.

"A token of esteem from Sedridge," he said, extending it to Kendricks. "He's having his bankers place his *Sizzle* stock with our bankers. Says you old boys must stick together and all that sort of thing."

Kendricks took the cigar, sniffed it appreciatively, and rolled it between his fingers near his ear. "That's not what the bastard said two years ago when we were bidding on that paper in Toronto."

"Two years ago you weren't so close to a knighthood or a peerage that he could practically taste it. It's quite the talk of London, you know. Suddenly you're the darling of all the old boys on Threadneedle Street. Has the Palace confirmed it yet?"

"No, but what is equally affirmative is that the Palace has in no way attempted to deny it, either. Her Majesty's sword is so close to my shoulder that I can feel its tap already." As though demonstrating the way he had bagged royal honors, he dropped the cigar into his breast pocket and patted it. "It will be interesting to see which of the old bastards who usually cut me will run to their clubs to propose me for membership, and how quickly their wives and daughters will rush to invite Mother to tea."

"If it turns out to be a peerage, maybe we can put the official portrait of you in your robes on the cover of *Sizzle*."

"That, of course," Kendricks said with a meaningful smile, "will be at the discretion of the new editor. First, though, we have to ensure that *Sizzle* will indeed be ours. Time is running out. How are you coming along in the wooing of the widow?"

"As I told you, Belmont seems to have the inside track there. I have a lunch date with her tomorrow, though."

"Lunch?" Kendricks raised his eyebrows. "I should think that a dinner, dancing, and bed date would prove to be a great deal more profitable for us."

"More likely, it would prove to be disastrous. I picked up a dose from Laura Leslie."

"Shit." Kendricks straightened in his chair, his face clouding.

He thought a moment, then asked, "How long would we have before she started feeling symptoms?"

"According to my doctor, she could wake up with a full-blown case within forty-eight hours. And this is herpes. There's no cure." Did Kendricks really expect him to take Louise Bailey to bed knowing full well that he would be infecting her? Obviously he did, for after mulling over Cliff's words for a moment, he said:

"That means that the earliest you could screw the old girl would be Thursday night, just one day before our deadline. We can't afford to cut things so close. See where hand-holding and lunch will get you. If you haven't made sufficient progress by Wednesday, I'll have to resort to my ace in the hole."

"What's that?"

"A copy of the coroner's report on Philip Bailey's death."

"How the hell did you get that?"

"My dear boy, after all the years we've worked together, how can you ask such a naive question? I had Nick plant someone with a camera and sticky fingers in the office."

"Sticky fingers?"

"Yes. I have a little bonus too. In short, I can have Marietta Wylford by her beautiful tits anytime I so choose."

Cliff sighed in confusion. "I don't understand. Why haven't you saved yourself a lot of time and trouble and used the information before now?"

"Because using it will create great embarrassment for Louise Bailey, and I much prefer to trap my flies with honey."

"Since when?" Cliff asked, raising one eyebrow.

Kendricks smiled. "Since it has been common knowledge that Philip Bailey was a very close friend of one who is near and dear to she who sits on the throne of England. And so, dear boy, you had better get to your hand-holding—and give it your all."

Cliff gave him a mock salute, gathered his papers, and took his leave. He had his hand on the doorknob when Kendricks suddenly added:

"And, Cliff, about that personal problem of yours…"

Cliff turned, his heart thudding. Kendricks did understand what he was going through and was about to offer sympathy after all. "Yes?" he said expectantly.

"You realize, of course, that the company flat is strictly for company use. I'm aware that while we're caught up in our current transactions you'll have no time to search for a place to live. But this business will be resolved by the end of the week. I'll expect you to move out over the weekend. And stay off the booze. Your eyes look like a road map of Las Vegas. There's no room in my organization for men who take their troubles to a bottle."

Cliff felt as though he had been slapped. Color drained from his cheeks, then flooded them again. "I assure you," he said, grasping the doorknob so hard his knuckles turned white, "that what happened this weekend was just a passing aberration."

"I'm pleased to hear that." The light caught on Kendricks's glasses, making him look as ominous as his voice sounded. "We both know—do we not?—that you have a great deal riding on this transaction."

Nodding, Cliff closed the door behind him.

Kendricks was wrong, he thought as he walked past the two secretaries, their fingers still flying over their typewriter keys. He had more than a great deal riding on the *Sizzle* transaction; now that he had lost Stephanie and the boys, it was all that gave purpose to his life.

Chapter Twenty

ON WEEKDAYS, FIVE-THIRTY was the time Marietta liked best. Most of the staff had departed by then, and those who remained knew better than to intrude upon her after hours. She could take a few minutes to unwind from the tension of the day, a look around the luxurious office reminding her that every pressure would have its inevitable payoff. Usually, she spent those moments with Melanie, catching up on corporate gossip and on what each of them had done to advance the interests of Wylford Enterprises. But Tuesday afternoon Melanie had taken off in pursuit of elusive *Sizzle* shareholders, and Marietta was left to spend the period alone.

With a sigh, she relaxed in her high-backed, white leather upholstered executive chair and took a brief mental survey of her day. It had been a productive one: she had fired two nonstarters, put the executive officers of a flagging subsidiary on notice that if they sent her a report that didn't show a considerable upturn in profits at the end of the quarter, they should be prepared to submit their resignations along with it, and hired a team of efficiency experts that would terrorize executives and employees alike at every subsidiary they visited.

Her gaze sweeping around the huge room, she tried to see it as it must appear to those who were summoned there. She had decorated it carefully, with an eye to creating an effect that would be part disarming, part intimidating. There were the pale blue walls and blue-green carpet and drapes, evoking relaxing thoughts of sea and sky. There were the lush plants, indicative of a warm, nurturing atmosphere. And then there was the harshly geometric art upon the walls and the stark white, sharply angled furniture, introducing a jarring, no-nonsense note of exacting severity. It amused her to see how people taking the long, nerve-racking walk from the door to her desk reacted to the conflicting messages. There weren't many who could pass the test. The overly self-assured evoked the same disdain as the fidgeters.

She looked at the Audemars Piguet watch on her wrist. Five forty-five. Even the stragglers must have left by now. She detested riding in the elevator with the lower echelons of her employees. There was a great deal to be said for keeping a distance and creating an air of mystery. She slipped on her jacket, picked up her burgundy leather briefcase from Bloomingdale's, and left, locking the door behind her.

As usual, Fred was standing at the curb beside her Rolls. Often on these cool, clear evenings she would dismiss him and walk home, but she had summoned Melanie and David to a strategy session at six and didn't want to be late. They were close to the countdown now. The moments were too precious to waste.

Bernice informed her when she arrived home that Melanie was already there and waiting for her in the living room.

"I've made some hors d'oeuvres, Mrs. Wylford, and fixed a cold supper for three, as you asked," Bernice said.

"Fine, Bernice. If everything's ready, you can leave. This is just an informal working session, and we'll serve ourselves." Marietta handed the housekeeper her jacket and hurried into the living room.

Melanie was curled up in an armchair, a cup in her hand. "Hi," she said with a weary smile. "I hope you don't expect me to get up and salute. I'm exhausted."

Marietta laughed. "You look like you can use something stronger than whatever Bernice gave you in that cup."

"Don't knock tea. The British won an empire on it."

"And then they drank too many soothing cups and lost it." She walked over to the bar. "How about a martini chaser?"

"Sounds tempting."

She got out the pitcher and the ingredients. "I was hoping you'd say that. You can mix them. No one makes them as well as you do."

With a mock sigh, Melanie rose to her feet. "I knew there had to be a catch."

Marietta sank down on the sofa. "How did it go this afternoon?"

"Not too bad. We won one and lost one. Tilden has gone over to the Kendricks camp, but Weicker has promised to come with us, and he has more shares."

"Yes, but not enough. Why the hell is Louise Bailey dragging her feet? David should have been able to pry her shares away from her by now."

"Go easy on him, Mari," Melanie said, stirring the contents of the pitcher. "It isn't his fault that Louise likes to play coy. Just remember that if it weren't for him, Kendricks would have had her in his pocket from the moment news of her husband's death broke."

"I suppose so," Marietta said, sighing. "But he'd better get her to take some positive action soon. There are only three days left. I have no patience with people who work in slow motion."

"Don't remind me how little time there is," Melanie said. "I'm off to Houston in the morning to twist a few more arms."

The doorbell rang and Bernice called out that she was still there and would get it. A moment later David walked in.

"Sorry I'm late," he said, "but I was spending some time with Louise, trying to undo the effects of a long lunch with the charming Clifford Langhton."

"How successful were you?" Marietta asked.

David shrugged, took the two martinis from Melanie and handed one to Marietta. "I think I'm holding my own, but it isn't easy to compete with someone who represents a man who's about to be made a lord of the realm in one of the few places where that kind of thing still counts."

"Find a way." Marietta gave him a long, cold stare, the one she knew struck terror in the hearts of her executives.

David did not look particularly terrified. "She hasn't run off to join the Kendricks camp yet, has she?"

"No, but she hasn't joined ours yet, either."

"We knew from the beginning," Melanie said with the soft tone of a peacemaker, "that Louise would be difficult for us. Maybe the most we can hope for is to keep her neutral through Friday. You can do that, can't you, David?"

He took a long swallow of his drink. "I'll try my damnedest."

Marietta was about to say that people who expected to remain in her organization didn't merely try their damnedest—they *did* their damnedest. But aware the barb would not have the desired effect, she refrained from making it. She wondered what David Belmont's skin was made of. It was annoying never to be able to get under it.

"What's holding things up with Martha Asquith?" she asked him instead.

"The pleasure of my company, it seems. She was supposed to tender her shares to our side yesterday, but she keeps coming up with cutesy questions to ask me. Don't worry about her. She'll come through in the end."

"See to it that she does, and that you keep Louise in line." Marietta reached for a pile of papers beside her. "If you can do that, we can still win, despite all the noises Kendricks is making to the contrary. He's overconfident now, and that can prove to be to our advantage. These last three days are crucial."

For the remainder of the evening, the three sat huddled together, examining figures, drawing up lists, planning strategy. Hardly aware of what they were eating, they consumed the cold dinner Bernice had painstakingly prepared for them, making jottings between mouthfuls, trying in every way to create a more optimistic picture than the one the figures projected. Harrison Kendricks was closer to victory than Marietta was prepared to admit openly. Even if Melanie were successful in Houston tomorrow and David also came through in Boston, they still would not have a comfortable margin.

"And what we have, we've brought in almost entirely on our own," Marietta said, throwing down her pencil. "Damn those acquisition lawyers! What the hell do they think I'm paying them for?" She pressed her fingertips to her eyes, trying to rub away some of the weariness and frustration. "If only we knew what Philip had on Kendricks! Where the hell could that bastard have hidden his information?"

"David and I have torn Philip's office apart three times, and David has searched the Bailey apartment." Her voice warm and comforting, Melanie reached over and touched Marietta's arm.

"Maybe there isn't any physical proof of whatever it was. Maybe Philip was carrying the facts in his head."

Marietta jerked away from Melanie's touch. "Don't try to soothe me as though I were a child. You're a lawyer. You know Bailey had to have concrete proof if he hoped to deal with a shark like Kendricks."

"Of course I do, but I'm not sure Bailey would have known it."

"He'd have known it," David said. "One last time, let's reconstruct his final actions. If he had received the evidence the night before, he could have dealt with it in many ways, but"—he turned to Marietta—"he gave you the impression that the evidence—whatever it was—came into his hands on that final day."

"Absolutely. He was very hyper. If he'd received it the night before, the surprise and the newness would have worn off."

David nodded. "Still, he gave you no idea what it was or where he'd hidden it?"

"I've told you that a thousand times." Marietta jumped up in a surge of impatience. "Why do we have to go through all this again?"

"Because this is the one thing that may win us the ball game. Think back, Marietta. Try to remember everything he said and did."

With a sigh, Marietta sank back down on the sofa. "What do you think I've been trying to do ever since that night? It's no use. All I can remember is how excited he was when he got here. He said he finally had the goods on Kendricks, something so hot it would make even a bastard like Kendricks back down. I tried every way I knew how to get him to share the news with me, but all he would say was something like he could nail Kendricks on Dallas. I know it couldn't have been anything as obvious as those pathetic real-estate deals Dutton unearthed."

"All right," David said, pacing the floor. "It's a waste of time to speculate on what it was. What we have to concentrate on is where it is." He ran a hand through his hair. "According to Dutton's report, Philip went directly to the office from home that day, and Louise swears he had no phone calls or visitors before he left the apartment. We know he taxied straight to Christ Cella for lunch and then directly back to the office. He didn't leave the office again until he taxied here. Also, we know that he sure as hell wouldn't have hidden it in one of the cabs he took. And it's even less likely that he jumped out of one of the cabs to dig a hole and hide it under a tree."

"That leaves only his office," Melanie pointed out, her voice weary, "and we know it isn't there—unless he was able to render it invisible." She stood up. "I could use a drink."

"Sit down," David said. "I'll get it."

Marietta's head was spinning. "Make one for me too while you're at it. I hope you're a better bartender than your late boss. He made the lousiest martinis I ever tasted."

"Give the guy a break," Melanie said. "He was within an hour or so of dying when he mixed those drinks. Maybe his reflexes were a little off."

David paused in the middle of pouring gin into the martini pitcher. He looked almost thunderstruck. "What did you say?"

"I said maybe his reflexes were a little off."

"No, before that." He shook his head, signaling that he didn't really expect her to repeat her words. "Never mind, I know—Marietta said he mixed the drinks." He slammed the bottle down on the bar. "Jesus! How could we have been so dense? We've been accounting for every minute of his time—except for the time he spent with Marietta. He could have hidden it here. It may be right under our noses."

Marietta's heartbeat quickened at the thought, then slowed with disappointment as reality took over. "But I was with him. I'd have seen him hide it."

"Not if he just casually slipped it behind something in the bar while he was mixing the drinks."

David's words were like a starter's gun to the two women. They jumped up and rushed to join him behind the bar. The three worked with a speed born of fresh hope, whisking out bottles and glasses, emptying drawers, running their hands along the tops and bottoms of shelves.

"Damn!" Marietta said when the search proved futile. The three of them were sitting on the floor, surrounded by bottles and glasses, jars of olives and onions and cherries, stirrers and straws.

As always when a new hope suddenly proves false, the disappointment that followed its demise was sharper than the frustration that preceded its birth. Melanie gazed blankly into space. Marietta felt cold and drained. Only David seemed still animated, unwilling to concede defeat.

"The bathroom!" he said, jumping up. "Did he go to the john?"

Melanie started to her feet too, but Marietta remained motionless except for the slow negative shake of her head.

"His heart may have been about to give out," she said dully, "but his kidneys were in perfect working order."

"Well, did you go to the john then? Or leave the room for even a moment?" David's glance darted around in search of possible hiding places.

"No, I was over there on the sofa every second." Sighing almost in unison, David and Melanie sank back down on the floor.

Melanie picked up the ice tongs and began fiddling with them absently. "I think we could all use that drink now," she said.

David nodded, and scowled at the profusion of bottles before him. "Where the hell did we put the gin and vermouth?"

Marietta continued staring straight ahead, but Melanie joined half-heartedly in the search. Suddenly, she gasped and jumped to her feet, her face and eyes alight. "In the kitchen!" she cried. "The gin and vermouth were in the kitchen!"

David and Marietta stared at her as though she had taken leave of her senses.

"How can they be in the kitchen?" Marietta asked. "They were here a few minutes ago."

"Not now—then!" Melanie said impatiently. "You never left the room that night—but Philip did. Don't you remember—after the police and paramedics left, you asked me to make some martinis. I couldn't find the gin and vermouth, and you told me Philip had made the drinks in the kitchen and had probably left the bottles there. That's where I found them—on Bernice's worktable."

"Of course!" The memory came rushing back, flooding Marietta's mind with every detail. "I'd forgotten all about it. He'd picked up the bottles and the pitcher and walked out, saying he needed ice, and that I shouldn't get up, he'd find his way around the kitchen. I remember telling him there was a mini-fridge with ice trays right there in the bar, but he just kept going, saying something ridiculous about ice from the kitchen always being better." She sprang up, hope and energy surging through her again. "It was just a ruse. He wanted to get out there alone and hide the damn thing!"

She ran out of the room, Melanie and David on her heels. They reached Bernice's sparkling kitchen, and stood frozen a moment, looking in dismay at the shiny counters and tabletops and seemingly endless cabinets and shelves.

"Where do we begin?" Melanie asked.

"Let's put ourselves in Philip's place," David said, getting down on the floor and examining the undersides of the tables and chairs as he spoke. "He had to do something quickly, because if he took longer than the time needed to mix the drinks, Marietta might come looking for him." He got to his feet, shaking his head.

"And he'd have to put it someplace where Bernice wouldn't spot it." Marietta opened a cabinet containing canned goods and began rummaging through its contents. "He'd have put it way in the back."

"He'd have done it immediately," Melanie said, pulling out detergents and cleansers from the cabinet beneath the sink, "because there was always the danger that Mari would decide to keep him company and follow him out here."

David paused in the middle of ransacking a cupboard that held pots and pans. "That's right. And he'd have looked like an ass and have had a lot of explaining to do if she'd walked in and caught him in the position any of us is in right now. He'd have wanted it to look like he was in the middle of the most natural thing in the world if she suddenly appeared in the room when he was hiding the thing—or when he was retrieving it. Because he certainly intended to come back within a day or two to pick it up." He walked over to the huge G.E. refrigerator-freezer and opened the top compartment. "And what would be more natural than to be caught with your hand in the freezer when you've already established that you were coming into the kitchen for ice?"

Melanie was already beside David, and Marietta joined them,

almost afraid to hope. He started passing the contents of the freezer to her and Melanie, and they systematically opened every unsealed carton and container. It began to look as if they were following yet another blind lead when he lifted up a large, square, foil-wrapped package from the recesses at the very back. The word *ravioli* and the date she had made and frozen it were written on the label in Bernice's rather childlike hand. At first glance, it had appeared to be on the very bottom of the freezer. But as he lifted it, David let out a shout. Beneath it lay a slim eight-by-ten manila envelope inside a translucent plastic bag. He grabbed the slim package and dropped the ravioli back into place.

"This is it! It has to be!" he cried.

Her heart pounding, Marietta snatched the package from him, tearing off the plastic bag and letting it fall to the floor. With trembling fingers she ripped open the envelope, then reached in to remove the contents. It was a glossy photograph. No, she realized, looking more closely, it was a contact sheet. Its rows of tiny photographs, each about an inch square and each numbered in the vertical margins that separated it from the others, brought back memories of the days when she had posed for pictures for swimsuit ads. These shots appeared to be pictures of a woman singing in a restaurant or night club. Confused, Marietta turned the sheet over. Stapled to the back was a narrow glassine envelope containing strips of negatives, and stamped in the center of the back were the words: PROPERTY OF GUS MAXWELL, PHOTOGRAPHER, followed by a Manhattan address and phone number. Beneath that were the handwritten words: *Wendy Carr, The Red Bull, Mexico City, 10/1/63.*

"Gus Maxwell," Marietta said. "Didn't Philip see him that last day?"

David nodded. "And obviously got these from him in addition to the shots of Mayor Koch he sent to me."

"But what is it?" Melanie asked.

"It's a contact sheet," David said, taking it from Marietta. "When photographers shoot a series of pictures for a newspaper or magazine, they take many more than can possibly be published. They're developed this way, and the editor goes over them and decides which ones he wants to use. Only those are processed. It saves a lot of money." He started out of the room. "We examine them through a powerful magnifying glass called a linen tester, because textile workers use them to count the threads in a square inch of cloth. I always keep a spare in my attaché case for working at home or out of town."

Marietta and Melanie followed him first to the hall closet, where he opened his attaché case and removed his linen tester, and then to the living room where he sat down at the end of the sofa near a lamp and began examining the pictures through the magnifier.

"What can Wendy Carr possibly have to do with anything?" Marietta asked, feeling at a total loss. "She's been dead for years!" She was beginning to wonder if Philip Bailey had been playing with a full deck. Maybe he had made up the whole thing.

"She was killed in an accident about twelve or fifteen years ago, wasn't she?" Melanie asked.

"Right." David didn't look up from the pictures. "It happened at the height of her career. These were taken toward the end of '63—about a year before her popularity began to soar. Lately, some of the kids have been building a kind of cult around her. Her records have been reissued and articles about her are being published all over the place. We featured her on a cover about a month ago."

"I don't understand," Melanie said, slumping down on the sofa beside him.

"That makes two of us." Marietta took a chair close by. "I don't remember any kind of scandal connected with Wendy Carr. And even if there was, how could it possibly hurt Kendricks all these years later?"

"Maybe it has nothing to do with Wendy," David said. "Maybe it's something else in one of the pictures."

"And maybe your boss was hallucinating." Marietta gave voice to her fears. "He told me he had the goods on Kendricks in Dallas—but these pictures were taken in Mexico City."

David didn't answer, just kept the linen tester moving slowly up and down along the rows, pausing to examine each picture meticulously. Suddenly his jaw tightened. "Jesus!" he cried.

Marietta and Melanie straightened. "What is it?" Marietta

asked, resisting an urge to grab the sheet away from him. "What do you see?"

David looked up, his face white. "I can't believe Maxwell sat on these pictures all these years." Holding the linen tester on a photo in the middle of the sheet, David handed the contact sheet to Marietta, who was now standing above him, her hand extended. "Look at that."

At first the picture looked blurred, but then she brought her eye down, almost touching the glass, and all the details suddenly became large and sharp. She saw Wendy Carr in the foreground, holding a hand microphone, her mouth open in song. She was standing on a postage-stamp-size dance floor. At the edge of it was a table where a young couple sat holding hands. "What's so terrible?" she asked, confused. "I don't see anything strange. Am I supposed to recognize the couple sitting near her?"

"Not them," David said. "Look at the man at the table near the wall."

Marietta returned her eye to the glass and studied the face of the man sitting alone at a table for two. He was youngish, slender, and his features looked familiar, but she couldn't place his face. "I'm sure I've seen him before," she said, "but I can't remember who he is."

"Does the name Lee Harvey Oswald ring a bell?" David's voice was grim.

Marietta looked up. "The guy who assassinated Kennedy?"

David nodded.

She looked down again. "My God! It *is* him. But I still don't see—"

"Just keep looking," David told her. "You'll see soon enough. Maybe you'd better sit down."

She did as he said, and continued to move the instrument slowly over the pictures as David talked to Melanie, telling her what Marietta was seeing. For the next two frames, Oswald continued to be alone, and then there were a few frames taken from a different angle, which didn't show the table near the wall. When it reappeared farther along, Oswald had been joined by a big man in tinted glasses, a man who was unmistakably recognizable as Harrison Kendricks. Again the table disappeared from the frames, but when it reappeared, Kendricks was reaching into his breast pocket. In the next frame, he was handing an envelope to Oswald, and in the frame that followed, Oswald was putting the envelope into his pocket. Two frames later, Kendricks was standing and shaking hands with the still-seated Oswald. In the remainder of the frames in which his table showed up, Oswald was alone.

Her heart pounding, Marietta looked up. All she could manage to say was, "Oh, my God!" She leaned over and handed the contact sheet and linen tester to Melanie.

"Now we know why Philip referred to Dallas," David said. "He meant he could link Kendricks to the assassination."

Melanie looked up, her face pale with shock. When she spoke, it was as a lawyer: "These pictures prove nothing except an association. We look at them and infer that Kendricks was giving Oswald either money or instructions relating to the Kennedy assassination, or both. But there's no way to prove that in a court. Kendricks could insist he was repaying a loan or giving Oswald a letter of introduction to a local parish priest."

"The key word there is *association*," David said. "These pictures are dynamite. I can't believe that Maxwell never came forward with them before. Their very existence is reason to launch a whole new investigation." He jumped up and began pacing the room in his excitement. "We just closed an issue, but we'll break the story in the next one. We already have the covers run off, but we'll destroy them and have new ones set up. It'll be a hell of an expense but worth every penny. We'll have to double our press run anyway. The issue will be an international sellout. I'll have to cancel that trip to Boston tomorrow to work on this. As soon as I've got things rolling at the office, I'll contact the authorities and—"

"No!" Marietta had had time to gather her thoughts, and they certainly weren't running in the same wild direction as David's. She knew exactly what had to be done, but she also knew she had to tread softly with David. She couldn't afford to have him spoil everything now.

David turned toward her, looking incredulous. "What do you mean, 'no'?"

"I mean this is too important a matter to go running off half-cocked on. It's going to take some thought."

"What kind of thought? This is the scoop of a lifetime. A journalist doesn't just sit and contemplate a story like this—he runs with it."

"You're more than a journalist now, David, you're a businessman. You seem to have forgotten Philip Bailey's purpose in getting this information."

David's jaw tightened. "Are you telling me you want this information suppressed?"

"Of course not," she said quickly. "What I'm telling you is that we have to be sensible and go slowly. I want to speak to the photographer myself and find out what kind of deal Philip made with him. I want to check the facts to be sure his dates are correct. For all we know, the pictures could have been taken years before he said they were. And in the meantime, I want to create an atmosphere of business as usual."

"What kind of neophyte do you think I am?" David protested. "Of course I intend to check all the facts. But I have to act immediately if we're going to make the next issue."

"For God's sake, David! The world has waited two decades for this information. Another day or so isn't going to make a damn bit of difference." She looked at her watch. "It's almost eleven. Will you have any trouble going to *Sizzle* to check the facts in the library files?"

"No problem. The night watchman is used to the odd hours I often have to keep."

"Good. Get down there, and as soon as you have the information, call me—I don't care what time it is. I'll talk to the photographer tomorrow. I want you to go ahead with your trip to Boston in the morning, and Melanie, I want you to go to Houston. We want everything to look normal."

"But the story—" David began.

Damn journalists and their one-track minds! "We'll discuss the best approach to that when you get back tomorrow," she said, careful not to let impatience show in her voice. "You'll both be tired after your trips. Let's all meet here after you've had a chance to eat dinner and rest. How does eight-thirty sound?"

"Sounds all right to me," Melanie said.

David nodded. He picked up the contact sheet, which Melanie had set beside her on the sofa. "I'll lock this in the office safe."

"I don't think that's a good idea." Marietta had no intention of letting the photographs out of her control. She stood up and held out her hand. "I'll take care of them. We can't take a chance on an outsider knowing about them until the right moment." David's eyes met hers, and she sensed his hesitation. "Philip trusted my freezer more than he trusted the *Sizzle* safe," she reminded him.

With obvious reluctance David placed the contact sheet in her hand. "But tomorrow night they go with me. We have a moral and legal responsibility to see to it that the authorities and the public are informed as quickly as possible."

"No one has to remind me of my responsibilities," Marietta told him.

Melanie left soon after David did, and once alone, Marietta placed the photographs in her wall safe, put on a pair of silk lounging pajamas, and curled up in bed with the latest issue of *Fortune* while she awaited David's call.

The phone rang as she was dozing over an article about how Japanese executives orchestrate the performance of lower-level functionaries.

"Everything checks out even better than we could have hoped." Despite the late hour, David's voice was full of energy. "Wendy Carr never left the States until September twenty-first, when she began a two-week engagement at the Red Bull, an obscure night club in Mexico City. She returned to Los Angeles October fifth, where she opened at the Golden Door and was spotted by Izzy Steinbrenner. He took her under his wing, and the rest is history. By the end of 1964, her popularity was exceeded only by that of the Beatles. In July 1965, while touring England, she drove her Ferrari over a cliff and was killed in the explosion." David paused, then went on, "I've gone over several reports of the accident, and they sound uncannily similar to the reports of the accident that killed Kendricks's brother the year before."

"Yes, yes," Marietta said impatiently, "but that's beside the point. What about Kendricks and the Kennedy connection?"

"I like that—'the Kennedy connection'—it's a good phrase. We'll use it on the cover."

"David…" Marietta prodded.

"Yes, I know—back to the point. Everything fits in with Kendricks too. In late '62 and early '63 he was what is euphemistically called 'director of special operations' in the Congo. During that time, he contracted a rare tropical disease which he was treated for in a hospital in Nairobi. He was released at the end of August 1963 with his vision irreversibly impaired, necessitating the wearing of tinted glasses. From that time until his sudden reappearance on his native shores on December first, 1963, he dropped out of sight. No one has ever been able to discover what he was doing during that period. Until now."

"Yes, until now," Marietta repeated, almost purring. "Tell me about Oswald."

"His tracks are a great deal easier to follow. He arrived in Mexico City on Friday, September twenty-seventh, and left on October second, after making several visits to the Cuban and Russian consulates. The whole world knows what he did in Dallas seven weeks later on November twenty-second."

"It was a conspiracy!" Marietta said, her heart racing with excitement.

"And the story's going to break in *Sizzle*. Are the pictures safe?"

"Of course. Not a word to anyone now."

"You don't have to tell me that," he snapped.

"Sorry," she apologized quickly, wanting to keep him in a mellow mood. "I know better. I guess the excitement has made me overzealous. You, of all people, can understand that, can't you?"

He laughed. "I guess I'm a little overzealous myself."

"Have a productive trip tomorrow. I'll see you in the evening."

"Don't worry—I won't be late."

No, she thought, hanging up, she was sure he wouldn't be.

THE NEXT MORNING Marietta thought it prudent to have Fred drive her out to Queens, where she had rented a safe-deposit box in a small neighborhood branch of a bank she had no personal or business dealings with. Alone in a private cubicle, she removed the contact sheet from her briefcase and placed it inside the box, turning the key with a sweet, satisfying sensation of finality. As one of the most influential women in the country, she knew full well the power she wielded over others, but she was never more exquisitely and pleasurably aware of it as when she watched the guard lock the little box away.

From Queens she went back to Manhattan, directly to the West Village address that had been stamped on the back of the contact sheet. It was a walk-up apartment house whose fancy brickwork and ambitious decoration recalled a bygone time when landlords took pride in their property, and whose present state of rot and decay attested to the current real estate philosophy of extracting a maximum of profit. Knowing that she would have the advantage over Maxwell if she appeared unannounced, without giving him time to think about terms, she hadn't called in advance. From what David had told her about Maxwell's illness, drinking, and stagnant career, she doubted that there was much chance he would be out.

Maxwell's apartment was at the top of three flights of stairs that looked as though they hadn't been swept in months. The door was opened by a thin, fiftyish woman with long, untidy graying hair. She wore a tattered terry robe, beat-up slippers, and a look of hopeless despair.

"Is Mr. Maxwell in?" Marietta asked in her most charming voice.

"No."

"When do you expect him back?"

"Never." The woman's voice was as lifeless as her expression.

"Do you mean he has left for good?"

"You could say that."

Damn the woman! Why couldn't she answer a question straight out? Marietta continued to smile sweetly. "Can you tell me where I can contact him then?"

"Lady, if you're a bill collector, you can forget it. You're not going to get another drop of blood out of him." The woman moved back a step, as though to shut the door.

"Oh, but you're wrong," Marietta said quickly, realizing that Maxwell was hiding from creditors in a back room. "I came to discuss business with him," she added in a louder voice, hoping Maxwell would hear. She expected to see him rush out and appear behind his wife. Instead, sudden tears filled the woman's eyes.

"You're a little late for that. He died two weeks ago."

Marietta's surprise was quickly followed by relief. Gus Maxwell was probably the only other person who knew about the pictures and he was dead. Fate seemed to be playing directly into her hands. Unless, of course, his wife knew about them....

"I'm so sorry," she said in her sincerest voice, reaching for the woman's hand. "You must be Mrs. Maxwell."

The woman nodded, her face unchanged, but she didn't pull away from Marietta's touch.

"May I come in?" Marietta asked. "There are a few questions you might be able to help me with."

With a shrug, the woman led the way into the living room, saying, "I don't know much about Gus's work."

Once it had been a cozy room—about twenty years ago. Now the springs sagged in the sofa and chairs, and the upholstery was spotted and threadbare. The lampshades were warped and discolored, and the once-bright rug was faded and worn. Tabletops were covered with yellowing mail, forgotten glasses and cups, and a layer of dust. Only the walls were attractive—covered with neatly matted and framed photographs of people and places, pictures that had no doubt been taken by Gus Maxwell in his prime. Several of the photographs were of a child in various stages of growth from infancy to about the age of two. In some of them, he was being held by a young, beautiful, adoring mother, her eyes filled with love and hope.

"He was a great photographer. It wasn't his fault that he was a weak man and a sick one." Gus Maxwell's wife stood beside Marietta, following her gaze along the wall.

Marietta turned, prepared to make some banal and sincere-sounding remark, but the words stuck in her throat. The woman was standing with her back to the light, the shadows softening the harsh lines on her face, obscuring the despair and bitterness in her eyes. Was it possible this shell of a person was the Madonnalike woman photographed with the child? Marietta turned back to the pictures for another look.

"Yes, it's me," the woman said. "Or maybe I should say, it *was* me. I'm not the same person I was back then. But who among us is the same person she was twenty or twenty-five years ago?" She turned away from the photograph. "Anyway, my name's still the same—Cora. What's yours?"

"Marietta."

"Fancy name." Cora gave her an appraising look. "But you're a fancy lady. It suits you. Want some coffee?"

Marietta shook her head. If the cups in the kitchen were anything like the cups scattered around the living room, it wouldn't be a hygienic idea.

"Have a seat," Cora said. She gathered up the newspapers strewn over the furniture and dumped them in a corner. "I called all the papers when Gus died. Not a single one devoted as much as a line of space for an obituary. Bastards." She gave the pile a little kick and sank down on the sofa, waving her hand around her. "Don't mind the mess. I used to try to keep it fixed up, but when your luck runs out, friends are always quick to follow suit. What's the sense of knocking yourself out when no one's going to be dropping in? Once, though, this place was really something. It was cozy and warm. I can't tell you all the people who used to hang out here. They'd come to talk to Gus—ask his opinion. How should they take a shot? What filter should they use? Things like that. But that was all a long time ago."

Marietta knew Maxwell had had a drinking problem. She was beginning to wonder whether his wife had one too. She hadn't smelled liquor on Cora's breath. Perhaps life was the only depressant she took.

"I'm associated with *Sizzle* magazine," Marietta said. "Your husband gave Philip Bailey some pictures before Philip died. Do you know anything about them?"

"Those shots of the reception at City Hall, you mean? The money from them went toward his funeral."

"No, not those. There were some other shots—old ones."

"Oh, you mean the Wendy Carr pictures." She shook her head. "Poor Gus. I think he went a little crazy at the end. He had these wild dreams of grandeur. The doctor said that happens sometimes with heart patients at the end—especially when they drink too much."

"What do you mean, 'dreams of grandeur'?" Marietta asked, keeping her voice casually curious.

Cora shrugged. "Gus knew he was dying. The doctor had told him he had six months at the most if he stayed off the bottle—a hell of a lot less if he didn't. He loved me, you know. He really did. He wanted to get some money together for me to live on after he was gone. We'd already taken out and used up loans against all his insurance. Anyway, he kept coming up with ideas for one-man shows no one would hold and picture books that no publisher would go for. A couple of weeks ago while we were having break-fast, a Wendy Carr song was played on the radio. Gus remem-bered that years ago when he was on assignment in Mexico, he stumbled across her while she was a nobody singing in some dive and had taken some shots of her that he'd never done anything with. He got this brainstorm that maybe Phil Bailey would want them for a story about her, and he tore the place apart looking for them. When he finally found them, he acted like he'd discovered gold. Kept saying they'd be our ticket to a better life.…" Her voice trailed off in a sigh.

"Did he show them to you?" Marietta asked.

Cora shook her head.

"Weren't you curious?"

"About pictures of a woman who's been dead for years sing-ing in a sleazy club? What could there have been to see? I knew it was just another of Gus's pipe dreams. It was better if I didn't look at them. That way it was easier for me to pretend that I believed him."

"Did your husband tell you what Philip said when he saw the pictures?"

Cora sighed. "Phil was a good friend to Gus all through the bad years—his only friend, really. I know he bought a lot of stuff from Gus that he didn't really need or want, but this time, I think he went too far in humoring him. Gus came home walking on air. Said Phil was wild to have the pictures. He said Phil told him it was too late in the day to get his hands on the kind of money they deserved, so Gus was to go down the next day and Phil would take him to the bank and draw out a big check, maybe even set up a trust fund." She shook her head. "Maybe Phil intended to let Gus down easy the next day, but he died that night. When Gus heard about it, he nearly went out of his head. I guess he'd been a little out of it already, the dreams he was spinning. Anyway, he began drinking twice as much as usual. His death was more suicide than anything else."

Everything was working out better than Marietta could have hoped. The photographer was dead, his wife had no idea what was in the photographs, and there were no large sums of money that had changed hands and might look suspicious at a future date.

"What you've just told me has cleared up a lot of things," Marietta said. "We found the photographs when we were cleaning out Philip's desk. They were of such poor quality that we wondered what he was doing with them, and when we checked the books, we could find no record of a payment made to your husband for them. I came here today to find out what the story behind them was. I didn't bring the pictures with me, but, of course, I'll return them if you want them."

Cora shuddered and pulled her robe tighter. "Throw them out. I never want to see the damn things."

"I'll do it the minute I get back to the office. I understand how you feel. They hold too many sad memories for you. Were you with your husband when he took them?"

Cora's dull, almost lifeless eyes turned toward one of the photographs of the little boy. "No, I never traveled with him in those days. We had a child back then and I…" She retreated into distant memories.

Marietta had all the answers she needed, though. She stood up. "I'm truly sorry to have intruded at such a sad time."

"No matter." Cora rose too and accompanied her to the door. "I'm used to sad times."

As she turned to say good-bye, Marietta found herself strangely moved by those vacant eyes so like and yet so unlike the ones that gazed lovingly at the child in the photographs. "I've suffered losses too," she said. "I hope you'll believe me when I tell you that someday things will be better for you."

"It's kind of you to say so," Cora said. "But the child I loved and the man I loved took all my somedays with them." She stepped back and closed the door softly behind Marietta.

MARIETTA WAS QUITE pleased with herself when she arrived at her office. She had just pulled off the perfect business deal: She had gotten something of extraordinary value for absolutely nothing, and the supplier would never know the difference. With the fervor of a conqueror she threw herself into the mountain of work awaiting her, moving it even more rapidly than usual. Nevertheless, there were moments when she would pause in the middle of dictating a letter or giving instructions to gaze off into space, moments when Katheryn, her secretary, would have to bring her back to the matter at hand with a polite, "Mrs. Wylford?" At those times, as she forced her mind to return to the present, she could never really be sure what she had been thinking about, but always there would be a vague image of Cora Maxwell's face before her eyes.

"That will be all for now, Katheryn," she said when it had happened for the third time. "We'll finish these letters later. Call Ed Stern and tell him I want to see him in my office immediately."

"Yes, Mrs. Wylford," Katheryn said, gathering up her papers and hurrying out.

Ed Stern had been head of the accounting department back when the only Wylford enterprise was Lady Sabrina Swimwear, and he had been her only ally when Harlan had taken her into the company. When Marietta convinced Harlan to branch out, he named Ed treasurer, and Marietta had kept him on in that position. He was loyal and hardworking and seemed to have the capacity to grow along with her conglomerate. Though a strong believer in new blood and quick to shed aging executives, Marietta considered Ed ageless and as close to indispensable as she would permit anyone to be. They never discussed the subject, but she knew that if he had not yet passed his sixty-fifth birthday, it would soon be upon him. She hoped, however, that he gave as little thought to the possibility of his retirement as she did. Next to Melanie, he was her most trusted employee.

As always when he entered her office, Ed had the slightly disheveled look of a man who likes to work in his shirtsleeves and who, to humor the boss, has just thrown on his jacket, straightened his tie, and run a hand over his hair. He walked the long distance from her door to her desk with the casualness of one who is well aware of the significance of his surroundings but feels welcome and at home in them. He carried a folder in his hand, and he handed it to her, saying, "I have those figures on the Cantwell Division for you. I think you'll find some surprises."

"Pleasant or unpleasant?"

He smiled his slow smile as he sank down in the chair opposite her. "Let's just say 'not unexpected,' as far as I'm concerned. The executives over there have tried to do some fancy footwork with their books. They don't know that a guy who's been around as long as I have is on to every trick of the trade with or without benefit of computers."

"They're about to find out. As soon as this *Sizzle* deal goes through, I'll have every one of these bastards on the carpet." Marietta patted the folder with satisfaction. "But I didn't send for you to talk about the swindlers at Cantwell. I have another assignment for you—a very simple one."

He leaned forward, looking mildly curious. "Oh? What's that?"

"Gus Maxwell, an old-time photographer who did some work for *Sizzle,* died a week or two ago. His widow's name is Cora. I want you to write out a check to her for ten thousand dollars in exchange for an option on his photographs."

"Have you seen the pictures?"

"No, but some of them may be valuable. He worked for *Look* years ago."

"I'll send her a letter making the offer today."

"I don't want you to make an offer and wait for an answer. I want you to messenger a check over to her." She wrote down Cora's address and held it out to him.

"But we shouldn't pay her unless we know she'll accept. Besides, we don't own *Sizzle* yet."

"Will you stop talking like a goddamn tight-fisted accountant? Get the check to her. She'll accept it. And do you really have any doubt that by this time next week you'll be up to your elbows reorganizing *Sizzle*'s accounting department?"

He took the paper with a smile. "If I had my jacket off, you'd see that my sleeves are rolled up already." He stood up. "I'll send someone over to Mrs. Maxwell with the check this afternoon."

How long, Marietta wondered as she watched him walk out, had Ed's shoulders stooped that way? The thought gave her a little chill. She didn't want him to grow old. He was one of the few people she could depend on.

Her phone rang, a welcome interruption to her thoughts. In a moment Katheryn buzzed her with the announcement that Harrison Kendricks was on line one. This seemed, indeed, to be her lucky day, Marietta thought, pressing down the appropriate button. Now she wouldn't have to take the initiative and call him.

"Hello," she said in a cool yet charming business voice.

Kendricks did not return the greeting. "The twenty days are almost up," he said in his clipped accent. "It's time we met and resolved this matter between ourselves."

So he was beginning to sweat. Good. "The same thought had occurred to me." Her mind raced ahead as she spoke. She hadn't had time yet to decide on the proper place for a meeting. It had to be somewhere private, but she didn't want to ask him to her apartment, and she knew he wouldn't come to her office.

"Excellent. I think it should be somewhere private," he said, putting her thoughts into words. "The press would make too much of it if we were spotted in public. We'll make it cocktails at my place this evening."

The son of a bitch. Men didn't tell her to come to their place for a drink. They asked her. Sometimes they begged her. Still, his place was the perfect solution. And soon she would be the one who had the upper hand. "That's agreeable to me."

"You have my address?"

"Of course."

"Five-thirty then." He hung up without another word.

"You British bastard," Marietta said softly. "It will give me great pleasure to have your balls." She gently replaced the receiver in its cradle.

WHEN IT CAME to business appointments, Marietta did not tolerate lateness in others and was never guilty of it herself. At precisely five-thirty, Fred pulled up her Rolls before the limestone mansion, in the East Sixties just off Fifth Avenue, that had been designed by one of New York's most prestigious architects at the turn of the century for one of the country's most infamous robber barons. Its gabled roof, high-arched windows, and ironwork balconies were as impressive eight decades later as they must have been in the days when the Morgans, the Fricks, and the Rockefellers had come to call.

"This may take anywhere from a few minutes to a few hours," Marietta said as she emerged from the car.

Fred stood erect by the door he held open for her, his face impassive; waiting was part of his job.

She swept up the stairs and rang the bell, knowing that she looked as regal in her burgundy Givenchy suit and pale pink silk blouse as any of the bluebloods in Harrison Kendricks's native land.

Almost immediately, the door was opened by a tall, thin man with sparse gray hair, wearing a black suit and tie. "Mrs. Wylford?" he said with an English accent and a perfect little bow. "You're expected, madam. Come this way, please."

The heels of her Gucci pumps clicking across the marble floor, she followed him through the magnificent hexagonal entranceway. Upon its two-story-high domed ceiling cherubim and lusciously rounded ladies from a Fragonard fresco that had once graced the home of a favorite in the court of Louis XV now continued their frolics, untouched by time, unharmed by revolutions.

Opening a pair of oak-paneled doors, the butler announced: "Mrs. Wylford." Then he stepped aside and withdrew, silently closing the doors behind him.

It was a beautiful setting for making an entrance: paneled walls, ceiling-high double windows that overlooked an English-style courtyard garden bursting with springtime color, a huge marble fireplace, genuine Georgian furniture and decorations including a Gainsborough, and a gleaming grand piano.

This time Kendricks, who had been sitting on a Sheraton settee covered in blue brocade, had the good grace to rise. He wore gray trousers and a navy-blue blazer. His white shirt, open at the throat, revealed a blue paisley ascot.

"Good evening," Marietta said, pretending she didn't notice that he had made no effort to cross the rug to meet her. She walked over to him instead, but since his hands remained in his pockets, she didn't extend her own.

"You're punctual," was his only greeting. "I like that in a woman."

They were face-to-face now, and she noticed his firm jawline, his mysterious eyes behind those sinister tinted glasses, his broad shoulders and his strong, taut muscles. She liked that in a man too, but she didn't tell him so. She raised her brows as she sat down gracefully on the settee, placing her purse beside her. "Only in a woman?" she asked. "That's strange. I like it in both sexes."

He didn't respond, but the corners of his mouth turned up slightly in a way that told her he had gotten her message and admired her for it. "What would you like to drink?"

"Scotch and soda."

He nodded, then tilted his head toward the silver tray bearing caviar and toast rounds, cheese and crackers, on the cocktail table. "Help yourself."

She picked up a little cube of Cheshire cheese as he walked over to a Pembroke table that had been set up as a bar beside a George III commode with magnificent marquetry, which was stocked with expensive liquors. He didn't speak as he mixed her drink and poured some Courvoisier for himself. His movements were graceful and deliberate, yet hinted at unfathomable depths of power. He reminded her of something, but she couldn't identify what it was until he walked smoothly across the room, his eyes never leaving hers as he extended her drink. Then she realized that he was like a panther stalking its prey. With a slow smile, she took the glass from his hand. She didn't mind in the least being stalked by him. In fact, it would be interesting to pretend to succumb before revealing that he had invited a tigress into his lair.

He sat down on the other end of the settee and raised his glass. "Cheers."

"Cheers," she returned, and sipped her drink.

Though Kendricks had a reputation for never mincing words and getting down to business immediately, he seemed in no rush to broach the subject. Through the first drink and then the second, they spoke instead in generalities—their shared interest in gardens, antiques, the theater. Since he had suggested the meeting, Marietta was determined that he be the one to initiate any discussion of a buyout or compromise. She would let him say his piece, then drop her bombshell.

At first, she thought he was avoiding the subject because he wanted to disarm her. But as their conversation progressed, she realized that he had more than business on his mind. Though the tinted glasses veiled his eyes, they did not hide them, and she was aware how often his gaze traveled from her lips to her breasts, to her calves and thighs. It was like a visual caress, and she began to respond to it, her nipples growing taut, her thighs tingling. Harrison Kendricks wanted her. It was possible, of course, that it was all part of his plan—that, with his gigantic ego, he thought that one roll in the hay with him and she would be eating out of his hand. But even if that had been his primary purpose, it was obvious he now wanted to satisfy a great deal more than corporate desires. Besides, what difference did his motivation make? She wanted him too. She wanted to see every inch of that firm, sleek body, to feel those muscular arms tight around her, to have those strong hands trace their way across her bare flesh. She had been made love to by many men—but never by such a dangerous one. The prospect was deliciously, wickedly exciting. She was aware that Kendricks, probably for the first time in his life, was faced with a problem in deciding what approach to take. For she had to be as unique to him as he was to her. He must know that the lines, looks, and moves that would tumble most women would be ineffectual in her case. She would have to find a way to help him. That gave her one more advantage.

Talk of the theater led Kendricks to make some unflattering observations about American musicals and music. "No one today seems to know what music is all about," he said.

"Except perhaps you?" Marietta asked.

He smiled. "There are a few others, I admit."

She nodded toward the piano. "Do you play?"

"Yes. Rather well, in fact. Schumann is my favorite. Does all that surprise you?"

"Nothing anyone does—whether admirable or despicable—ever surprises me."

"So you're an absolute cynic."

"Not a cynic—a realist. I see things as they are. For example, I'm very much aware that you would like to get me into bed."

"Really?" he said, raising an eyebrow.

"Don't play coy. It's out of character."

"All right. I'll admit that I find the idea of making love to you rather attractive."

"And I find it rather attractive too. So I wonder why, busy people that we are, we're sitting here wasting each other's time sipping drinks and chatting. Why don't we simply go up to your bedroom?" she said, rising.

"You're an extraordinary woman."

"If I weren't, you wouldn't be so interested in taking me to bed, would you?"

He followed close behind her as she walked across the room. When she paused at the big double doors, he reached around her and opened them, probably the first time in his life that he had performed such a courtesy for a woman other than his mother. Smiling to herself, she passed through them, then preceded him up the winding marble staircase.

"It's the second room on the left," he said.

She waited for him to open that door also.

It was a large paneled room with a fireplace, furnished in the Georgian style, but she couldn't see the furnishings in detail, for the heavy drapes at the windows were tightly drawn and Kendricks quickly closed the door behind them, shutting out the light from the hall and plunging them into darkness.

"Where's your light switch?" she asked, groping along the wall. Alone in the pitch dark with a man like Harrison Kendricks, she suddenly found herself feeling vulnerable rather than sexually aroused.

"There is none." His voice came from so close that she could feel his breath on her cheek and she jumped. His hand closed over hers and brought it down to her side. "This room is kept dark on purpose. It's the one place where I can remove my glasses safely. I use only a small night light. You'll be surprised how much light it can diffuse."

He let go of her hand, and she sensed rather than heard him move across the room. A moment later a pinpoint of bluish light began to glow from the direction of the mantel.

"Your eyes will adjust soon." He was beside her again, his hands gripping her shoulders. How had he gotten back so quickly? How could a man of his size move with such stealth? Her heart pounded, but she was determined to sound calm and cool as she answered him with a quick-witted observation. But before any words could pass her lips, his mouth was upon hers in a kiss that left her reeling. She reached up and wound her arms around his neck, as much to keep her balance as to return his embrace.

Slowly, they made their way toward the bed without being conscious of the movement, kissing, caressing, shedding clothes.

He was right, Marietta discovered, when at last she was lying on the silk sheets. Her eyes had adjusted to the darkness. He stood above her in naked splendor, his perfectly proportioned body glowing in the dim light. At some point, perhaps even before he had taken her in his arms, he had removed his glasses, and for the first time there was no barrier between her gaze and his. She hadn't expected it to make such a difference. Without his glasses, he looked even more exotically sinister than with them. A delicious little shiver surged through her.

Neither spoke, but words were unnecessary. They were two of a kind, creatures who had fashioned themselves in the image of their own wants and needs. They understood each other as no other person on earth could. What they felt was neither love nor hate, but admiration coupled with disdain, and it led to an all-consuming desire to come together for one single moment in time in an act that symbolized both destruction and renewal— and then to part forever. She stretched her arms out to him, and he sank down beside her, gathering her in a crushing embrace. They rolled on the bed in a frenzy of passion, kissing, biting, squeezing, panting. Marietta's heartbeats thundered in her ears, and the low, moaning, animal sounds that escaped from her throat were matched by deeper, almost growling, sounds from Kendricks. When at last they came together, it was in the wild, lustful, explosive coupling of two magnificent jungle beasts, and, her heart feeling as though it were about to burst, Marietta nearly fainted with delight.

For a long time they lay side by side, as close as it was possible to be without touching. Marietta was as aware of Kendricks's ragged breathing as of her own. At last her mind and body came back to normal, but she made no move to get up or change her position, and neither did Kendricks.

"You're aware, of course, that you cannot possibly win."

It was not at all surprising to her that he should initiate their business discussion now, when they were lying together naked in bed. They had satisfied one desire; it was time to move on to the next.

"I'm aware of no such thing." Her voice was as boardroom cool as his.

"My dear woman, surely you know that by Friday I shall have enough shares to take over the control of the company."

"No, I don't know that—and neither do you. If you did, you would never have bothered to invite me here today."

He was silent a moment, and then he said, "I invited you here today to give you the opportunity to withdraw gracefully."

"I appreciate your thoughtfulness, but I have no intention of withdrawing. Did you really think that what just happened between us would turn me into some kind of love slave, ready to do your bidding?"

"Neither of us is that naive. I have a much stronger inducement for a change of mind on your part."

She laughed. "Don't tell me you intend to try to buy me off?"

"Obviously, you haven't done your homework, Mrs. Wylford." He propped himself up on his elbow and looked down at her, his eyes and teeth gleaming in the dimness. "A little research would have shown you that I never buy off opponents—I destroy them."

"Do you really now?" She smiled up at him. "And just how do you intend to destroy me?"

He traced a finger along her jawline, down her neck, to the hollow of her throat "What would you say, my dear lady, if I told you that I have irrefutable proof that Philip Bailey was fucking you at the moment he dropped dead and that I plan to publish it?"

Marietta remained unruffled. "I'd say you were bluffing."

"And if I told you that I can produce a copy of the coroner's confidential report and a false eyelash that was custom-made for you and that was found oh-so-cozily enmeshed in the pubic hairs of the gentleman in question?"

For a second, Marietta's heart sank and she felt a sudden rush of anger. Then she remembered what she had on Kendricks. "In that case," she said calmly, "I'd quote one of your own prime ministers to you: 'Publish and be damned.'"

He laughed softly. "Now who's bluffing? When that story hits the front page of the *Clarion*, you can kiss Louise Bailey's options good-bye—and with it, all chance of gaining a controlling share of *Sizzle*." His hand moved down to her breast, rested there a second, then squeezed. "I have you, my dear lady, by the tits."

"That," she said with soft deliberation, "is what you think." Her eyes held his. "If you are under the impression that I came here today simply to hear what you had to offer, you know even less about me than you assume I know about you. You see, my dear man, I, too, do my homework. I came here today to induce you to withdraw. What I have found out about you makes that coroner's alleged findings look about as exciting as a weather report."

He burst into laughter. "You *are* naive, after all. You forget that I've built my reputation on being a scoundrel and a blackguard. That's why I command so much respect. Do you really believe that there is anything you could reveal that would actually hurt me?"

"How," she asked sweetly, "does collusion in the assassination of President John F. Kennedy sound?"

The laughter died on his lips, and his hand froze on her breast.

"Contrary to any ideas that stories about our Wild West may have given you, Mr. Kendricks, we Americans do not take kindly to the bumping off of our presidents. I have it on good authority that the Queen of England looks rather askance at it too. You would wave bye-bye to that peerage I've been hearing so much about, and you would do it from the inside of an American prison cell."

"I think you've gone bonkers. I don't know what the hell you're raving about." His voice was clipped and calm, but she could hear the rage behind each word.

"Oh, yes, you do. Even in this dark room, I can see it written all over your face. I'm talking about the night of October first, 1963—the night you met Lee Harvey Oswald in a Mexican dive known as the Red Bull and gave him an envelope containing his pay and his instructions. There was an unknown singer there that evening by the name of Wendy Carr. When she became popular a year or two later, you remembered her, didn't you? And you became afraid that one day she might remember you and Oswald as well. Is that why she died in an accident so like the one that took your brother's life? The similarities between the two are bound to come out in the investigation that will be held."

"How do you know about all this?"

"You remembered Wendy Carr when she became famous, because she'd been in the spotlight that night. What you didn't know was that there was a photographer there who was capturing her—and you and Oswald—forever on film."

"What photographer?"

"What difference does it make? He's dead. But he gave me the pictures and the negatives."

"Where are they?"

"In a very safe place."

"Who else knows about them?"

"I'm the only one."

"Really?" For the first time, the tension slipped out of his voice. "How very foolish of you to say so." His hands slid up to her neck.

Her heart beat faster, but her voice remained calm. "You wouldn't be foolish enough to strangle me in your own bed."

"True," he said just as calmly. "But let me give you an anatomy lesson. There's a certain spot at the base of the skull. I need only to exert enough pressure there, and you will die instantly and peacefully without a sign of violence—no bulging eyes or protruding tongue. People will think that, like poor Philip Bailey, you simply had one fuck too many."

"Then perhaps I should tell you that I have taken the precaution of sending letters to high-level law enforcement officers both here and in your country that are to be opened immediately upon my death—natural, accidental, or violent. Those letters will lead them directly to the proof we've just discussed. So you see, my dear man"—she turned on her side and slid her hand along his body—"it is I who have you—by the balls." She emphasized her words with a not-too-gentle squeeze. "Now, I'm a simple businesswoman, not an intelligence agent. I'm willing to keep our little secret in return for your dropping all interest in acquiring *Sizzle* and a promise never to cross my path again in any corporate battle. What do you say to that?"

"I say you're a conniving whore and a scheming bitch."

"And I say that there's an old American maxim it's time you became familiar with: 'It takes one to know one.' But you still haven't answered my question."

"Those pictures would never stand up in a court of law. They prove nothing except an acquaintance with Oswald."

"The scandal they'd provoke would be enough to make you *persona non grata* here for the rest of your life and to rob you of any hopes of a peerage at home. But we both know it wouldn't end at just that. Americans wouldn't rest until the full truth became known. Publication of those pictures would start an investigation the likes of which have never before been seen in this country. And all you have to do to prevent it is to go along with my generous terms."

"You bitch."

"I take it that means *yes*."

He didn't answer.

"I expect to see the announcement of your withdrawal in the papers tomorrow, along with the suggestion that those who tendered their options to you now transfer them to my bankers."

"I'll pay you back someday."

"I doubt that very much. You're too smart to play with this kind of dynamite." She withdrew her hand from his scrotum, and got out of bed. Neither of them spoke as she dressed.

"I'll see myself out," she said. She picked up her purse and walked to the door, then paused before opening it. "I doubt very much that you're a religious man. But if I were you, I'd begin praying now for a long life for Marietta Wylford—one that will exceed yours by at least a day."

Chapter Twenty-One

HARRY HAD ASKED for the Rolls at seven-thirty. It was now a quarter to eight. Nick had been sitting in the car, waiting, for almost a half hour. He had turned onto the street at about seven-fifteen, just in time to see that Wylford bitch emerge from the townhouse. Immediately her own Rolls had pulled up to the curb, the chauffeur springing out and opening the door for her so fast it looked like he was practicing for some new kind of Olympic event. On the other hand, the Wylford dame had approached the car slowly, as if she were a queen leading a royal procession, maybe a dozen imaginary handmaidens following behind to lift her ermine robes from the ground. Nick had to hand it to her: Her head had been held high, her step sure and firm; no one would know, to look at her, that she had just suffered a resounding defeat.

Maybe that was why Harry was late. Maybe he was having a little private celebration. But it wasn't like him to forget the time.

After drumming his fingers on the steering wheel another five minutes, Nick got out of the Rolls and went into the house.

Williams told him that Kendricks was in the library. The library was where Harry conducted all his business when he was home. No doubt there were some mop-up operations he wanted to activate before leaving the house.

Nick sat on the Darby and Joan chair in the vestibule, where he could have a view of the closed double doors that led to the library, and waited. At last one of the double doors swung open and Kendricks emerged. He wasn't dressed for dinner, but was wearing gray flannel slacks and a white shirt. There was no ascot at his throat, and he hadn't put on a jacket. Nick tried to remember when he had seen Harry without at least a blazer or lounging jacket on in the house. He got to his feet, perplexed.

"I've canceled my dinner engagement," Kendricks said, catching sight of Nick.

Harry's jaw was tight, his lips a thin line, his eyes narrowed with rage. The last time Nick had seen that look on his face had been back when they had been running guns to the IRA. Some hotshot in the CID had found a shipment of grenades. Harry had lost a quarter of a million on that deal. The hotshot eventually lost his life; the murder, of course, had been blamed on the IRA.

Since Harry didn't close the doors to the drawing room behind him, Nick followed him inside. He watched in silence as Kendricks poured himself a drink, downed it, then poured himself another. Before drinking it, he turned and faced Nick.

"The bloody bitch has pulled the rug out from under me."

Nick shook his head, not sure he had heard right. But Harry's expression matched his words. "How could she do that? Didn't you tell her about the report? The eyelash?"

"She doesn't give a damn about them."

"She will when they're published. She's just bluffing, Harry. She can't win without Louise Bailey's stock—and she'll never get it once the story runs."

Kendricks took a swig of his drink and sat down. "We're not running the bloody story."

"Why the hell not?"

"Because she's got a bloody story of her own."

"What story? What do you mean?"

"I mean she's managed to find out something about me that I thought no living human being could ever uncover. The one thing that could ruin me."

A terrible coldness washed over Nick, and his mind shot back to that September night in the Congo, the night when he'd been the lookout as Harry had tampered with the engine of that plane. No one had seen them. He could have sworn no one had seen them.

He sank down on a chair. "Jesus, Harry! Did she find out about Hammarskjöld?"

Kendricks didn't answer. He didn't have to.

And then another, even more horrible thought followed. Nick jumped to his feet.

"Harry, I never told her! I never told anyone!"

"Don't be an ass. Of course I know you didn't. Do you think you'd be alive and breathing now if I thought you had? Go fix yourself a drink. You look like a candidate for an intensive-care unit."

Nick paused for a moment, staring at the array of bottles. In his own room he had a couple of six packs in the refrigerator for relaxing, and a bottle of Johnny Walker Black on the shelf for more serious drinking. It made things simpler. He poured himself a double of Courvoisier. What the hell? It wasn't often he and Harry drank together these days.

The liquor felt like warm gold running down his throat and into his gut, chasing the chill before it. Feeling in control of himself again, he resumed his seat.

"I can take care of her for you, Harry."

"What works with petty pains in the neck wouldn't work with Marietta Wylford. The investigation would stink to heaven."

"Let it stink. They'd never find anything. I could fix her car, the way I took care of that singer back home. Her death made headlines around the world, but Scotland Yard couldn't find a thing."

"No. It's not the answer. This isn't some dumb-broad entertainer we're dealing with. This woman has the mind of a computer and the instincts of a killer shark. She has thoroughly examined all our options and her own. She has arranged for her proof to be brought to the attention of the authorities in the event of her demise by any means, foul, accidental, or natural."

"What proof?"

"Photographs and negatives. She says she has them all, and I believe her. She's much too clever to allow anyone else around her to see and handle such dynamite."

"But what about the photographer?"

"Dead. Of natural causes, according to her. But, of course, she would say that."

"I can't understand why the guy sat on the pictures all these years. Why didn't he try to blackmail you?"

Kendricks's eyebrows shot up. "Coming from you, that's a rather naive question. You know exactly what would have happened to him if he had attempted blackmail. Obviously, so did he."

"Okay, but then why didn't he go to the press? He'd have gotten a bundle from the media."

"The man was a crook who wanted to make the most of what he had. He was waiting for the right time and the right person."

"All these years?" The whole business was beginning to smell decidedly fishy. Nick leaned forward. "Harry, the world is filled with your filthy-rich enemies. The guy could have gone to any one of them years ago and had his pockets lined with gold. The dame's bluffing. She's clever, that's all. She knows your reputation, knows when you were in Africa. She went to a history book and looked up some of the things that happened while you were there. Then she took a lucky stab in the dark."

His nostrils flaring with rage, Kendricks leaned forward too. "Do you think there is a single person on the face of this earth who could con me? Why the bastard waited so long to sell his wares, we can never know. But, no doubt to his misfortune, wait he did. And now Marietta Wylford has proven to me beyond a doubt that she has it in her hot little well-manicured hands."

"What does she intend to do with it?"

"Nothing—as long as I back out of the *Sizzle* skirmish and won't attack any of her other ventures."

"And you agreed?"

"I've just been on the telephone drawing up an announcement of my withdrawal from the field in the *Sizzle* takeover battle. I've released all the options that would have been tendered to our side."

"They'll go to Wylford?"

"The owners are free to do as they please. What pleases them is turning a profit. I assume they'll go to her."

"That's it, then?" Nick couldn't believe Harry would knuckle under like that.

Kendricks took a sip of his drink. "That's it," he said, "for now."

Nick relaxed a bit. He liked the sound of that *for now.* "Meaning?"

"Meaning that with time against me, I had no choice but to retreat from this battle. Nevertheless, I have no intention of tiptoeing around that woman for the rest of my life. It may take years, but one day I'll find out where she has hidden the evidence, and I'll destroy it."

"And then we'll destroy her."

"We'll do no such thing." He leveled a hard look at Nick. "Don't get any ideas about acting on your own. You're never to touch one silky hair on that gorgeous, scheming little head."

"But you're not going to let her get away with it?"

"Why not? Even the kings of old allowed noble adversaries their lives and their freedom. And she is a noble adversary. The only real match I've ever met. She played by my rules, and she beat me fair and square." Kendricks smiled appreciatively. "We shall meet again one day on the corporate battlefield. I look forward to it." He sat back, his eyes filled with thoughts of future battles. "Be a good chap, and tell Williams that I have changed my mind. I'll dine after all. Ask him to have the cook prepare a full meal."

After delivering Harry's message, Nick left to return the Rolls to the garage. All these years, and he still didn't understand Harry. He wondered if he ever would.

Chapter Twenty-Two

I T HAD BEEN a productive but exhausting day for Melanie. She had obtained the options in Texas, and as she slipped the key into her lock at a quarter to eight, she wished she could reward herself with a lazy, languid bath, a good mystery novel, and an early bedtime. But there was still the eight-thirty meeting at Marietta's looming ahead of her. She did allow herself the luxury of a hot shower, and once out of it she ignored the Halston suit she had laid out on her bed and pulled on a pair of comfortable jeans and a bright red blouse.

She had bought the blouse and several other equally colorful outfits at Saks the week before on the same day she had gone to Kenneth's and had her hair cut. She still wasn't sure why she had done it. She told herself that the change of wardrobe and the new hairdo with soft, short curls had nothing to do with what David had said that night in Marietta's roof garden. She had wanted a change, that was all. Every woman did now and then. She didn't have to have the idea put into her head by some man. Of course, that didn't explain why she had felt annoyed and rather hurt when David didn't even comment on the change the next time they were together. She had been aware that he was looking at her as they went over some papers, but when she met his gaze, his eyes seemed to hold censure rather than admiration, and she quickly turned away. David had been an enigma to her from the beginning, but back then there had been some light, even warm moments. Those moments had all disappeared after the Saturday night he had shown up drunk at her door. Now when they had to be together, he was cool and remote, and she found herself feeling awkward and even rather lonely in his company.

Well, she thought as she applied a touch of blush and lip gloss, after Friday the rush for options would be over. David would concentrate on being the editor of *Sizzle* and she would return to the piles of work awaiting her at the office. She would probably never have to see him again on business, for *Sizzle* was Marietta's pet project. That thought should have brought a welcome rush of relief, but it didn't. As she left her apartment, Melanie found herself vaguely wishing that David would get plastered again one night soon.

Looking tired, but thoroughly sober, David was already at Marietta's when Melanie arrived. In contrast, Marietta seemed to be bursting with energy. "Now the celebration can begin," she said as soon as Melanie sat down on the sofa. She nodded toward a bottle of Piper-Heidsieck chilling in a silver ice bucket and asked David to do the honors.

"Don't you first want to hear how my trip went?" Melanie asked.

"I know without asking that it went well. So did David's. But at this point, it wouldn't make a damn bit of difference if you'd both fallen flat on your faces." Eyes bright and cheeks flushed, Marietta seemed barely able to contain herself as she took a glass from David. Melanie had seen her that way before—always on the eve of great successes; for Marietta, as for most business moguls, manipulating a corporate coup was the ultimate high.

David handed Melanie a glass before raising his own. "What are we drinking to?" he asked, and Melanie noticed how warily he was watching Marietta.

"To *Sizzle* of course," Marietta said, "the newest link in the golden chain of Wylford Enterprises."

Melanie took a sip from her glass. "It sounds like you had a pretty interesting day."

"'Interesting' doesn't come close to describing it. Try 'fantastic' or 'stupendous.' It's as though some special force has been guiding us all along—straight to this moment when everything falls into our laps. It's all over and we've won. It couldn't have gone better if we'd planned it every step of the way." Marietta drained her glass, then got up and refilled it. "You wouldn't believe how great everything has turned out for us. That photographer who took the pictures was the only one besides Philip who knew what was in them, and he died over a week ago."

David turned pale. "Gus is dead?" he murmured, sinking down on the other end of the sofa.

"As a doornail." Marietta sounded as though she were announcing a happy event she had been instrumental in planning. Her face sobered a bit when she saw David's reaction. "Why do you look so surprised? You told me he was a very sick man."

"Sure, I knew he was sick," David said. "And that he had a lot of problems—particularly with booze. I'm not so much surprised by the news as saddened by it. I don't like to hear that anyone has died—especially someone I knew and liked."

Melanie squirmed, and wished that Marietta hadn't sounded so callous about Gus. She knew that Marietta's feelings really ran deep, and she hated it when Marietta played right into David's false image of her as a self-centered and self-serving woman.

As though realizing that she had gone too far, Marietta adopted a more serious and sympathetic expression. "I'm sorry if you've lost a friend," she said, "but the man was dying anyway, and I don't think I can be blamed for noting that his death has been rather lucky for us. Alive, he might try to bleed us dry, or get a little too drunk one day and let something slip to the wrong people. I spent the morning with his widow. All he told her was that he had come across some pictures he'd taken of Wendy Carr when she was unknown and that Philip was so pleased to have such rare shots he was going to buy them for a fantastic sum. The banks had already closed when he'd visited Philip, so he'd left the photos and they'd agreed to meet the next day and take care of everything. The next morning, of course, Philip was dead, and the news seems to have hastened Maxwell's end. His widow thinks the photos are actually worthless, that Philip was just trying to make Gus feel good for old times' sake. She thinks he probably would have given Gus no more than a token amount and tossed the pictures out—which, by the way, is what she told me to do—throw the pictures away. I told her I would, but, of course, my conscience wouldn't let it go at that. I sent her a very generous check this afternoon with the stipulation that it was for giving *Sizzle* exclusive option on all her husband's unpublished photographs."

Melanie wondered just how generous the check had been. She knew that when it came to business deals, Marietta tended toward extreme exaggeration in her employment of the word. Still, she noted that David seemed pleased to hear that Marietta had attempted to right things with Maxwell's widow. She hoped he wouldn't ask for figures. He didn't. Instead, he pointed out:

"When we publish the pictures, she'll realize exactly how valuable they are."

"No, she won't," Marietta said.

"Of course she will. We'll have to give Maxwell credit, and the story will be picked up all over the world."

Marietta shook her head, and Melanie began to feel apprehensive rather than uncomfortable.

"We're not going to publish the pictures." Marietta's voice was calm and matter-of-fact.

"Mari!" Even Melanie was taken by surprise.

David jumped up. "What the hell are you talking about?"

Marietta, resuming her chair, looked amused by their reactions. "Calm down, you two," she said soothingly. "There's no need to publish them. I've just come from a meeting with Kendricks. I told him all about the pictures. For the first time in his life, that man is shitting in his pants. The morning's papers will carry the announcement that he's no longer interested in acquiring *Sizzle*. I already told you—we won."

"You can't just throw those pictures away because Kendricks has agreed to leave the field clear for you, Mari," Melanie said.

"Oh, I have no intention of throwing them away. They're in a very safe place. They're my insurance that that British bastard will never attempt to step on my toes again." She smiled and took a sip of her champagne.

David had been standing there looking thunderstruck, but suddenly he came to life. "Goddamn it! These aren't just some compromising shots of a married man with his pants down— something that might put him in the doghouse with his wife if they got out. They're proof of involvement in a plot to assassinate a president of the United States—a plot that obviously didn't stop with Kendricks. He was a soldier of fortune who always worked for the highest bidder. An investigation would be bound to uncover who paid him to hire Oswald. You can't take evidence like that and sit on it!" He turned to Melanie. "You're a lawyer. Tell her she can't do it."

"He's right, Mari. Suppressing evidence is a serious crime. You could be fined or sent to jail or both." Knowing she would score more points with logic than emotion, she kept her voice calm and tried not to show how upset Marietta's announcement had made her.

"Come off it, Melanie." Marietta appeared unruffled by the threat of prison. "You know that no court would accept those photographs as evidence of a crime. You said as much last night when you pointed out that the most they prove is an acquaintanceship."

"But they would lead to an investigation," David said impatiently, "an investigation that would be bound to reveal a crime."

Marietta shrugged. "What difference does it make after all these years? It wouldn't bring Kennedy back or change the course of history."

"How can you say that?" Melanie was beginning to lose some of her lawyer's composure. "Justice would be done—that's the difference it would make."

"Justice." Marietta almost spat the word out. "Justice is a game you lawyers play. You created it as a scheme to keep yourselves in business, and you always see to it that it goes to the highest bidder."

The crack left Melanie smarting. She had won the dismissal of enough suits that had been justifiably filed against Wylford Enterprises to recognize the truth in Marietta's words.

"Well, it will be done in this case," David insisted. "I'm publishing those pictures, Marietta, and I'm delivering copies of them to the authorities."

"What pictures?" Marietta spread her hands. "I don't see any pictures."

"You didn't destroy them, did you?" He looked as though he'd like to inflict that fate on her.

"Of course not. I'm not that stupid. If I destroyed them, I'd have no hold over Kendricks, would I? I've put them in a place a hell of a lot safer than my freezer—and one only I know about and have access to. Now will you stop ranting, David, and sit down?"

"Damn it! Don't talk to me like I'm a spoiled kid who has asked for one too many lollipops! We're involved with political assassination and international intrigue here."

"Correction: *We're* not involved with it in any way—and what little we know about it, we're going to forget."

"I'm not going to forget it and neither are you. Something like this can't be buried. If you won't give me the pictures, then I'll go to the authorities and report that you have them."

"And what do you think they'll do—come barging in here with a search warrant? That's quite unlikely when someone has made such an outlandish accusation against an upright citizen, isn't it, Melanie?"

Melanie's head had been spinning as she listened to the two arguing. She had known Marietta to do some underhanded, even barely legal things, to further her business interests but never anything as despicable as this. Maybe if she had some time alone with her, she could convince her—

"Well, isn't it?" Marietta prodded.

"Yes, of course, it's unlikely," Melanie said. "But, Mari, you have to remember that—"

"That's all I wanted to know." Marietta cut her off, and turned back to David. "So you see, it would boil down to your word against mine—and no one would believe you."

"Don't be so sure about that," David said. "I'm an upright citizen myself, and a highly respected journalist. Any accusation I made would carry a lot of weight."

"That depends on the circumstances."

The cold look that had come into Marietta's eyes made Melanie shudder, but David seemed unaffected by it. "What do you mean by that?" he asked.

"I mean that when I tell the authorities that you're trying to get revenge because I replaced you as the editor of *Sizzle,* they'll dismiss the story as a wild fabrication."

David's eyes narrowed. "I take it that you're telling me to keep my mouth shut about this if I want to stay on as the editor."

Marietta raised her glass to him. "I always said that you were an extremely intelligent and perceptive man." She sighed impatiently. "Oh, for heaven's sake, David! Stop standing there looking outraged and offended. This won't be the first time in your life that you've ever dumped a story. You can't tell me that you haven't killed plenty of articles because your ad men suddenly sent word that they would offend an advertiser, or Philip said it would hurt a personal friend."

"Sure, I admit it. Every editor does it now and then. But this story is different."

"Don't be such a goddamn hypocrite. This isn't different, it's only bigger. Do you think cops would say that murdering someone six-feet-two is more of a crime than killing a midget? You've relaxed your precious journalistic standards before. There's no reason why you shouldn't do it again—especially when it's for such a good cause."

"What good cause?"

"The cause of Wylford Enterprises. In future operations, we can get a hell of a lot more mileage out of suppressing that information than out of releasing it."

"You mean *you* can get more mileage out of it. You're Wylford Enterprises—not I."

Suddenly Marietta looked as though she was growing weary of the argument. "You're right: you're not a part of Wylford Enterprises—yet. You had better make up your mind whether you want to be. Because if you don't, I intend to make certain that you never again work as a journalist in any major city—here or abroad."

It was a face-off. Melanie looked from one to the other, knowing Marietta would never back down, hoping David would come to his senses and make the right decision. In time, maybe they could get Marietta to change her mind about releasing the pictures.

"There are other things a man can do for a living," David said, and Melanie's heart plummeted.

Marietta looked him up and down distastefully. "Not in two-hundred-dollar shoes."

He shrugged. "They've been pinching my feet a lot lately."

"Then there's nothing more to be said. You know your way out."

"There's a lot more to be said. I intend to go to the authorities."

Marietta laughed. "They'll think you're just a spiteful fool—out to get revenge on both Kendricks and me in one blow."

"You seem to forget that I have a witness. Melanie saw the pictures too."

"And you think she'll back you up?"

"Yes, I do."

Melanie felt the blood drain from her face as they both turned to her. Why did they have to put her in the middle of their fight? She knew that David was in the right, but how could he expect her to turn against her best friend, the person who had done everything for her?

When she didn't speak, David's eyes hardened. "I see," he said quietly.

But he didn't see—he couldn't possibly see. She had to say something to erase that awful look of disgust from his face. "You don't understand, David," she said. "Even with my support, no one would believe you. We'd have no documentary proof. We'd come out looking like cranks and publicity hounds, lunatics. There's nothing that can be done. Accept that."

Suddenly he looked very tired. "You're right, of course. With or without you, I'd be laughed out of the FBI's offices. But when you can't rectify a situation that stinks, you can do something about it—you can refuse to be a part of it and walk away. That's what I'm doing. You can do it too."

The blood that had left her face came rushing back, burning her cheeks. "No, David, I couldn't. I've told you before—I belong with Marietta."

Their eyes locked for a long moment, and it was as though he were trying to penetrate some depth inside her that she wasn't even sure existed. The disgust left his eyes, but it was replaced by a sadness that cut through her even more as he said:

"Once I asked you, 'What are we letting Marietta do to us?' That was a cop-out question. It should have been: 'What are we doing to ourselves?'" He turned to Marietta. "As you reminded me before—I know my way out." He gave Melanie one last, searching look, and then spun round and rushed out of the room.

Both women sat in silence, waiting to hear the click of the hall door closing behind him. When it came, it went through Melanie like a knife. Marietta, on the other hand, sprang to her feet, picked up the champagne bottle, and refilled their glasses.

"Good riddance," she said. "He was always a bit too sanctimonious for my taste."

Melanie didn't answer; she couldn't get any words past the lump in her throat. She sipped her champagne, hoping it would wash the lump away, but it succeeded only in shrinking it a bit. "He's right, you know, Mari," she said finally. "It's not necessary to publish those pictures, but they should at least be turned over to the authorities. It's your duty as a citizen."

"Now don't you start in on me too." Marietta's voice was light, but her eyes were steely. "I do my duty as a citizen every time I pay my taxes, which must be more than enough to cover the missile program. Nobody has a right to ask any more of me than that. The government has had two decades to solve Kennedy's murder. In that time they should have stumbled across Kendricks. Those pictures are worth a lot more to me than they could ever be to any investigator. Because of them, Kendricks will never again try to rustle away a business deal I'm interested in."

"That's really all those pictures mean to you, isn't it?" Melanie asked. It was as though a veil had suddenly been lifted. For the first time she found herself looking at Marietta through the clear, objective eyes of an adult and a lawyer, not through the rose-tinted glasses of an adoring, grateful child. She was appalled by what she saw. When had Marietta changed into such a totally self-serving person? Or had she always been that way, and had Melanie simply refused to recognize it? She said with sudden anger:

"Does it mean nothing to you that as a result of the transaction taking place in those photographs, a woman was widowed, two little children were left fatherless, a nation was robbed of its duly elected president, and the world was deprived of a man who might have proved to be a great leader? And that the man who initiated that transaction has gone scot-free?"

"Now you're talking like a romantic. Maybe you've had too

much champagne." Marietta smiled indulgently and shook her head. "You make it sound as though the shots were fired yesterday instead of all those years ago. That widow you mention was young, beautiful, and rich, and she later married a man who made her even richer. The little children were left fabulously wealthy and have long since grown up. The nation had another president in minutes, and the world has so many different leaders, all pulling in different directions, that one more or less never has and never will make a damn bit of difference. As for Kendricks going scot-free, you of all people should know that bringing him to trial wouldn't change that. He'd hire the smartest lawyers in the country, and for a whopping fee, they'd get him off without a hitch. If it's retribution you're after, then you can rest assured that my keeping the pictures will make Kendricks sweat a hell of a lot more and a hell of a lot longer than my releasing them ever would. They're staying right where they are."

"And where is that?"

"Where they'll be safe."

Marietta said the words lightly, but her tone was one of dismissal, and it hit Melanie like a slap. She had always thought that Marietta trusted her completely. Obviously she didn't. Perhaps she never had. "I'm your lawyer—don't you think I should know?" She tried to match Marietta's light tone.

"The fewer people who know about this, the better."

"I wasn't aware that you lumped me with 'people.'"

"Don't pout," Marietta said impatiently. "It isn't like you. I just think it's a lot safer for everyone if I'm the only one who knows the whereabouts of the photos."

"And that way it makes it a lot easier for you to maintain that they don't exist too."

"You see, you do understand."

"Understanding and condoning are two very different things. If you won't release those pictures for the right reasons, Mari, maybe I can convince you to do it for the wrong one. You're a sitting duck for Kendricks as long as he thinks you're the only one who knows about them. He has killed before. You've just given him a strong motivation for killing again."

Marietta laughed. "Those pictures are the best life insurance policy I could possibly have. I told Kendricks that law enforcement officers here and in England have in their possession sealed letters that are to be opened upon my death—letters that will lead them directly to the photographs. He's so eager to get that goddamn peerage he'll probably underwrite a search for the fountain of youth just for me."

"And have you written those letters?"

"Two of them. I'll get to the rest first thing in the morning. The next order of business after that will be to fix David Belmont's wagon. Now stop sitting there looking so serious. Nothing's going to happen to me. I've come out of this stronger than ever before. I might be even stronger if I used the information to ruin Kendricks completely, but I've made it clear to him that as long as he stays out of my way I don't intend to be greedy. There's plenty of room out there for the two of us."

"There's plenty of room," Melanie said, her voice dulled by the depression that was washing over her. "There are more than enough companies for you both to plunder, more than enough people for you to trample upon and ruin if they dare to cross you or get in your way. You're two of a kind, aren't you?"

Marietta made a wry smile. "I'd say 'three of a kind' would come closer to the truth. You seem to be conveniently forgetting everything you've done over the past several years."

"Oh, I'm not forgetting it." Melanie shook her head. "Like Marley's ghost, it seems to be rising up before me right here in this room. And its stink makes me want to throw up. But at least I know I didn't do those things for self-gain and self-aggrandizement. I did them for you."

"So it's all my fault." Marietta looked amused. "I don't recall ever having to force you to do any of the shameful things you seem to have in mind."

"I'm not blaming you. I saw you through the eyes of a child, and I excused my behavior with a child's rationalizations: I thought the woman I loved and revered as a mother, sister, and friend all rolled into one could do no wrong, and that anything I did in her name could never be wrong, either. But tonight I've stopped being a child. I see you for what you are, and myself for what I've become. And both of us make me sick." Her eyes filled with tears. "We can change, Mari. It's never too late to change."

"What would you have me do—give away all my worldly goods and go forth with a begging bowl?" Marietta's eyes hardened. "No, thank you. I came into this life with a begging bowl, and I have every intention of leaving it with a solid-gold spoon in my mouth. Your problem is that you weren't poor long enough to learn the real facts of life. I saved you from that. Well, let me sum them up for you in one simple sentence: Money and power are all that matter in life, and when it comes to acquiring them, there's no such thing as right and wrong—there's only expediency."

The observation wasn't a new one. Melanie had heard Marietta air it many times over the years. What was new was that at last Melanie realized Marietta truly believed it and had centered her life around it. "Who are you?" she asked softly. "Have you always been this way, or did you change somewhere along the line, and I was just too blind to see it?"

"You know as well as I do that I haven't always been this way. I had an alcoholic father and a mother who died of overwork and underpay. I had a bright, handsome brother who died an addict's death, and a beautiful little sister who was killed because the powers-that-be put safety matting only in parks where the rich kids played. Of course, I changed. Change means survival. If I'd followed in my family's footsteps, I'd have starved to death long ago."

She got up and refilled her champagne glass. "Don't tell me that the change wasn't for the better, either. And I don't mean just for me. The world is a better place because I'm rich—never forget that. I'm directly responsible for the employment of the thirty thousand people who work for all the subsidiaries owned by Wylford Enterprises, not to mention the people who work for companies we give our business to. I donate money to charity, and the taxes I pay build schools and roads and hospitals and bombs to scare off or kill our enemies. Look at my mother and your mother—then look at me and tell me who has had the more meaningful life. Our mothers died because they lacked ambition."

"No!" Melanie cried. "They died because others had too much of it. Your mother died because she couldn't afford decent health care. And why couldn't she afford it? Because her boss cared only about profits, not employees' wages and health benefits, and because the best doctors are interested only in treating patients who can fill their pockets fastest. And my mother died because landlords are concerned with making a maximum profit for a minimum investment—not with the well-being of their tenants and the upkeep of their property. As for the thousands you employ—how about the thousands you throw out of work when you merge with other companies instead of creating new ones, or transfer your factories to Korea or China?"

Marietta's face paled with anger, but still Melanie rushed on: "Don't talk to me about the glories of ambition. In the mouths of people like you, it's just a euphemism for greed. Not all the tax-deductible donations you make to charity or all the money that can't slip through tax loopholes can make atonement or restitution for the deaths of people like our mothers or the broken lives left in the wake of every business deal."

"I think you've said enough." Marietta's voice was edged with rage. "Don't presume on our friendship too much."

"You've made it quite clear that I can't presume upon it at all." Melanie's eyes filled with tears. "Besides, I'm not sure we can be friends anymore."

Marietta nodded thoughtfully, then said with a wistful smile, "Tender words of gratitude from the girl I rescued from the gutter."

"You rescued me from poverty—not from depravity, Mari. I'm rescuing myself from that right now. And you're wrong. Since I was sixteen, I've been grateful to you for all you did for me, and over the past five years, I've done all I possibly could to repay you. If it wasn't enough, I'm sorry. But I just can't do any more. You said a moment ago that change means survival. That's one thing I think we can agree upon. What we don't agree upon is what survival means. I can't survive in your world anymore, Mari. I don't want to. I have to change and make a world of my own."

"You'd better think twice about walking out on me. I can make it very hard for you."

"No one knows that better than I do, Mari. I've seen you destroy too many people over the years. Your revenge is swift and devastating. I know exactly what I'm letting myself in for."

"Then change your mind," Marietta said. "That's an option I've never given to anyone else."

"I imagine that I'm supposed to appreciate that." Melanie sighed and shook her head. "Don't you see that it means absolutely nothing compared to the fact that after all the closeness we've shared, you can still lump me with the people you consider to be your enemies? People whose careers you've wrecked with less emotion than you'd feel after swatting a mosquito. There's a big difference between those people and me, though, Mari. They all wanted to continue operating on the same level. I don't. I'm through with your type of big business."

Marietta dismissed the idea with a sneer and a wave of her hand. "You'll starve."

"No, I won't. You seem to forget Harlan saw to it that nothing like that would ever happen to me. But then, you seem to have forgotten all about Harlan, haven't you? I can't remember the last time you mentioned him. For me, he was the father I never had. For you, he was no more and no less than everyone else who has passed through your life—just a means to an end."

"Are you quite through?" Marietta turned her back, indicating that she was.

Melanie rose and walked over to Marietta. For a moment she stood in silence behind her. Then, tentatively, she reached out and touched her shoulder.

With a sharp, jerking movement, Marietta shrugged off her hand. "You're wrong about Harlan," she said, not turning around. "He meant more to me than you'll ever know. Of all the things you've said tonight, that's the vilest." Her voice caught on the last words, and she paused a second, as though to regain control. When she spoke again, it was with her earlier coldness: "I think we have nothing more to say to each other."

"It's not too late to change," Melanie repeated.

Marietta's back remained rigid.

Melanie sighed and shook her head. "Good-bye, Mari."

She was halfway across the room when Marietta spoke again.

"Don't expect to come back when everything comes tumbling down on your head."

Turning, Melanie saw that Marietta had been watching her

leave. Maybe it was the lighting, but she thought she saw a glint of tears in her eyes.

"There's no chance of that," she said quietly, and added, "But I want you to know that if you ever need me, I'll be there."

"Need *you?*" Marietta laughed, and made a wide gesture that seemed to encompass her entire penthouse apartment. "How could I possibly ever need you?"

Melanie shrugged. "I wasn't talking about money. I forgot that that's the only point of reference you have." Suddenly the room with its elegant furnishings and masterpieces became oppressive. She turned and hurried out of it.

Downstairs, she refused the doorman's offer to flag a cab and went out into the street. She knew it wasn't wise to walk alone at night, but she needed time to sort out her thoughts and the emotions that were rushing around inside her too quickly for her to identify them. She always thought better when she walked, and home was only fifteen blocks away....

A cool late-April breeze wrapped around her like a protective cloak, slowing her jagged breathing, calming her pounding heart. At first she felt sadness and a deep sense of loss, the same emotions she had experienced upon the deaths of her mother and sister and then Harlan. But as the tears slipped down her cheeks, she began to realize how foolish she was. How could she mourn the end of a relationship with someone who had never really existed? The Marietta she had believed in had been the creation of her child's mind. Over the past hour she had grown up, freed herself from bondage to false images and warped principles. That wasn't something to cry about—that was something to exult over. Her tears drying and her mind suddenly bursting with plans, she quickened her steps. She was her own person now, on the brink of a new life. There was a whole world out there just waiting for her brains, her talent—a world that people like Marietta, obsessed with getting and spending, had turned their backs on. But there was so much more to life than amassing wealth and power. Now she could live life as it was meant to be lived, savoring its gifts, creating a world that would, perhaps, be just a little better because she had passed through it.

Waiting for a traffic light to change, she looked up at the sky studded with stars that had fought their way through the city's haze, and she took a deep breath of the cool, clear air. Once again her eyes filled with tears, but these were tears of joy. Never before had she felt so free, so alive, so aware of and a part of her surroundings. No, that wasn't true. Once before she had experienced the same feeling—just two weeks ago, when she had left Anne Frank's hiding place in Amsterdam. It had taken her twenty-eight years to discover what the child Anne had learned in two—that life is too precious a gift to be squandered in the pursuit of false gods, that human love and understanding are worth more than all the gold that passes through the world's money exchanges year after year.

She crossed the street, almost running with the joy of discovery: That was what David had wanted her to see. He had dangled it before her, but he had known that for it to have any real meaning she would have to reach for the prize herself. And then her heart sank and her footsteps slowed. Now that she held the prize, how much could it really mean if she couldn't share it with David? For at last she faced the strongest realization of all—the one she had been running from since the day he came into her life: She was in love with David Belmont. And the worst part was that she finally realized he had loved her too. That was why he had gone along with so many of Marietta's demands, even though they went against his grain. All the time, he had been trying to awaken her, Melanie, from her self-deluding dreams. Even at the very end, when he could take it no longer, when it was obvious that he had probably given up hope of getting her to come to her senses, he had made one last effort to prod her into leaving with him. But idiot that she was, she had slept on, and now she had lost him forever.

Or had she? Surely, it wasn't too late. She had awakened, after all.

It was well past midnight, but she didn't care. She had to go to David and find out if she was too late. She turned in the direction of Lexington Avenue and began running. She knew exactly what she was looking for, and prayed that she would find it. After three blocks she did. The man behind the counter of the all-night pizzeria didn't bat an eyelash when she ran up to him and panted, "I want the biggest pepperoni pizza you can make." He did glance down at her waistline, though, before he set to work. Maybe he thought she was pregnant.

HALF AN HOUR LATER, balancing the huge pizza box, Melanie disentangled herself from the backseat of a cab in front of David's apartment house. She had been there a few times while they were working together, and she hoped the doorman would recognize her and agree not to call David to seek permission for her entrance. He was sitting by the intercoms, reading the early edition of the *Daily News*.

"Hi," she said, giving him her most charming smile. "Remember me? I'm Mr. Belmont's friend. Can you let me in without announcing me? I don't want to spoil my surprise."

"Rules are that everyone's to be announced, miss." His tone said he was willing to be convinced otherwise, and he eyed the box with interest.

She moved a little closer, the better for him to smell the contents. "It's his birthday," she said in a conspiratorial whisper, "and I got him a pepperoni pizza—his favorite. I wanted to arrive at a minute after midnight, but I was delayed at the pizza place. Why don't you take a slice? It will add a little spice to your evening."

"Oh, I couldn't..." He moistened his lips.

"Of course you could. He'd be hurt if you didn't. He'd want you to help us celebrate."

"Well, if you think so..." He opened the box and took out the largest slice. "Thanks a lot."

"Thank *you*," she said, slipping into the lobby and heading for the elevators.

"You're lucky you were delayed," he called after her. "Mr. Belmont just got in a little while ago."

Heart pounding, she stepped out of the elevator at David's floor and walked slowly toward his apartment, trying to steady her breathing. She paused for a moment before his door, then thrust her finger firmly against his bell.

What if he wouldn't let her in?

No, she wouldn't think that way. She rang the bell again.

And then at last she heard David's voice demanding: "Who is it?"

"I—it's—" Her tongue suddenly felt like a foreign body in her mouth, and as she tried to command it to function properly, she heard David manipulating the locks.

The door swung open, and they were standing face-to-face. David looked as though he wasn't sure he could believe what he saw.

"I've had a very busy evening," Melanie said, the box trembling in her hands. "So busy that I'm not quite sure who I am anymore. But I hope that one of the people I'll turn out to be is your pepperoni-pizza girl. Is is there a good movie on TV?"

"The hell with TV," he said, his voice husky, and he took her arm and gently propelled her inside.

She hadn't felt so nervous and unsure of herself since she was a kid. "I hope you like extra cheese," she babbled as she walked past him and placed the box on the table in his foyer. "There's a piece missing, though."

"What happened?"

"I bribed your doorman with it so he'd let me come in unannounced."

"I wasn't asking about the pizza."

His eyes, when she looked into them, were warm and reassuring. "You told me once that I was viewing Marietta through the eyes of a child. I finally grew up and declared my independence."

"Welcome to the ranks of the unemployed," he said, and took her in his arms.

She felt many things as his lips came down on hers. There was the pounding of her heart, the roaring in her ears, the delicious slow-motion whirlpool that engulfed her entire body. But most of all, there was the sweet, warm, unique sensation of comfort and contentment; after years of lonely wandering she had finally come home.

"If that's what's meant by unemployment compensation," she said shakily when they finally drew apart, "I think I'm going to love being jobless."

Tenderly he brushed the hair back from her face. "Do you know how long I've wanted to do that?" he asked.

She shook her head.

"From the first moment I saw you."

"You could have fooled me. You were so cold sometimes, so distant."

"Not cold and distant, just hopeful and waiting, maybe not too patiently. It was the real you—the woman I saw beneath the surface—that I wanted. And I knew that you were the only one who could set her free."

"What if I hadn't?"

"I guess, little by little, I would have died inside. It began to happen tonight, you know, when you didn't walk out with me. I waited awhile in front of Marietta's building, hoping I'd see you walk through the door. When you didn't, I thought I'd lost all hope of ever having you."

"And it mattered to you so very much?" Her eyes misted with tears.

He took her face between his hands. "I thought lawyers were supposed to be able to read between the lines. What I've been standing here telling you is that I love you."

She never thought she would hear those words spoken to her with such sincerity. Tears welled up in her eyes and began to flow down her cheeks. "What lawyers can read between the lines," she said, "women like to hear spelled out for them."

"Men aren't any different when it comes to that."

"I love you," she said, her lips trembling as they formed the words. "When I finally admitted it to myself tonight, I thought I'd burst with joy. Oh, David, kiss me again!"

His eyes searched hers. "I want to do so much more than that."

"Yes," she whispered. "Oh, yes."

He took her hand and led her into his bedroom. Together, slowly, almost as if they were performing a ritual, they removed the bedspread and turned the blankets down. Then she stood before him trembling. What if he was disappointed in her figure? What if she didn't please him? It had been a long time since she had made love—and never with someone who meant so much to her. And then he was standing before her, and all her fears fled at his nearness.

"Are you protected?" he asked softly.

Only by the time of month, but it would be sufficient. She

nodded, and slowly, tenderly, his hands reached for the buttons on her blouse. At the same time, she reached up and began unfastening his shirt. One by one they removed their garments, their eyes locked, their hands moving deftly, almost automatically. Melanie felt as though she were suspended on a plane far beyond the need for conscious thought. She was aware only of this moment, this place, this man. Her entire body tingled with anticipation.

When their last garments had fallen away, they stood before each other in awe.

"How very beautiful you are," he whispered.

"And you," she said, her voice catching. His shoulders were broader, his arms more muscular than she had imagined. Unable to resist, she reached out and ran a hand over the short, crisp mat of hair on his firm, strong chest. With a moan of delight, he pulled her to him, and his mouth came down on hers in a kiss that set the room spinning. Gently, never taking his lips from hers, he eased her down upon the bed.

It was as if all their lives they had been preparing for that moment. Every kiss, every caress seemed to fan a magnificent, all-consuming flame of desire until finally, flesh to flesh and heart to heart, they were consumed by it and melded into one. Then, slowly, with tender kisses and caresses, they brought each other back to earth again.

There were tears on Melanie's cheeks as she lay curled against David, her head nestled on his chest, and she knew that they were not entirely her own. "I never knew love could be so beautiful," she whispered.

"Nor I," he said, running his hand through her hair. "But that's because neither of us knew what real love was before."

"And what is it?" She knew, of course, but she longed to hear him put it into words.

He propped himself up on one elbow and looked down upon her. His gaze was like a gentle caress, his smile a tender kiss.

"It's finding the one person in all the world who means more to you than life itself. It's the end to loneliness and the search for meaning, for you've found that meaning in another's eyes. It's the one touch of sanity we can cling to in the midst of a world gone mad. At least, that's what it is for me."

She reached up and traced a finger along his cheek. "When I was a little girl, I read a myth about creation. It said that at first, the gods created men and women joined together as one inseparable being. But then humans became too presumptuous, and the angry gods cleft them in two and dispersed them, forcing them ever after to roam the earth in search of their other half. I know now that's not just a story. All my life, I've been searching for you. And now that I've found you, I'm finally complete."

"We're not nearly as complete as I long for us to be," he said, kissing her. "I want to be your husband. I want to know you'll be beside me for the rest of my life."

She snuggled closer. "If that's a marriage proposal, my answer is 'yes.'"

He kissed the top of her head. "I hope you won't change your mind when you hear what I've been up to since I left Marietta's place."

She propped herself up on one elbow and looked down at him. "Did you go to the authorities after all?"

He shook his head. "No. I realized the futility of that. But I was mad—damn mad, sick to death of the likes of Marietta Wylford and Harrison Kendricks always getting their way. I went to see Louise, to tell her that I was washing my hands of the whole deal, that Kendricks had pulled out, and that she had a choice of selling to Marietta or holding on to her stock." He reached up and gently smoothed Melanie's hair back from her face. "You should have seen her, darling. She was like a different woman. She hadn't had a drink since Saturday, and had been going to AA meetings. She apologized for throwing herself at me. Can you imagine—she apologized to me! She said it had been liquor and loneliness and self-pity speaking. And she thanked me for never taking advantage of it. Because, you know, despite the conclusions you and Marietta jumped to, I could never bring myself to do that to Louise. It was hard enough for me to live with the other ways I was manipulating her—I couldn't take her to bed."

Tears came to Melanie's eyes. "Oh, darling," she whispered, "I'm so glad to hear that."

Smiling, he traced a finger along her lips. "You ain't heard nothing yet. We had a long talk. Louise said that even if she were starving, she'd never sell her shares to Marietta. She offered them to me—along with Mark Bailey's. She got on the phone right then and called him in Amsterdam, telling him that in exchange for a new letter of intent letting her or me buy the shares, she'd cast a friendly eye on his requests for money from his trust fund. The letter of intent is on a jet plane with a special messenger right now. That would give me thirty-five percent of the company. All I'd need is another sixteen. Maybe I'm crazy. I don't know if any bank or investment group will back me, but I've got to try. I may be tilting at windmills, but—God!—how I'd love to keep greedy conglomerates away from that magazine."

"You're not tilting at windmills!" Melanie sat up, her eyes sparkling with excitement. "You can do it. *We* can do it. Darling, I have connections in all the best places. Just one phone call in the morning, and I know I can get all the backing we'll need. And as for that other sixteen percent—have you sold your one percent to Marietta's bankers yet?"

He shook his head. "I haven't had time."

"I never bothered to dispose of mine, either. Then there's the three percent owned by the other officers of the magazine. They've been sitting on the fence with it. Call them—tell them it's a whole new ball game."

"Now? At this time of night?"

"Now!"

He sat up and reached for the bedside phone.

While he was talking, Melanie picked up the pad and pencil on his night table and began making notes.

"They were mad as hell when I woke them," David said when he hung up after his last call, "but ready to kiss me when I told them we'd found a way to keep the conglomerate wolves from our door. They'll sell to us."

"I knew they would. With our two percent, that makes five, and with—"

The phone rang, cutting her off. She went back to her figures as David talked.

"That was Craig Campbell," he said when he hung up a few minutes later. "I called him when I got home, asked if he'd come in on the deal with me. He was very nice about it, but said he'd given Marietta his word that she could have his stock, and he wouldn't break his promise. He offered to see what he could do along other lines, though. He just called to say that there's a part in his next movie that Laura Leslie could handle, and he's offered it to her as a reward for tendering her shares to us. She agreed. Brent Allen said he'd go with Wylford now that Kendricks is out of the picture, though."

"Who needs him?" Melanie hugged David and held out her paper. "With Laura's two percent, we have seven. We know Mrs. Asquith will give you her two percent—that's nine. Ronald Bennett has known me since I was a kid—he was Harlan's friend, not Marietta's. He'll come through for us with the four percent he controls—I know he will. That makes it thirteen percent to add to the Bailey thirty-five. An additional three percent—and we've won! We'll get it—and more! I'm sure we can count on Wallace Carlyle, and besides him there are a lot of people who went over to Kendricks because they don't like Marietta. Now that Kendricks is releasing them, they'll come to us. Darling, I guarantee you that by noon tomorrow, everything will be in the bag."

"And we'll be in debt up to our ears."

"Who cares? There's always junk bonds. We'll beat the conglomerates at their own game. We'll be free and independent, with our own business, one we can run by our own rules the right kind of rules. And we'll have each other."

"That," he said, holding her close, "is the best part."

They talked about the future then, where they'd live, what they'd do, their plans for the magazine. Melanie would run the business end, but she wanted to make sure she had some time for other things, like working with poor people who needed legal advice. David, too, wanted to take time out to teach evening classes in journalism. And they didn't intend to forget what they knew about Harrison Kendricks. They didn't need Marietta's pictures. They would begin their own investigation. It wouldn't be easy, and it wouldn't be quick. But they were determined that someday, even it if took years, they would unearth the facts that would bring Kendricks to justice. On one point, however, Melanie was adamant: Marietta was not to be touched by the scandal that would ensue; they would make their case without mention of the photographs. David understood. When Melanie had needed someone desperately, Marietta had been there for her. Old kindnesses are never to be forgotten.

There was more to discuss, of course, but they had a lifetime ahead of them to work out the details. For the moment, there was the newness of their love and the wonder of discovery, and once again, they lost themselves in the breathtaking world that only they could create.

Later, David put on a pair of jeans and Melanie slipped into his comfortable old corduroy robe. Then they went into the living room, and, snuggled together on the couch, wrapped in a warm cocoon of love, they ate cold pepperoni pizza, watched an old horror movie on TV, and waited for the new day to begin.

Epilogue

Late April 1988

A T FIVE O'CLOCK on Friday, Marietta's secretary opened her door and asked as she always did before leaving for the day, "Will there be anything else, Mrs. Wylford?"

"Nothing, thank you, Katheryn," Marietta said. "Have a nice weekend."

For a few minutes after the door had closed behind Katheryn, Marietta sat gazing at it as though she expected Melanie to open it and come in for their usual end-of-the-day roundup. But it didn't happen, of course. Never again would Melanie stroll in to talk over the day's events. From now on, no doubt, Melanie would be sharing that ritual with David Belmont.

With a shake of her head, Marietta stood up and walked over to the window. She was sorry she had told Fred to pick her up at the usual time. She had no desire to linger in the office tonight. The huge room seemed eerily deserted, and yet, at the same time, filled with ghosts. Her mind was still spinning from the way Melanie and David had pulled the rug out from under her on the *Sizzle* deal. What she found even more difficult to understand than their disloyalty was her own inertia when it came to fighting back. There were calls she could have made, arms she could have twisted to keep those two traitors from succeeding in their eleventh-hour takeover. Yet her own arm had seemed to freeze every time she reached for the phone, and when her acquisition bankers called for instructions, all she could say was: "Let them have it and be damned." What had gotten into her, she wondered.

Her eyes stinging, no doubt from the glare of the setting sun, she turned away from the window, wishing she hadn't declined two invitations to dinner. Suddenly the prospect of a long evening alone was unappealing. She ran a hand over her face. Why was she allowing her thoughts to drift in such a depressing direction? She had purposely planned to spend the evening—the entire weekend, in fact—alone. She had so much thinking to do. She had to pull herself out of this depression, this lethargy. What she needed was a new project, something exciting, something that would get the juices running again.

Briskly, she started across the room toward her rack of business publications, intending to leaf through them in search of an idea. But she stopped when she saw her reflection on her television screen. It was like a sign from the god or demon in charge of the business world. What could offer her more excitement, more challenge than taking over a television network? She would have Melanie get on it right away!

And then she remembered that Melanie was no longer with her.

She sank down on the chair behind her desk. That had been one of the things she had been going to think about over the weekend—getting someone to take over Melanie's job. It wouldn't be easy. Not that Melanie was irreplaceable, she reminded herself quickly. No one was irreplaceable. It would just be a little more difficult in Melanie's case, because Marietta had not been expecting the desertion and, therefore, had not been conducting the executive searches she usually made when she wanted to replace someone. Searches took time, time she couldn't afford to waste if she wanted to get the TV project launched. She would have to rustle someone from the competition—someone who knew the ins and outs of takeovers as well as Melanie did.

Immediately, Clifford Langhton came to mind. His being one step ahead of her so often on the *Sizzle* skirmish had infuriated her before, but now it intrigued her. What better person to have on her team? No doubt Kendricks had promised him the editorship of *Sizzle*. Everyone knew Kendricks was always promising Langhton an editorial plum—and then whisking it away the moment it was within reach, because, otherwise, he would lose the services of a valued second in command. Clifford Langhton was a handsome, charming, brilliant and extremely competent man. With Kendricks the loser in the *Sizzle* battle, he no doubt was also a very disappointed man. Maybe she could interest him in new worlds to be conquered.

She thought of Harrison Kendricks. How he must be laughing because, despite her victory over him, she had lost *Sizzle* in the end—screwed by a rank amateur in league with her own trusted employee. If she could rustle away his own right-hand man, she could have the last laugh. It would be delicious!

In her desk she had a special book in which she kept the names, addresses, and telephone numbers of all her business adversaries. She was disappointed to see that Clifford Langhton lived in Scarsdale, which meant if he were on his way home, it would be a while before she could reach him. But maybe, like a diligent assistant, he was still tidying up the week's work. She dialed the direct line listed for his office.

The phone was answered by a man with a British accent. "Gibson here."

"I'm calling Clifford Langhton. Perhaps I have the wrong number."

"Until yesterday it was the right number. He's no longer associated with Kendricks International."

"Really?" That was interesting. "Thank you. No doubt I can reach him at home then."

"Not if you mean his place in Scarsdale. He's no longer living there, either. Try the St. Regis. He told me he'd be staying there until he finds a flat in the city."

At the St. Regis, Clifford Langhton picked up the phone on the first ring. His voice was sober and alert, which meant that he had probably terminated his employment with Kendricks, rather than the reverse. That pleased her.

"This is Marietta Wylford," she said. "I'd like you to meet me this evening to discuss a business opportunity I have in mind."

"What kind of opportunity?"

She could almost hear the wheels of his mind spinning. "I am going to branch out into television. It occurred to me that you might be just the person to help me do it. Are you interested?"

"Perhaps."

He refused to sound overeager. She liked that. "Good. I'll meet you at the Four Seasons at six forty-five."

She would have made it earlier, but as she heard his voice, she remembered how very handsome he was, and she decided that she wanted to go home and change. Feeling almost lighthearted, she quickly hung up the phone, collected her things, and left the office.

At home, she slipped out of her suit and walked into her closet, studying the racks of dresses. She finally decided on a navy-blue knit she had recently picked up at Martha's. Its long sleeves and jewel neckline gave it a most businesslike look, but it clung to her figure in an alluringly unbusinesslike fashion. After studying her image in the mirror, however, she decided the neckline was a little too severe and needed something to soften it—a scarf perhaps, such as that little red silk with flecks of blue that she had bought in Gucci's a year or so ago. She pulled out her scarf drawer and began rummaging through it. It had to be there somewhere. Finally she came across it at the bottom toward the back. As she reached for it, her fingers touched something hard and smooth. She moved away the scarves covering it and discovered a little white pasteboard box.

Curious, she pulled out the box and opened it. Upon a yellowing piece of cotton was a tiny gold heart with the word *Forever* etched across it. At first, she couldn't place it in her mind. And then she remembered Craig—and the Christmas that had changed her life and started her on the road to all she had today.

As she picked up the heart and held it in her hand, a vision of Craig as he had looked nearly twenty years ago came back to her. Her eyes misted and she smiled. How happy they had been back then. And then she remembered what he had said to her less than two weeks before in Paris. Her lips tightened, and her fingers clamped around the heart. He expected too much of her. He always had. So had Melanie. She had become what she had to be in order to survive and come out on top in this jungle called life. And the top was the only place worth being, the only place of safety. Harlan had understood her. Melanie had been wrong; she hadn't forgotten Harlan and she never would.

How could she? He was the only person she had ever felt close to who had accepted her, totally and completely, exactly as she was. Or had he? The memory of his last moments, when he had called out to Jane, came rushing back to her. Had he, too, despite his blinding love, somehow seen her as flawed? But she wasn't flawed. It took strength, not weakness, to create and sustain an industrial empire.

Her hand was clenched so tightly that the heart began to cut into her palm. Slowly, she uncurled her fingers and looked at it. Why had she held on to this cheap, silly little thing all these years? She flung it into the wastebasket. Why was she wasting time with such foolish, morbid thoughts? She had an appointment to keep. Pretending she didn't notice that her fingers were trembling, she tied the scarf around her neck. It added just the right touch of color and flair. A dab of Opium behind her ears, and she was once again the indomitable business magnate, ready to go out and conquer new worlds.

CLIFFORD LANGHTON had come early, and was seated at one of the tables on the balcony in the Bar Room. He spotted Marietta as soon as she arrived, and rose to his feet and smiled while the maître d' led her past the azaleas and birch trees and the huge bar with Lippold's sculpture created from brass rods dipped in gold. Even at a distance, Marietta noticed the change in him, and as they shook hands, she wondered how someone's appearance could alter so much in a week or two. He seemed older somehow. The lines on his face seemed to have deepened and his eyes had lost their sparkle. Though he stood as tall and as straight as ever, there was something about the rigid line of his shoulders and back that indicated that his fine posture was now a matter of strong conscious effort. It crossed her mind as she eased herself onto the Mies van der Rohe chair, now upholstered in its beige spring finery, that perhaps Clifford Langhton had not left Kendricks International of his own free will, after all. She couldn't afford to have losers on her team, and having ordered her drink, she turned to him and said:

"I understand that you're no longer with Kendricks International."

"That's right." His eyes didn't shift from hers. That was a good sign.

"Why did you leave?"

"Personal reasons."

"Yours or your boss's?"

He looked amused. "If you mean, did I quit or was I fired—I quit. I'm surprised that you weren't aware of that by now. Kendricks has been exerting pressure all over town to make sure I don't land on my feet. He never makes such efforts with people he fires—they're already ruined. Hasn't he gotten to you yet?"

Marietta laughed, relaxing. "I'm the last person he would ever contact—about anything."

"How *did* you get him to surrender on the *Sizzle* bid? I've never known him to do such a thing before."

"That," she said with a mysterious smile, "is an off-limits subject. No one will ever know the truth about it except Harrison Kendricks and me."

"That could put you in a very dangerous position."

"On the contrary, it makes me stronger than you could possibly imagine. I often take business risks, but never personal ones."

"Whatever type risk, that last one doesn't seem to have paid off. You lost *Sizzle* in the end. Or is it as Kendricks suspects—you were just a stalking horse, and you wanted to clear the field for your friends?"

She thought it best just to smile mysteriously.

The waiter brought their drinks. Cliff raised his glass. "To your successful risks, then."

"And yours." She smiled and took a sip. "Is that why you left Kendricks—because he lost out on *Sizzle,* which meant you lost out on being its editor?"

"With Kendricks, there would always be another publication waiting in the wings." He shook his head. "I left him because I'd finally had a bellyful of the dirty games I had to play to make him come out a winner. The minute *Sizzle* was lost, he began talking about strategy for gaining control of another publication, possibly *Reader's Digest.* I'd had enough."

"I'm not sure I like what I hear," Marietta said. "You seem to be telling me that you can't be depended on as a team player."

His eyes never wavered from hers. "What I'm trying to do is to be honest with you right from the beginning. I'm a very ambitious man, and I guess I always will be. But my life has changed a lot over the past week—and so have I. I've learned that if I'm going to live with myself, I have to set my own limits."

"My, that sounds terribly profound," Marietta said, trying for a light tone. "Don't tell me you found religion."

"It isn't what I've found—it's what I've lost. Because of the things I've done, my wife is divorcing me."

"Maybe now that you've set your limits, she'll change her mind."

"I set them too late. The harm has been done. I can never again be the man she thought and hoped I was. I've lost her for good."

His eyes became sad, almost haunted, and Marietta shuddered as he talked about Stephanie and their marriage. She had seen that look somewhere before. But where? When? And then she remembered: She had seen it in her mirror less than two weeks ago—the night Craig walked out on her in Paris. Sitting there, watching Cliff and listening to him speak of all he had lost, she grasped for the first time that she had lost a great deal too. All those years, ever since the day they met at the photo studio, she had been in love with Craig and had never admitted it. And now that she finally was able to face up to it, it was too late. His wife and Marietta's own irreversible past would forever stand between them. Like Cliff, she could never again be the person the one she loved had thought and hoped she was.

"Are you all right?" Cliff's voice seemed to break in on her thoughts from far away. "You look rather pale all of a sudden."

"I'm fine," she said, reaching for her drink. "I just had a slight chill. It's over now."

"Are you sure? Would you like me to take you home?"

She shook her head. "No, really, I'm fine." She liked the way he looked at her—with sincerity and concern. Not many men had looked at her that way. The two who had were lost to her forever. "You were saying... ?"

"Far too much, no doubt." His smile had a touch of the boyish. "I guess I've rambled because this is the first time I've had a chance to talk about what has happened. But I wanted you to know exactly where I stand. I've finally learned that there are more important things in life than zeroing in on the next big buck and the next big deal. As far as I'm concerned, some sacrifices that have to be made for business just aren't worth it."

As she looked at him across the table, Marietta realized that they were very much alike. She felt a little flutter of pleasure at the thought. "If that's supposed to turn me off," she said, "it doesn't. I've made a few discoveries myself in the past few days. I used to think that every man had his price. Now I've learned that everything I've done to further myself has had its price too." Her eyes misted as she thought of Craig and Melanie, and of Harlan, who had loved her so much and yet had felt unable to turn to her at the end. She took a sip of her drink to steady herself. "I think we both know that there is no way to go back and recover the people and the chances for happiness we forfeited in the past. But if we can't go back, we can at least profit by our mistakes and go forward. Would you like to go forward with me, Mr. Langhton?"

"It depends on what you're going forward to—and how you intend to get there."

"A fair point," she said. "When I asked you to meet me, I intended that we'd discuss taking over a television network. I've changed my mind. I prefer that we brainstorm about starting a new one—from scratch, no dirty deals involved."

He searched her eyes for a moment, and she held her breath.

"In that case, Mrs. Wylford," he said finally, "I think I'd like very much to go forward with you."

As he smiled at her, she realized how afraid she had been that he might turn her down. She smiled back. "Then there are two things that we're going to have to do immediately."

"And they are?"

"First, we're going to have to start calling each other by our first names, and second, we're going to have to extend this meeting to include dinner so that we can discuss our plans."

He laughed. "Those are the best business conditions I've ever been offered."

IT WAS LATE when Marietta got home, but as tired as she was, she felt exhilarated too. She was convinced she had found a kindred spirit in Cliff. True, he wasn't Craig. But then, she wasn't Cliff's Stephanie, either. They understood each other, though, and that made up for a lot. They would help each other over the rough spots, see to it that they never again lost sight of life's real goals as they conquered new worlds and pursued success.

Before she went to bed, she foraged through her wastebasket until her fingers at last came in contact with the necklace Craig had given her so long ago. How could she have decided earlier that it was cheap and ugly? As she held it in her hand, her tears made it sparkle more brilliantly than any of the jewels locked away in her safe.

From the back of her night table drawer she removed the framed wedding portrait of Harlan and herself that had occupied a place of honor on his desk during his lifetime. Gently, she dusted it, then set it down on her dresser, draping the thin gold chain over it. She wanted the necklace and the photograph out where she would always be able to see them. Someday, she hoped, she might even feel worthy of the little gold heart and the adoration in Harlan's eyes.

If you enjoyed this book—and I hope that you did—
please consider posting a review at Amazon.com and
www.goodreads.com. Thank you.

Barbara Brett

DISCUSSION QUESTIONS

1. *Sizzle* is about the loves and ambitions that drive its principal characters into a fierce battle to seize control of the nation's most popular and prestigious journalistic plum. On one side are the ruthless British media mogul, Harrison Kendricks and his henchmen. On the other, the glamorous, self-made corporate wizard Marietta Wylford and her entourage. Which one did you hope would win?

2. As the book opens, we find Marietta in a compromising position with Philip Bailey, the current publisher of *Sizzle*. How did she handle the situation? What would you have done if something like that ever happened to you?

3. When you learned of Marietta's early life, did you sympathize with her determination to escape her miserable home life and desperate poverty at any cost? Did her situation remind you of other people you have known or public figures you have read about?

4. Early in their affair, Marietta tells the struggling actor Craig Campbell not to get serious about their relationship. Do you think it was fair of her to continue with the affair since she had made it clear that it could go nowhere?

5. What do you think of the way Marietta gets the wealthy widower Harlan Wylford to take notice of her, and of how she manipulates him into falling in love with her?

6. Do you like Harlan? Why or why not? Do you think that there was a point when he became aware that Marietta was manipulating him into marriage?

7. Once they are married, Marietta devotes herself to being a good wife and to helping Harlan grow his business. Do you think this makes up for the way she went about getting him to propose?

8. Were you surprised that Marietta wanted to take in teenager Melanie Danielle when she was orphaned in the fire that gutted the tenement where Marietta grew up? Did the love and care she and Harlan gave to Melanie change the way you thought about Marietta? Why?

9. Though much of the book occurs in some of the most glamorous places and homes in New York City, the action also takes the reader to such exotic places as the Riviera, Paris, Bermuda, and Amsterdam. Which of these areas appealed to you most? Why?

10. When the battle to gain enough shares to take over *Sizzle* begins, Marietta wins David Belmont, its editor, over to her side. Do you like David? How do you feel about the things he is willing to do to help Marietta gain shares? Melanie seems to be attracted to him. Did you think the feeling was or ever could be mutual?

11. When Melanie must travel to Amsterdam to convince the son of Philip Bailey to release his shares to the Wylford camp, David tells her that while there she should make a point of visiting Anne Frank's house and Our Dear Lord in the Attic church, adding, "They're more important for people like us to see than all the art treasures in the museums." Why do you think he said that? And why do you think that Melanie, when she returned, could not bring herself to tell him that she had seen them and how much they moved her?

12. When Marietta travels to Paris and meets with Craig Campbell to try to get him to tender his shares in *Sizzle* to her, were you surprised that the old spark seemed to reignite between them? How did you feel about Craig's final reaction? Do you think Marietta should have told him that she was responsible for the big break that set him off on his successful career?

13. What do you think of Clifford Langhton, Harrison Kendricks's second in command? Did you warm to his wife and family? Did you understand why he did what he had to do to win shares over to the Kendricks side? Do you think his wife was right to react as she did when she was affected by the results of his actions?

14. Just before he died, Philip Bailey told Marietta that he had come into possession of proof that Harrison Kendricks had been involved in something so vile that Kendricks would be forced to back out of the takeover battle when he was confronted with it. All through the book, Marietta, Melanie and David struggle to find out what it was. Were you shocked when they finally unearthed the secret?

15. What do you think of the meeting between Marietta and Kendricks? Were you surprised by his reaction when she revealed that she had proof of what he did? Do you think that the precautions Marietta took will keep her safe?

16. How do you feel about the outcome of the takeover battle for *Sizzle*?

17. By the end of the book, did your feelings for Marietta or any of the other characters change? If so, how and why?